CONSOLATION

Born in 1970, Anna Gavalda was a teacher whose collection of stories, *I Wish Someone Were Waiting for Me Somewhere*, shot her to fame (published in Vintage together with her novella, *Someone I Loved*). Her novel *Hunting and Gathering* (*Ensemble c'est tout*) was a bestseller in several countries, selling over two million copies, and was made into a film. Her books have been translated into thirty-six languages. The mother of two children, she lives and writes just outside Paris.

ANNA GAVALDA

Consolation

TRANSLATED FROM THE FRENCH BY
Alison Anderson

VINTAGE BOOKS
London

Published by Vintage 2011

2 4 6 8 10 9 7 5 3

Copyright le dilettante 2008

English translation copyright © Alison Anderson 2010

Originally published in French as *La Consolante*

Anna Gavalda has asserted her right under the Copyright, Designs
and Patents Act 1988 to be identified as the author of this work

First published in Great Britain in 2010 by
Chatto & Windus

Vintage
Random House, 20 Vauxhall Bridge Road,
London SW1V 2SA

www.vintage-books.co.uk

Addresses for companies within The Random House Group Limited
can be found at: www.randomhouse.co.uk/offices.htm

The Random House Group Limited Reg. No. 954009

A CIP catalogue record for this book
is available from the British Library

ISBN 9780099531920

The Random House Group Limited supports The Forest Stewardship
Council (FSC), the leading international forest certification
organisation. All our titles that are printed on Greenpeace approved
FSC certified paper carry the FSC logo. Our paper procurement
policy can be found at www.rbooks.co.uk/environment

Printed and bound in Great Britain by
CPI Bookmarque, Croydon, CR0 4TD

As selfish
and illusory
as it might seem,
this book, Charles,
is for you.

He always stood off to one side. Over there, away from the fence, out of harm's way. His gaze febrile, his arms crossed in front of him. More than crossed – twisted tightly, straitjacketed. As if he were cold, or had a stomach ache. As if he were clinging to himself so as not to fall over.

Defying us, every one of us, but not looking at anyone. Seeking out the shape of one lone little boy and clutching a paper bag to his chest.

In it was a chocolate croissant, that I knew, and every time I would wonder if it hadn't got completely squashed, what with . . .

Yes, that's how he hung on – the bell, their scorn, the trip by way of the bakery, and all the little spots of grease on his lapel as if they were so many medals, unhoped-for.

Unhoped-for . . .

But . . . In those days, how could I possibly know that?

In those days, I was afraid of him. Shoes too pointy, nails too long, and index finger too yellow. Lips too red. And coat too short and much too tight.

And a dark line all round his eyes, too dark. And a voice that was too weird.

When at last he caught sight of us, he'd smile and open his arms. Leaning forward, silently, he'd touch his hair and shoulders and face. And while my mother moored me firmly to her body, I would count all his rings as he held them against my friend's cheeks, fascinated.

He had one on each finger. Real rings, beautiful rings, precious, like my grandmother's . . . It was always just then that my mother would turn away, horrified, and that I let go of her hand.

As for Alexis, no. He never turned away. Just handed over his

1

schoolbag and, with the other hand, he ate his snack, and they headed off towards the Place du Marché.

Alexis with his extraterrestrial in spiky high heels, his circus freak, his primary school clown, felt safer than I did, and was better loved.

Or so I thought.

But one day I did ask him, all the same, 'Well, um, is it a man or a woman?'

'Who?'

'The, um, the person who comes to fetch you in the evening.'

He shrugged his shoulders.

Of course it was a man. But he called him Nana, his nanny.

And so Nana had promised, for instance, to bring him some golden jacks and he'd swap them with me for that marble, if I wanted, or even . . . she's late, Nana, today . . . I hope she hasn't lost her keys . . . Because she always loses everything, you know . . . She often says that some day she'll forget her head at the hairdresser's or in a fitting room at Prisunic and then she laughs, and says, thank God she's got legs!

But it's a man, you can tell.

What a question.

I can't recall his name. And yet it was something extraordinary . . .

A music-hall sort of name, echoes of worn velvet and stale tobacco. Something like Gigi Lamor or Gino Cherubini or Ruby Dolorosa or . . .

I can't remember and it's driving me mad that I can't remember. I'm in a plane headed for the ends of the earth, I have to sleep, I simply must sleep. I've taken some pills, just for that. I have no choice, I won't make it otherwise. I haven't slept in so long . . . and I . . .

I won't make it.

Nothing doing. Neither chemistry, nor grief, nor exhaustion. Over thirty thousand feet, so high up in the void, and I'm still struggling like a cretin to rekindle these poorly extinguished memories. And the harder I blow, the more my eyes sting, and the less I see, the further down I fall on to my knees.

My neighbour has already asked me twice to switch off the overhead light. Sorry, but I can't. It was forty years ago, Madame . . .

forty years, don't you see? I need the light to find the name of that old drag queen. That amazing name which of course I've gone and forgotten, since I used to call her Nana, too. And I adored her. Because that's the way things were with them: you adored each other.

Nana who surfaced like a ruin in their life, one hospital evening.

Nana who spoiled us rotten, who fed us, stuffed us, consoled us, deloused us, genuinely hypnotized us, enchanted us and disenchanted us a thousand times. Read our palms, told our cards, promised us the life of a sultan, a king, a nabob, a life of amber and sapphire, of languorous poses and exquisite love; Nana who left our life one morning with a dramatic flourish.

Dramatic, which was fitting. Fitting for him, fitting for them, the way everything had to be with them.

But I . . . Later. I'll go into that later. I've no strength left right now. And I don't feel like it, anyway. I don't want to lose them again just now. I'd like to sit a bit longer on the back of my Formica elephant, with my kitchen knife stuck in my loincloth, with all his turbans and make-up and gold chains, from the Alhambra cabaret.

I need my sleep and I need my little light. I need everything I've lost along the way. Everything they gave me and then took back.

And everything they ruined, too . . .

Because, well, that's the way things were, in their world. That was their law, their creed, the way they lived, like heathens. They loved one another, bashed into one another, they'd cry and dance all night and set fire to everything.

Everything.

There should have been nothing left. Nothing. Ever. Nada. Bitter expressions, wrinkled, broken, twisted lips, beds, ashes, ravaged faces, hours spent weeping, years and years of loneliness, but no memories. Least of all. Memories were for other people.

Overcautious people. Accountants.

'The best parties of all, you'll see, duckies, are the ones you've forgotten by the next morning,' he used to say, 'the best parties happen *during* the party. There's no such thing as the morning after. The morning after is when you take the first metro and they start harassing you all over again.'

★

And what about her? Yes, her. She used to talk about death, all the time. All the time . . . To defy the bastard reaper, to crush him. Because she knew as much, she knew we would all end up there some day, it was her livelihood to know as much, and that was why we had to touch one another, love one another, drink, bite, take our pleasure and forget everything.

'Burn it, kids. Be sure you burn it all.'

It's her voice and I can still . . . I can still hear it.

Wild things.

★

He cannot switch off the light. Or close his eyes. He is going to go – no, he is going – mad. He knows it. Sees himself in the black depths of the window and . . .

'Sir? Are you all right?'

A stewardess is touching him on the shoulder.

Why have you abandoned me?

'Is something wrong?'

He would like to reply, No, everything's fine, thank you, but he can't: he is weeping.

At last.

I

1

Early winter. A Saturday morning. Paris Charles de Gaulle airport, terminal 2E.

Milky sun, smell of aeroplane fuel, immense fatigue.

'Don't you have a suitcase?' asks the taxi driver, pointing to the boot.

'I do.'

'Well, you've got it well hidden, then!'

He chuckles, I turn around.

'Oh, no . . . I . . . the carousel . . . I forgot to . . .'

'Go get it! I'll wait!'

'No, never mind. I haven't the strength just now, I . . . never mind . .'

He's no longer chuckling.

'Hey, you're not just going to leave it there, are you?'

'I'll get it another day. I'm coming back the day after tomorrow anyway . . . I feel as if I lived here, I . . . No . . . Let's go, I don't care. I don't want to go back in there just now.'

'Hey, you, clap, clap, *my God, yes you, I'll come to you on . . . horseback!*

Oh yeah, yes, on horseback!

Hey, you, clap, clap, *my God, yes you, I'll come to you on . . . a bike!*

Oh yeah, yes, on a bike!'

Pretty lively stuff in Claudy A'Bguahana's Peugeot 407 number 3786. (His permit is taped to the back of the seat.)

'Hey, you, clap, clap, *my God, yes, you, I'll come to you . . . in a hot air balloon!*

Oh yeah, yes, a hot air balloon!'

He calls out, looking at me in the rear view mirror, 'I hope you don't mind hymns, by the way?'

I smile.

'*Hey, you*, clap, clap, *my Lord, yes you, I'll come to you in a . . . jet propelled rocket!*'

If we'd had hymns like this, we might not have lost our faith quite so soon, would we?

Oh, yeah!

Oh, yes . . .

'No, no, it's fine. Thanks. This is perfect.'

'Where did you come in from?'

'Russia.'

'Hey! It's cold there, isn't it?'

'Very.'

Among sheep from the same flock, I would have *fervently* liked to behave in a more brotherly fashion, but . . . Mea culpa, here I have to beat my breast, and that is something I know how to do, beat my jet propelled breast, because I just can't.

And that is my great sin.

I'm too jet-lagged, too exhausted, too dirty and too dried out to take communion.

At the next motorway exit ramp:

'So do you have God in your life?'

Fuck. Jesus. This would have to happen to me . . .

'No.'

'You know what? I could tell that right away. A man who leaves his luggage just like that, I said to myself, he doesn't have God in his life.'

He says it again, hitting the steering wheel.

'No-God-in-his-life.'

'Guess not,' I confess.

'But He is there all the same! He is there! He is everywhere! He is showing us the w—'

'No, no,' I interrupt, 'the place I've just got back from, where I've come from . . . He isn't there. I assure you.'

'Why not, then?'

'Poverty . . .'

8

'But God *is* in poverty! God performs miracles, don't you know that?'

I glance quickly at the speedometer, 90, so no way to open the door.

'Take me, for example . . . Before, I was . . . I was nothing!' He was getting excited. 'I was drinking! Gambling! Sleeping with loads of women! I wasn't a man, you see . . . I was nothing! And the Lord took me. The Lord plucked me like a little flower and He said, "Claudy, you . . ."'

I'll never find out what sort of pap the Old Man had fed him: I'd fallen asleep.

We were outside the entrance to my building when he squeezed my knee.

On the back of the receipt he'd written the address to paradise: *Aubervilliers Church, 46–48 Rue Saint-Denis. 10.00am to 1.00pm.*

'You have to come next Sunday, right? You have to say to yourself, If I got into that car, it was not by chance, because chance . . . (great big eyes) doesn't exist.'

The window of the passenger seat was down so I leaned in to bid farewell to my shepherd, 'So then . . . um . . . You . . . you don't sleep with women any more . . . um, not one?'

Big smile.

'Only the ones the Lord sends my way.'

'And how do you know which ones they are?'

Very big smile.

'They're the most beautiful ones.'

*

We've been taught the wrong way round, I reflected, pushing open the front door; as for me, as far as I can recall, the only time when I was sincere was when I would repeat, 'I am not worthy to receive you.'

At that moment, yes. At that moment I truly believed.

And *you, clap, clap,* as I was climbing, *yes you,* my four flights of stairs, I realized to my horror that I had that bloody refrain stuck in my head, *in a taxi, yes, in a taxi.*

Oh, yeah.

The security lock was on and these ten last centimetres where I found my home resisting me were infuriating. I had come from too far away, I'd seen too much, the plane had arrived too late and God was too tactful. I blew a fuse.

'It's me! Open up!'

I was screaming, pounding on the doorframe, 'Will you bloody open this door!'

Snoopy's muzzle appeared in the gap.

'Hey, it's okay . . . Calm down, all right? Calm down . . .'

Mathilde slid open the bolt, stepped back, and had already turned away from me when I crossed the threshold.

'Hello!' I said.

She merely raised her arm, limply wiggling a few fingers.

Enjoy, commanded the back of her T-shirt. Well now. For a split second there I entertained the notion of grabbing her by the hair and breaking her neck to force her to turn around, and saying it to her again, to her face, those two oh-so outmoded little syllables, Hel-lo. And then, oh . . . I let it go. And anyway, the door to her room had already slammed shut.

I'd been gone a week, I was leaving again in just two days and how . . . how important was all that anyway.

Well? How important? I was just passing through, wasn't I?

I went into Laurence's room, which was also my room, as far as I knew. The bed was impeccably made, the duvet was smoothed, the pillows were plumped, paunchy, haughty. Pathetic. I hugged the wall and carefully set my buttocks on the very edge of the mattress so as not to crease anything.

I looked at my shoes. For a fairly long while. I looked out of the window. The roofs just below and the Val-de-Grâce in the distance. And then her clothes on the back of the armchair.

Her books, her water bottle, her address book, her glasses, her earrings . . . It must all mean something, but I could no longer quite grasp what. I . . . I didn't get it any more.

I toyed with one of the little tubes of tiny round pills that sat on the night table.

Nux Vomica 9CH, difficulties sleeping.

Yes, that must be it, that's what this place is about now, I thought with a grimace, and stood up.

Nux Vomica.

It was the same, and it was worse, every time. I was no longer here. The shoreline was receding ever further, and I . . . .

Stop it, come on, I castigated myself! You're tired and you're winding yourself up. Stop it.

The water was scorching. With my mouth open and my eyelids closed, I waited for it to wash away all my rough scales. From the cold, the snow, the lack of daylight, the hours of traffic jams, my endless discussions with that bastard Pavlovich, all the battles lost from the start and all the faces still haunting me.

The bloke who'd tossed his hard hat in my face the night before. The words I couldn't understand but which I could easily guess. The building site, which was getting out of control . . . On all sides . . .

What the hell had I been thinking to go and get involved in such a thing, honestly? And now! I couldn't even find my razor in the midst of all these beauty products! Conceals blemishes, period pains, luminous skin, firm abdomen, seborrhoea, fragile hair.

What the hell did all this crap mean! What the hell was the point?

And for what moments of tenderness?

I cut myself and swept the lot into the wastebasket.

'You know . . . I think I should make you a coffee, no?'

Mathilde, her arms crossed, stood slouching on one leg in the door to the bathroom.

'Good idea.'

She was staring at the floor.

'Oh . . . um . . . I knocked over a few things, you see . . . I'll . . . don't worry about it.'

'Oh, no. I'm not worried. You do this every time.'

'Oh?'

She shook her head.

'Have a good week?' she went on.

I didn't reply.

11

'Right. A coffee, then.'

Mathilde . . . As a little girl she'd been so hard to get close to . . . So hard . . . How she'd grown, good Lord.

Fortunately we still had Snoopy, on her T-shirt.

'Feeling better now?'

'Yes,' I went, blowing into my cup, 'thanks. I get the feeling I've finally landed. No school today?'

'Nah.'

'Laurence working all day?'

'Yes. She'll meet us at Granny's. Oh, noooo. Don't tell me you'd forgotten. You know perfectly well it's her birthday party tonight.'

I had forgotten. Not that it was Laurence's birthday the next day, but that we were in for another charming little soirée. A proper family dinner, just the way I liked them. All I needed, truly.

'I haven't got a present.'

'I know. That's why I didn't go and sleep over at Lea's. I knew you'd need me.'

Adolescence . . . What an exhausting yo-yo.

'You know, Mathilde, you have a way of blowing hot and cold that will never cease to astound me . . .'

I stood up to help myself to more coffee.

'Well at least I'm astounding someone.'

'Hey,' I replied, placing my hand against her back, 'enjoy.'

She arched her back. Ever so slightly.

The way her mum did.

We decided to go on foot. After a few silent streets, where each of my questions seemed to pain her even more than the previous one, she began to fiddle with her iPod and wiggled the head-phones into her ears.

Very well then, looks like I ought to get myself a real dog, no? Someone who'd love me and would literally jump for joy when-ever I got back from a trip . . . Even a stuffed one, why not? With big moist eyes and a little motor that would cause his tail to wag when I touched his head.

Oh, I love him already . . .

'You in a mood, now?'

Because of her gadget she'd said the words more loudly than necessary and the woman on the crossing with us turned round.

Mathilde sighed, closed her eyes, sighed again, removed her left earplug and stuck it into my right ear.

'Here, I've got something for you that's just your age group, it'll perk you up.'

And there in the midst of the noise and traffic, on the end of a very short wire that still connected me to a faraway childhood, a few guitar chords.

A few notes and the perfect, hoarse, slightly drawling voice of Leonard Cohen, singing 'Suzanne'.

'Better now?'

I nodded my head, just like a moody little boy.

'Brilliant.'

She was pleased.

Spring was still a long way off but the sun was working on heating things up a bit, stretching lazily over the dome of the Panthéon. My-daughter-who-was-not-my-daughter-but-who-was-nothing-less-either gave me her arm so she wouldn't lose the sound, and there we were in Paris, the most beautiful city in the world – I'd finally come round to admitting the fact by virtue of leaving it behind so often.

Wandering through this *quartier* I loved so, turning our backs on the Great Men, just the two of us, little mortals who could astound no one, amidst the tranquil weekend crowd. Feeling relaxed, our guard down, to the very rhythm of *for he's touched* our perfect bodies *with his mind*.

'This is wild,' I said, shaking my head, 'and you still listen to this stuff?'

'Looks that way . . .'

'I must have come along this very street humming this, over thirty years ago . . . See that shop, there?'

With my chin I pointed towards the shopfront of Dubois, the art supply place on the Rue Soufflot.

'If you knew how many hours I spent drooling over their window . . . It all set me dreaming. Everything. The paper, the pens, the tubes of Rembrandt. One day I even saw Prouvé come out of there. Jean Prouvé, can you imagine! And, well, on that particular day I must have been waltzing along murmuring that Jesus *was a sailor* and all that stuff, I'll bet you anything . . . Prouvé . . . when I think back . . .'

'Who's Prouvé?'

'A genius. Well, not even. An inventor, a creator, an incredible bloke . . . you know, the designer and architect; I'll show you some of the books. But, um, to get back to our cheery lad, there . . . My favourite was *Famous Blue Raincoat*, haven't you got that one?'

'No.'

'Jeez! What are they teaching you at school these days, anyway? I was mad about that song, absolutely crazy. I think I must have worn the cassette right through from rewinding it so many times.'

'Why?'

'Oh, I don't remember . . . I'd have to listen to it again, but as I recall, it's the story of a guy who's writing to one of his friends, a bloke who'd gone off with his wife at some point, and he was saying that he thought he'd forgiven him. There was something about a lock of hair, I remember, and for someone like me who was incapable of chatting up a single girl, I was such a great lump, awkward and so moody it was pathetic, well, I thought that sort of story was very *very* sexy. As if it were written for me, in a way . . .'

I was laughing.

'And listen to this. I even pestered my dad so he'd give me his old Burberry, and I tried to dye it blue and screwed up completely and utterly. It went this greenish-yellow colour. So ugly, you can't begin to imagine.'

She was laughing.

'But do you think that stopped me? Not likely. I wrapped myself inside the thing, with the collar up and the belt undone, "my fists in my torn pockets" like Rimbaud's Bohemian, and off I went . . .'

I mimed the loser I must have been. Peter Sellers in his prime.

'. . . taking these great long strides, right through the crowd, mysterious, elusive, ever so careful to avoid the gaze of all those people who weren't even looking at me. Oh, he must have laughed, old Leonard off on his promontory among the great Zen masters, let me tell you!'

'And now?'

'Well . . . he's still alive, far as I know.'

'Nah, the raincoat.'

'Oh, that! Vanished, along with everything else. But you can ask Claire tonight if she remembers it.'

'Okay . . . And I'll download it.'

I frowned.

'Hey, that's enough already! You're not going to do your head in about all that *again*. He's earned enough as it is.'

'It's not a question of money, you know that perfectly well. It's more serious than that. It's –'

'Stop. I know. You've told me a million times. The day there are no artists left, we'll all be dead and blah blah and all that.'

'Exactly. We'll still be alive but we'll all be dead. Hey, look, speaking of which . . .'

We were standing outside Gibert's books and music store.

'Come on in. I'll buy it for you, my lovely sickly green raincoat.'

I stood frowning hesitantly at the till. Three other CDs had miraculously appeared on the counter.

'Oh, come on!' she said, as if it were fate, 'I had been planning on downloading those ones, too.'

I paid and she grazed her cheek against mine. Just a touch.

Once we'd rejoined the flow of people on the Boulevard Saint-Michel, I grew bolder. 'Mathilde?'

'Yes.'

'Can I ask you a delicate question?'

'No.'

Then a few metres farther along, she covered her face with her hands. 'I'm listening.'

'Why have things got this way between us? So . . .'

Silence.

'So what?' asked her hood.

'I don't know . . . predictable. Cash-oriented. I get out my credit card and only then am I entitled to a tender gesture. Well, tender . . . A gesture, at any rate. How . . . so what's the going rate for a kiss from you at the moment, anyway?'

I opened my wallet and checked the receipt from Gibert's. 'Fifty-five euros and sixty cents. Right.'

Silence.

15

Tossed the receipt into the gutter.

'You know it's not just a question of money really, I was happy to give them to you, but . . . I really wish you could have said hello earlier on when I came in, I was so −'

'I *did* say hello.'

I pulled on her sleeve so she'd look at me, then I lifted my hand to imitate her limp-fingered greeting. Or the limpness of her intention . . .

She pulled her arm away abruptly.

'And it's not just with me, anyway,' I went on, 'I know it's like this with your mum, too. Every time I call her, even though I'm far away and I might like a little . . . That's all she talks about. Your attitude. Your rows. This sort of ongoing blackmail . . . A little bit of kindness for a little bit of cash. All the time. All the time. And −'

I stopped in my tracks and took hold of her again.

'Answer me. How did it get like this between us? What did we do? What did we do *to you* to deserve this? I know . . . Some might say it's adolescence, the awkward age, the dark tunnel and all that rubbish, but you − You, Mathilde. I thought you were more intelligent than the others, I didn't think it would affect you like them. I thought you were far too clever to get caught up in their statistics −'

'Well you were wrong.'

'So I see.'

She'd been so hard to get close to. Why had this ridiculous pluperfect sprung to mind above my coffee cup earlier on? Simply because she'd taken the trouble − the immense trouble − to push a capsule into the coffee machine and press the little green button?

Hey. I'm a bit obtuse myself, at times.

And yet, when I think back −

She was − how old, at the time? Seven, maybe eight, and she'd just lost in the finals at the gymkhana. I can still see her flinging her riding cap into the ditch, lowering her head and ploughing into me without warning. Bam. A battering ram. I even had to grab hold of a post to keep from falling over.

I was dazed, moved, breathless, my hands all tied in knots and in the end I'd managed to pull the flaps of my coat around her

16

while she spilled tears and snot and horse dung all over my shirt, with her arms squeezed round my girth as tight as could be.

Could you call this gesture 'taking someone in your arms'? Yes, I decided; yes. And it was the first time.

The first time . . . and when I say she was eight, I'm almost certainly wrong. I'm hopeless with ages. Perhaps it was even later. Good Lord, it took years, then, didn't it?

But then she was there, really there. Her entire little self fitted inside the lining of my raincoat and I let it last as long as I could, despite my frozen feet and my aching legs, soon to be stuck at the edge of that bloody riding ring in Normandy, and I hid her from the world, with a silly smile on my face.

Afterwards, in the car, she curled up in a ball on the rear seat, and I said, 'What was your pony's name again? Pistachio?'

No reply.

'Caramel?'

Missed again.

'Wait, I've got it! Popcorn.'

Silence from the rear.

'Hey, what could you expect from such an ugly stupid pony, with a name like Popcorn to boot . . . huh? Honestly. That was the first and last time he'll ever make it to the finals, that fat Popcorn of yours, let me tell you!'

I was useless. I was overdoing it and I wasn't even sure of the animal's name. Come to think of it, I seem to recall it was Peanut . . .

Well, in any case she'd turned away.

I straightened the rear view mirror and clenched my teeth.

We had got up at dawn. I was exhausted, and cold, and I was scrambling to keep up and had to stop off at the agency that very evening for yet another all-nighter. And I'd always been afraid of horses. Even little ones. Especially little ones. Dear God . . . all of this did not bode well when you were stuck in a traffic jam. Not at all . . . And while I was at it, churning my thoughts round and round, irritated and tense and ready to burst, suddenly there came these words:

'Sometimes I wish you were my father.'

I didn't say anything, afraid I might spoil it all. I'm not your father, or I'm like your father, or I'm better than your father, or no, what I mean is, I am . . . Phew . . . My silence, it seemed, would say all that much better than I ever could.

But today? Now that life has become so . . . so what? So laborious, so *inflammable* in our one hundred and ten square metres. Now that we almost never made love any more, Laurence and I; now that I was losing my illusions at the rate of one a day, and a year of my life per construction site, and I found myself rambling away to Snoopy T-shirt while saying nothing, and I was obliged to key in my PIN code just to feel loved, I regretted not heeding those distress signals.

I should have seen them that time, obviously.

I should have pulled over onto the emergency lay-by, so aptly named, should have got out into the night and opened her door and pulled her out by the feet and gently smothered her in turn.

What would it have cost me? Not a thing.

Not a thing, because there wouldn't have been any other words to say . . . Or at least, that's how I imagine it, the botched scene: silent, and effective. Because words, for Christ's sake, words – they're not something I've ever been good at. I've never had the kit.

Never.

And now that I'm turning towards her, there outside the gate of the School of Medicine, and I can see her face, hard and set and almost ugly, because of one little question, and here am I who never asks questions, I tell myself I'd have done better to keep my mouth shut this time round, too.

She was walking ahead of me, taking long strides, head down.

'Anyouinkbetter?' I heard her mumble.

'Excuse me?'

She spun around.

'And you? Do you think you're any better?'

She was furious.

'You think you're any better, you guys? Huh? You think you're any better? You guys think you're not predictable?'

'You guys who?'

'Who, who do you think? Well, the two of you! You guys! You and Mum! I really wonder what sort of statistic you two belong in! Maybe the crap couple category, the ones who . . .'

Silence.

'Who what?' I ventured, idiot that I am.

'You know what I mean,' she murmured.

Yes, that I knew. And that is the reason why we both stubbornly stood there not speaking.

Lucky kid with headphones: here was I, with nothing but my own inner turmoil to listen to.

My own negative feedback and a moth-eaten raincoat.

When we reached the Rue de Sèvres, opposite the posh department store that was already making me feel discouraged, I veered off in the direction of a café.

'Do you mind? I need a coffee before the battle.'

She followed, making a face.

I burned my lips while she fiddled with her gadgets again.

'Charles?'

'Yes.'

'Can you tell me what he's singing, here? 'Cause I get some of it but not all . . .'

'No problem.'

So we shared the sound again. She got the Dolby, I got the stereo. One ear each.

But the opening chords of the piano were quickly drowned by the noise of the espresso machine.

'Wait –'

She dragged me down to the other end of the counter.

'Ready?'

I nodded.

Another man's voice. Warmer.

And I began my simultaneous translation for her, into French, '*If you were the road, I would go* . . . Wait . . . Because this could be either road or path in French, it depends on the context. Do you want the poetry or word for word?'

'Oh,' she moaned, cutting off the sound, 'you fuck everything up. I don't want an English lesson, I just want you to tell me what he's saying!'

'Right,' I said impatiently, 'let me listen to the whole thing once through on my own, and then I'll tell you.'

I took her little thingammies and covered my ears with both hands while she looked at me out of the corner of her eye, febrile.

I was blown away. More than I would have imagined. More than I would have liked. I was . . . simply blown away.

Bloody love songs. The way they sneak up on you . . . Enough to make you surrender, in less than four minutes. Bloody banderillas planted in hearts already riddled with statistics.

I handed the earpiece back to her with a sigh.

'Good stuff, isn't it?'

'Who is it?'

'Neil Hannon. An Irish singer. Right, the whole thing through, now?'

'The whole thing.'

'And no stopping, right?'

'*Don't worry sweetie, it's gonna be all right,*' I drawled, best cowboy fashion.

She smiled again. Well done, Charley, well done.

So I picked up the road where I'd left it, because it was surely a road that was meant, no doubt about that.

If you were the road/ I'd go all the way . . . If you were the night/ I'd sleep in the day . . . If you were the day/ I'd cry in the night . . . She was sticking right by me now, not to lose a single word . . . *'Cause you are the way, the truth and the light./*

If you were a tree/ I could put my arms around you . . ./ And . . . you . . . you could not complain/ If you were a tree . . ./ I could carve my name into your side/ and you would not cry,/ 'Cos trees don't cry . . . (there I took some liberties with the French to translate, "Cos trees don't cry', okay, right, Neil, you'll forgive me, won't you? I've got this teenager on my back at the other end of the wire) *If you were a man/ I would still love you . . ./ If you were a drink/ I'd drink my fill of you . . ./ If you were attacked,/ I would kill for you . . ./ If your name was Jack/ I'd change mine to Jill for you . . ./ If you were a horse,/ I'd clean the crap out of your stable/ and never once complain . . ./ If you were a horse/ I could ride you through the fields at dawn . . ./ Through the day until the day was gone* (uh . . . no time to polish that) . . . *I could sing about you in my songs* (not brilliant either) . . . (She didn't care and I could feel her hair against my cheek.) (And smell her scent, too. Her Body Shop Tea Tree Oil, a whiff of young teenager with rips in her sleeve.) *If you were my little girl/ I would find it hard to let you go . . . / If you were my sister* uh, 'find it doubly' oh, let's just take a stab,/ *I would find it doubly so. / If you were a dog, / I'd feed you scraps from off the table* (sorry) *Though my wife complains . . . / If you were my dog* (and now his voice is rising) *I am sure you'd like it better. / Then you'd be my loyal four-legged friend, / You'd* (almost shouting now) *never have to think again* (now he was really yelling but in a sad sort of way)/ *And we could be together till the end* (Right to the *eeeeeennnddd* in fact, but you could tell the affair was hardly in the bag either . . . not a sure thing at all . . .).

I handed her property back without a word and ordered a second coffee that I really didn't want at all to give her the time to let the credits roll by. The time to get used to the light and shake herself down.

'I love this song,' she sighed.

'Why?'

'Dunno. Because . . . because trees don't cry.'

'Are you in love?' I ventured cautiously, walking on eggshells.

A slight pout.

'No,' she confessed, 'no. When you're in love you don't need to listen to this sort of lyric, I don't suppose, like duh.'

After a few minutes during which I scraped conscientiously at the treacle in the bottom of the cup, she said, 'To get back to what you were saying . . .'

She directed her gaze over there, towards the question I'd asked earlier.

I didn't budge.

'The dark tunnel and all that. Well, um, I think that . . . we should just leave things as they stand . . . Like not get too greedy with each other, know what I mean?'

'Uh, not exactly, no . . .'

'Well, you can count on me to help you find a present for Mum, and I can count on you to translate the songs I like, and . . . and that's it.'

'That's it?' I protested mildly. 'That's *all* you have to offer?'

She'd put her hood back up.

'Yes. For the time being, yes. But, yeah it's quite a lot, in fact. It's . . . like . . . it's a lot.'

I stared at her.

21

'Why are you smiling like an idiot now?'

'Because,' I replied, holding the door for her, 'because if you were my dog, I could sneak you the scraps and you'd be my loyal friend at last.'

'Ha, ha. Very clever.'

And while we stood motionless at the edge of the pavement, watching the stream of cars, she lifted her leg and pretended to piss against my trouser leg.

She'd been very honest with me, and on the escalator I decided to pay her back in her own coin.

'You know, Mathilde . . .'

'What?' (in a tone of, *now* what?)

'We are all cash-oriented.'

'I know,' she replied, without hesitating.

The ease with which she'd put me in my place left me pensive. It seemed to me we were a more generous lot, back in Cohen's time . . .

Or perhaps we simply weren't as clever?

She took a step away from me.

'Hey, then, let's drop these mega-boring conversations, right?'

'Right.'

'And so what shall we get for Mum?'

'Whatever you like,' I replied.

A shadow passed over.

'I've already got my present,' she said, clenching her teeth, 'it's *yours* we're talking about.'

'Sure, sure,' I said with forced cheerfulness, 'give me time to think, let's see . . .'

So that's what it meant, to be fourteen years old in this day and age? To be lucid enough to know that everything has its price here on earth and, at the same time, stay naïve and tender enough to want to go on giving your hands to the adults on either side of you, and stay with them, right between them, maybe not skipping any more but squeezing their hands hard, keeping a firm grip, to keep them *together* in spite of everything.

That was already something, no?

Even with all those great songs, it must be quite a burden.

What was I like, at her age? Completely immature, I suppose.

I stumbled as we arrived at the next floor. Huh. It wasn't important. Absolutely pointless. Absolutely.

And besides, I can't remember any of it.

Let's go, kid, I'm fed up already, I suddenly realized, clinging to the handrail. Let's have a look and find something and get it wrapped and we're out of here.

A handbag. Yet another . . . The fifteenth, I suppose.

'If Madame is not pleased with the item, she can always come and exchange it,' cooed the saleswoman.

I know, I know. Thank you. Madame frequently exchanges. And that is why I don't go to more trouble than this, any more, you see.

But I kept my mouth shut and paid up anyway. I paid up.

No sooner were we out of the store than Mathilde vanished again and I stood there like an imbecile in front of a newspaper kiosk, reading the headlines without taking them in.

Was I hungry? No. Did I feel like going for a walk? No. Wouldn't I do better to go and lie down? Yes. But no. I'd never get up again.

Could it be that . . . A bloke shoved past me to grab a magazine and I'm the one who said sorry.

All alone, with no imagination, the odd one out in the middle of the ant farm, I raised my arm to hail a cab and gave him the address of my office.

I went back to work because that was the only thing I knew how to do any more at that point. Time to see what sort of fuck-ups they'd got into here while I was away checking on the ones they'd got into over there. That's about what it had come to, my profession, for the last couple of years. A lot of huge cracks, a tiny knife, and plenty of filler.

The promising architect had become a little stonemason as he rose through the ranks. He was a regular Mr Fix-it for his colleagues, when they needed help in English; he did no more drawings, clocked up his frequent flier miles at an alarming rate and fell asleep lulled by the gentle drone of warfare on CNN, in hotel beds that were far too big.

The sky had clouded over. I put my forehead against the cool windowpane and compared the colour of the Seine with that of the Moskva, while holding an utterly pointless present on my lap.

Was God there?

Hard to say.

2

They've come, they're all here.

Let's run the credits in order of appearance, it will be easier.

The fellow who opens the door saying to Mathilde, oh, how you've grown, a regular little woman now, that's my older sister's husband. I have another brother-in-law, but this one's really my favourite. Say, you've gone and lost some more, he adds, ruffling my hair, did you remember to bring back some vodka this time? Hey, what exactly are you doing with the Russkies, anyway? Dancing the kazatchok or something?

What did I tell you . . . He's a good sort, no? He's perfect. Okay, let's shove our way in a bit here and this very upright gentleman who's taking our coats, just behind him there, is my father, Henri Balanda. He, on the other hand, isn't much of a one for words. He's given up. Now he lets me know that I've got some mail by pointing to the console over to my left. I give him a kiss, but I don't linger. The kind of mail that shows up at my parents' place is usually of the please-donate-to-your-school-your-college-your-university variety. Promotional meetings, subscription reminders for journals I haven't read in twenty years, and invitations to conferences I never attend.

Fine, I say to my father, already looking for the wastebin that isn't a wastebin, or so my mother will inform me with a frown a few minutes from now, since it is an umbrella stand, might I remind you. A well-worn script, how long have I been telling you this?

Yes, and that's my mother you can see there from behind, at the end of the corridor, in her kitchen, tied up in her apron while she bastes the roast.

Now she's turning around and kissing Mathilde and saying, my how you've grown, you're a real young lady now! I wait until it's my turn and I greet my other sister, not the wife of Jolyon Wagg

25

but of the tall skinny guy sitting over there. He's not at all the same type. He's manager of a Champion supermarket out in the country but he has a perfect understanding of the concerns and economic policies of Bernard Arnault. Yes, that Bernard Arnault, the tycoon of the LVMH group. He's sort of a . . . colleague, you might say. Because they're in the same profession, you see, and . . . well, I'll stop there. We'll enjoy ourselves all the more later on.

That woman there is Edith, and we'll be hearing from her as well. She'll talk about how much the children's schoolbags weigh, and about the PTA meetings, no really, she'll add – as she refuses a second helping of cake – it is unbelievable how little people contribute these days. The end-of-year fête, for example, who do you think came to fill in for me at the fishing booth, *who?* No one! So if the parents are dropping out, what on earth can you expect from the children, I ask you? Well, we shouldn't hold it against her, her husband is a Champion manager when really he was cut out to be a superstore manager, he's proven as much, and the puddle of sawdust in the fishing booth at the Saint-Joseph primary school fête is her little corner of paradise, so no, we shouldn't hold it against her. It's just that she gets very tiresome and she ought to change the record from time to time. And hair-style too, while she's at it. Let's follow her into the living room where the other side is waiting for us: my sister Françoise. Number One. Madame Kazatchok for those who haven't been following or who stayed behind dawdling in the kitchen. Now she does change her hairstyle quite frequently, but she's even more predictable than her younger sister. And anyway, there's no need to prove it, all you have to do is cut and paste the very first thing she says: 'Oh, Charles, you look frightful . . . And you've put on weight, haven't you?' Well, may as well include the second thing she says, too, otherwise I'll be accused of being biased: 'You have! You've filled out since the last time, I assure you. Not to mention the fact that you're as badly dressed as ever.'

No, don't feel sorry for me, in a few hours they'll have vanished from my life. At least until next Christmas, with a bit of luck. They can't come into my room any more without knocking, and by the time they snitch on me I'm already long gone.

I've saved the best for last. The one you don't see, but you can hear her laughing up on the first floor with all the teenagers in the house. Let's go and track down that lovely laugh, too bad about the cashew nuts.

★

'Noo! I can't believe it!' she cries, rubbing the scalp of one of my nephews, 'do you know what these cretins are talking about?'

Kisses along the way.

'Look at them, Charles. Look how young and handsome they all are. Look at their gorgeous teeth! (lifting up poor Hugo's upper lip), just check it out, they're the flower of youth! All these thousands of kilos of hormones overflowing all over the place! And do you know what they're talking about?'

'No,' I go, relaxing at last.

'About their gigabytes, for Christ's sake . . . They all sit there wanking about with their MP3 players, comparing gigabytes . . . Disturbing, don't you think? When you realize that this is what is going to be paying for our retirement . . . pinch me. I guess after this you'll go comparing the tariffs on your mobiles, right?'

'Done that,' sniggers Mathilde.

'No, I mean it, I really feel for you, kids . . . At your age you're supposed to be dying of love! Writing poetry! Planning the Revolution! Stealing from the rich! Filling up your backpacks and taking off! Changing the world! But gigabytes, I don't know . . . Gigabytes . . . Pfff . . . Why not your building society accounts while you're at it?'

'And you?' asks Marion the ingénue, 'what did you talk about with Charles when you were our age?'

My little sister turns to me.

'Well, we . . . we were already in bed at this time,' I muttered in turn, 'or we were doing our homework, weren't we?'

'Absolutely. Or you were helping me to do my essay on Voltaire perhaps?'

'Quite likely. Or we'd use the time to get ahead with the work for the week . . . And then, remember how we used to recite our geometry theorems by heart?'

'Exactly!' exclaims their beloved aunt, 'or equati—'

The pillow that has just landed in her face prevents her from finishing the sentence.

She answers immediately with a yell. Another cushion goes flying, then a trainer, other war cries, a sock rolled into a ball, then a –

27

Claire grabs me by the sleeve.

'Come on, let's go. Now that we've got the fun going here, let's go and stir things up downstairs.'

'That's going to be harder.'

'Oh, we'll see about that . . . All I need to do is suck up to that other cretin and tell him how wonderful the products are at Casino and it's in the bag . . .'

Then she turns round in the stairway and adds solemnly, 'Because they still give out bags at Casino! Whereas at Champion, don't hold your breath!'

She bursts out laughing.

That's who she is. That's Claire. And she's some consolation for the other two, after all. At least, she's always been a consolation to me.

'What on earth have you been getting up to up there?' fusses my mother, pulling at her apron strings, 'what's all that screaming?'

My sister pleads innocence, showing her palms. 'Hey, it's not me, it's Pythagoras.'

In the meantime Laurence has arrived. She is sitting at the end of the sofa and is already deep in the huge restructuring plan for the condiments department.

Right, I know, it's her evening, her birthday and she's been working all day but . . . still . . . We haven't seen each other for almost a week . . . Couldn't she have looked for me? Got up? Smiled? Or even just glanced over my way?

I slide in next to her.

'No, no, but it's a good idea to put the ketchup together with the tomato sauce, you're right . . .'

This is what my hand on her shoulder has inspired.

Enjoy.

As we are on our way to the dining room, she finally grabs me, as the kids upstairs would say.

'Good trip?'

'Excellent, thanks.'

'And did you bring back a present for my twentieth birthday?' she simpers, clinging to my arm, 'perhaps some jewellery from Fabergé?'

I guess it really runs in the family . . .

'Russian dolls,' I grumble, 'you know, one lovely woman, and the more interest you show in her, the tinier she turns out to be . . .'

'Are you talking about me?' she quips, walking away.

No. About me.

She quips.

She quips, walking away.

It's because of an aside like that that I fell in love with her, years ago: her foot was finding its way up my leg just as her husband was explaining to me what he expected from my business . . . He was fiddling with the ring around his cigar, making a to and fro movement with that innocent little piece of paper that I found to be . . . extremely unwise.

Yes. Because another woman would have been more predictable, more aggressive. Are you talking about me? she would have said, mocking or grating or scoffing or biting or scathing or shooting daggers with her eyes or something less cruel, but not this woman. No, not her. Not the beautiful Laurence Vernes.

It was winter and I had met them in a posh restaurant in the 8th arrondissement. 'For coffee,' he'd taken care to point out. Yes, indeed, for coffee . . . I was a supplier, not a client.

A little treat, at most.

Finally, I introduced myself.

Out of breath, slovenly, bulky. With my helmet in one hand and the tubes of blueprints in the other. Pursued by a waiter who was as horrified as he was obsequious, pestering me to take my rags off me, fussing in my wake. He took my dreadful biker jacket and went off, inspecting his pale carpet. Searching, no doubt, for traces of dirty oil or mud or similar vile excretions.

The scene only lasted a few seconds but it was enchanting.

So there I was, sly and mocking, pulling off my long scarf and shivering one last time, when by chance my gaze met hers.

She thought, or knew, or hoped that my smile was meant for her, but in fact it was for the absurdity of the situation, for the stupidity of a world, her world, which fed me in spite of myself (in those days it seemed to me that to come and give an estimate to a bloke who'd made his fortune in leather, in order to redo his new duplex 'without touching the marble', was proof of an utter lack of taste on my part . . . But the social security contributions, my God! This was Le Corbusier they were assassinating!). (I've changed since then. I've lost a few holes in my belt at business lunches and I've accumulated some useful complaints against the social security contribution collection agency. I've learned to live with my clear-sightedness, when all is said and done. Even with marble . . .) So, as I was saying, in spite of myself, a world that had not invited me just asked me to sit down in front of a stained tablecloth while some other fool swept up the last crumbs.

My nastiness in exchange for a smile. We were even, then.

The first smile.

But a nice one . . .

A nice one, already a bit charged, and I would realize fairly quickly, alas, that her self-confidence, and the way she was eyeing me up, all bold and flattering, owed more to the virtues of Monsieur Taittinger than to my improbable charm. But anyway . . . It was indeed her big toe I could feel, there, in the hollow behind my knee, while I was trying to concentrate on the gentleman's desiderata.

He was asking for details about the bedroom. 'Something spacious and intimate at the same time,' he said, over and over, peering at my specifications.

'Don't you think, darling? Do you agree?'

'Sorry?'

'The bedroom!' he whispered, with an exasperated puff on the cigar. 'Try to keep up please.'

She agreed. Only her lovely foot had wandered off.

I loved her, knowing full well what she was like, and I don't really see how I can complain now just because she wanders off with a flippant remark . . .

She was the one overseeing the site. We began to meet more and more frequently and as the work progressed my perspective became more vague, her handshakes less energetic, the load-bearing walls less of an obsession, and the workers increasingly in the way.

Finally one evening, on some flimsy pretext that the parquet was too dark, or too light, she hardly knew which, she demanded I meet her within the hour.

So we were the first to inaugurate the magnificent bedroom. On a painter's sheet, spacious and intimate, among the fag-ends and pots of white-spirit . . .

But after she'd got dressed in silence she took a few steps, opened a door, closed it again at once, came back to me smoothing her skirt, and announced, quite simply, 'I shall never live here.'

There was no arrogance for once, no bitterness or aggression. She would never live there.

We switched off the lights and went down the stairway in the semi-darkness.

'I have a little girl, did you know?' she confided between two floors, and while I was knocking on the concierge's door to give her the keys, she added in a very low voice, for herself alone, 'A little girl who deserves something better than this, I think.'

Ah-hah! The seating arrangements! Always the best moment of the evening.

'So . . . Laurence . . . on my right,' declares my old dad, 'then you, little Guy (poor Laurence . . . refrigerator department, shoplifters and havoc among the personnel coming right at you), Mado, you're here, then Claire, then —'

'No!' protests my mother irritably, tearing the paper from his hands. 'We said Charles, then Françoise, here . . . Oh, no, that doesn't work . . . We're one man short now.'

What would become of us without our seating arrangements?

Claire is watching me. She knows we are one man short. I smile to her and she shrugs her shoulders in a gallant sort of way to shake off my tenderness, which is making her uncomfortable.

Our gazes are worth more than that absent man's, after all . . .

Without any further hesitation she grabs the chair before her, unfolds her napkin and calls out to our favourite grocer, 'Come on, come over here, little Guy! Come and sit next to me and tell me again what I'm entitled to with my three discount points!'

My mother sighs and throws down her weapons. 'Oh, well, sit wherever you like, then.'

Such talent, I muse.

Such talent . . .

But the intelligence of this marvellous girl, who is capable of sabotaging your seating arrangements in a split second, who can make a family gathering bearable, who can stir up a group of blasé adolescents without humiliating them, who can find favour with a woman like Laurence (needless to say, she never got along with the other two, something that gladdened my heart), and is respected by all her colleagues, who is called Our Little Vauban in the plush offices of certain elected officials (I read one day in an ultra-serious urban planning journal this paraphrase of a certain famous phrase, 'A case fought by Balanda is a case won, a case defended by Balanda is an unwinnable case') – all of this, all her finesse and common sense, stop short once you get anywhere near the region of her heart.

The man who is missing this evening, and who has been missing for years now, does actually exist. Except that he too must be surrounded by his family this evening. With his wife (at his Maman's, said Claire, her smile a bit too forced to be honest), and his napkin ring.

Such a hero.

And cutting such a fine figure, modern man in his well-worn slippers . . .

The point is he very nearly came between us, the fat bastard . . . 'No, Charles, you can't say that . . . He's not fat . . .' That's the sort of feeble rejoinder she'd come out with back in the days when I was still doing my Don Quixote act and would try to struggle against that flailing windmill of words. But I have since given up, it's pointless. A man who, even if he is thin, can say calmly and without irony to a woman like her, 'Be patient, I'll leave when the girls are grown up,' is not even worth the hay you'd feed to old Rosinante.

He can go to hell.

'But why do you stay with him?' I have asked her, formulating the question every possible way.

'I don't know. Because he doesn't want me, I suppose.'

And that is all she has to say in her own defence. Yes, her defence. Our own little . . . Our lovely beacon and the terror of every court of law.

A hopeless case.

But I've given up. Out of fatigue, and from a sense of honesty, and because here am I incapable of cleaning up my own back yard.

I'd make a lousy prosecutor, my arm isn't long enough.

And there are other things going on underneath all that, other renunciations and shadowy regions and slopes that are far too slippery, even for the kindred spirit of a brother like me. So we don't talk about it any more. And she switches off her mobile. And shrugs her shoulders. So that's life. And she laughs. And she doesn't mind getting lumbered with the resident champion, to take her mind off things.

There's no point describing the rest. It's all too drearily familiar.

The little feast. Saturday evening dinner in the home of nicely brought-up people, where everyone valiantly follows the score. The best dishes, the dreadful knife-rests in the shape of a basset hound, the glass that gets knocked over, the kilo of salt that gets poured onto the tablecloth, the debate about televised debates, the 35-hour working week, France going down the tubes, all the taxes we pay and the police radar we didn't see, the bad guy who says that Arabs have too many kids and the good girl who answers back that you shouldn't generalize, the hostess who insists it's over-cooked just for the pleasure of being told it isn't, and the patriarch who fusses over the temperature of his wine.

Go on then. I'll spare you all that. You know them only too well, these interludes that are always warm and rather depressing at the same time, that are referred to as family and that remind you from time to time that you really haven't come that far . . .

The only thing worth saving is the laughter of those kids upstairs, and wouldn't you know, it is Mathilde who is laughing the loudest. And her giggles take us back to the concierge's *loge* on the Boulevard Beauséjour, and the whispered confidences of the superb wife of the man who'd hired me for this job, and she's just run off with my heart and my senses wrapped up in a dirty old painter's sheet.

I'll never know what it was exactly that her little girl had been spared, nor what it was she deserved, in fact, but I do know how she made my work easier. After that last 'site meeting' I heard nothing more from Laurence. She didn't come any more, I couldn't get hold of her, and what's worse, I began to think I'd dreamt it all, and I sent off my final proposals into the void.

And yet she haunted me. I was haunted. And since she was too beautiful for me, I had to use some cunning.

My Trojan horse was made of wood, too. And I worked on it for weeks.

This was the school-leaving project I had never had the courage to finish. My craftsman's masterpiece, my dreams cobbled together with a tube of glue, my little pebble tossed into the deepest well . . .

The less it seemed I'd ever see her again, the more time I spent on the finishing touches. I found ways to challenge the best suppliers in the Faubourg Saint-Antoine, I made my way through all the model-making shops, I even used a trip to London as an excuse to lose myself among the cats of an astonishing old witch, *Mrs Lily Lilliput*, who could even fit Buckingham Palace into a thimble and to whom I paid a small fortune. Now that I recall, she even flogged me an entire set of copper cake moulds no bigger than ladybirds. 'An essential in the kitchen, indeed', she insisted, drawing up her . . . oversized invoice. And then one day I had to face the facts: there was nothing more to add and it was time to go looking for her.

I knew she worked for Chanel so I took my courage in both hands, interlocking two C's for Conquest and Concupiscence, but I left my bravado behind: it was more a case of Cold Feet and Cupid, to be honest, as I pushed open the door on the Rue Cambon. I'd shaved too closely, even nicked myself here and there, but my collar was clean and I had new shoelaces.

They called her, she acted all surprised, fiddled with her string of pearls, was charming, casual and . . . Oh, it was cruel . . . But I didn't get flustered and I asked her to stop by the agency the following Saturday.

And when her little girl discovered my present, her present that is, and I showed her how to light up the loveliest doll's house in all the world, I knew I was on the right track.

But after the mother had made the customary exclamations, she stayed on her knees a little bit too long . . .

At first she was full of wonder, then awkward and silent, and she must have already been asking herself what she would have to pay in exchange for so many hours of painstaking hope. It was time for me to fire my last round: 'Look,' I said, bending over her nape, 'there is even some marble, just there . . .'

And then she smiled and let me love her.

'And then with a smile she loved me' would have been snappier, no? Would have been stronger, more romantic. But I didn't dare . . . Because I've never known how, I guess . . . And when I look at her now, sitting on the other side of the table, light-hearted and affable, indulgent, so *magnanimous* with my family, and still just as attractive, just as . . . No, I've never known how . . . After the carpet

34

at the Bristol and the false charms of alcohol, perhaps Mathilde was the third misunderstanding in our relationship . . .

It's something new, feeling dizzy like this. Being so introspective, asking these useless questions about our relationship, and it really isn't like me. Been travelling too much, perhaps? Too much jet lag, too many hotel ceilings and restless nights? Or too many lies . . . Too many sighs . . . Too many mobile phones snapping shut whenever I show up in silence, too many forced poses and mood swings, or . . . Too much of nothing, if truth be told.

This wasn't the first time Laurence had cheated on me and up to now I'd usually got off fairly lightly. Not that I particularly liked it, but as I've already said, I'd thrown myself to the lions, trying to pat the kitty on my way into the coliseum. It hadn't taken me long to figure out that I was out of my league. She'd always refused to marry me, didn't want a child with me, didn't . . . And then . . . I was working so hard, was away so often myself . . . So I just learned to bite the bullet and sweet-talk my pride to keep it docile.

I managed pretty well, actually. I even think that her . . . slippages often acted as a fuel for our semblance of coupledom. Our pillows, in any case, were delighted.

She'd seduce, embrace, get bored, and come back to me.

Come back to me and talk to me in the dark. She pushed back the sheets and lifted herself up a bit, stroked my back, my shoulders, my face, a long time, slowly, tenderly . . . and always ended up murmuring something like 'You're the best, you know . . .' or 'There's no one else like you . . .' I kept my mouth shut, lay there motionless, never tried to resist her wandering hand.

Because even if the skin was mine, it often felt as if those nights of strategic withdrawal were for her scars, not mine, and that she was somehow trying to contain something, appease something, by massaging those scars, very gently.

But this time we haven't got that far. Nowadays she's trusting her insomnia to homeopathy and even in the dark she won't let me see what it is that's beating out of synch beneath her beautiful suit of armour . . .

Who is to blame? Mathilde, for growing up too fast, like Alice in Wonderland when she bursts her way out of her tiny house, blasting it to smithereens? She hardly needs me any more to hold her stirrup for her, and soon she'll be speaking English much better than I do . . .

Or Mathilde's father, for his carelessness that once upon a time seemed downright criminal but now seems almost funny? Irony has replaced bitterness and so much the better, but as a result I suffer by comparison. Even if I never mix up the dates of the school holidays, unlike some . . .

Or maybe the passage of time, no longer doing such a great job? I was young when I met Laurence, younger than her, I was her 'toy boy'. Now I've caught up. Maybe even overtaken her.

There are days when I feel so old.

So old . . .

Or could it be my profession − the constant struggle, no sooner have you persuaded them than you have to start all over again. Nothing is ever sure, and here I am nearly fifty years old and I sometimes get the feeling I'm still this frantic student high on caffeine rattling on about how 'I've got to rush, I'm running late,' to whoever will listen, and screw up with the drawings when presenting the umpteenth project to the umpteenth jury, and the only difference now is that the old sword of Damocles has lost none of its trenchancy over the years − it just cuts differently.

Yes, that's how things stand . . . Nothing to do with getting good marks and moving on to the next year, it's all about money. Lots and lots of money. Money, power, and megalomania too.

Not to mention politics, of course. No, let's not go there.

Or perhaps love is to blame? The way it . . .

'And you, Charles? What do you think?'

'Sorry, what?'

'About the Museum of Primitive Mankind at the Quai Branly?'

'Oh! I haven't been there in a while . . . I went to the site a few times, but . . .'

'At any rate,' says my sister Françoise, 'it's the worst place to try to have a pee . . . I don't know how much that thing cost but they definitely saved on the partition walls in the lavatory, that much I do know.'

I can't help but try and imagine the expression on the faces of Nouvel and his crew if they were here tonight . . .

'Yeah . . . they did it on purpose,' says her oaf of a husband, 'you think primitive mankind had a problem with toilet partitions? They just jumped behind a bush and bingo!'

Uh, no. Just as well they aren't here.

'Two hundred and thirty-five million,' says my other, unfunny brother-in-law, clutching his napkin.

And as no one at the table has reacted, he continues, 'Euros, of course. That thing, as you so kindly describe it, my dear Françoise, will have cost the French taxpayer the trifling sum of . . . (he pulls out his glasses and his mobile, fiddles with it and closes his eyes) . . . one billion, five hundred and forty million francs.'

'Old francs?' chokes my mother.

'Of course not,' he retorts, leaning back comfortably, 'new ones!'

He is exultant. This time he's got them. They're hooked. The assembly is in an uproar.

I try to catch Laurence's gaze; she returns a commiserating little smile. There are some things in my life, like this, that she still respects. I go back to my dinner.

The conversation is moving again, rumbling along in a mix of common sense and common stupidity. A few years ago they bleated on about the Opéra Bastille or the Bibliothèque Nationale, so this was just rehashing the same old stuff.

Claire, sitting next to me, leans over. 'How's Russia going?'

'It's 1812 and the Berezina all over again,' I confess, with a smile.

'No way.'

'Yes, I assure you. I'm waiting for the thaw to count my dead . . .'

'Shit.'

'Yup. Or *chort*, as they say.'

'Is it a problem?'

'Pff . . . not for the agency, no, but for me . . .'

'For you?'

'I don't know . . . I don't function well as Napoleon . . . I am missing his *vision*, I suppose . . .'

'Or his madness.'

'Oh, that will come!'

'You're joking, aren't you?' she adds, worried.

'*Da*!' I reassure her, sliding my hand between two shirt buttons, 'from the top of this disaster, forty centuries of architecture have not sufficed to look down on me!'

'When do you have to go back?'

'Monday.'

'Really?'

'Yup.'

'Why so soon?'

'Well, the latest is – get a load of this – the cranes are disappearing. Overnight, puff, they vanish.'

'That's impossible.'

'Yeah, you're right . . . It takes them a few more days than that to spread their long wings. Specially as they take the other machines with them, the excavators, and cement mixers, and drills. The whole lot.'

'You're having me on.'

'Not at all.'

'So? What are you going to do?'

'What am I going to do? Good question . . . To start with, hire a security company to keep an eye on our security company, and then once that one turns corrupt too, I'll . . .'

'You'll what?'

'I don't know . . . Send for the Cossacks, I suppose.'

'What a mess.'

'You said it.'

'And you're in charge of this shit?'

'Not at all. You can't be in charge. At all. You want to know what I'm doing?'

'Drinking!'

'Not only. I'm rereading *War and Peace*. And thirty years on I'm falling in love with Natasha just like the first time. That's what I'm doing.'

'Oh, Christ . . . And don't they send you some sublimely pretty girls so you can relax a bit?'

'They haven't yet . . .'

'Liar.'

'What about you? What news from the front?'

'Oh, me,' she sighs, reaching for her glass, 'I chose this job to save the planet and here I am trying to hide people's shit underneath a carpet made of genetically modified lawn, but other than that everything's fine.'

She chuckles.

'And that business with the dam?' I add.

'It's over with. They were had.'

'You see.'

'Pfff . . .'

'What do you mean, pfff? That's enough, hey, you need to follow the instructions on Mathilde's T-shirt!'

'In other words?'

'Enjoy!'

'Charles?'

'Mmm?'

'We should go into business together, you know . . .'

'To do what?'

'To build an ideal city.'

'But we *are in* an ideal city, love, you know that perfectly well . . .'

'Oh, I don't know that I'd say that . . .' she says, making a face, 'we need a few more Champion supermarkets here and there, don't you think?'

No sooner are the words out of her mouth than tring! his master's voice, our brother-in-law, butts in, 'Did you say something?'

'No, it was nothing. We were talking about your latest advertising campaign for caviar.'

'I'm sorry?'

Claire smiles at him. He shrugs his shoulders and goes back to his little speech. 'What the hell do they *do* with our tax money?'

All of a sudden I feel tired. Tired, tired, tired, so I pass the cheese plate round, without taking any, just to make things move a little faster.

I look at my father, always so discreet, courteous, and elegant. I look at Laurence and Edith telling their stories about stubborn stick-in-the-mud teachers and clumsy cleaning women, or was it the other way round, I look at the décor in this dining room where nothing has changed in fifty years, I look at . . .

'When do we do the presents?'

The kids have come charging downstairs, bless them. This means my bed can't be that far away.

'Clear the plates and come and join me in the kitchen,' their grandmother orders.

My sisters get up to go and fetch their packages. Mathilde winks at me and points to the bag containing our bag and John James Rockefeller Sainsbury ends the debate and wipes his mouth, 'And in any case, we're headed straight for disaster!'

There. You said it. In general, he waits until the coffee is served but now, with what might be prostate problems I suppose, he's got ahead of himself. Right . . . now put a sock in it.

Forgive me, but I'm tired, as I was saying.

Françoise comes in with her camera, switches off the lights, Laurence discreetly adjusts her hair, and the children scrape at the matches.

'There's still some light in the hallway!' someone shouts.

I volunteer to take care of it.

But as I am searching for the switch, I notice an envelope on the top of my pile of mail.

A long white envelope with black handwriting that seems familiar although I don't recognize it. The postmark means nothing to me. The name of a town and a postal code that I can't locate on the map, but the handwriting, on the other hand . . .

'Charles! What are you up to?' someone complains, and the cake is already quivering in the reflection in the window.

I switch off the light and come back to join the others.

But I'm no longer here.

I don't see Laurence's face in the bright candlelight. I don't start singing Happy Birthday. I don't even try to applaud. I . . . I'm like the other bloke when he bit into his madeleine, except that for me it's all different. I'm already retracting. I don't want to let anything in. I sense that a whole dimension of a forgotten world is opening up beneath my feet, I can sense the void beyond the fringe of the carpet and I'm transfixed, looking instinctively for a doorframe or a chairback to cling to. Because, yes, I do know that handwriting and there's something wrong. Something in me is resisting, something is already afraid of it. I'm looking. The clicking in my brain has been set in motion and is hiding the rush of sound from outside. I cannot hear their shouts, I cannot hear that they're asking me to put the lights back on.

'Char-ley!'

Sorry.

Laurence is rummaging through her presents and Claire hands me the cake server. 'Hey, what are you up to? You going to eat standing up?'

I sit down, take a slice of cake, attack with my little sp . . . I get back up again.

Because it's intimidating, I open the letter very carefully with a key in order not to tear it. The sheet has been folded in three. I lift the first fold, feel my heart pounding, then the second, and my heart stops.

Three words.

No signature. Nothing.

Three words.

Then the sound of the blade falling. Shlack.

Lift the blade back up.

As I look up I meet my own reflection in the mirror above the console. I feel like shaking that guy, feel like telling him, What the hell did you think, trying to fool us with your Proustian nonsense just now? Because you knew all along . . .

Didn't you?

He has nothing to say.

He looks at me and as I don't react he eventually murmurs something. I can't hear a thing but I can see his lips trembling. Something like, You stay. Just stay there with her. I'll go on in. I'm obliged to, you see, but you just stay there. I'll take care of everything.

So he goes back to his strawberry gateau. Hears sounds, voices, laughter, takes the glass of champagne someone hands to him and chinks it against others with a smile. The woman who has been sharing his life for years goes round the table with a kiss for everyone. She kisses him too. She says, it's just lovely, thank you. He protects himself from this surge of tenderness by admitting that it was Mathilde who picked it out and hears Mathilde contradicting him vehemently, as if he'd betrayed her. But he has smelled her perfume, and reaches for her hand, only she has already left, and she's kissing someone else. He holds his glass out for more. The bottle is empty. He gets up, goes to fetch another one. Opens it too quickly. A geyser of foam. Helps himself, empties his glass, starts again.

'Are you okay?' asks the woman next to him.

He says nothing.

'What's wrong? You're all pale. You look as if you'd seen a ghost . . .'

He drinks.

'Charles,' murmurs Claire.

'Nothing. I'm exhausted.'

He drinks.

Cracks inside. Fissures. He's crazed with tiny lines. Doesn't want this.

The varnish cracks, the hinges give way, the bolts snap.

He doesn't want this. He struggles. He drinks.

His older sister is giving him a funny look. He raises his glass in a toast to her. She persists. He declares with a smile, carefully detaching each syllable, 'Françoise . . . Just for once, just for *one time* in your life . . . try not to piss me off . . .'

She looks for her valiant knight of a stupid ass of a husband to come to her rescue, but he fails to grasp her outraged sign language. Her face falls. Fortunately, ta-da! her other sister is there.

Edith gently reprimands Charles with a shake of her headband, 'Charley . . .'

He raises his glass to her as well, and is in the process of finding his words when a hand comes to rest on his wrist. He turns, her grip is firm, he goes quiet.

The noise and chatter continue. Her hand is still there. He looks at her.

He asks, 'D'you have any cigarettes?'

'Well . . . You stopped smoking five years ago, might I remind you . . .'

'Well do you?'

His voice frightens her. She pulls her arm back.

★

They are standing together with their elbows on the railing of the terrace, their backs to the light and to the world.

Opposite them is the garden of their childhood. The same swing, the same impeccably manicured flowerbeds, the same incinerator for dead leaves, the same view, the same lack of horizon.

Claire pulls her pack from her pocket and slides it along the stone. He is about to grab it but she doesn't let go.

'Do you remember how hard it was, those first months? Do you remember what a rough time you had stopping?'

He tightens his hold on her hand. He is really hurting her now, and he says, 'Anouk is dead.'

3

How long does a cigarette last?

Five minutes?

If so, they stand there for five minutes without a word.

She gives in first, and her words overwhelm him. Because he was dreading them, because —

'So you've heard from Alexis?'

'I knew you were going to ask,' he says, in a very weary voice, 'I'd have staked my life on it and you cannot imagine how I —'

'How you what?'

'How it bothers me, how it upsets me . . . How I resent you for it. I thought you'd be a bit more generous, given the circumstances. I thought you'd ask me, "How did she die?" or "When?" or . . . I don't know. But to ask about him, fuck . . . No, not him. Not straight out of the blue like that . . . He doesn't deserve that any more.'

Another silence.

'How did she die?'

He takes the letter from his inside pocket.

'Here . . . And don't say, "It's his handwriting," or I'll kill you.'

She unfolds it, then folds it up again, and murmurs, 'Yes. It is his handwriting.'

He turns to her.

There are so many things he would like to say to her. Tender things, terrible things, words that cut and words that soothe, crazy words, words of a brother in arms or words of a sister of mercy. Or he could shake her, or knock her about, or split her down the middle, but the only thing he manages to moan, is one syllable.

'Claire . . .'

And doesn't she call his bluff and smile. But he knows her well, so he simply throws down his cards and grabs her by the elbow to bring her back to earth.

She twists her ankles in the gravel and he's talking to himself. Talking into the night.

He's talking for her sake and for his own, he's talking to the incinerator and the stars, and he says, 'There. It's over.'

Tears up the letter and tosses it into the bin in the kitchen. When he lifts his foot from the pedal and the lid falls back down, bang, he has the feeling he has managed to close some sort of Pandora's box, just in time. And since he's right there by the sink, he splashes his face, groaning.

Goes back to join the others, back to life. Feels better already. It's over.

★

And the soothing impression of a splash of cold water on an exhausted face, how long does that last?

Twenty seconds?

Time's up. He searches for his glass, downs it in one, and pours himself another.

And goes to sit on the sofa. Right up close to his partner. She tugs on her jacket.

'And you, you . . . Be kind to me, you . . .' he warns, ''cause I've already had a few, y'know . . .'

She doesn't find it funny at all, if anything she's ruffled, put out. And this has a sobering effect on him.

He leans over, places his hand on her knee and looks up at her: 'You know that you're going to die someday, too? You know that, my sweet? That you too are going to snuff it?'

'He really has had too much to drink!' she protests, forcing a laugh, then thinking better of it: 'Get up, please, you're hurting me.'

There is an uneasy silence over the sugar bowl. Mado looks questioningly at her youngest daughter; Claire signals to her to go on drinking her coffee as if there were nothing wrong. Stir, Maman, stir. I'll explain. Kazatchok makes a joke that falls flat, and the country bumpkin grows restless.

'Right,' sighs Edith, 'let's get going. Bernard, will you call the children, please?'

'Good idea!' adds Charles, 'pack 'em all up in the big SUV!

Hey, champion? Now that you've got that lovely SUV? I saw it just now . . . Smoked glass, an' all . . .'

'Charles, please. You're not funny any more.'

'But . . . I've never been funny, Edith. You know that perfectly well.'

He gets up, stands at the bottom of the stairs and shouts, 'Mathilde! Come on, heel, dog!'

Then turning to the assembly of dumbstruck jurors: 'Don't panic. It's a private joke.'

Embarrassed silence suddenly broken by delirious yapping.

'What'd I tell you?'

He spins around, holding onto the brass knob, and says sharply to the queen of the party, 'It's true she's a pain, your kid, these days, but y'know what? She's the only beautiful thing you've ever given me.'

'Right. Let's go,' says Laurence, who's had enough, 'and give me the keys. I'm not letting you drive in that state.'

'Well said!'

He buttons his jacket, submits.

'Good night, all. I'm dead.'

4

'But how?' asks Mado.

'That's all I know,' replies Claire, who has stayed behind after the last farewells to help them shake out the tablecloth.

Her father has just joined them in the kitchen with a pile of dirty plates.

'Now what's going on in this madhouse?' he sighs.

'Our old neighbour died . . .'

'Which one this time? Old Madame Verdier?'

'No. Anouk.'

Oh, how heavy the plates seem suddenly. He puts them down and sits at the end of the table.

'But . . . When did it happen?'

'We don't know.'

'An accident?'

'We don't know, I said!' says his wife, annoyed.

Silence.

'And yet she was young, she was born in . . .'

'She was sixty-three,' murmurs her husband.

'Oh . . . it can't be. Not her. She was . . . too alive to go and die . . .'

'Maybe it was cancer?' suggests Claire.

'Yes, or . . .'

Her mother glances at an empty bottle.

'Mado . . .' frowns her husband.

'What, Mado? What, Mado? She drank, and you know it!'

'She moved away such a long time ago . . . We don't know how she lived after that.'

'Always ready to defind her, aren't you?'

How nasty Mado seemed all of a sudden. Claire reckoned that

she had missed a few episodes, but had never imagined they'd still be at this point this evening . . .

Charles, herself, and now her father . . . A fine game of skittles.

Oh, it was such a long time ago, all that. But no, on the other hand . . . Charles losing his grip and now you, Papa. I've never seen you look as old as in this light . . . You . . .

Anouk. Anouk and Alexis Le Men. When will you leave us in peace? Just look at them, Charles and his dad . . . The grass never grew back after you'd been through here.

Right. Now get out of here. Get lost.

You don't go shooting at convalescents.

'Pass me the glasses, Maman.'

'I just can't believe it.'

'Maman . . . Enough, now. She's dead.'

'No. She isn't.'

'What do you mean, she isn't?'

'People like her lot never die.'

'They do, too! Proof is . . . C'mon, give me a hand, I've got to get going.'

Silence. Purr of the dishwasher.

'She was mad.'

'I'm going to bed,' announces her father.

'Yes, Henri, she was mad!'

He turns around, very weary. 'All I said was that I'm going to bed, Mado.'

'Oh, I know what you're thinking!'

She was silent for a moment, then in a flat voice, looking away, out of the window, at a shadow that no longer existed, not caring whether anyone heard or not: 'One day, I recall – it was at the beginning, I hardly knew her – I'd given her a plant . . . or a flower in a pot, I don't remember . . . To thank her for having Charles over, I suppose . . . Oh! It was nothing special, right. A silly little plant that I must have brought home from the market . . . And a few days later, when I'd utterly forgotten about it, she rang at the door. She was in quite a state and she was bringing my present back to me and shoving it into my hands.

'"What is it?" I muttered, "is something wrong?" "I . . . I can't

47

keep it," she spluttered, "it . . . it's going to die . . ." She was white as a sheet. "But why do you say that? The plant looks absolutely fine!" "No, look . . . There are some leaves that have turned yellow, there, look . . ." She was trembling. "Oh go on," I said, laughing, "that's perfectly normal. You just pull the leaves off, and that's it!" And then – I remember as if it were yesterday – she began to sob and she pushed against me to put the plant down at my feet.

'We could not get her to calm down.

'"Forgive me. Forgive me. But I can't," she hiccupped, "I just can't, you see . . . I haven't the strength. I have no more strength . . . For people, yes, for the children, yes, I can make an effort . . . but sometimes even then it does no good, I . . . they'll leave me anyway, you know . . . But now, when I see this plant is dying, too, I . . ." A veritable fountain. "I can't. And you can't make me. Because . . . it's not as important, you understand . . . Huh? Don't you see, it's less important?"

'She frightened me. It didn't even occur to me to offer her a coffee or tell her to come and sit down for a while. I watched her blow her nose in her sleeve with her eyes popping out and I said to myself, This woman is mad. She is completely bonkers.'

'And then?' asked Claire.

'And then, nothing. What did you expect me to do? I took the plant, put it with the others in the living room, and I probably had it for years.'

Claire was struggling with the bin liner.

'What would you have done in my place?'

'I don't know,' she murmured.

The letter . . . She hesitated a split second, then tossed the left-overs from the plates, the bits of fat and the coffee grounds on top of all she had left of Alexis. The ink ran. She pulled the liner closed with all her strength, the plastic tie snapped. Oh shit, she moaned, shoving the bin into the pantry. Oh, shit.

'But . . . you do remember her, don't you?' insisted her mother.

'Of course . . . Could you just move, there, so I can wipe here with the sponge?'

'And you never thought she was mad?' she went, putting her hand on Claire's to force her to pause for a moment.

Claire straightened her back, blew sideways on a lock of hair that was tickling her eyes, and looked at her mother. Her mother, this woman who had lectured her so often with her principles, her morals, and all her good manners: 'No.'

Then, concentrating again on the grain of the wood, 'No. I never thought she was mad. At all.'

'Oh?' went her mother, somewhat disappointed.

'I always thought . . .'

'Thought what?'

'That she was beautiful.'

Wrinkles of disapproval: 'Of course she was pretty, but that's not what I'm referring to, am I, I was talking about *her*, her behaviour . . .'

I figured that much, reflected Claire.

Rinsed out the sponge, wiped her hands, and suddenly felt old. Or was it that she felt like a child all over again, the littlest one.

Which amounted to the same thing.

She kissed her mother's worried brow and went off in search of her coat.

From the front door she called out a farewell to her father. He had remained within earshot, that she knew, and she closed the door behind her.

Once she was in the car she switched on her mobile – no messages of course – put her sidelights on, glanced in the rear view mirror before pulling out and saw that her lower lip had doubled in size. And that it was bleeding.

Stupid idiot, she scolded herself, while continuing to nibble at exactly the spot where the pain felt so good. Poor little black robes, when you wear them you're capable of holding back millions of cubic metres of water while you lean against a monstrous dam, but you're utterly incapable of stopping three little tears: soon you'll be carried away on the current, drowned by a ridiculous sorrow.

Go to bed.

5

She had followed him into the bathroom.

'Air France left a message. They found your suitcase.'

He mumbled three words, rinsing his mouth. She added, 'Did you know?'

'Sorry?'

'That you left your case at the airport?'

He nodded and their reflection deterred him. She turned away and started to unbutton her shirt.

She continued, 'Any reason why?'

'It was too heavy.'

Silence.

'So you left it.'

'That's a new bra, isn't it?'

'Any chance I can find out what is going on?'

The scene was taking place in the mirror. Two half-length portraits. A second-rate Punch and Judy. They went on staring at each other for a long time, very close but never really looking.

'Any chance I can find out what's going on?' she repeated.

'I'm tired.'

'And it's because you're tired that you humiliated me in front of everyone?'

No answer.

'Why did you say that, Charles?'

No answer.

'About Mathilde, that is.'

'What is this? Is it silk?'

She was on the verge of – then thought better of it. Left the room, switching off the light.

*

She sat up when he leaned against the armchair to take his shoes off, and it was a relief. If she had actually fallen asleep without removing her eye make-up, that would have been a sign that the situation was really quite serious. But no, she hadn't reached that point yet.

She would never reach that point. It might flood, but only after she'd done her eyeliner. The earth might tremble, but you go on moisturizing.

You go on moisturizing.

He sat on the edge of the bed and felt fat.

Or heavy. Yes, heavy.

Anouk . . . he stretched out with a sigh. Anouk.

What would she have thought of him nowadays? What would she have recognized? And the postmark . . . Where was that place, exactly? What was Alexis doing living so far away? And why hadn't he sent a proper announcement? An envelope with a black border. A more precise date. A place. Names of people. Why? What was this? Punishment? Cruelty? A simple piece of information, my mother has died, or an ultimate spit in the face, and you'd never have known a thing if I hadn't had the immense kindness to spend a few cents to announce it to you.

Who was he nowadays? And how long ago did she die? Charles hadn't had the presence of mind to look at the date on the postmark. How long had the letter been waiting for him at his parents'? How far had the maggots got? What was left of her? Had Alexis donated her organs the way she had so often made him promise he would?

Swear you will, she said. Swear on my heart that you will.

And he swore.

Anouk . . . Forgive me. I . . . Who was it that got you, in the end? And why didn't you wait for me? Why did I never go back there? Yes. I know why. Anouk, you . . . Laurence's sighs put an abrupt end to his ravings. Farewell.

'What did you say?'
  'Nothing, sorry. I . . .'

He reached over, found her hip, placed his hand there. She'd stopped breathing.

'Sorry.'

'You're so hard on me,' she murmured.

He didn't know what to say.

'You and Mathilde . . . You are . . . It feels like I'm living with two teenagers . . . You make me tired. You wear me out, Charles . . . Who am I now, for the two of you? The woman who opens her wallet? Her life? Her sheets? What? I just can't take it any more, I – do you understand?'

Silence.

'Did you hear what I said?'

He said nothing.

'Are you asleep?'

'No. Please forgive me . . . I'd had too much to drink and –'

'And what?'

What could he say? How much would she understand? Why had he never talked to her about all that? What was there to tell, anyway? How much was left of all those years? Nothing. A letter.

An anonymous letter ripped to shreds, at the bottom of a rubbish bin at his parents' house . . .

'I just found out that someone died.'

'Who?'

'The mother of one of my childhood friends.'

'Pierre?'

'No. Someone else. Someone you don't know. We . . . we're not friends any more.'

She sighed. Class photos, buttered toast, *The Magic Roundabout* on telly, not really her thing. Nostalgia was a bore.

'And you suddenly turn unbelievably obnoxious because the mother of some guy you haven't seen in forty years just died? That's what you're saying?'

That was exactly what he was saying. What a fabulous gift she had, she could always sum it all up, fold, label, put away, and forget. And how he had loved that side of her, her common sense, her vitality, her ability to toss it all out, the better to see which way things were headed. How he had clung to that, all these years. It was so . . . comfortable. And it was probably what had saved him.

So he clung to it, once again. To her spirit, to whatever credit he still had left with her, so that he could move his hand and slide it down her thigh.

Turn this way, he begged in silence. Turn this way. Help me.

She didn't move.

He pulled his pillow closer to hers and curled up against the back of her neck. His hand continued winding up her nightgown.

Give me some slack, Laurence. Show me something, I beg you.

'And what was so special about this woman?' she asked jokingly, 'was she good at baking cakes?'

He let go of the silk folds.

'No.'

'Did she have big breasts? Did she take you on her lap?'

'No.'

'She –'

'Sshhh,' he interrupted, parting her hair. 'Sshhh, stop now. Nothing. It was nothing. She's dead, that's all.'

Laurence turned round. He was tender, he was attentive, she liked it and it was dreadful.

'Mmm . . . funerals suit you,' she eventually sighed, pulling the duvet up.

Her words threw him and for a split second he was sure that – no, it was nothing. He clenched his teeth and banished the thought from his mind before it could even take shape. Stop right there.

She fell asleep. He got up again.

★

As he took his BlackBerry from his briefcase, he saw that Claire had tried to ring him several times. He winced.

He made a coffee and settled in the kitchen.

It took a few clicks and then he found it. Dizzying.

Ten numbers.

Ten numbers were all that separated them, and he had invested so much bitterness, so many days and nights, in widening the gap.

How mischievous life could be . . . ten numbers for a dial tone. And pick up.

Or disconnect.

And like his sister, he was hard on himself. His screen was now displaying all the details of the path that could lead him there. The number of kilometres, the motorway exits, the cost of the tolls, and the name of a village.

Taking this trembling as an excuse, he went to fetch his jacket and, on the pretext that he had it on his shoulders, pulled out his diary. He looked for some useless pages – August, for example – and jotted down the itinerary for an improbable voyage.

Yes . . . In August, perhaps? Perhaps . . . He would see.

Jotted down the contact information in the same way: like a sleepwalker. Perhaps he would send him a word, one evening . . . Or two, or three?

Just as he had done.

To see if the guillotine was still working . . .

But would he have the courage? Would he even feel like it? Or be weak enough? He hoped not.

He closed his diary.

His mobile rang again. He ignored the call, got up, rinsed out his cup, came back, saw that she had left him a message, hesitated, sighed, gave in, listened, groaned, swore, lost his temper, cursed her, switched off the light, took his jacket and went to lie down on the sofa.

'He would have been nineteen years old, three months from now.'

And the worst of it was that she had said these words quite calmly. Yes, calmly. Just like that, in the middle of the night and after the beep.

How could she say such a thing to a machine?

Or even think it?

And take pleasure in it?

He felt another burst of fury. What was she thinking with this bloody soap opera?

Disconnect, old girl, disconnect.

He called her back to give her a piece of his mind.

She picked up the phone. You're being ridiculous. I know, she replied.

'I know.'

And the softness of her voice pulled the rug out from under his feet.

'Everything you're about to say to me, Charles, I already know. No need to shake me or laugh in my face, I can do it on my own. But who else can I talk to about all this besides you? If I had a decent girlfriend, I'd wake her up, but . . . you're my best girlfriend.'

'You didn't wake me up.'

Silence.

'Talk to me,' she murmured.

'It's because it's night-time,' he continued, hoarsely. 'Night fears . . . She used to talk about it really well, do you remember? How people would freak out, just lose it completely and drown themselves in their glass of water while she held their hand . . . Things will be better tomorrow. Time to sleep now.'

Long silence.

'D'you –'

'I –'

'D'you remember what you said to me that day? In that shitty café across from the clinic?'

He didn't reply.

'You said, "You'll have other kids."'

'Claire . . .'

'I'm sorry. I'm going to hang up now.'

He sat up. 'No! That's the easy way! I'm not going to let you off so easily. Think about it. Think about yourself for once. No, that's not something you know how to do . . . Okay, think about yourself as if you were a really complicated lawsuit. Look me in the eyes and tell me straight: do you regret your decision? Do you really regret it? Be honest, my learned friend . . .'

'I'm going to be for—'

'Shut up. I don't care. I just want you to answer yes or no.'

'—ty-one years old,' she continued, 'I loved a man I could have died for, and then I worked hard to forget him and I worked so hard that I lost myself along the way.'

She sniggered.

'It's bloody stupid, huh?'

'He wasn't a good bloke . . .'

She didn't say anything.

'The only time he was ever straight with you was when he told you he wanted nothing to do with the pregnancy . . .'

She remained silent.

'And I said pregnancy on purpose, Claire, so as not to say . . . Because it was nothing. Nothing. Just –'

'Shut up,' she spat, 'you don't know what you're talking about.'

'Nor do you.'

She hung up.

He would not give up.

Got her voicemail. Tried her landline. At the ninth ring, she gave in.

She'd switched her rifle to the other shoulder. Her voice was cheerful. Something she'd learned in court, no doubt. Dissembling in order to save her defence.

'Yes, this is SOS Pathos, good eeevening. This is Irma here, may I help you?'

Smiling in the dark.

He loved this woman.

'Having trouble coping, is that it?' she continued.

'That's right . . .'

'In the old days, we'd have gone to the *Bistro Chez Louis* with your little classmates and we would have drunk so much that we would never have come out with such utter crap . . . And then, you know what? We would have had a *good* night's sleep . . . A good, good night's sleep . . . Until noon at least . . .'

'Or two . . .'

'You're right. Two o'clock, quarter past . . . And then we'd be hungry . . .'

'And there'd be nothing to eat . . .'

'Yeah . . . and the worst of it is that there weren't even any Champion supermarkets back then . . .' she sighed.

I could picture her in her room with her smile, all crooked, her piles of files at the foot of her bed, her cigarette butts drowning in a last swallow of herbal tea and the dreadful flannelette nightgown she called her old maid's negligee. What's more, I could hear her blowing her nose in it . . .

'It's really bloody stupid, isn't it?'

'Bloody stupid indeed,' I said.

'Why am I such an idiot?' she implored.

'Blame the genes, I reckon. Your sisters got all the intelligence.'

I could hear her dimples.

'Right, I'll hang up now,' she concluded, 'but you too, Charles, you've got to look after yourself . . .'

'Oh, I'll –' I waved myself away, wearily.

'Yes, you. You never say a thing. You never confide in anyone and you go off hunting bulldozers as if you were Prince Andrei . . .'

'Nicely put.'

'Bah. It's my job, may I remind you. Right, good night.'

'Wait, one last thing.'

'Yes?'

'I'm not really sure I like being your best girlfriend, but hey, let's just suppose I am. So I'm going to speak to you like the best of best girlfriends, okay?'

She didn't reply.

'Leave him, Claire. Leave that man.'

Silence.

'You're too old for this. It's not Alexis. This isn't the past. It's that man. He's the one who's hurting you. One day, I remember, we were talking about your work and you said, "It's impossible to be just, because justice doesn't exist. But injustice, on the other hand, does exist. Injustice is easy to fight because it stares you in the face and everything becomes crystal clear." And, well, we've reached that point. I don't give a fuck about that bloke, about who he is or what he's worth, but what I do know is that *per se*, this is an *unjust* thing in your life. Throw him on the dump.'

Still nothing.

'Are you there?'

'You're right. I'm going to go on a diet and then stop smoking, and after that I'll get rid of him.'

'Now you're talking.'

'Easy-peasy.'

'Right, go to bed and dream about a nice boy . . .'

'Who'll have a gorgeous SUV,' she sighed.

'Humungous!'

'And a flat screen.'

'Well, obviously. Right. Hugs and kisses.'

'Same . . . (sniff) here.'

'Christ, you're a pain. I can hear you, you're still crying.'

'Yes, but I'm okay now,' she sniffled, 'really I am. It's a good big fat cry and it's all because of you, you worm.'

And she hung up again.

He grabbed a cushion and wrapped himself in his jacket.

End of this week's *Play for Today*.

★

If Charles Balanda – one metre eighty, seventy-eight kilos, bare-foot, baggy trousers and belt undone, his arms crossed over his chest and his nose stuffed into that old blue cushion – had finally fallen asleep, the story would have ended there.

He was our hero. He would have turned forty-seven, a few months from then, and he'd had a life, but not much of one. Not much at all . . . He wasn't very good at it. He must have been telling himself that the best was behind him, and he didn't dwell on the matter. The best, you said? Best of what? And for whom . . . No, never mind, he was too tired. The words were missing, for him and for me. His case was too heavy, and I didn't really feel like carrying it for him. I understood him.

I understood him.

But.

There was something she had said . . . Something which kept creeping up on him, to squeeze a sponge soaked in water onto his face, when in fact he was half dead over in his corner.

Dead and already defeated.

Defeated and totally indifferent. The prize too paltry, his gloves too tight, life too predictable.

'Three months from now.'

That was what she said, wasn't it?

Those four words seemed more terrible than all the rest. So, she had been keeping track from the beginning? From the first day of the end of her last period? No . . . It wasn't possible.

And all these ellipses, this pitiful mental calculating, all the weeks and months and years living at a low ebb obliged him to look back.

He was suffocating, in any case.

His eyes are open wide. Because she said, three months from now, he thinks, okay, that means April . . . And the machine starts up again and he too is counting the gap on his fingers.

That makes July, that makes September since it had already been two months. Yes, that's it, he remembers now . . .

End of summer. He had just finished his internship at Valmer's and was getting ready to fly to Greece. It was the last evening, they were celebrating his departure. She had stopped by, on the off chance.

It's lucky you stopped by, he said, pleased, come over here, let me introduce you, and when he turned round to take her by the shoulders, he understood that she . . .

Yes. He remembers. And because he remembers, he is devastated. That *unbearable* message was the poacher's snare, sprung from a poorly wound ball of wire and, by opening his hand and letting out nine months – twenty years, in other words – in the dark, he had got caught in the trap.

Never mind. Too bad for him. He won't fall asleep. The story is never-ending. And at least he is still honest enough to admit that those three months were nothing more than a pretext. If she hadn't said that, he would have found something else. The story is never-ending. The bell has just rung and he has to get back to his feet.

Go back into the ring, get pounded some more.

Anouk was dead, and Claire, that night, had not stopped by on the off chance.

6

He had followed her down the street. It was a beautiful evening, soft, warm, elastic. The asphalt gave off a good Paris smell and the outdoor cafés were packed. Several times he asked her if she wasn't hungry, but she kept walking ahead of him, the distance between them ever greater.

'Right,' he said, getting cross, '*I'm* hungry and I'm fed up. I'm stopping here.'

She turned around, took a paper out of her bag and placed it on top of his menu.

'Tomorrow. Five o'clock.'

An address in the *banlieue*. An utterly improbable place.

'At five o'clock I'll be on the plane,' he said with a smile.

But not for long.

How could you smile at such a face?

★

Later, she had come into that café bent double. As if she were trying to hold back what she had just lost. He had got up, put his hand on the back of her neck, and let her cry her fill. Behind her, the café owner was sending him anxious looks which Charles waved away with his other hand as best he could, flattening the air around them with his palm. Afterwards he had left a big tip, to make up for the embarrassment, and had taken her to see the sea.

It was a crazy idea but what else could he have done?

He closed the door to the toilet and put on a jumper before going back to collapse on the sofa.

What else could he have done?

They had gone on long walks, drunk a great deal, smoked all sorts of amusing grasses and even danced, on occasion. But most of the time they did nothing.

Sat there and observed the light. Charles drew, dreamt, haggled down in the port, and made their meals, while his sister read the first page of her book again and again before closing her eyes.

And yet she never slept. If he had asked her a question, she would have heard and would have responded.

But he didn't ask.

They had been brought up together, had shared the same tiny flat for almost three years and had both known Alexis for ever. Nothing could resist them.

And there was not a shadow on this steep terrace.

Not a single one.

On the last evening, they had gone to the restaurant and, as they started on the second bottle of retsina, he tested the atmosphere: 'Will you be okay?'

'Yes.'

'Sure?'

She nodded vigorously.

'Do you want to come back home to live?'

She shook her head vigorously.

'Where will you go?'

'To stay with a friend . . . a girl from college . . .'

'Okay.'

He had just shifted his chair so he could share the street scenes with her.

'You still have keys, anyway.'

'And you?'

'What about me?'

'You never talk to me about your love life.' She made a face. 'Um love, well, your life, what's going on . . .'

'Nothing terribly exciting, I should think.'

'What about the surveyor you were seeing?'

'She went off to take some other measurements . . .'

She smiled.

Although he was tanned, his face seemed extremely brittle. He filled their glasses again and forced her to drink to better days.

After a long while she tried to roll herself a cigarette.

'Charles?'

'That's my name.'

'You won't tell, will you?'

'What am I supposed to tell him?' he sniggered. 'Talk to him about honour?'

Her cigarette paper tore. He took the packet from her hands, painstakingly sprinkled a gutterful of tobacco into the paper and lifted it to his lips to lick it.

'I meant Anouk.'

He froze.

'No,' he said, spitting out a flake of tobacco, 'no. Of course not.'

Handed her the cigarette and shifted his chair to make more room.

'Are . . . are you still in touch with her?'

'Rarely.'

His glasses had just fallen down onto his nose. She didn't push him any further.

★

In Paris it was raining. They shared a taxi and parted at Les Gobelins.

'Thanks,' she murmured into his ear. 'It's over, I promise you. I'll be all right.'

He watched as she hurried down the steps into the metro.

She must have felt his eyes on her back because she turned round halfway down to make a diver's O with her thumb and index finger, and gave him a wink.

A comforting little gesture, reassurance that all was well.

He'd believed her, and he'd gone off with an easy heart.

Young and naïve in those days . . . Believed in signs.

It was yesterday, and in a few weeks, it would be nineteen years.

She'd fooled him, good and proper.

7

He was dozing and when he came round, Snoopy was gazing at him silently. It was Snoopy from the old days, with a round face, puffy with sleep, rubbing her ear with her front paw.

Dawn tapping at the window; he wondered for a moment whether he was not still dreaming. The walls were so pink . . .

'Did you sleep here?' she asked him sadly.

Dear Lord, no. This was life. New round.

'What time is it?' he yawned.

She'd already turned round and was headed back to her room.

'Mathilde . . .'

She froze.

'It's not what you think . . .'

'I don't think anything,' she replied.

And vanished.

Six twelve. He dragged himself to the coffee maker and put in a double dose. It was going to be a long day . . .

Frozen stiff, he locked himself in the bathroom.

With one buttock on the edge of the bathtub and his chin crushed against his fist, he let his mind drift amidst the bubbling water and warm steam. What was absorbing him at the moment did not require many words: Balanda, you're pissing me off. Stop it right now, and get a grip.

Up to now you have always been capable of finding your way without giving it too much thought, so you're not going to start today. It's too late, you understand? You're too old for the luxury of this sort of disaster. She's dead. They're all dead. Pull the curtain and take care of the living. Behind that wall there's a little Dresden doll who's acting tough, but actually she looks like she's having a hard time. She gets up far too early for her age . . . Turn off that bloody tap and go and yank those headphones from her ears for a second.

He knocked gently and went in and sat on the floor, at her feet, his back against the side of her bed.

'It's not what you think.'

Silence.

'What you up to, my loyal friend?' he murmured, 'are you sleeping? Are you listening to sad songs under your duvet or are you wondering what this old fool of a Charles has come to bore you with?'

Still she said nothing.

'If I was sleeping on the sofa, it's because I couldn't sleep, actually . . . And I didn't want to disturb your mum.'

He heard her turn over and felt something of hers, perhaps her knee, brush his shoulder.

'And even as I'm telling you this, I figure I'm wrong . . . Because I don't have to justify myself to you . . . None of this is any of your business, or, rather, it doesn't *concern* you. It's grown-up business, well, between adults, and –'

Oh, what's the bloody use, he thought, why go getting up to your neck in . . . Talk to her about something else.

He looked up and inspected her wall in the half-light. It had been a long time since he had actually looked closely at her little world, and yet he adored everything about it. He adored seeing her photos, her drawings, her mess, her posters, her life, her memories . . .

The walls in the room of a growing child are always a funny sort of ethnology lesson. Square metres that are constantly vibrating and taking new forms as they gobble up the Blu-tack. What was she up to these days? Had she been with a few girlfriends to take goofy photos in a photo booth? What were the latest trinkets, and where had she hidden it, the face of the one who'd do better to be a tree one could put one's arms around and it could not complain?

He was surprised to find a photo of Laurence and himself that he had never seen. A photo she had taken when she was still a child. In the days when her index finger always showed up somewhere in the sky. They looked happy, and you could see the mountain of Sainte-Victoire behind their smiles. And there was a gel capsule in a transparent bag where you could read *Be a Star Instantly*, a poem by Prévert copied out on large-squared paper, and which ended with:

In Paris
On earth
Earth that is a star.

Photos of blonde, fleshy-lipped actresses, codes for internet sites copied out on beer mats, key rings, idiotic cuddly toys, painstaking flyers for concerts out in the sticks, ribbon bracelets, an ad for a Monsieur G who *brings back your loved one and ensures you'll pass you're exam the frist time round*, Corto Maltese's smile, an old ski resort day pass, and even the reproduction of the Aphrodite of Callimachus which he'd sent to her to put an end to a prickly phase.

Their first major crisis . . .

He'd gone berserk because she was exposing her belly.

'Dye, tattoos, piercing – anything you like!' he'd shouted, 'even feathers out your bum if that turns you on! But not your belly, Mathilde. Not your belly . . .' He'd oblige her to lift her arms to the sky in the morning before she left for school and he'd send her back to her room if her T-shirt rose above her bellybutton.

There ensued weeks of very bitter bad moods, but he'd stood his ground. It was the first time he resisted her. The first time he took on his role of old fart.

Not her belly, no way.

'A woman's belly is among the most mysterious things on earth, one of the most moving, beautiful, sexy things, as they might say in your idiot magazines,' he waffled, under Laurence's condescending gaze. 'And . . . no . . . Cover it. Don't let them steal it from you . . . It's not that I'm trying to play Father Morality here, or to talk to you about what's decent and what isn't, Mathilde . . . I'm talking to you about love. Lots of blokes are going to try to guess the size of your arse or the shape of your tits, and that's fair enough, but your belly, keep it for the man you'll love some day, you . . . Do you understand?'

'Yes, I think she gets the picture, now,' said her mother dryly; she wanted to move on to other things. 'Go and put on your nun's habit, my child.' Charles had looked at her, shaking his head, and finally said no more. But the next morning he went to the shop at the Louvre and sent her that postcard, where he'd written, 'Look, it's because you can't see it that it's so beautiful.'

Her face, her clothes grew longer, but she never mentioned the postcard. He was even sure she'd chucked it out. But she hadn't, here it was . . . Between a rap singer in string underwear and a half-naked Kate Moss.

He went on exploring . . .

'You like Chet Baker, do you?' he asked, surprised.

'Who?' she grunted.

'This guy, here.'

'I don't even know who he is. I just think he's buff.'

It was a black and white shot. When he was young and looked like James Dean. A more febrile version. More intelligent, more emaciated. He was slouched against a wall, holding on to the back of a chair to keep from slipping farther.

His trumpet on his knees and his eyes staring off into space.

She was right. Buff.

'It's funny . . .'

'What is?'

He could feel her knee against the back of his neck.

'When I was your age . . . No, we were a little bit older . . . I had a friend who was crazy about Chet Baker. Completely utterly crazy. Fall down dead crazy. He must have worn the same T-shirt, and I'll bet he knew this photo inside out and backwards . . . And it's precisely because of him that I spent the night freezing my arse off on the sofa . . .'

'Why?'

'Why did I freeze my arse off?'

'No . . . why did he like him so much?'

'Because it was Chet Baker, that's why! A great musician! A bloke who could speak every language and every feeling on earth with his trumpet. And his voice, too . . . I'll lend you my record-ings and then you'll understand why you think he's so handsome.'

'Who was your friend?'

Charles sighed a smile. This business isn't over yet . . . Not right away, in any case, he'll just have to get used to it.

'His name was Alexis. And he played the trumpet, too. Not just the trumpet, either. He played everything . . . Piano, harmonica, ukulele . . . He was –'

'Why are you talking about him in the past tense? Is he dead?'

This business isn't over, I said . . .

'No, but I don't know what became of him. Or whether he went on with his music.'

'Did you fall out?'

'Yes. So much so that I thought I'd wiped him from my memory . . . I thought he no longer existed and –'

'And what?'

'I was wrong. He still exists. And it's because I got a letter from him last night that I slept in the living room.'

'What did the letter say?'

'You really want to know?'

'Yes.'

'It informed me that his mother had died.'

'Great . . . That's cheerful,' she grumbled.

'You said it.'

'Hey, Charles?'

'*Hey*, Mathilde?'

'I've got a gi-normous mega hard physics project for tomorrow . . .'

He got to his feet, making a face. His back . . .

'So much the better!' he cheered. 'Good news. That's just what I needed. Mega hard physics along with Chet Baker and Gerry Mulligan. A dream Sunday ahead. Right . . . Go back to sleep, now. Try and get a few more hours, sweetheart.'

He was looking for the door handle when she added, 'Why did you fall out?'

'Because . . . precisely because he acted like he was Chet Baker, he wanted to do everything like him . . . And doing everything like him also meant doing a lot of stupid things.'

'Such as?'

'Such as drugs, for example.'

'And so?'

'Well, my little girl,' he grumbled, his hands on his hips in imitation of the big teddy bear in her childhood kiddie programme, 'the sandman has just been through here, and I'm headed back up to my ccc-loud. Another bedtime story for you to-mor-row. And only if you're a ve-ry good girl. Ta-dah!'

He saw her smile, faintly lit by the clock radio.

★

He ran some more hot water and sank into a tub near to over-flowing, submerging his hair and thoughts too, then he rose to the surface and closed his eyes.

★

And, contrary to all expectations, it turned out to be a beautiful late winter day.

A day full of pulleys and the principle of inertia. A day for *My Funny Valentine* and *How High the Moon*. A day that was utterly indifferent to the laws of physics.

His foot kept time under the little desk that was far too cluttered for clear thinking and, with a 20-centimetre ruler in his hand, he tapped her rhythmically on the head whenever her thinking went astray.

And for a few hours he forgot his fatigue and his files. His colleagues, his migrating cranes, and his deadlines, all overdue. For a few hours, forces in movement became compensating forces.

Truce. Knockout by default. Brass instrument therapy. Placed on a drip of nostalgia and 'black poetry,' as they said in one of the album booklets.

The speakers on Mathilde's computer weren't very good, alas, but the track titles scrolled onto the screen, and it was as if each and every one were addressed to him.

To them.

In A Sentimental Mood. My Old Flame. These Foolish Things. My Foolish Heart. The Lady Is A Tramp. I've Never Been In Love Before. There Will Never Be Another You. If You Could See Me Now. I Waited For You and . . . *I May Be Wrong.*

A disturbing sort of short-cut, he mused. And also . . . perhaps . . . Something that might serve nicely as an oration, no?

He would have had to be extremely naïve to use such worn-out words. Said over and over again and so poorly tailored that they could clothe any bloody idiot on the planet. But never mind, he'd deal with it. It felt good to be back in these titles, this music, these songs, the way he used to be. To be the tall gangly bloke again, confining his life within other people's emotions.

A guy blowing into his trumpet and there you were. Jericho.

★

He didn't like the word 'tramp', which was ambiguous. Vagabond, rather. A barefoot beggar she may well have been, but where the rest was concerned, her foolish heart could defy even Newton.

September Song.
He opened his hand. They'd heard that track together . . .
Such a long time ago. At the New Morning jazz club wasn't it? And how handsome he still was, then.
Terrifyingly handsome.
But a mess. All thin and gaunt and toothless and ravaged by alcohol. And he winced, and moved oh-so cautiously, as if he'd just taken a beating.

After the concert, they'd had a row precisely because of that. Alexis couldn't stay still, he was in a trance again, swaying back and forth and drumming on the bar with his eyes closed. And he could *hear* the music, could even *see* it, could read a score the way other people flip through a page of advertising, but it wasn't really his thing, reading scores . . . Charles, on the other hand, had left the concert feeling depressed. The guy's face was so full of suffering and exhaustion that he couldn't listen to him, he was too scared to sit there staring at him in silence.
'It's horrible. To have so much talent and fuck yourself up like this.'
His friend had leapt at his throat. The wrong chorus. A torrent of insults on the very friend who'd offered him the ticket.
'You don't get it,' said Alexis in the end, with a nasty smile.
'No.'
And Charles buttoned up his jacket.
'I can't.'
It was late. He was supposed to be up early the next morning. He was working.
'You never get anything, anyway.'
'No, of course not.' He got rid of his change. 'I know, and I understand less and less. But at your age, he'd already done amazing things.'
He'd said the words so quietly that Alexis couldn't possibly have heard him. And in any case he'd already turned his back on Charles.

But he had heard them. He had a sharp ear, the swine . . . Never mind, his friend was already pushing his glass across the counter . . .

Charles leaned over to pick up Mathilde's rubber, and as he rose to the surface, he knew that he would call Alexis.

Chet Baker threw himself out of a hotel window a few years after that concert. Passers-by stepped over him, assuming he was some wino, fast asleep, and he spent the night like that, dislocated, on a pavement in Amsterdam.

What about Anouk?

He wanted to know. He wanted to understand, for once.

Just understand.

'Charles?'

He didn't answer.

'Hello? Hello? Control tower to Charlie Bravo, do you copy?'

'Sorry. Right . . . where were we? So what is opposed to the weight of your mobile?'

'Huh?'

'What?'

'I can't take your music any more.'

She switched off the sound with a smile. He'd got what he wanted.

End of improv.

He would call.

*

When Laurence came home from the Turkish bath with her friend Maud, Charles took all his little gang to the pizzeria on the corner, and they celebrated her birthday once again, to the sounds of *Come prima*.

They put a candle on her slice of tiramisu, and she pulled her chair closer to his.

For the photo.

To make Mathilde happy.

So they could smile together on the tiny screen of her mobile.

Since he had to get a plane at seven the next morning, he set his alarm for five and rubbed his cheeks.

He slept badly, and not enough.

They never really found out whether he'd thrown himself from the window, or fallen.

Sure, there were traces of heroin on the table, but when they finally turned his ethereal carcass over, he was still clutching the window handle.

Charles switched off the alarm at four thirty, shaved, gently closed the door behind him and didn't leave a note on the kitchen table.

How did Anouk die? Had she fussed with some bloody window catch, too, to let the others off the hook?

She had watched so many people die. She'd stopped counting, one window, one annoyance more or less . . . Particularly back then. The heyday of the New Morning, in the early 1980s, when Aids was killing off all the healthy young men with a vengeance.

They'd had dinner together in those dark days and, for the first time, he'd seen the doubt on her face:

'The hardest thing is when you have to tell them.'

She was choking up, already.

'Because of the risks of infection, you see . . . You have to tell them that they're going to die like a dog and that there's nothing you can do for them. That's actually the first thing you tell them . . . So that they're careful not to go off and shoot someone when they leave. Yes, you're going to die but hey, don't waste any time. Go quick and tell the others, the ones you've loved. So they know straight away that they're next in line, too . . . Go on! Run! And see you next month, all right?

'And you know, this is the first time we've been through something like this. The first time. And we're all in the same boat, fat cat doctors and little helpers alike. We've all been swept away by this bloody thing. There's no stopping it, either, it's bombarding us, bloody bitch of a disease. No quarter. We're all utterly useless. You know . . . I've closed a few eyes in my time, and up until now, well, it's been my life, so what. Yes, of course, you know me. And even if I always clenched my teeth, I would call the nursing auxiliary when the body had gone down to the fridge and we were doing the room. Yes, we'd put on fresh sheets for the next one, and then we'd wait for him, and when he arrived, we'd take care of him. We'd smile, and look after him. We *looked after* him, you hear? Isn't that the very reason we've chosen such an insane profession?

'But now, with this? What are we supposed to do?'

She stole my cigarette.

'This is the first time in my life that I've had to learn to be creative, Charles . . . First time I've seen Death like this, with a capital letter. You know, that thing in your French homework, that thing all the teachers used to love, what was it called?'

'Anthropomorphism.'

'No, it had a smoother sort of ring to it.'

'Allegory?'

'That's it! I'm allegorizing death. I can see it lurking about with its skull and its bloody scythe. I see it. I can sense it. When I start my shift I can smell it in the corridor and often I even turn around with a start because I can hear it walking behind me and . . .'

Her eyes were shining.

'Have I gone stark raving mad? D'you think I'm losing my mind, too?'

'No.'

'And the worst of it is that there's another new element along with all the rest . . . Shame. Shameful disease. Sex, or drugs. Hence, solitude. Death *and* solitude. The families don't come, you use complicated words to confuse the cretinous parents who still go round sniffing their children's sheets . . . Yes, Madam, it's a lung infection, no, Madam, there's no treatment. Oh, yes, you're right, Sir, you might say it does affect the other organs, indeed . . . Very perspicacious, I see. How many times have I felt like screaming and grabbing them by the collar and shaking them to get rid of every last bloody prejudice, till every last one comes crashing down at the foot of . . . Of what? Of what's left of their child? Of . . . there's not even a name for it, what we . . . Those beds where they've lost even the strength to close their eyes, so they won't have to put up with it any more . . .'

She looked down.

'What is the point of having kids if they don't have the right to talk to you about love when they grow up, huh?'

She shoved her plate back.

'Huh? So what's left? What's left if we can't talk about love, or pleasure? Our pay slips? The weather?'

She was losing her temper.

'Children – they are life, damn it! And it's because we had a fuck, too, that they are here, no? Besides, who gives a damn about another person's sexual orientation! Two boys, two girls, three boys, a whore, a dildo, a doll, two whips, three sets of handcuffs, a thousand fantasies – where's the problem, huh? Where is the problem? It's night-time, no? And at night, it's dark! Night is holy! And even when it's daytime, it's . . . that's fine, too . . .'

She was trying to smile, and she poured herself another glass between each question mark.

'You see, for the first time in my career, I – I've become utterly useless . . .'

I touched her elbow. I felt like taking her in my arms, I . . .

'Don't say that. Hey, if I had to die in the hospital, I'd want to be near –'

She interrupted me just in time. Before I fucked everything up, yet again.

'Stop. We're not talking about the same thing. You see a tall, pale young man stretching out his hand towards some bloody allegorization, whereas I'm talking about the runs, and herpes, and necrosis. And when I said like a dog just now, I was miles off. A dog at least, when it's suffering too much, they put it down.'

The people at the next table were giving us funny looks. I was used to that. It had been going on for twenty years. Anouk always spoke too loudly. Or laughed too quickly. Or sang too shrilly. Or danced too soon, or . . . Anouk always went too far and people would look at her and whisper crap. Never mind. Under normal circumstances, she would have got back at them by raising her glass. 'Here's to love!' she'd have winked at the model father and husband, or 'Here's to sex!' or something even worse, depending on how many glasses she had already raised by then, but that evening, nothing. That evening, the hospital had won. People who were sound in body no longer interested her. Could no longer save her.

I didn't know what to say. I thought about Alexis, whom she hadn't seen in several months. About his downward spiral, and his pupils that were always dilated. Her son who reproached her because he'd been born a white man, and who wanted to live like Miles Davis, Charlie Parker, and all the others.

Who was overdoing it. Who was fed up with stamping his feet impatiently. Who sought himself wherever he went, by lying in bed all day.

And who blinked in the daylight.

Had she been reading my thoughts?

'With the junkies it's another story altogether . . . Either there's no one, or else the parents are so devastated that it's as if they need looking after as well. And those parents, the ones who are still there, the ones who have *always* been there, do you know what they say?'

I shook my head.

'"It's our fault."'

Around the time we had that dinner – it must have been in '85 or '86 – Alexis was still relatively clean. I think he was smoking, mainly. I don't remember, but he wasn't yet into the tourniquets and the long sleeves, otherwise I'd remember what I'd said. In this case she was talking about other people's parents, and I was quietly agreeing. Other people.

What I do remember is that I had managed to change the subject, and we were chatting about things that were not so serious – my studies, our respective desserts, the film I'd seen the weekend before, when her smile suddenly froze.

'I was on duty Sunday,' she continued, 'and . . . And there was this kid there . . . scarcely any older than you . . . a dancer . . . He showed me some photos . . . A dancer, Charles. A *magnificent* body and –'

She flung her head back, staring at the ceiling to drive it all away, saliva, snot, everything that was blurring her vision, and then she came back and took aim at me again.

'And on that Sunday morning, I was cooling his body with camphorated water, which means I really wasn't doing much at all, it was just a sham, really, I helped him bend over so I could do his back and do you know what happened, right there in my hand?'

She showed me her hand.

'Beneath this hand, right there . . . The hand of a registered nurse who has dressed thousands of patients for over twenty years?'

I didn't react.

'On –'

She broke off to empty her glass. Her nostrils were throbbing.

'On the crest of his spine his skin —'

I handed her my napkin.

'— tore apart . . .'

★

He had just claimed his suitcase and was waiting impatiently at the check-in counter. He could already hear Russian all around him and three girls were giggling and gushing as they compared the contents of their respective shopping bags.

You could see their bellies.

He felt like a coffee.

And a cigarette . . .

As he pulled out his book, he dropped the stub from his previous boarding card that he'd been using as a bookmark. No panic, they'd be giving him a new one a few metres from here . . .

XXXIII

The main action of the battle of Borodino took place over a stretch of seven thousand feet between Borodino and Bagration's flèches. (Outside that stretch, on one side, there was a show of Uvarov's cavalry in the middle of the day, and on the other side, beyond Uti—

Not a window . . .

She'd always had vertigo . . .

—tsa, Poniatowski's collision with Tuchkov; but these two were detached and feeble actions in comparison with what took place in the cen—

He could not understand a thing.

His mobile was vibrating: the agency. This early?

No. The message was from the night before. Philippe. One of Pavlovich's minions had sent a catastrophic e-mail. The second screed would have to be completely redone, there was a balls-up in their calculations, the blokes from Voradin didn't want to know and they'd found a bloke dead on the western site. A bloke who wasn't registered anywhere, obviously. The police would be coming by again.

Right then . . . Why hadn't the guy just disappeared?

There was no more concrete?

He took a deep breath to expel his anger, looked for an empty seat, closed his book, put the two emperors and their half a million dead each in the bottom of his briefcase and pulled out his files. Checked his watch, added two hours, got voicemail, and began to swear again in English. *Good Lord*, he went at it with relish. The fucking bastard wouldn't listen to his message to the end anyway.

All of a sudden, it all vanished. Alexis and his pathetic cruelty, Claire and the little chapels on Skopelos, Laurence's moods, Mathilde's pouting, his memories, their future, the lapping of the past and all that quicksand. Off it went. Deleted. The shambles on the site was beginning to seriously piss him off and he'd get back to his life later on.

Sorry, mate, but there just wasn't time.

So Balanda, with his engineering degree, his Master of Sciences, his School of Architecture, his government certification, his membership of the Society; Balanda the workhorse, with his awards and medals, everything you can imagine, yes, everything you can imagine, everything you could possibly fit onto a business card when you've had enough, tossed that other, wobbly, self out.

Aaah. That feels better.

Everyone, at some point or another, had reproached him for giving too much importance to his work. His fiancées, his family, his colleagues, his collaborators, his clients, the cleaning ladies who officiated at night, and even a doctor, once. Well-intentioned people said he was conscientious; others said that he was needy or even worse, academic, and he'd never really known what to say in his own defence.

Why had he been working so hard for so many years?

What was the point of all these sleepless nights? Life on a scale of 1:100? This relationship that was so shabbily constructed? This nagging little stiffness in his neck? This urge he had to climb the walls?

Or was it simply a trial of strength, lost from the start?

What . . . No, he'd never known how to justify himself to obtain absolution. He'd never felt the need, to be honest. But now, yes. Now he did.

That morning, as he got up and took out his passport, surprised yet again at how light his luggage was, to the sound of *Passengers on Air France flight 1644 departing at seven ten for Moscow Sheremetyevo are kindly requested to proceed to gate 16*, he had his answer: it was so that he could breathe.

Just breathe.

The hours, the little we've seen of him thus far, the abyss, might all seem to suggest, how to put it . . . that we should have some doubts as to just how clear-sighted Charles's explanation really is, but anyway . . . Let's give him the benefit of the doubt for once.

Let's let him breathe as far as gate 16.

8

The flight reached its cruising speed of nine hundred kilometres an hour. He'd scarcely had time to switch on his laptop when the captain came on to inform them that the temperature was two degrees Celsius at their destination, wishing everyone a pleasant flight, and the usual blah blah from SkyTeam.

He located Viktor, his chauffeur with the gentle smile (a hole, a tooth, a hole, two more teeth); Charles would discover, after dozens of hours of traffic jams (in no other country in the world had Charles spent so much time on the rear seat of a car. Puzzled at first, then worried, then annoyed, then enraged, then . . . resigned. Oh! So this was the legendary Russian fatalism? Watching, through a steamy car window, as one's goodwill dissolves into the endless ambient confusion?), that Viktor, in another life, was a sound engineer.

He was talkative, and told countless amazing stories that his passenger did not understand, all the while smoking dreadful-smelling cigarettes that he pulled out of charming little packets.

And when Charles's mobile rang, when his client began putting on the pressure again, he would hasten to turn on the music at full volume. Out of discretion. No balalaikas or Shosta, no, just the local rock group, his own. The needle well into the red.

Bloody hell.

One evening, he had taken his shirt off to show Charles his life. Every era quivering on his skin: firmly tattooed. In front of a petrol pump, he had spread his arms and whirled like a ballerina while Charles gazed at him, wide-eyed.

It was . . . remarkable.

He met up with his little French comrades, his little German comrades, and his little Russian comrades. Managed to bullshit his way through several meetings, and equal quantities of sighs, taking the piss, and doing bugger all, a luncheon that lasted far too long, and then on with the hard hat and the boots once again. Everyone talked at him, voluminously, everyone confused him, slapped him on the back, and eventually he had a good laugh with the blokes from Hamburg. (The ones who came to install the air con.) (But where?)

Yes, in the end he had a laugh. One fist on his hips, one hand to his brow, and his feet deep in shit.

Then he headed over to the bosses' prefabs where two fellows were waiting for him, two blokes straight from a Karl Marx Brothers comedy. Larger than life with their big cigars and their air of second-rate cowboys. Nervous, pale, already flushed with excitement. And already so eager.

Militsia, they announced.

Right, who else.

All the others who were called as witnesses, most of them workers, only spoke Russian. Balanda was surprised that his usual interpreter was not there. He called Pavlov's office. A young guy was on his way, they assured him, he spoke excellent French. Good. And here he is now, knocking at the door, red-faced and out of breath.

The discussion began. Or rather, the interrogation.

But when it was his turn to defend himself, he quickly realized that Starsky and Hutchov's eyebrows were wiggling in the oddest fashion.

He turned to his interpreter: 'Do they understand what you're saying?'

'No,' went the interpreter, 'they say the Tadzhik not drinking.'

Er . . .

'No, but what I said to you before, about Mr Korolev's contracts . . .'

He nodded, started again, and the militsiamen's eyeballs grew ever rounder.

Well?

'They say you guaranter.'

What?!

'Forgive me for asking, but . . . how long have you been learning French?'

'In Greynooble,' he replied, with an angelic smile.

79

Oh, fuck.

Charles rubbed his eyelids.

'*Sigaryet*?' he inquired of the younger of the two sheriffs, tapping his index and middle fingers against his lips.

Spasiba.

He let out a long breath, a delicious puff of carbon monoxide and pure discouragement as he contemplated the ceiling where a broken neon hung crookedly between two darts.

And he suddenly felt for Napoleon . . . That genius of a strategist who, as he'd read a few chapters earlier, failed to win the battle of Borodino because he'd been suffering from a head cold.

Go figure; suddenly he felt great solidarity with the man. No, kid, they won't hold it against you . . . You've been fighting a losing battle from the start . . . Those guys are far too crafty for the likes of us. Far, far too crafty.

Finally Pavlovich arrived, Fiat Lux, accompanied by an 'official'. A friend of the brother-in-law of the sister of the stepmother of Luzhkov's right-hand man, or something like that.

'Luzhkov?' exclaimed Charles, 'you mean . . . the . . . the mayor?'

Pavlovich didn't even bother to reply, already too absorbed by the presentations.

Charles went out. In cases like this, he always went out, and everyone was always grateful.

He was joined at once by his Berlitz wonder boy, and decided to show some enthusiasm of his own: 'So, you spent some time in Grenoble?'

'No, no!' corrected the interpreter, 'I am live here at day!'

Right.

Dusk had fallen. Machines switched off. Some of the workers greeted him, while others shoved them from behind to get them to move along faster, and then Viktor drove him to the hotel.

He was entitled once again to a Russian lesson. The same one, over and over.

Roubles were *rubli*, euros were *yevrà*, dollar, ha, that's *dollar*, imbecile of the 'Move, c'mon, let's go' type was *kaziol*, imbecile of the 'Let me pass, arsehole!' was *mudak*, and 'Move your arse!' was *sheveli zadam*.

(Among other things.)

Charles was going over things absent-mindedly, hypnotized by the kilometres and kilometres and kilometres and kilometres of rows and rows of rabbit hutches. That was the thing that had struck him the most on his first visit to Eastern Europe, when he was still a student. As if the very worst of the peripheral suburbs in Paris, the most depressing of all the council housing tower blocks, could not stop reproducing, ad infinitum.

And yet Russian architecture . . . Yes, Russian architecture, that was something else . . .

He recalled a monograph by Leonidov that Jacques Madelain had given him . . .

It was a familiar refrain . . . Anything beautiful had been destroyed because it was beautiful, hence, bourgeois; and then an entire nation had been crammed into . . . into this, and the little bit of beauty that remained, well, the Nomenklatura had appropriated it.

Yes, we know. No need to pontificate about miserable little lives from the back seat of a leather-upholstered Mercedes, where it was twenty degrees warmer than in their stairwells.

Right, Balanda?

Yes, but?

C'mon, let's go . . . *Sheveli zadam.*

*

While the water was running he called the agency and summed up his day for Philippe, who was the most concerned among his associates. Certain e-mails had been forwarded to Charles that he must read within the hour in order to give his instructions. And he had to call the planning board.

'Why?'

'Well . . . it's about the screed . . . Why are you laughing?' They were worried, in Paris.

'Sorry. It's nerves.'

Then they talked about other sites, other estimates, other margins, other fuck-ups, other decrees, other rumours in their little world and, before hanging up, Philippe informed him that Marquesin and his lot had got Singapore.

Ah?

He didn't know whether to laugh or cry.

Singapore . . . ten thousand kilometres and seven time zones . . .

And suddenly, that very instant, he remembered that he was

extremely tired, that he hadn't had the sleep he was owed for . . . months, years, and his bath was about to overflow.

As he came back into the room, he looked for sockets where he'd be able to recharge his various batteries, tossed his jacket across the bed, undid the top buttons of his shirt, squatted down, paused for a moment of bewilderment in the cold clarity of the minibar, then went and 'sat down next to his clothes.

He pulled out his diary.

Pretended to be interested in the next day's appointments.

Pretended to leaf through it before putting it away.

Just like that. The way you fiddle with a well-worn personal object when you're far away from home.

And then, what do you know . . .

He came upon Alexis Le Men's number.

Well I –

His mobile was still on the night table.

He looked at it thoughtfully.

No sooner had he dialled the area code and the first two numbers than his stomach betrayed him . . . He made a fist and dashed to the toilet.

When he looked up again, he slammed into his own reflection.

His trousers round his ankles, his white calves, his knock knees, his arms wrapped round his torso, his tight face, his pitiful expression.

An old man.

He closed his eyes.

And emptied himself.

The bath felt lukewarm. He was shivering. Who else could he call? Sylvie . . . the only real female friend he'd ever known Anouk to have . . . But . . . How could he find her? What was her last name, again? Brémand? Brémont? And had they still been in touch? Towards the end, at least? Would she be able to give him more information?

And did he even want to know?

Anouk was dead.

Dead.

He would never hear the sound of her voice again.

The sound of her voice.

Or her laugh.

Or her fits of anger.

He'd never see her twisting her lips again, or see them tremble or stretch to an infinite smile. He'd never look at her hands again. The inside of her wrist, the tracings of her veins, the hollow of the circles beneath her eyes. He'd never know what she was hiding, so well, so poorly, so far away, behind her weary smiles or her silly faces. He'd never sneak sidelong glances at her. Never take her arm by surprise. Never –

How could it help just to replace all of that with a cause of death? What would he gain? A date? Details? The name of an illness? A stubborn window handle? One last stumble?

Honestly . . .

Was the sordid truth really worth the candle?

Charles Balanda put on some clean clothes and tugged at his shoelaces as he ground his molars.

He knew. That he was afraid to know the truth.

And the braggart in his soul placed a hand on his shoulder, and began to sweet-talk him: Oh, go on . . . Give it a rest . . . Just keep your memories . . . Remember her the way she used to be . . . Don't ruin her . . . That's the greatest tribute you can pay her, and you know it . . . Keep her the way she was . . . Absolutely alive.

But there was the coward, too, breathing down his neck, murmuring in his ear: You know very well what happened, hey – she might have left the world the way she lived?

Alone. Alone, and in a mess.

Totally adrift in a world that was far too small for her. What was it that had killed her? Not hard to guess. Her ashtrays. Or all the drink, which never seemed to give her peace. Or the bed she never turned down any more. Or . . . And what about you? What the fuck do you think you're doing now, piling on the flattery? Where were you before all this? If you'd been there, you wouldn't be shitting your knickers like this now . . .

Please, have some dignity, my boy: you know what she would do with your compassion?

Shut your face, he grated; just shut your face.

And because he was so proud, it was the coward who redialled the number of his worst enemy.

What would he say? 'Balanda here' or 'It's Charles . . .' or 'It's me'?

By the third ring, he could feel his shirt sticking to his back. By the fourth, he closed his mouth to try to work up some saliva again. By the fifth . . .

On the fifth ring he could hear an answerphone click on, and a female voice chirping, 'Hi, you have reached the home of Corinne and Alexis Le Men, please leave us a message and we will get back to you as soon as . . .'

He cleared his throat, let a few seconds of silence go by for a machine to record his breathing thousands of kilometres away, and hung up.

Alexis . . .
    He put on his raincoat.
Married . . .
    Slammed the door.
To a woman . . .
    Rang for the lift.
A woman called Corinne . . .
    Stepped in.
And who lives with him in a house . . .
    Went down six flights.
A house with an answerphone . . .
    Walked across the lobby.
And . . .
    Headed in the direction of the draughts.
And . . . what about his slippers?

'Please, Sir!'

He turned around. The concierge was shaking something above the counter. He came back, hitting his forehead with his palm, took his set of house keys and handed over the room key in exchange.

Another chauffeur was waiting for him. Far less exotic, this one, and in a French car. The invitation had been nicely put, but Charles had no illusions: the good little soldier was headed back to the front. And when they drove through the Embassy gates, he finally decided to switch off his mobile.

He did not eat much, and this time he did not admire the sublime bad taste of the Igumnov mansion, but he answered the questions he was asked and reeled off the anecdotes they wanted to hear. Played his role to perfection, stood up straight, held tight to the handle of his knife and fork, did not hesitate to stick his neck out, responded with jokes and allusions, shrugged his shoulders when it was called for, gave his opinion, and he even laughed on cue – and all the while he was quietly going to pieces, falling apart, cracking up.

He watched his knuckles tightening, going white along the stem of his glass.

Snap the glass, maybe he'd bleed, get up and leave the table . . .

Anouk had come back. Anouk was once more taking her place. Taking up all the space. Like before. Like always.

Wherever she was, wherever she had come from, she was looking at him. Making fun of him, gently, and commenting on his neighbours' manners, the arrogance of these people, and just look at the jewels on those ladies, and isn't it all just as it should be, and what was he doing among these people?

'What are you doing here, Charles my dear?'

'I'm at work.'

'Oh, really?'

'Yes.'

Quizzical silence.

'Anouk . . . please.'

'So you remember my name?'

'I remember everything.'

And her face grew darker.

'No, don't say that . . . There are certain things, times . . . that I want you to forget.'

'No. I don't believe that. But . . .'

'But?'

'Maybe we're not talking about the same . . .'

'I hope not,' she smiled.

'You –'

'I . . .'

'You are still just as beautiful.'

'Shut up, you daft fool. And get up. Look . . . they're going back into the salon . . .'

'Anouk?'

85

'Yes, kid?'

'Where were you?'

'Where was I? But that's for you to tell me . . . Go on, go and join them. Everyone's waiting for you.'

'Is everything all right?' asked his hostess, pointing to an armchair.

'Yes, thank you.'

'Are you sure?'

'Just tired . . .'

Well, well.

That's it, blame fatigue. For how many years had he been using that excuse, tucked snugly in the loose folds of his trousers? Such a respectable smokescreen, and so very very useful . . .

It's true, fatigue is quite chic when it comes in the wake of a fine career. Flattering, even. A nice medal pinned to an idle, restless heart . . .

He went to bed thinking about her, and he was struck, yet again, by how pertinent certain clichés could be. Well-worn phrases that you pull out once the nails have all been hammered in: 'I didn't have time to say goodbye . . .' or, 'If I'd known, I would have said goodbye in a better way . . .' or, 'I still had so many things to say to her.'

I didn't even say goodbye to you.

He did not hope for an echo this time round. It was night-time, and at night, she was never around. Either she was at work, or she was telling herself her own story, or her vast battle plans, leaving it to Johnnie Walker and Peter Stuyvesant to turn the pages and to send out the light brigade, until eventually she ended up forgetting, or surrendering, and fell asleep at last.

My Anouk . . .

If there were a heaven, you'd already be vamping St Peter . . .

Yes.

I can see you.

I can see you twiddling his beard and taking his keys from his hands, to make them glitter against your hip.

When you were feeling good, nothing could stand in your way, and when we were children you could take us to heaven whenever you felt like it.

How many doors did your smile break down? How many queues did we jump? How many yards did we sneak ahead? How many signs did we overturn, bypass, disobey?

How many times did we give them the old V-sign, all those grumpy old sods; and to hell with all the barriers, and everything forbidden?

'Give me your hands, guys,' she'd conspire, 'and everything will be fine . . .' And we loved it, the way you'd call us 'guys' even though we were still sucking our thumbs, and you would crush our knuckles as we launched the attack. We'd get the jitters, and sometimes it even hurt, but we would have followed you to the ends of the earth.

Your decrepit Fiat was our vessel, our flying carpet, our stage-coach. You'd spur on your little four horsepower steed, swearing like Hank in *Lucky Luke*, Yeah! Giddy-up y'ole nag! Your whip would crack all along the Paris *périphérique* and you'd chew on your cigarette just for the pleasure of startling us when you spat the wad out of the window.

With you, life was exhausting, but the telly remained silent. And everything was possible.

Everything.

Provided we never let go of your hand . . .

You even did it again once the Marlboros had replaced the tubes of Nestlé's condensed milk, remember? We were on our way back from Caroline's wedding and we must have been sleeping off the confetti in the rear seat when your anxious cries woke us.

'Hello, hello, XB 12, do you copy?'

We emerged, grumbling, in the middle of a field; all the headlights were off and you were conversing with the cigarette lighter in the dim glow of the overhead lamp. 'Do you copy?' you pleaded, 'our vessel is stranded, my Jedi are stuck in the mud and I've got the Rebel Alliance on my tail . . . What should I do, Obi-Whatsit Kenobi?'

Alexis was despondent and muttered fuck in a thick voice, while a fascinated cow looked him over, but you were laughing too hard to hear him. 'Why do you take me to see such idiotic films?' Then we got back on the tracks of hyperspace and I observed your smile in the rear view mirror for a good long while.

I saw the little girl you must have been, or should have been if they had only let you get up to mischief back then . . .

Sitting behind you I looked at your neck and thought, Is it because she had such a rotten childhood that she's so good at enchanting our own?

And I realized that I was growing older, too . . .

Several times I touched your shoulder to make sure you weren't falling asleep, and at one point you put your hand on mine. The toll booth took it away from me again, but there were still a lot of stars around our vessel that night, weren't there?

So many stars . . .

Yes, if there is a paradise, you must be making quite a shambles of it up there . . .

But . . . what could there be?

What could there be after you?

He fell asleep with his hands by his sides. Naked, feeling queasy, and all alone on Ulitsa Smolenskaya, in Moscow, in Russia. On this little planet which had become – and that was his last conscious thought – terribly boring.

9

He got up, returned to his quagmire, shut himself inside a smoke-filled hut once again, handed over his papers once again, took the plane, claimed his luggage, climbed into a taxi where the hand of Fatima was dangling from the rear view mirror, came home to a woman who no longer loved him and a young girl who did not yet love herself, gave each of them a kiss, showed up at his appointments, had lunch with Claire, hardly touched his food, assured her that everything was fine, sidestepped the issue when the conversation strayed from classified green light areas and programmed maintenance operations on buildings resulting from decentralization, realized that the deep crevasse was gaining ground when he watched her disappear round the corner and his heart was in his boots, shook his head, tried to dissect his feelings on the Boulevard des Italiens, drilled himself into silence, analyzed the quality of the terrain, concluded that he was dealing with a display of sheer self-indulgence, despised himself, flogged himself, turned on his heel, put one foot in front of the other and started again, changed his currency, began smoking again, was incapable thereafter of swallowing the tiniest drop of alcohol, lost weight, won tenders, shaved less often, felt the skin on his face flaking off in places, stopped scrutinizing the drain plug whenever he washed his hair, became less talkative, parted with Xavier Belloy, made another appointment at the ophthalmologist's, came home later and later, and often on foot, suffered from insomnia, walked as much as he could, found himself skirting the edge of the pavement, crossed outside the zebra crossing, went over the Seine without looking up, no longer admired Paris, no longer touched Laurence, realized that she was forming a trough in the duvet between their bodies whenever she went to bed before him, began watching television for the first time in his life, was stunned, managed to give Mathilde a smile when she told him her mark in physics, no longer reacted when he came upon her doing her shopping on LimeWire, couldn't give a fuck about the ambient looting, got up in the middle of the night, drank litres of water on the cold kitchen tiles, tried to read, gave up on Kutuzov and his troops at Krasnoye, replied when he was asked a question, answered no when Laurence threatened him with a real conversation, repeated himself when she asked whether it was out of cowardice, tightened his belt, had his Derby shoes resoled, accepted an invitation to travel to Toronto for a conference on environmental issues in the construction industry which left him utterly indifferent, lost his temper with an intern, ended up unplugging the intern's computer, grabbed a pencil in passing and thrust it in his hands, go on, losing his patience, show me, *you*, show me what I am supposed to see, launched a project for a hotel complex near Nice, made a cigarette hole in the sleeve of his jacket, fell asleep at the cinema, lost his new glasses, found his book on Jean Prouvé, remembered his promise and went to knock on the door to Mathilde's room one evening and read her this passage out loud, 'I recall my father saying to me, "You see how the thorn clings to the stem on this rosebush?" And he opened his fist and ran his finger over his palm: "Look . . . Like the thumb on your hand. It's all well made, it's all solid, both are shapes with equal resistance, in spite of everything it's flexible." I've never forgotten. If you look at some of the furniture I've made, nearly everywhere you'll find a design of things that . . .', realized she couldn't give a toss, wondered how that could be possible, she used to be so curious about things in the old days, left her room walking backwards, put the book back any old place, leaned against the side of the bookshelf, looked closely at his thumb, closed his fist, sighed, went to bed, got up, went back to his quagmire, shut himself inside a smoke-filled hut once again, handed over his papers once more, took the plane, claimed . . .

It lasted for weeks, and it could have gone on for months or years.

Since it was the braggart, in the end, who'd won the bet.

And it all made sense . . . It's always the braggarts who win, no?

★

90

For nearly twenty years he'd lived next door to her, never seeing her, so why should he be so impressed by three little words that hadn't even had the manners to come forward and introduce themselves? Sure, it was Alexis's handwriting . . . and so what? Who was that Alexis, anyway?

A thief. A bloke who betrayed his friends and left his girlfriend to have an abortion all alone, as far away as possible.

An ungrateful son. A little whitey. A talented little whitey, perhaps, but so spineless.

It was years ago now, when he had . . . No, when Anouk had . . . No, when life, let's say, had given up on them, Charles realized – and this was very painful – that he was having great difficulty in reading the specifications for this project that others called life. He didn't really see how any of it could hold together when the foundations were so shaky, and he even wondered if he hadn't made a mistake right from the start . . . Charles? This pile of gravel? Build something? That's a good one. He went along with it because he didn't have a choice, but God, it was . . . tedious.

And then one morning he stretched and grunted and got his appetite back, took pleasure in pleasure and enjoyed his profession. He was young and gifted, they kept telling him. He was weak enough to believe them once again, he forced himself, and started piling up his bricks like everyone else.

He denied her. Worse still, he belittled her.

Reduced the scale.

Anyway . . . That is what he had cobbled together for himself. Until one Sunday afternoon he happened on a magazine that was lying around at his parents' . . . He tore the page out and read it over again, as he was standing in the metro, with his doggy bag under his arm.

It was all there, clear as day, between an ad for a health spa and the letters to the editor.

It was more of a relief than a revelation. So, this is what he'd got? Phantom limb syndrome? They'd amputated, but his idiot brain hadn't followed and still sent him erroneous messages. And even if he had nothing left, because there was nothing there any more – and that he couldn't deny – he continued to perceive very real sensations.

'Heat, cold, stinging, prickling, cramps, even pain, at times,' said the article.

Yes.

Precisely.

He was suffering from all of those things.

But in no one place.

He'd scrunched it up into a ball, given some slices of cold roast to his flatmate, lowered the lamp and raised the table. His was a Cartesian mind that needed proof in order to keep going. And this proof convinced him. And calmed him.

Why should things have changed, twenty years on?

It was that phantom that he loved, and you know what? Phantoms never die.

So he went through the events enumerated above, but without suffering any worse than that. He lost weight? Actually rather a good thing. He was working harder? No one would notice the difference. He'd started smoking again? He'd stop, all in due course. He bumped into passers-by? He was excused. Laurence was losing it? Her turn now. Mathilde would rather watch a brainless soap? Too bad for her.

Nothing serious. Just a bad blow to the stump. It would pass.

Perhaps it would, indeed.

Perhaps he would have gone on living like that, but taking things more lightly. Perhaps he would have done away with the commas, and taken the trouble to start a new paragraph more often.

Yes, perhaps he would have started up again with his rubbish about breathing and fresh air . . .

But he'd eventually given in.

To her entreaties, to her gentle blackmail, to her voice, made to sound quavering as she twisted the phone line.

All right, he sighed, all right.

And he went once again to dine with his elderly parents.

He paid no attention to the cluttered console and mirror in the entrance, he hung up his raincoat with his back turned, then joined them in the kitchen.

They were models of propriety, all three of them, chewing slowly on each bite, and they were careful to avoid the subject that had brought them together. During the coffee, however, and with an air of oh-I-know-it's-really-foolish-but-I-was-about-to-forget, Mado gave in and turned to her son, looking somewhere well beyond his shoulder:

'Oh, by the way, I heard that Anouk Le Men is buried near Drancy.'

He managed to strike the right note: 'Oh, really? I thought she was in Finistère . . . How did you find out?'

'Through the daughter of her former landlady.'

Then he gave up.

'Well, then, you finally got round to chopping down the old cherry tree?'

'Yes, we were obliged to . . . Because of the neighbours, you know . . . Guess how much it cost us?'

Saved.

Or at least that is what he thought, but just as he was getting to his feet, she put her hand on his knee and said, 'Wait.'

She leaned over the coffee table and handed him a large brown envelope.

'I was tidying up the other day, and I came across some photos which might amuse you . . .'

Charles stiffened.

'It all went by so quickly,' she murmured, 'look at this one. How sweet you look, the pair of you . . .'

They were holding each other by the shoulder, Alexis and him. Two beaming Popeyes, smoking a pipe and inflating their tiny biceps.

'Do you remember? There was that odd chap who used to dress you up all the time . . .'

No. He wasn't in the mood for remembering.

'Right,' he interrupted, 'I've got to get going now.'

'You should keep these.'

'No, thanks. What am I supposed to do with them?'

He was looking for his keys when Henri came up to him.

'Have mercy,' he joked, 'don't tell me she's wrapped up the apple pie!'

Charles looked at the envelope trembling beneath his father's thumb, let his gaze wander over the ribbing on his waistcoat, the worn buttons, his white shirt, the impeccable tie he had knotted every God-given morning for over sixty years, his stiff collar, his transparent skin, the furrows of white hairs that the blade had missed, and finally, his gaze.

The gaze of a discreet man who had spent his entire life with a bossy woman, but who hadn't given in to her on everything.

No. Not everything.

'Take them.'

He obeyed.

As long as his father went on standing there motionless he couldn't open the car door.

'Papa, please . . .'

His father said nothing.

'Hey! You need to move, now.'

They stared at one another.

'Are you all right?'

The old gentleman, who hadn't heard him, stepped to one side with a confession: 'For me, it wasn't as –'

A lorry went by.

As long as the road allowed it, Charles watched his father's figure growing smaller as the horizon receded.

What was it that he had muttered?

We shall never know. As for his son, he had a hunch, but he lost it at the following traffic light in the pages of his guide to the suburbs.

Drancy.

They were hooting their horns at him. He stalled.

10

His plane for Canada was at seven in the evening, and she was a few kilometres from the airport. He left the agency at lunchtime.

'With his heart slung over his shoulder': a lovely expression from a French pop song.

So he left with his heart slung over his shoulder.

Nothing in his stomach, filled with emotion, as nervous as if he were on a first date.

Ridiculous.

And not quite exact. He wasn't on his way to a dance, but to a cemetery, and it wasn't so much slung over his shoulder as wrapped up in a sling, that crippled little muscle of his.

It was beating, true, but any old way. It was pounding as if she were alive, as if she were looking out for him among the yew trees, and would tick him off, to start with. Ah, at last! You certainly took your time! And what are these horrible flowers you've brought me? Here, put them over there and let's get out of here. And what were you thinking, telling me to meet you in a boneyard? Did you fall on your head, or what?

Yet again, she was exaggerating . . . He glanced quickly at the bouquet. They were fine, those flowers . . .

His heart in a straitjacket – that, yes.

Hey, Charles . . .

I know, I know. But leave me alone.

A few more kilometres, my last cigarette, Mr Executioner . . .

★

It was in the outskirts, a little provincial cemetery. No yew trees, but wrought iron gates, the Holy Ghost on the windows of the tombs, and ivy on the walls. A cemetery with a verger, a rusty tap, and zinc watering cans. It didn't take long to walk around it. The newest arrivals, that is, the ones with the ugliest tombs, dated from the 1980s.

He shared his puzzlement with a little woman who was polishing up her dearly departed.

'You must be confusing it with the cemetery in Les Mévreuses . . . It's over there that they bury people nowadays. We've got a family plot here . . . And even so, we had to fight, you know, because the –'

'But . . . Is it far?'

'Do you have a car?'

'Yes.'

'Then the best thing is to take the national road as far as the big DIY and . . . Do you know where it is?'

'No,' said Charles hesitantly; he was beginning to find his bouquet rather awkward. 'But, uh, go on, I'll find it . . .'

'Otherwise you can get there from Leclerc shopping centre . . .'

'Oh?'

'Yes, you pass that, then under the railway lines, and after the waste dump, it's on the right.'

What sort of cock-up was this?

He thanked her, and went off lost in thought.

No sooner had he unbuckled his seatbelt than he fell to pieces.

It was exactly as she had described it: after the DIY and the Leclerc shopping centre, there it was: a dog pound for stiffs, right up next to the Regional Motorway Maintenance offices. With the RER suburban train directly overhead, and the cargo jumbos playing softly in the background.

Recycling bins in the car park, plastic bags clinging to the bushes, and walls made of concrete slabs that served as pissoirs for all the local taggers.

No. He shook his head. No.

And yet he wasn't the squeamish sort. It was his job to notice when developers fucked up, but this, no.

His mother must have made a mistake. Or that other woman mixed things up. The landlady's daughter – what were they talking about? And that landlady had fucked about with Anouk's mind too, she was a right one. It wasn't hard to make an impression on a young woman who was raising her son on her own, who came home knackered just when the bitch was taking her ratters for a shit on the square . . . Yes, that was it, it was all coming back to him. Madame Fourdel. Anouk's heart was in her boots whenever she saw her, one of the few people on the planet who could make her feel that way . . . The rent. The rent for old Mrs Fourdel.

The absurdity of this car park must be the last dirty trick on the part of that usurer. A mean trick, a gossipy mistake, an address remembered the wrong way round. Anouk had nothing to do with this place.

Charles kept his hand squeezed tight round the keys, and the keys were in the ignition.

Right. One quick look round.

He left the flowers behind.

Poor dead people . . .

The sheer weight of so much bad taste . . .

Marble lids which shone like kitchen Formica; plastic flowers; open books made of craftily cracked porcelain; hideous photos in yellowed Plexiglas; footballs; three aces; sculptures of lively looking pike; pathetic epitaphs; words dripping with lame regret. All of it carved there, for all eternity.

A gilt German shepherd.

Sleep, Master, I lie watching by your side.

It was probably not as bad as all that, or at least there might have been a touch more tenderness, but our Charles had decided to despise them all.

On Earth as it is in Heaven.

A typically French cemetery, laid out in a grid like an American town. Numbered rows, graves all lined up tight together, signposting for the soul in B23 and eternal rest for H175, aligned chronologically, the really cold ones towards the front, the more lukewarm ones towards the rear, the gravel neatly raked, a sign warning about recycling rubbish and another one about some crap manufactured in China and endlessly, ceaselessly, the infernal racket overhead, those bloody trains thundering right through their sleep.

This time it was the architect who was protesting. Surely there were terms and conditions to be respected where the dead were concerned, too? At least a bare minimum? Just a little bit of peace, excuse me – you mean it isn't included?

Why should it be . . . They'd been taken for a ride when they were alive, crammed into those wretched prefabs that had cost them three times what they were worth and left them in debt for twenty years – so why should anything change now that they'd snuffed it? And how much had they paid to have a view of the waste dump, until kingdom come?

Oh . . . that's their problem after all. But what about his belle dame? If he found her in this tip, he –

Go on. Finish your sentence. What would you do, you wanker? Start scratching at her grave to get her out of there? Dust off her skirt, take her in your arms?

What's the use. He can't hear us anyway. There's a freight train going by, lifting the carrier bags, depositing them a little farther along.

★

It wasn't the Fiat any more, nor was it Han Solo's Millennium Falcon, not yet, so it must have been during the glorious years of her little red Peugeot, her first *brand new* car, and the action takes place about the time they were ten years old. Or maybe eleven. Were they already in secondary school? He can't remember. Anouk didn't look her usual self. She was all dressed up, and she wasn't laughing. She was chain-smoking, and she forgot to turn off the windscreen wipers, she didn't get their silly Toto jokes at all, and she told them every five minutes that they had to be a credit to her.

The boys replied yes, yes, but they didn't really understand what she meant by that, being a credit to her, and since Toto had drunk all the beer, he went wee wee in his dad's glass, and . . .

She was taking them to see her family, to her parents' place, and she hadn't seen them for years; Charles was along for the ride. And for Alexis's sake, probably. To protect him from whatever was already making her so nervous, and because she felt stronger when she could hear them snorting with laughter about Willies, Sausages and Co. in the rear.

'When we get to Granny's you leave off all the Toto business, all right?'

'Yeah, yeah . . .'

It was in the cheap housing district on the outskirts of Rennes.

That much Charles recalled quite clearly. She was trying to find the way, driving slowly, cursing, complaining that she didn't recognize a thing, and Charles, as in Russia thirty-five years later, could not take his eyes off the row upon row of brand new blocks of flats that were already so unspeakably dreary . . .

There were no trees, no shops, no sky, the windows were tiny and the balconies full of junk. He didn't dare say anything but he was somewhat disappointed that part of her came from here. He had always thought she'd arrived on their street from the sea . . . on a scallop shell . . . Like in the painting of Spring that Edith was so fond of.

She'd brought heaps of presents, and she'd forced them to tuck their shirt-tails into their trousers. She'd even combed their hair, out in the car park, and it was at that point that they understood that being a credit to her meant not behaving the way they normally did. So they didn't squabble to see who would get to press the button on the lift and they watched her growing paler and paler as they rose towards the top floor.

Even her voice had changed . . . And when she handed her the presents, her mother put them away in the next room.

Alexis asked about it on the way home: 'Why didn't they open the presents?'

She took a while to answer.

'I don't know. Perhaps they're keeping them for Christmas.'

The rest is vague. Charles recalls that there was far too much to eat and that he had a stomach ache. There was an odd smell. They talked too loudly. The television was on all the time. Anouk gave some money to her younger sister, who was pregnant, and to her brothers, and some medicine to her father. And no one had thanked her.

And in the end he had gone downstairs with Alexis to play in the empty lot next door, and when he'd gone back up, on his own, to use the toilet, he'd asked that fat woman, who seemed tricky: 'Excuse me, ma'am . . . Where's Anouk?'

'Who are you talking about?' she'd retorted, as if he'd said something wrong.

'Uh . . . Anouk.'

'Don't know her.'

And she'd turned back to her kitchen sink with a grumble.

But Charles had a *really* bad tummy ache.

'Alexis's mum . . .'

'Ah! You mean Annick?'

What a nasty sweet smile she gave him . . .

'Because my daughter's name is Annick, isn't it! There's no such person as Anouk. Those are names for little Parisian folk like yourself. What she says when she's ashamed, like, you see? But here she's called Annick so get that into your skull, lad. And why are you wriggling like that?'

Her older daughter came in and showed him the place he was looking for. When he came back out she was gathering up all their belongings.

'I didn't say goodbye,' said Alexis worriedly.

'It doesn't matter.'

She ruffled his hair.

'Come, my princes. Let's get out of here.'

For a long time they didn't dare say a thing.

'Are you crying?'

'No.'

Silence.

And then she rubbed her nose: 'Okay, well, let's see . . . Toto goes to buy some sweets in a grocery shop in Paris, and he leaves his bicycle outside the shop. But it gets stolen.

'Since he is too far from home to walk all the way back before dark, he sneaks into a hotel and hides under a bed to spend the night.

'A pair of lovers come into the room and stretch out on the bed.

'The man says to the woman, "I can see all of Paris in your eyes," and at that very moment Toto comes out of his hiding place and exclaims, "Can you see my bicycle in her eyes?"'

She was laughing so hard she was crying.

Later, on the motorway, when Alexis had fallen asleep: 'Charles?'

'Yes?'

'You know, if I'm called Anouk now, it's . . . it's because I think it's a prettier name . . .'

He didn't reply right away, because he was trying to think of an answer that would be really super.

'Do you understand?'

She shifted the rear view mirror so she could catch his eye.

But he couldn't find a good enough answer. So he just nodded his head and smiled.

'Does your tummy feel better?'

'Yes.'

'Me too, you know,' she continued, lowering her voice, 'I always get a tummy ache when . . .'

And didn't finish her sentence.

Charles didn't think he could still recall memories like this. So why did the boomerang suddenly come back? The Toto joke, the forgotten presents, the hundred-franc notes on the table and the smell in that flat, of burnt fat and rancid envy?

Because . . .

Because on the tomb in plot number J93, you could read, above the dates:

LE MEN ANNICK

'Bastards.' All he could say by way of reverent contemplation.

He went back to the car with a hurried step, opened the boot and rummaged about in his clutter.

It was a fluorescent marker he used on site. He shook the aerosol, knelt down beside her, wondered at first how he would manage to link the 'n' and merge the 'i' with the 'k', then he decided to cross the whole thing out and give her back her true identity.

Well done! A round of applause, now! What gallantry!

What a magnificent tribute!

Forgive me.

Forgive me.

An old crone who was visiting the neighbouring gravestone looked at him with a frown. He put the cap back on his marker and got to his feet.

'Are you a family member?'

'Yes,' he replied curtly.

101

'No, I mean don't mind my asking . . .' Her mouth went into a twist. 'Because . . . there is a guard here, but . . .'

Charles's gaze left her disconcerted. She did her little house-keeping and said goodbye.

That must have been Madame Maurice Lemaire.

Maurice Lemaire who had a lovely slab paid for by his hunting mates, with a dandy rifle in relief.

Could you dream of a better neighbour, now, my dear Anouk? Say . . . You will really be treated like a queen here . . .

As he was leaving the place, he saw the man who was 'a guard here, *but* . . .'

He was black.

Ah, that explains it.

Everything was clear, now.

Climbing into the car, Charles was bothered by the smell of the flowers. He tossed them into a skip and looked at his watch.

Right. He'd have just enough time to call the bastard before boarding.

His assistant was trying to reach him and rang several times. He ignored her and eventually switched the phone off.

Staring straight ahead, his thumbs planted deep into the fat of the steering wheel, he felt his head begin to whirl.

Turn around . . . Invent an accident . . . Claim he'd missed his plane, add 'only just', bypass Paris, take the Océane motorway, exit at Thingammy, head for Whatsit, look for Rue What-d'you-call-it, and shove open the door at number 8.

Find him at last.

And plant his fist right in his face.

He should have done it twenty years ago anyway. But no regrets. In the meantime he had put on at least twenty pounds and stock-piled a bit of resentment. His jaw would appreciate the fact.

But that's not what happened. Little Rocky in a tweed jacket switched on his indicator and dropped back into the left-hand lane. He'd committed himself. He would go and get bored in one of the lounges at the Toronto Park Hyatt, and he'd come home with his head and his briefcase stuffed with *Advances in Building Technology* which would restore neither his cranes nor his faith.

Yes . . . There'd be a bit of vagueness in that obit, too . . . An architect, you say?

Oh? I had forgotten. It's funny: all these years I've had the impression, rather, that I was running an agency . . . Running. That's the word. Like a little carthorse with its blinkers on, numbly trotting with its load to market.

Where had Jean Prouvé's guiding hand got lost in all this dust? And all the hours spent glued to the architectural notebooks of Albert Laprade, at an age when others were collecting football stickers? And what about the abbey at Le Thoronet? And the clean, sculptural lines of the great Alvaro Siza? And all those study trips, with nothing but his drawings for currency?

And always, always, the impression, the *seal* of Anouk Le Men on these busy little efforts that would serve nicely as a career, as a life . . .

Because she did hesitate, yes, she did spit in her palm to flatten their cowlicks, yes, she had dropped all her packages when she slammed the boot, and yes all of a sudden she was speaking so roughly to them, but that hadn't stopped her from turning round, from following with her gaze the dismay of the little boy who'd been born with his silver spoon, and from lifting her chin up, too, and waiting for him, and declaring solemnly when he had reached her side: 'Charles . . . You know you draw so well . . . You should be an architect when you grow up . . . And you must do whatever you can to stop them from putting up places like that . . .'

And the little boy who drew so well, who looked away discreetly when Pavlovich handed out his envelopes, who flew Business most of the time, who was about to go to a useless and extremely costly conference at a FiveStar Alliance hotel where – so it said on the programme – he could enjoy full Spa service with *waterfalls* and *streams*, and who would probably doze between his headphones from having consumed too much good food; yes, that guy, that wretch, he missed the exit ramp for Terminal 2 and roared out loud in his tin can shell.

Roared.

Bloody hell and a thousand bleeding wankers.

He'd have to drive all the way round again.

11

'Hello?'

Unfortunately, it wasn't his voice, and what was worse, it chimed.

'Um . . . is this the home of Alexis Le Men?'

'Yuh, it is,' said the little voice.

He was disconcerted.

'May I speak with him, please?'

'Daddy! Telephone!'

Daddy?

That was all he needed . . .

And everything he'd been rehearsing over and over for nearly an hour, in the car park, on the escalators, in the various queues, and finally by the big plate glass windows – the way he would introduce himself, the first words he'd say, his plan of attack, his bite, his anger, his venom, his sorrow – it all vanished, quite simply.

All he could find to torpedo him with after all these leaden years was: 'You . . . you've got a kid?'

'Who's this?' asked the voice on the phone, curtly.

Christ, no. This wasn't at all the way he'd envisaged things, our super hero . . .

'Is that you, Charles?'

'Yes.'

And the voice was gentler.

Far too gentle, alas.

'I've been waiting for you.'

A long silence.

'So you got my letter, then?'

The crack opened wider. In an alarming way. Charles got up, headed for a corner, and nestled against the wall. Lowered his forehead to the wall and closed his eyes. The world around him had become . . . seemed to be burning . . .

It was nothing. It would pass. Fatigue. Nerves.

'Are you still there?'

'Yes, yes . . . sorry . . . I'm in an airport.'

He was ashamed. Ashamed. He raised his head.

'But I'm okay, it's okay . . . I'm here.'

'I was asking you if you got my –'

'Of course. Why else would I be phoning you?'

'I really don't know! Because you wanted to! To hear my news, to –'

'Stop it.'

That did it. It had all come back. To hear that voice again, oozing charm, the voice he adopted to arse-lick anyone who crossed his path: it was enough to clear Charles's mind in a split second and restore his anger.

'You cannot leave her where she is . . .'

'Sorry?'

'In that crap cemetery.'

Alexis began to laugh; it was a horrible sound.

'Ha, ha! You haven't changed, I can see . . . Always the fine prince on his white charger, is that it? You haven't lost your style, have you, Balanda!'

Then his voice changed completely.

'But hey . . . You've turned up a bit late now, haven't you? Your nag's on its last legs! There's no one left to save, didn't you know?'

Silence.

'I can't leave her there, I can't leave her there,' he hissed, 'but she's dead, mate! She's dead! What difference does it make if she's there or elsewhere? You know what? I'm sure she doesn't give a fuck!'

Of course he knew. He was the more rational of the two, after all. Methodical, geometrical, the good pupil, buttoned up to his collar, the class delegate, the designated driver who could blow into the balloon, the . . . But . . . Not any more. His wires were beginning to overheat, and whatever he could say in her defence, out it came:

'You can't leave her there. It represents everything she always despised . . . The cheap district council housing, racism . . . Everything she tried to avoid for ye—'

'What . . . what the hell are you on about now, racism, what?'

'Her neighbour.'

'What neighbour?'

'In the tomb next door.'

Stunned silence.

'Hang on a sec. Is this Charles Balanda speaking? The son of Mado and Henri Balanda?'

'Alex, please . . .'

'No but what the *hell* are you on about? Hey, seriously . . . Are you all right? Nothing broken on top? Maybe you forgot to put on your hard hat or something?'

Silence.

'Hello?'

'And the waste dump on top of all that.'

'I'm coming!' shouted Alexis, away from the receiver, 'start without me! On top – the dump? Are . . . Charles?'

'Yes.'

'After all this time . . . I have to confess something very important to you.'

'I'm listening.'

He, um, cleared his throat, very solemnly.

Charles covered his other ear.

'When people are dead, you know, well . . . they don't see anything any more . . .'

What a bastard. Play the old something-to-confide trick all the better to take the piss out of him. Typical, absolutely typical.

Charles hung up.

He hadn't even reached the boarding stairs when suddenly he felt the void beneath his feet: he'd forgotten to ask him the most important thing.

★

They served a glass of champagne and he used it to swallow yet another sleeping tablet. It was a really stupid cocktail, he knew that, but he'd stopped counting all the stupid things he'd been doing, so one more or less . . .

For several weeks now his life had been little more than a succession of undesirable side effects, and the machine had kept running, so . . . At best in a few minutes he'd collapse, at worst he'd go and lean over the toilet seat.

Yes, chuck it all up, that might not be so bad, why not . . .

He pulled the pin on another miniature bottle.

When he took out his files, the envelope from his parents slipped beneath his seat. Fine. Let it stay there. He'd had his fill, now. Ridicule didn't kill you, that's as may be, but at a certain point, all the same, it was healthier to get into gear. He could no longer stand what he'd become: a complaisant man.

Right then, go on. Trample on all that. Memories, weakness, wailing. Let's have some air!

He loosened his tie and unbuttoned his collar.

In vain.

He seemed to have forgotten that the air, where he was, was *pressurized*.

When he came to, he'd been drooling so much that the shoulder of his jacket was soaking. He looked at his watch and could not believe his Lexomil: he'd only slept for an hour and a quarter.

Seventy-five minutes of respite . . . That's all he'd been entitled to.

The woman sitting next to him was wearing an eye mask. He switched his light on, wriggled this way and that to retrieve the envelope, smiled when he saw the magnificent tattoos on their little sailors' forearms, wondered who it was who must have drawn them, closed his eyes. Of course . . . his mother was right. It was him. That funny little man with the dyed hair. He sought his face, his name, his voice, found him again outside the school gates and was back at square one.

As are we.

II

1

'The guy in 6A?'

'Yes.'

'What's wrong with him?'

'I've no idea, some kind of nervous attack. D'you have any ice cubes left?' she asked her colleague, who was waiting on the other side of the cart.

Somewhere up above the ocean, one of their passengers had unfastened his seatbelt.

He was sobbing, hiding his entire face behind his hand.

'Are you all right?' asked his neighbour anxiously.

He did not hear her, submerged as he was, drifting off in his own zone of turbulence; then he stood up, climbed over her, holding on to the headrests, went round to the other side of the curtain, found an empty row and collapsed into it.

End of business class.

He pressed his face against the window and covered it with vapour.

They sent a steward to see him.

'Do you need a doctor, Sir?'

Charles raised his head, tried to smile, and pulled out his bull-shit secret weapon: 'Just tired . . .'

The steward was reassured and they left him in peace.

Rarely has an expression been so misused.

In peace? When has he ever lived in peace?

The last time, he was six and a half years old and was walking up the Rue Berthelot with his new friend.

A boy in his class, whose name was Le Men, in two words, and who had just moved in next door. He had noticed him from the very first day because he wore his house key round his neck.

It was really something, in those days, to have your house key round your neck. It made a man of you, in the schoolyard during break . . .

He'd already come to Charles's place several times for afterschool snack, but that day it was his turn, and Alexis had said, taking his shoes off, 'You know, you have to be quiet, because my mum is asleep.'

'Oh?'

Charles was impressed. There were mums who could sleep in the afternoon?

'Is she sick?' he asked in a very low voice.

'No, she's a nurse, but since she leaves very early in the morning, she often has a nap . . . Look, the door to her room is closed. That's our code.'

It all seemed very romantic. Because it was an added game, to play that way, to roll their little cars without having them collide; to whisper, catching each other by the sleeve; to cut their slices of gingerbread all by themselves.

The two of them all alone in the world, starting at the slightest pschitt from the lemonade bottle . . .

Yes, and even then peace was not such a sure thing, because every time he went by that door he could feel his heart beat.

A little.

It was as if Sleeping Beauty, or a very weary princess, who'd been condemned, or perhaps disfigured? were hiding behind that door . . . He walked on tiptoes, held his breath, and made his way to his friend's room placing his feet just so on the parquet floor so that he wouldn't fall over.

The corridor was a bridge suspended above crocodiles.

Charles went there several more times, and he was always fascinated by the closed door.

He must have wondered if she were dead, in fact. Perhaps Alexis was lying to him. Perhaps he managed on his own all the time, and lived on biscuits . . .

Perhaps she looked like one of those statues in their history book?

And she was shrouded in a stiff veil, with her feet sticking out at the other end?

112

But no, it couldn't be, because the kitchen table was always a mess . . . Bowls of coffee and half-finished crosswords, strands of hair in a slide, an orange peel, torn envelopes, crumbs . . .

And Charles watched Alexis cleaning it all as if it were the most natural thing in the world, to empty your mum's ashtrays, and fold her cardigans.

Thus, no longer was his friend the little boy the teacher had put in the corner a few hours earlier, he was . . .

It was strange. Even his face changed. He stood up straighter, and he counted the cigarette butts with a frown.

That particular day, for example, he'd shaken his head and broken the silence: 'Pfff . . . It's disgusting.'

Three butts stuck into a yoghurt that had hardly been touched.

'If you want,' he added, confused, 'I have a new marble, a gigantic one . . . It's on my night table.'

Charles removed his shoes and set off on an expedition.

Oh, oh. The door was wide open. He looked to one side on the outward trip, but on the return he could not keep from taking a quick look.

The sheet had slipped and you could see her shoulders. And even half of her back. He stood still. Her skin was so white and her hair so very long . . .

He had to get away from there, he really must, he was *about* to, when she opened her eyes.

How lovely she was. Lovely like in Bible stories. Silent and still, but with a sort of light all around her.

'Hey. Hello there,' she said, lifting herself up slightly in order to wedge her palm under the back of her neck.

'You're Charles, isn't that right?'

He couldn't reply because you could see a bit of her . . . Well, her . . .

He couldn't reply so he ran off.

'What are you doing? Are you leaving?'

'Yes,' mumbled Charles, struggling with his shoelaces, 'I have to do my homework.'

'Hey!' exclaimed Alexis, 'but it's Saturday tomor—'

The door had already slammed.

113

2

Let's forget that whole thing about peace, whether stolen or condemned. He had been protesting too much to be honest. Of course Charles, once he was in the street, had knelt down and dealt with his shoelaces the way he should, passing the big loop around the small one, then off he set again best foot forward.

Of course.

What's more, he could smile about it now. Talk about Holy Virgins . . .

He was amused by the little boy he'd been, illuminated and touched by grace, yet still puzzled. Yes, puzzled. A boy who lived surrounded by girls but would never have imagined that there was another colour, that bit he saw . . .

He didn't lose his peace, but he gained a sort of agitation, a disturbing feeling that would grow as he did, lengthening at the same pace as his trouser legs. It would hide his scrapes, circle his hips and expand at the bottom. It would be flattened by his mother's iron and reproved by his father's elegance. As time passed it would start to get frayed. It would roll up in a ball and get covered with marks. Then it would gain in maturity, therefore in quality, and acquire an impeccable crease, and turn-ups too, and it would demand to be dry cleaned, only to end up all wrinkled amidst the gravel of a creepy cemetery.

He lowered his seat back and blessed the sky.

How lucky he was to be on a plane, in the end. Flying so high, and high on other things, with an empty stomach; how lucky he was to have found them again, to have recalled Nana's perfume and its scent of old tart; how lucky to have known them, to have been loved by them, and never to have recovered.

At the time, he thought of her as a lady, but now he knows this was not the case. Now he knows that she must have been twenty-five or twenty-six and that this age business – which had so haunted him – had finally proved him right: it did not matter in the least.

Anouk was ageless because you could not pigeonhole her, and she would fight any attempt to circumscribe her.

She often behaved like a child. She'd curl up in a ball in the middle of their Meccano games and fall asleep in the way of their toy truck convoy. She'd sulk when it was time for homework, would copy her son's signature, write exaggerated excuses for them, could go for days without speaking, fell in love without care or caution, spent her evenings waiting for the phone to ring, giving it dark glances, exasperated them with her repeated questions, did they think she was beautiful, no, she meant *really* beautiful, and ended up telling them off because there was nothing for dinner.

And then there were other times . . . no. Other times when she saved people's lives, and not only at the hospital. People like Nana, and so many others who worshipped her as the most solid of idols.

She was not afraid of anything or anybody. Stepped nimbly aside when the sky was falling. Dealt with things. No fear of crossing swords. Took the rap. Batted her eyelashes, clenched her fists or raised her middle finger, depending on the enemy, and eventually understood that the line had gone dead, hung up, shrugged her shoulders, put on some fresh make-up and took them all out to a restaurant.

Yes, her age, the difference in their ages, were the only figures that proved elusive to this good pupil. An inequation left in the margin . . . Too many unknowns . . . And yet he remembers how her face had affected him, the last time. But it wasn't her wrinkles, or her white roots that were disconcerting, it was her withdrawal.

Something, someone, life itself, had switched off the light.

They offered him a coffee, revolting dishwater that he accepted joyfully. He sipped the burning plastic, his forehead against the pane of glass, while he observed the trembling of the wing, and he tried to distinguish the stars from other long-haul aircraft; then he wound back the hands of his watch and forged onwards into the night.

*

The second photo was one he'd taken . . . He remembers because his uncle Pierre had just given him the camera, a little Kodak Instamatic that he'd been dreaming about for ages, and he'd rolled up the sleeve of his communion gown to be able to christen it.

Alexis and he had just taken first communion, and everyone had gathered in the family garden. Beneath the cherry tree that had just been chopped down the week before, to be precise . . . His uncle must have been driving him nuts telling him over and over that he had to read the instructions first, and check the light, and make sure the film was properly loaded, and . . . did you wash your hands, first? but Charles wasn't listening: Anouk was already posing.

She'd wedged a lock of hair between her nose and her upper lip and, making faces, seemed to be sending him an enormous moustachioed kiss from beneath her straw hat.

If he'd known he would go cross-eyed staring at this photo several lives later, he would have paid more attention to his uncle's advice . . . It was poorly framed and the focus left something to be desired, but, oh well . . . It was Anouk. And if it was blurry, it was because she'd been clowning around . . .

Yes, she was clowning around. And not just for the photo. Not just to rescue Charles from his four-eyed uncle. Not just because the weather was splendid and in the viewfinder of someone who loved her she felt trusting. She was laughing, licking the edge of her glass when the foam spilled over, she pelted them with sugared almonds, and even made vampire's fangs out of nougatine, but it was just . . . to create a distraction . . . To forget, and above all, make them all forget, that her entire family, the only human beings with whom later in life she would be able to say, 'Don't you remember? It was at my little boy's communion, you know . . .' and who had agreed at the last minute to act as godfather and godmother when it was time to sign the register, were a colleague from work and an old trouper whose beehive was bigger than ever . . .

Ah, speaking of which. There he is . . . The magnificent Nana . . . Flanked on either side by his two cherubs, proud as Punch and scarcely taller than they were, despite his little heels and his expandable hairdo.

'Oh, ducks! Do be careful with your candles! With all the spray Jackie put on my head, I'll just explode! Touch it, you'll see . . .'

They had touched it, and it was indeed just like the sugary frosting on top of the fanciest cakes.

'What did I tell you . . . Right, go on, big smile now!'

And they were smiling for the photograph. Smiling. Clinging tenderly to his arm, to wipe their fingers on his alpaca sleeve.

Alpaca . . . That was the first time Charles ever heard the word. They were all out on the square in front of the church, deafened by the racket from the bells, and peering into the distance, twisting the cord of their communion gowns because Nana was late.

Mado could make neither head nor tail of it all, and just when they had given up, oh well, time to go in, there he was, climbing out of a taxi as if it were a limousine at Cannes.

Anouk burst out laughing, 'But Nana – you look fabulous! Really!'

'Please,' he replied, primly, 'it's just a little alpaca suit, after all . . . I had it made for Orlanda Marshall's tour in . . .'

'Who was she?' I asked, as we headed towards the sacristy.

Long dramatic sigh.

'Oh . . . A good friend of mine . . . But she never made it . . . The tour was cancelled . . . someone was getting his leg over, if you want my opinion . . .'

Then, kissing his index finger and touching their foreheads (with his *Rouge Baiser* lipstick, the best of all holy oils): 'Off you go, my little Jesus boys, . . . And if you see the light, no kidding you look down, all right?'

But Charles had recited his Lord's Prayer with his eyes wide open, and he'd seen her, smiling her crooked smile, hanging onto her neighbour's hand for dear life.

At the time, it had annoyed him a bit. But not now, hey. Pax. She wasn't going to start weeping now, was she? But today . . . Our emotion, which art in heaven . . . Hallowed be thy name, thy will be done. It was the first communion of her only child, a day full of grace, a little *official* truce in the midst of a life full of thorns, and her only past, her only shoulder, the only fingers she could crush during all the organ grinding, were those of Orlanda Marshall's old girlfriend, with her patent leather boots and her rosary on a chain over her violet suit . . .

It was nothing.

And yet it was a great deal.

Any old rubbish.

It was her life.

Nana had offered Charles a pen, which had belonged to 'Monsieur Maurice Chevalier, if you please', but no one could get the cap off any more.

'Well? Isn't your heart going pitty-pat, now?' he'd added, when he saw Charles's embarrassed smile.

'Uh, yes . . .'

And when the little boy had wandered off, it was the pout on Anouk's face that he felt obliged to deal with: 'What are you looking at me like that for?'

'I don't know . . . Last time, you told me that damned pen belonged to Bing Crosby . . .'

'Oh please, sweetheart . . .'

A great, alpaca weariness.

'It's the dream that matters, you know that . . . And anyway, I thought that Maurice Chavelier, for a communion, well it would be . . . it would be better.'

'You're right. Bing Crosby, that's a Christmas fantasy.'

She burst out laughing; he frowned.

'Oh, c'mon dear Nana . . . Where would I be without you?'

He blushed beneath his foundation.

Charles put the photos back onto the tray. He would have liked to go farther, but that old strolling player had to be in the lime-light, as usual. And you couldn't hold it against him. The stage, the show, was his raison d'être: '*Ze show must go on*,' he would say, in his thick Frenchy accent . . .

Right, he mused, off we go. After the little dogs wearing fake fur collars and before the lights come back on, Ladies and Gentlemen, exceptionally, this evening, straight from his triumphal New World Tour, in front of your very own bedazzled eyes, I give you the One, the Only, the Unforgettable: Nana!

*

One night in January, 1966 (when she told him the story, much later, Anouk, who never remembered a thing, would use this reference: the night before, a Boeing had crashed into Mont Blanc), an old lady died in cardiology. That is, three floors up. That is, light years away from the immediate concerns of Nurse Le Men, who, in those days, worked in *shock* recovery. Charles is using the word *shock* on purpose: it's his word, but just to be clear: in the emergency unit. Anouk – and it suited her so well – was an *accident and emergency* nurse.

Yes, an old lady had died, and why should Anouk have known anything about it, since there is nothing more hermetic than a hospital ward. Each department has its own parties, its own victories, its own misfortunes . . .

But that's without taking rumours into account. Or the humming of the coffee machine, to be exact . . . On that particular day, one of her colleagues was complaining about a weirdo who was beginning to get on their nerves upstairs, because he kept coming to visit his late mother with fresh flowers every day, and was surprised that they dare try and send him away. Then he would laugh about it and ask the assembled company if someone was willing to sign him into the psych ward.

At the time she paid no particular attention. Her heart and her paper cup were equally crumpled before she tossed them into the bin. She had enough on her plate.

It was only when security got involved and they wouldn't allow him to go upstairs that the weirdo in question entered her life. At all hours of the day or night, whether she was going on duty or off again, she would find him there, in the reception lobby, seated between two potted plants and the accounting office. He was devastated, he was tolerated, buffeted by draughts and the flow of crowds, shunted about to the rhythm of the empty seats, his face constantly turned towards the doors of the lifts.

But even then she wouldn't look at him. She had her own fate, her own sorrow – the bodies pulled from the wreckage, the scalded infants, the winos' puke, the firefighters who were too slow, her babysitting crises, her money problems, her solitude, her . . . She looked away.

And then one evening, who knows why, because it was a Sunday and Sundays are the most unfair days on earth, and her shift was over, and because Alexis was safe and sound with their kindly neighbours, and because she was too exhausted to notice her fatigue just yet, because it was cold, because her car had broken down and the very idea of walking all the way to the bus stop stuck in her throat, and because he was bound to die at this rate, sitting there motionless: instead of slipping out the service entry, she walked out into the light and, instead of looking away, she came and sat next to him.

For a long time she remained silent, racking her brains to think of a way to make him give up his bouquet without breaking him into a thousand pieces, but she couldn't find one, and, head down, she'd eventually had to concede that she herself was far too badly off to help anyone at all.

'And so?' asked Charles.

'Um . . . I asked him if he had a light.'

He doubled over with laughter. 'Hey! Incredibly original way to start a conversation!'

Anouk was smiling. She'd never told anyone this story, and she was surprised that she remembered it this well, for someone who'd forget her own head if it weren't screwed on.

'And then? Did you ask him if he came here often?'

'No. Afterwards I went out to take a few puffs to work up my courage and when I came back in I told him the truth. I had never confided in anyone the way I spoke to him that night. Never. Poor thing, when I think back . . .'

'What did you say?'

'I said that I knew why he was there. That I'd asked around, and I'd been told that his mother had passed away, very quietly. I'd like to think that I deserved at least that much some day. She'd been fortunate to have him there with her. One of my colleagues had told me that he came every day and held his mother's hand right up to the end. I envied the two of them. I hadn't seen my mother in years. I had a little boy who was six years old and she had never taken him in her arms. I'd sent her a card when he was born and she'd sent back a dress for a little girl as a present. It probably wasn't meant unkindly, but in fact it was worse. I spent nearly every waking hour of my life bringing relief to other people, but no one had ever taken care of me. I was tired, had trouble sleeping, lived alone, and on occasion I drank, in the evening, so that I could fall asleep, because just the thought that there was a child asleep in the next room whose life depended on mine was enough to make me horribly anxious . . . I had never heard from his father, although he was a man I could still dream about. I had to apologize for telling him all this. He had his sorrows, too, but there was no need for him to keep coming back to the hospital, because he must have buried her in the meantime, no? He shouldn't go on hanging about a place like this when he was in good health, because it was an insult to those who were in pain, but the fact he was still coming, it meant he must have a certain amount of spare time on his hands, and if that was the case, um . . . wouldn't he like to spend it at my place instead?

'And I told him that before moving here I had worked nights at another hospital, and in those days I lodged with friends who could look after my kid, but for the last two years I'd been living alone and spending a fortune on nannies. Because the boy had been learning to read since starting school in the autumn, I'd taken on the most exhausting schedule in order to be there when he got home from school. He was only this high, but he still woke up alone every morning and I was always worried about whether he'd had his breakfast and . . . I'd never told a soul because I was too ashamed . . . He was so small . . . Yes. I was ashamed. I was going to have to work during the day as of the very next month. My supervisor gave me no choice and I hadn't dared tell the boy yet . . . Nannies never have time to go over the children's lessons or make them do their page of reading, at least not those nannies I could afford and . . . I would pay him, naturally! He was a very sweet child, who was used to playing all alone and . . . it wasn't very nice at my place, but it was at least a little bit more welcoming than here, and . . .'

'And?'

'Well, after I'd said all that, nothing . . . And since he didn't react, I wondered if he wasn't deaf or . . . I don't know . . . A bit simple-minded, you see . . .'

'And?'

'And it seemed to take him for ever, Good Lord! As if we were both in some psych ward somewhere! And I put us both in the same basket, you see? Two nutcases in amongst the yuccas . . . Oh, when I think about that night . . . I must really have been desperate. I had gone up to him thinking I could help him somehow and there I was begging him to rescue me . . . it was pathetic, Charles, pathetic . . .'

'Go on.'

121

'Well then, at one point I had to get up, after all. And he stood up with me. I went to catch my bus, and he followed me. I sat down, and he sat down across from me and uh . . . I was beginning to freak out.'

She was laughing.

'Shit, I thought, this just simply isn't on! I asked him to come to my place, but not right away. Nor for ever. Help. I put on a good face, but I swear, my heart was in my month. I already pictured myself dragging him off to the police station. Good evening, Officer, well here's the situation . . . I've got this orphaned chick who thinks I'm his mother and he follows me wherever I go . . . What . . . what am I doing? So as a result I didn't dare look at him any more and I tried to disappear into my scarf. But he didn't stop looking at me. Great atmosphere . . . And at one point he just said, "Your hand." "Sorry?" "Give me your hand . . . No, not that one, the left hand . . ."'

'What did he want?'

'I don't know . . . To see my CV I suppose . . . To make sure I'd told him the truth. So he read my palm and added, "The little boy . . . What's his name?" "Alexis." "Oh?" Pause. "Like Sverdjak . . ." And when I didn't react, "Alexis Sverdjak. The greatest knife thrower of all time." And with that – believe me I said to myself I must have fucked up yet again . . . He looked such a complete nutter with his old-granny head scarf . . . And then I really felt guilty. You really go looking for trouble, don't you, went the lecture in my head as I sat there looking at my nails. Shit, this is your kid you're talking about! Who in hell is this circus freak Mary Poppins you've dug up?'

'Was he wearing make-up and everything?'

'No, it was something even harder to pinpoint . . . Like some very old dolly . . . With his blotchy face and his eyes like jelly, and his anything-but-kid gloves and his really scary collars . . . It was dreadful, I tell you . . .'

'And did he follow you to your place?'

'Yes. He wanted to see where I lived. But he refused to come up for a drink. And God knows I did insist, but it was impossible to persuade him.'

'And then?'

'And then I said goodbye. I told him I was sorry to have bothered him with all my woes and he could come back whenever he felt like it. He would always be welcome, and my little boy would surely be happy to learn all about Thingammy-jig, but, above all, he must not go back to the hospital . . . Promise?

'I walked away, looking for my keys, and I heard him say, "You know, sweetheart, that I was an artiste, too?" Well, who are you kidding, of course I assumed he was! I turned around to say goodbye one last time.

'"I was in vaudeville . . ."

'"Oh?"

'And at that point, Charles . . . Try to picture the scene . . . It's night-time, there's his shadow, his really odd voice, it's cold, there are dustbins and . . . Frankly, I felt pretty stupid . . . I could already see myself in the morning paper . . .

'"Don't you believe me?" he added. "Look . . ."

'He thrust his hand into the neckline of his little coat and do you know what he pulled out?'

'A photo?'

'No. A dove.'

'*Magnifique.*'

'Exactly. We had our share of shows with him, didn't we? But that one will always remain the most beautiful one for me . . . It was both so completely crazy, so sort of old-fashioned and incredibly poetic . . . It was . . . That was Nana all over. If you could have seen his face . . . How proud he was. And at that point I felt this smile spread across my face and I couldn't get rid of it. I drank my coffee, I brushed my teeth and I went to bed with that smile . . . And you know what?'

'What?'

'That night, for the first time in years — years and years — I slept *well*. I knew he was going to come back. I knew he was going to take care of us and that . . . I don't know . . . I just had faith. He'd seen it, seen that my luck line was even shorter than my heart line . . . He'd called me sweetheart and had caressed his birdy's head and given me this smile full of his rotten teeth, and . . . He was going to love us, of that I was certain. And you see, for once I was not mistaken . . . The Nana years were the best years of my life. The least difficult, at any rate. And that bloody fireworks display they set off two years later, for me, it was all meaningless: what

mattered was Nana. He was the pyrotechnician. That little Zebedee
– he was my revolution and . . . oh . . . he was so good for us.'

'Er . . . , forgive me for being so mundane, but . . . all that time
he was there, at the hospital – did he have the bird in his pocket?'

'It's funny you should ask, because that is precisely what I asked
him not long afterwards, and he never wanted to give me an
answer . . . I felt he was uneasy about it so I didn't press him. It
was only years later, one day when I must have been feeling particularly pathetic, and I must have broken down yet again, that he sent
me a letter. The only letter he ever wrote to me, actually. I hope
I haven't lost it. He said all these very kind things, compliments
of the sort no one had ever paid me, yes, it was a love letter now
that I think back on it, and at the end, he wrote:

*Do you remember that night at the hospital? I knew I would never
be going back to my house and that is why I had Mistinguett in my
pocket. To let her go before I . . . And then you came along, so I went
home after all.'*

Her eyes were shining.

'And when did he come back?'

'Two days later . . . At tea time. All spruced up, with a new hair
colour, a bouquet of roses and some jelly babies for Alexis. We
showed him the house, the school, the shops, your house . . .
And . . . There we are. You know the rest.'

'Yes.'

My eyes were shining.

'The only snag, in those days, was Mado . . .'

'I remember. I wasn't allowed to visit you any more.'

'Yes. And then look what happened . . . he even managed to win
her over, in the end.'

★

At the time, I hadn't dared to contradict her, but it hadn't been as
easy as all that . . .

My mother wasn't exactly a little white dove who closed her
eyes when you stroked her head. Alexis was still welcome to come
over, but I was not allowed to visit at number 20.

I heard new words, words that didn't seem to be very polite
where Nana was concerned. Morality, morals, danger. Words which
to me seemed utterly ridiculous. What danger? That I might get

cavities because he bought us too many sweets? That I might smell like a girl because he gave us too many kisses? That I might not work as hard at school because he kept telling us over and over again that we were princes and that we'd never have to work later in life? But, Maman . . . We didn't believe him, you know that . . . And in any event, they were all rubbish, his predictions. He had sworn we would win the mini Le Mans sweepstake at the local fête and we didn't win a thing, so there . . .

No, the reason she finally gave in was because for once I resisted. I went twelve hours without eating, and nine days without speaking a word to her. And then the events of May '68 finally made her relent somewhat . . . Since the world was going to hell, well then, my son, go ahead. Go and play marbles.

So I was allowed to go back there, but I was not allowed to forget her special concession, and I had all sorts of instructions and a very strict time table. There were warnings, about gestures, my body, his hands, and . . . Sentences I could make neither head nor tail of.

Nowadays, of course, I see things differently. And if I had a child, would I entrust him or her to a babysitter as hybrid as Nana? I don't know . . . I would probably have a few reservations as well. But in fact . . . we had nothing to fear. In any case, there were never any feelings of unease. How Nana spent his nights was another matter, but with us he was the most modest of men. An angel. A guardian angel who wore Ô mon amour scent and left us in peace to play our war games.

And then he became a pretext. It was Anouk who bothered my mother, and that too, I can understand. It was enough to see my father's distress the other day, which says it all.

I was allowed to go and play marbles, but there came a time when I was not to say her name in the house. Just what had happened, I never knew. Or knew all too well. There wasn't a man on earth would have wanted to live with her, but they were all prepared to swear the contrary . . .

When she was cheerful, when her dizzy spells left her alone, when she'd let her hair down and go barefoot, when she remembered that her skin was soft and that . . . well, she was like a sun. Wherever she went, whatever she said, heads would turn and everyone wanted a piece of her. Everyone wanted to grab her by the arm, even if they hurt her a bit – preferably hurting her a bit – just to stop the jingling of her bracelets for a second. Just a second. The time it took for a grimace or a look. For a silence, a withdrawal, anything from her. Anything at all, really. But just for oneself alone.

Oh yes . . . She must have heard her share of lies, in her time.

Was I jealous? Yes.

No.

I had learned to recognize those looks; how could I not? And I no longer feared them. All I needed was to get older, and I was working hard at it. Day by day. I had faith.

And then everything I knew about her, what she had given me, what belonged to me, is something that they, all the others, could never have. For them she changed her voice, spoke too quickly, laughed too loudly, but with me, no, she was herself.

So, I was the one she loved.

But how old was I to be reasoning like this? Nine? Ten?

And why did I have this crush on her? Because my mother, my sisters, my teachers and cub mistresses and all the other women around me filled me with despair. They were ugly, they didn't understand a thing, all they cared about was finding out whether I'd learned my tables or had remembered to change my vest.

Of course.

Of course, since I had no other aim than to grow up so I could be rid of them.

Whereas Anouk . . . Precisely because she was ageless, or because I was the only person in the world who would listen to her and who knew when she was lying, she never *leaned towards* me, and she could not stand it when people called me Charley or Charlot, and she said my name was gentle and elegant, and it suited me, and she always asked for my opinion and conceded that I was often right.

And why did I feel so self-assured, looking down my snotty little nose?

Because she'd told me as much, by Jove!

I'd spent the night at their place and, before we'd left for school, she'd slipped our snacks into our schoolbags.

When it was time for the break, we joined the others with our bagfuls of marbles in one hand and our little foil parcels in the other.

'Oh!' Alexis exclaimed with enthusiasm when he unwrapped his 'Talking biscuits!'

I was already kneeling down, clearing a path in the gravel.

'*You're on the tip of my tongue* and *You make me laugh*,' he read out, before scoffing them down.

I was rubbing my palms against my thighs.

'And what have you got?'

'Me?' I said, a bit disappointed to see that I had only one biscuit.

'Well?'

'Nothing . . .'

'There's nothing written on the biscuit?'

'No, it says, "Nothing".'

'Oh, that's crummy . . . Well, anyway . . . Whose turn to start?'

'Go ahead,' I went, standing up to put the biscuit into my jacket pocket.

We played, and I lost a lot that day . . . All my cat's eyes . . .

'Hey! You're really useless today, y'know that?'

I smiled. First there, in the dust, and then at my desk, inside my pocket, and then in my locker, and finally in my bed, after I'd got back up three times to change the hiding place, I was smiling.

Crazy about you.

With forty years' hindsight, Charles could not recall a more direct declaration . . .

The little wafer had crumbled to bits and he'd eventually had to throw it away. He'd grown up, gone away, come back, and she had laughed. And he'd believed her. Then he got older, and put on weight, and . . . and she was dead.

And that's it.

Go on, Balanda, it was only a biscuit. You know what they call them in retro grocery shops nowadays? *Funny biscuits.* And besides, you were only a kid.

It's all rather ridiculous, isn't it?

Ridiculous.

Yes, but . . .

He didn't have time to plead his case. He'd drifted off.

3

A chauffeur was waiting for him at the airport with his name on a sign.

A room was waiting for him at the hotel with his name on a television screen.

On the pillow were a piece of chocolate and the weather forecast for the following day.

Cloudy.

Another night was beginning, and he wasn't sleepy. Here we go, he thought, I'm going to get fucked by jet lag again. In the past, he wouldn't have given it a thought but today his old bones were grumbling. He felt . . . disheartened. He went down to the bar, ordered a bourbon, read the local papers, and took a moment to realize that the flames in the fireplace were fake.

As was the leather in his armchair. And the flowers. And the paintings. And the woodwork. And the stucco on the ceiling. And the patina on the lamps. And the books on the bookshelves. And the odour of wax polish. And the laugh of the pretty woman at the bar. And the thoughtfulness of the gentleman who stopped her slipping off her bar stool. And the music. And the candlelight. And . . . Everything, absolutely *everything*, was fake. It was Disney World for the rich, and however lucid he might be, he was one of them. All that was missing was a pair of Mickey Mouse ears.

He went out into the cold. Walked for hours. Saw nothing but dull, charmless, utilitarian constructions. Slipped a plastic card into the slot of room 408. Turned off the air conditioning. Switched on the television. Turned off the sound. Turned off the picture. Tried to open a window. Swore. Gave up. Turned around and, for the first time in his life, felt trapped.

```
03:17   lay down
03:32   and wondered
04:10   calmly
04:14   unhurriedly
04:31   just what he
05:03   was doing there.
```

Charles took a shower. Ordered a taxi. And went home.

4

Never had he paid so much for a plane ticket, nor wasted so much time. Two entire days. Lost. Irretrievable. Not a file, not a phone call, no decisions to make and no responsibility. At first it seemed utterly absurd to him, and then, terribly exotic.

He bummed around Toronto airport, did the same during the stop in Montreal, bought dozens of newspapers, some trinkets for Mathilde, a carton of cigarettes and two crime novels that he forgot on the counter.

It was eight in the morning when he went to get his car. He rubbed his eyelids, felt the stubble on his cheeks, and crossed his arms over the steering wheel.

Lost in thought.

Since he couldn't see clearly about anything else, he located himself geographically on the planet, set his sights on the simplest thing, was sorry that he didn't have something more splendid to hand, then figured that as matters stood, any old stones would be good to touch . . . He had a look at his maps, turned his back on the capital and, with neither pilgrim's staff nor any purpose other than that of forgetting the ugliness that had been clouding his retinas and clinging to his soles for weeks, set off to visit the abbey at Royaumont.

And while he was winding his way through the succession of zones that were earmarked as urban, industrial, commercial, development, residential, or for even more far-fetched purposes, he remembered the surreal conversation he had had with the taxi driver the morning of the day he learned of her death. Was God in his life? No, obviously not . . . But His architects were, yes. And always had been.

*

Even more than to Anouk's prayer at the foot of those concrete monstrosities (the one that had helped her to turn her back on her family for good) it was to the Cistercians he owed a large part of his vocation. Something he had read as a teenager, to be exact. He remembered it as if it were yesterday . . . In his little suburban bedroom, beneath the eaves of a house located a stone's throw from the new ring road, there he was, feverishly devouring that book, *The Stones of the Abbey*, by Fernand Pouillon.

Absorbed in the stories of the convivial monk who struggled against doubt and gangrene with each passing season and each successive hardship, and raised his masterpiece of an abbey from the arid earth. The shock had been so great that Charles had never allowed himself to reread the book. Let one part of him, at least, despite all the disillusions that would follow, remain intact . . .

No, he would not relive the trials and tribulations of master Paul in his desolate quarry, nor the Rule to which the lay workers were subjected, nor the terrible death of the mule, disembowelled beneath his shaft, but he had never forgotten the opening sentences, and from time to time, he still recited them in a quiet voice, to feel again the handles of the tools and the grain of the ochre stone, and all the exultation of being fifteen years old:

Third Sunday of Lent

The rain has soaked our clothing, the frost has hardened the heavy fabric of our cowls, frozen our beards, stiffened our limbs. Our hands, feet and faces are splattered with mud, the wind has covered us with sand. The movement of walking . . .

'. . . no longer makes the icy folds sway over our emaciated bodies,' he intoned very quietly, after rolling down the window to rid himself of the smoke.

Rid himself of smoke . . . What sort of roundabout phrase was this, now? Come now, Charles, didn't you simply mean, 'to get some air'?

Yes, he smiled, puffing on his cigarette, exactly. I can't hide a thing from you, I see . . .

At the very moment he should have been fretting in Uncle Scrooge's mansion, having to put up with the patter of reinforced concrete vendors, he was, instead, blinking furiously to keep from missing the exit.

He took a breath of fresh air, shook the heavy fabric of his cowl, and drove towards the light.

Towards his broken vows, his naïveté, the rough draught of his youth, or the faint remnant of himself that still pulsed with life.

He shivered. Didn't try to decide whether it was with pleasure, cold, or panic, he just rolled up the window and began to hunt for a genuine bar where he could drink a real coffee with real odours of stale tobacco, real grimy walls, real tips for the fifth race, real shouting matches, real boozers and a real proprietor in a really bad mood behind his real moustache.

★

The church's impressive architecture, whose dimensions are comparable to those of the cathedral at Soissons, is the fruit of a compromise between the pomp of the royal abbey and Cistercian austerity . . .

Charles, lost in thought, raised his head and . . . saw nothing.

. . . but not long after the Revolution, continued the notice, *the Marquis de Travalet, who had already converted the abbey into a mill, razed it to the ground in order to use the stones for housing for his workers.*

Oh?

What was this? Why hadn't they chopped his head off along with all the others?

So, there are no monks at the abbey in Royaumont nowadays.

But there are artists in residence.

And a tea room.

Right.

Fortunately, there was the cloister.

He walked through it, his hands behind his back, then leaned against a column and took his time to observe the shape of the swallows' nests hanging from the ribbed vault.

Now there were some real builders . . .

The place and the moment seemed absolutely perfect for a final curtain call.

Goodnight, goodnight, my swallows sang Charles Trenet. Nana didn't get the chance to wear his lovely suit for their solemn communion.

One day he did not show up. Nor the day after. Nor all that week.

Anouk reassured them: he surely had other things to do. And

surmised: perhaps he went to see his family, he mentioned a sister in Normandy, I think . . . And rationalized: and besides, if there were a problem, he would have told me . . . And fell silent.

She fell silent and got up during the night to ask the first bottle neck she could find if, by any chance, it had had any news.

The situation was disturbing. They knew all about their Nana with his false eyelashes, his Bobino and Tête de l'Art and Alhambra cabarets, and all the caboodle, but they didn't know his name, nor where he lived. And it was not for a lack of asking, but . . . 'Over that way,' he dithered, waving his rings above the roofs of Paris. They didn't press him. His hand had already fallen, and over that way seemed so far away . . .

'You want me to tell you where I live? I live in my memories . . . A world that vanished a long time ago . . . I told you how we used to heat our eyebrow pencils under the lamp to soften them, and . . .'

The boys sighed. Yes, you told us, a million times. André Whatsit singing about his pink cherry tree and his white apple tree, Master Yo-Yo and his tame nightingales, curtain up every evening, and that Russian with his hands tied so that when he wanted to drink his bottle of vodka he had to bite off the bottle neck, and the *patronne* over at Jacob's Ladder who locked a journalist in the coal cellar, and Lord Hooligan, and the mongrel belonging to Johnny Boy from Flanders that would jump on the tables and stick his muzzle into the champagne glass of an attractive customer then deliver it to his drunken master, not to mention the evening when the singer Barbara got up on stage at l'Ecluse, and you had to re-apply your make-up because you'd been crying so hard and . . .

Our display of bad faith would cause Nana to sulk, and the only way to make him stop his song and dance was to ask him to do his imitation of the tragic Fréhel. You had to beg a bit, to be sure, then he would puff out his cheeks, steal a cigarette from Anouk, stick it to his lower lip, wedge his hands on his hips and belt out in a husky voice,

> 'Hey there booooys!
> C'mon and have one on meeee!
> I'm all alone t'daaaaay . . .
> He's gone and died on me this mornin!'

There, they'd have a good laugh, and the Stones could just wait for another day. They'd have to find their satisfaction elsewhere.

'And when I'm not in my memories, I'm living with you, can't you see that?'

Right, but *where* have you been all this time, then, if you say that we're your greatest love story?

Anouk did some research at the hospital, found his mother's records, picked up the telephone, explained her worries to that sister they'd heard all about, listened to her reply, put down the receiver, and fell off her chair.

Her colleagues helped her to her feet, insisted on taking her blood pressure and eventually handed her a lump of sugar that she spat back out in a gob of saliva.

When the boys saw her face as they left school that evening, they knew that Nana would not be waiting for them ever again.

She took them for a hot chocolate.

'We didn't realize, because of his make-up and everything, but you know, he was actually very old . . .'

'How did he die?' asked Charles.

'I just told you. Old age . . .'

'So we'll never see him, ever again?'

'Why did you say that? No . . . I . . . I'll always . . .'

It was their first funeral and the boys hesitated an instant before tossing their handfuls of sequins and confetti onto the coffin: Who was this Maurice Charpieu?

No one came to greet them at the graveside.

The paths emptied. Anouk took their hands, stepped forward to the edge of the grave and murmured, 'So, my Nana . . . Are you there? Did you find all those wonderful people you used to go on about so often? You must be having a wild time of it up there, no? And . . . and your little poodles? Tell us, are they up there too?'

Then the children went off for a walk, and she sat next to him just as she had done years before.

She tossed tiny pebbles on his head for the pleasure of seeing him roll his eyes heavenward one last time, and she smoked a last cigarette in his company.

Thank you, said the swirls of smoke. Thank you.

They were silent on the ride home and, just when they must have been thinking, all three of them, that life was the most rotten cabaret act of all, Alexis leaned forward to turn up the volume.

Léo Ferré was singing that life was grand, and yes, just then – but only because it was Ferré and Nana had known him before he was famous – they were prepared to believe him for the three minutes his bloody song lasted. And then Alexis switched off the radio, talked about something else, and had to repeat that year at school.

One evening Anouk, who had been fretting over this business for a long time, came out with it: 'Tell me, kitten . . .'

'What?'

'Why do you always change the subject when we talk about Nana? Why haven't you cried? He was someone important in your life, wasn't he?'

He focused on his macaroni, then was obliged to raise his head and meet her eyes because of the strings of Gruyère, and he simply replied, 'Every time I open my trumpet case I can smell him. You know, there's this sort of old musty smell and . . .'

'And?'

'And when I play, it's for him and . . .'

'And?'

'When people tell me I'm playing well, it's actually because I think I've been crying . . .'

If she could have, she would have taken him in her arms at that very moment in their lives. But she couldn't. He didn't want her to, any more.

'But . . . are you sad, then?'

'Oh, no! Absolutely not! I feel good!'

She smiled instead. A little smile with arms and hands, a neck and two cheeks grazing.

Charles looked at his watch, turned round, glanced at a tiny grotto in the style of Lourdes (*On the path of Saint-Louis*, said the arrow. What rubbish . . .) and waited until he got back to the car park to be done with it and spew out his *Dies Irae*.

'Yes. And then, he even managed to win her over, in the end,' echoed Anouk's voice.

No, he hadn't tried to contradict her on that score. His mother . . .
His mother had found other fish to fry, soon enough. She had her
house to run, her marriage, her social status, her flowerbeds and all
the rest. And then de Gaulle was back in power. So she'd eventually
relaxed.

Not on that score, but:

'Anouk?'

'Charles . . .'

'Today you can tell me . . .'

'Tell you what?'

'How he died.'

Silence.

'Old age, you said it was, but you were lying. Weren't you?'

'Yes.'

'Was it suicide?'

'No.'

Silence.

'You don't want to tell me?'

'Sometimes lies are better, you know . . . Particularly where he's
concerned . . . He gave you so much to dream about . . . And all
those magic tricks he knew . . .'

'Did he get run over?'

'Got his throat cut.'

Charles sat in stunned silence.

'I knew it,' she said, cursing herself, 'but why do I always do
what you want, anyway?'

She turned around to ask for the bill.

'You see, Charles, you have only one fault, but dear Lord . . .
and it's a sad one . . . You are too intelligent. But, believe me, there
are things in life that don't figure in the operating instructions . . .
when I got here earlier and I saw all that maths you were stuck
with, I felt sorry for you even when I was hugging you. I thought
to myself that for your age you are spending far too much time
trying to fold the world up into neat little squares. I know, I know.
You're about to say that it's your studies and all that, but . . . But
here's the thing. From today on, when you think about the final
hours of the most wonderful mother hen there's ever been, you're
no longer going to picture a little old man sleeping in his shawls
in the midst of his memories, no, and you've only got yourself to

blame, sweetheart, you're going to go and shut yourself away with your calculator and you won't be able to concentrate, because all you'll see in your bloody paragraphs full of x this and y that ad infinitum, is an old man they found naked in a public urinal . . .'

Silence.

'His dentures gone, his ring gone, all his papers gone and . . . An old man who waited nearly three weeks at the morgue before this woman stiff with shame would condescend to go and get him out of there, forcing herself, but for the last time in her life, God be praised, to admit that yes, they were blood relations because yes, that gaping wreck was her kid brother . . .'

Then she took me back to school, turned around, and fell into my arms.

It wasn't me she was smothering, it was the memory of Nana, and if the next class seemed even more confusing than what she'd predicted, teeth clenched, it wasn't the old rogue's fault – he had died on stage, after all – no it was my own fault, because despite my best efforts to visualize a label attached to a cold toe, I couldn't help making her aware of how upset I was through the cloth of my trousers and . . . Oh, why go round the houses? She'd given me a hard-on and I was ashamed, that's all.

For two hours or more we'd been labouring through d'Ocagne and his lessons on infinitesimal geometry, so don't let her go telling me I was intelligent, just because I knew more or less what the teacher was driving at . . . Shit, no, she could see perfectly well that I was, on the contrary, completely lost! And besides, she had turned away, shaking her head.

As usual, I waited for her to invite me for another lunch, and I waited a long time, as I recall.

That sordid, pointless confession, one I had begged for, bloody fool that I was, ended up meaning quite simply this: my childhood died that day with Nana, for good.

*

It was too early to head back to Paris, where no one was expecting him, so he pulled out his diary and dialled a number that he'd been postponing for months.

'Balanda? I'd given up on you! Of course I'm expecting you, what were you thinking?'

Philippe Voernoodt was a friend of Laurence's. A bloke who'd made a fortune in the property market . . . Or the Internet . . . or was it property on the Internet? In short, a bloke who drove a grotesque automobile and who probably didn't have time to go to the dentist any more, since he was constantly fiddling on his Palm with a moist toothpick.

Whenever Philippe gave him a friendly slap on the back, Charles always lost a few centimetres and couldn't help wondering whether his friend's powerful but rather short hand had ever found its way higher than his beloved's forearm . . .

No, he assured himself, no. She had better taste than that.

They arranged to meet in the north of Paris at an old printing works that forward slash forward slash Voernoodt dot com had bought for peanuts (naturally . . .) and that he wanted to convert into a sublime loft (ditto). Not that many years ago, Charles would not even have bothered. He didn't like working for private individuals any more. Or else he chose the ones who inspired him. But in this case . . . The banks . . . The banks, in the meantime, had forced him to put some water in his wine, so to speak, and were bottling up his existence. So when he found a client who was a solid megalomaniac who could help him pay his expenses, he tucked his second thoughts into his back pocket, and drank his bitter wine down to the last estimate.

'Well? What d'you think?'

The place was magnificent. The space, the light, the density, even the echo of silence – everything had . . . integrity.

'And it's been abandoned like this for over ten years,' said Philippe, crushing his cigarette on the mosaic floor.

Charles didn't hear him. He felt as if this were merely the lunch break, and the workers would all be coming back any minute now, to start up their machines, pull over their stools, joke, pull open the hundreds of extraordinary printers' drawers, lift up the bottle of ink that had been left there, glance at the enormous clock looking down on them and set everything working again amidst a hellish racket.

He moved off, and went to look through the window into the office.

The handles on the drawers, the backs of the chairs, the wooden stamps, the bindings of the registers: everything in this place had been finely polished by the years, by human hands.

'Well, you can't really get a fix on it because of all the mess, but imagine what it'll be like once it's cleaned up . . . It's a great space, isn't it?'

Charles was admiring a tool, some sort of very strange magnifying glass, which he slipped into his pocket.

'Don't you think?' He jangled the keys of his SUV.

'Sure, sure . . . A great space, like you said.'

'So how do you see it? What would you do?'

'Me?'

'Well, yeah, you . . . I've been waiting for you for months, I'll have you know! And I've had the property tax people on my tail in the meantime! Ha! Ha!' (He laughed.)

'I wouldn't do a thing. I wouldn't touch any of it. I'd live elsewhere and I'd come here to relax. To read. To think . . .'

'You're having me on, right?'

'Yes,' lied Charles.

'Hey, you're a bit odd today aren't you?'

'Jet lag. Right . . . You have the prints?'

'In the car.'

'Okay. Let's get going, then.'

'Going where?'

'Back.'

'But aren't you going to take the tour?'

'What tour?'

'I don't know – outside?'

'I'll come back.'

'But . . . you haven't even asked me what I want . . .'

'Oh,' Charles sighed. 'It's all right, I know what you want. You want to keep just a little of the rustic touch, just the right amount, but you want it comfortable, just the right amount. You want concrete flooring, or a sort of rough wood like the floor of a railway carriage, you want a footbridge with a glass floor and brushed steel handrails, there, you want a high tech kitchen, professional equipment, something like Boffi or Bulthaup, I imagine . . . You want lava or granite or slate. You want light, pure lines, noble materials, and all of it eco friendly, naturally. You want a big desk, made-to-measure shelving, Scandinavian fireplaces and I'm sure you want a projection room too, no? And outdoors, I have just the landscape designer for you, a bloke who'll do you a garden *in motion*, they call it, with sustainable seeds and an integrated watering system. And even one of those swimming pools priced over the top that will save your eco-reputation. You know, a "wild pool" you can actually drink from . . .'

His hand was stroking the beams.

'Not forgetting the access control kit with alarm system, digital camera and automatic gate, that goes without saying . . .'

Philippe was staring at him.

'Am I wrong?'

'Uh, no . . . But how did you guess?'

'Huh . . .'

He was already outside and refused to turn round and look at the impending destruction.

'It's my profession.'

He waited while Philippe fussed with the lock (dear Lord, even his key chain was worth its weight in elegance . . .), spoke to someone through his earplug, gave a few tongue lashings to the support staff, and handed him the keys at last: 'How soon can you do it for me?'

'It': that was the word he used.

'Say . . .'

'For Christmas?'

'No problem. You'll have a fine manger.'

His new client gave him a funny look. He must have been wondering if he were dealing with the ox or the ass.

Charles gave his little hand a warm handshake and headed for his car, his fingers trailing along the fence.

Tiny bits of paint lodged under his fingernails.

Well, at least I've rescued that much, he mused, putting the car in reverse.

Between the Russians, HSBC, and this ear-wired cretin, there was plenty of food for thought for the way home. So much the better, too, because now he found himself buffeted by the rush hour traffic.

What –

What a strange life.

It took him a moment to figure out that it was the radio, above all, that was unbearable. He switched off the squawking of listeners who should never have been allowed to phone in, and settled for a non-stop jazz station.

Bang bang, my baby shot me down lamented the crooning chanteuse. Bang bang, too easy, he retaliated.

Too easy.

'You're too intelligent . . .' But what exactly did that mean?

Yes, I did fold the world up into neat little squares. Yes, I was looking for the way out. Yes, I was on my way home when others were getting ready to go out. Yes, I wore myself out fashioning very complicated little origami figures where the lies were always under the fold of paper, and I went on seeing Alexis and suffering from it and letting him eat me alive, and the only reason I did it was so that I could say to her, 'He's fine,' in between a sip and a smile which, by then, was no longer meant for me.

He's fine. He stole from me, is stealing from me, and will go on stealing from me. He stole from my parents and traumatized my grandmother so that he could get his fill up to there, but yes, he's fine, I promise.

She isn't. I think she died of it. She was an old lady whose weakness was holding on to her memories . . .

But . . . Wasn't he doing precisely the same thing? Letting himself be annihilated by a load of dusty old trinkets?

Precious, perhaps, but what were they worth today?

What were they worth?

Bang bang, at the Porte-la-Chapelle stop, so close to his goal but so far from home, Charles felt, physically, that the time had come to toss out all that stuff once and for all.

Sorry, but I can't.

It's not even fatigue any more, it's . . . weariness.

Futility.

You see . . . I'm still that poor blighter who checks over his essay, sends the rent in on time, and ruins his eyesight over his drawing table. And yet I did try to believe you. Yes, I tried to understand you and follow you but . . . where has it got me?

Stuck in a traffic jam?

And you, Alexis, who were so condescending with me the other

141

night, with your Corinne and your cottage and your carpet slippers: you were not so proud when I came to fetch you at the police station in the 14th arrondissement, were you?

No, you don't remember a thing, of course, but put me back on your answerphone for a second so I can describe the pitiful shit you were back then . . . It took me for ever to get you dressed, holding my breath all the while, and I carried you out to the car. Carried, do you hear me? Not helped, carried. And you were crying, and you lied to me yet again. And that was the worst thing of all. The way you still, after all these years, after all our oaths as kids and the force of the Jedi, after Nana and the music, and Claire, and your mother, and mine, after all those faces I no longer recognized, after all you'd laid waste to around me – you still tell me a load of bullshit.

I ended up hitting you so you'd finally shut up, and I dropped you off at the emergency entrance of the Hôtel-Dieu hospital.

For the first time, I didn't stay with you and, you know, I regretted it.

Yes, I regretted I hadn't let you just die right there, that night . . .

But you're back on your feet, it looks like. You're strong enough now to send anonymous letters, expedite your mother to the junkyard, and laugh in my face. So much the better. And you know what? When I think about you, I can still smell it, that stink of piss.

And puke.

I don't know how Anouk died, but I remember that Sunday afternoon when I came to see the two of you before heading back to my dormitory . . .

I must have been about Mathilde's age, but I was nowhere near as streetsmart as she is, sadly . . . I wasn't abrasive, the way she is. Mathilde hadn't yet taught me to beware of adults, or how to squint when life came creeping up on me. No, I was a child. An obedient little child, who brought you cake and regards from his mummy.

I hadn't seen the two of you for a long time, and I unbuttoned the top buttons of my shirt before ringing at your door.

I was so happy to get away from my holy family for a few hours to come and get a breath of your fresh air. To sit in your messy kitchen, gauge Anouk's mood by the number of bracelets she was wearing, hear her beg you to play something for us, but I already knew that you'd refuse; so I was happy to talk with her, to yield to the weight of her questions, let her touch my arms and shoulders and hair and look down when she went on, My, how you've grown, such a handsome lad, where has the time gone, but . . . why? And wait for the moment when she'd reminisce about Nana, unconsciously placing her hand on her wrist to silence it before placing it on her forehead and laughing again. I could be certain that you'd soon give in, and you'd sprawl on the first armchair you could find to tune in to our little gossip and give a pleasing texture to our silences . . .

The two of you couldn't possibly know, you've never known, but what was left for me, there, on those long evenings with the stifling presence of all the other boys, and the school supervisors who were such wankers? I had you two.

You were my life.

No. You would never have been able to understand. People like you who never obeyed anyone, and didn't know the meaning of the word discipline.

So perhaps I idealized the pair of you? That's what I used to tell myself, at any rate, and you have to admit it was tempting . . . I was trying to convince myself, I blurred your outlines, I experimented on you with the great da Vinci's *sfumato* – he was my absolute idol at the time – and I would smudge my memories to soften you, until the time came when, sitting once again in my usual seat at the end of your table as I painstakingly resumed picking at your rotten old oilcloth tablecloth and listened to the two of you squabbling, I could at last feel my heart beating again.

My blood, my blood was circulating.

'Why are you smiling like a great oaf?' Alexis would ask.

Why?

Because I could feel solid ground.

For fifteen years they'd been telling me, two gardens farther over, that life was nothing more than a succession of duties and flagellations of all sorts. Nothing could be taken for granted, everything was based on merit, and that merit – while we're at it – had become a very wobbly notion in a society that no longer respected a thing, not even the death penalty. Whereas you. You . . . I was smiling because your empty fridge, your open door, your psychodramas, your half-baked solutions, your downright barbarian philosophy – you were so sure that there could be no substituting one word for another down here on earth, and that happiness was in the here and now, eating any old thing provided it was eaten with heart – all proved exactly the contrary.

To Anouk's way of thinking, our only merit was that we were neither sick nor dying, and the rest was not important. The rest would follow. Eat, boys, eat, and you, Alexis, just give it a rest, you're driving us mad with your cutlery, you've got your entire life ahead of you to make noise.

But that day I'd knocked a few times and I was just about to turn away and go home when I heard a voice I didn't recognize: 'Who's there?'

'Little Red Riding Hood.'

Silence.

'Hey! Hallo? Is anyone home?'

Still no answer.

'I've brought a cake and a little pot of butter!'

The door opened.

She had her back to me. A figure in a bathrobe, bending over, her hair dirty, a pack of cigarettes in her hand.

'Anouk?'

She didn't reply.

'Are you all right?'

'I'm afraid to turn around, Charles. I . . . I don't want you to see me like this, I . . .'

Silence.

'Okay . . .' I said eventually, 'I'll just put the plate on the table and . . .'

Then she turned around.

It was her eyes, above all. Her eyes terrified me.

'Are you sick?'

'He's gone.'

'Sorry?'

'Alexis.'

And while I was heading for the kitchen to get rid of my sickly strawberry gateau, I was already sorry I'd come, and had the confused

144

certainty that I didn't belong here and that very soon I would be out of my depth.

I had homework to do. I could come back later.

'Where did he go?'

'He left with his father.'

This much I knew. That his prodigal father had reappeared on the scene a few months earlier, driving a superb Alfa. 'Is he nice?' I'd asked. 'He's okay,' said Alexis, and that's as far as it got, those two words. Blasé. Harmless, or so it seemed at the time.

Oh, woe. I must have missed a few episodes. What was I supposed to do, now? Call my mother?

'But, uh . . . he'll be back.'

'Do you think so?'

I didn't know what to say, then.

'He took all his things, you know . . .' She paused, then, 'It will be like with you. He'll come back on Sundays to eat cake . . .'

Followed by a smile I would have preferred she'd kept to herself.

She tipped a few bottles upside down and eventually poured herself a big glass of water that she swallowed in one go before choking on it.

Right. I was trying to find a way to get round her to go back out into the hall. I didn't want to witness any of this. I knew she drank, but I had always refused to know how much. It was something about her that didn't interest me. I'd come back when she'd got dressed.

But she didn't move. She gave me a hard look. Touched her neck, her hair, rubbed her nose, opened and closed her mouth as if she were drowning. She looked like an animal caught in a trap, ready to devour her own paw before going to die in the room next door.

As for me, I looked away, through the window at the clouds.

'D'you know what it means, bringing up a kid on your own?'

I didn't answer. It wasn't a question, anyway, it was an abyss she was opening so that she could stumble into it. I wasn't very brave, but I wasn't a complete idiot, either.

'You're so good at figures: how many days does it make then, fifteen years?'

That, on the other hand, was a question.

'Um . . . a little more than five thousand, I think . . .'

She put her glass down and lit a cigarette. Her hand was trembling.

'Five thousand . . . Five thousand days and five thousand nights . . . Can you imagine? Five thousand days and five thousand nights all alone . . . So you end up wondering if what you're doing is okay . . . You worry . . . You wonder if you'll manage . . . And you work. You forget about yourself. Five thousand days of slogging and five thousand nights locked indoors. Never a moment for yourself, never a single day off, no parents, no sister, no one to take your little boy so you can catch your breath for a while. No one to remind you that you were quite pretty once upon a time . . . Millions of hours wondering why he did that to us and then one fine morning, there he is, the bastard, and you know what you say, then? You say you miss that time already, those millions of hours, because that was nothing compared to the hours still to come.'

She struck her forehead against the wall.

'You think . . . A father who's a pianist in fancy hotels, that's better than a pathetic nurse now isn't it?'

She was shouting at me, but I refused to fall into her trap. She was shouting in the wrong ear. I was too young for this sort of thing, it's not for you, as my father would say. No, it wasn't up to me to tell her whether she was right or wrong. She'd have to manage on her own for once.

'You have nothing to say?'

'No.'

'You're right. There is nothing to say. I fell right into the trap, too, so . . . I can understand him . . . There's nothing worse than musicians, believe me . . . You mix everything up. You think they're Mozart or I don't know what, but really they're just con artists who look the other way when they realize they've got what they want. That you're done for. They close their eyes with a smile, and then they . . . I hate them.

'I know perfectly well that I've never been a good mother, but it was hard, you know? I wasn't even twenty when Alexis was born and . . . he'd disappeared . . . It was the midwife who went to register him during her lunch break and she came back all proud and handed me this thing they call a family booklet. I started crying again. What was I supposed to do with a family booklet when I didn't even know where I'd be living a week from then? The woman next to me in the ward kept saying, "Hey, don't cry like that, it'll make your milk go off . . ." But I didn't have any milk! I didn't have any, bloody hell! I looked at that wailing baby and I . . .'

I clenched my teeth. Please, be quiet, have mercy, be quiet. Why was she telling me all this? All this bloody women's stuff I could never understand? Why was she imposing it on me – hadn't I always been loyal to her? I'd always stood up for her . . . At that moment in time I would have given anything to be at home with my family. Normal people, well balanced, *deserving*, who didn't shout, who didn't pile up empty bottles under the sink, and who had the tact to send us packing to our bedrooms when they did need to pour out their feelings.

Her cigarette ash had fallen into her sleeve.

'Never a sign of life, never a letter, no help, no explanation, nothing . . . Not even curious to know his son's name . . . He was in Argentina, it seems . . . That's what he told Alexis, but I don't believe him. Argentina my arse. Why not Las Vegas while you're at it?'

She was crying.

'He left me to do all the hard part, and now that the kid is weaned, up he rolls, one screech of the tyres, two promises, three pressies and ciao, old lady. You know what I think? It stinks.'

'I have to go or I'll miss my train.'

'That's right, go on, be like them. You too, go on, abandon me . . .'

As I walked by her, I realized I'd grown taller than her.

'Please . . . stay . . .'

She'd caught hold of my hand and pressed it against her belly. I pulled away, horrified; she was drunk.

'Sorry,' she muttered, pulling her bathrobe tighter, 'sorry . . .'

I was already on the landing when she called out: 'Charles!'

'Yes.'

'Forgive me.'

I didn't reply.

'Say something . . .'

I turned around.

'He'll be back.'

'Do you think so?'

★

147

Stuck on the Place de Clichy behind the number 81 bus and in another century, with absolute clarity he recalled her incredulous little smile, when she finally resolved to lift her chin. And her face, so disturbing, so . . . naked, and the sound of the door in his back, and the number of steps that separated him from the world of the living: twenty-seven.

Twenty-seven steps in the course of which he felt himself getting thicker, heavier. Twenty-seven times his foot in the void and his fists crammed ever tighter into his pockets. Twenty-seven steps to realize that this was it, he'd gone over to the other side. Because instead of sympathizing with her sorrow and blaming Alexis for his behaviour he could not help but be pleased: Alexis had left his spot vacant.

And when his mother started to nag because he'd forgotten to bring back the cake dish, for the first time in his life he told her where to get off.

He'd left his little boy skin in that stairway.

He didn't revise for his lessons in the train, and that night he fell asleep reconciled with his right hand. After all, it was she who'd grabbed hold of it. But he didn't feel any less ashamed for all that, he was just . . . older.

As for the rest, I was right, yet again. Alexis did come back.

'When is your father coming to get you?' asked Anouk at the end of the Easter break.

'Never.'

Thanks to my mother and her charitable works, they offered Alexis a place at the Collège Saint-Joseph, and I followed in his wake . . .

I was relieved. Anouk must have struck a bargain with fate, or with the devil, more like it, and she changed her life. Stopped drinking, cut her hair very short, asked to work in the operating theatre, and stopped letting her patients get her down. Was content just to lull them to sleep.

She also decided to repaint their flat, just like that, with a snap of her fingers after she'd drunk her coffee:

'Go and get Charles! This weekend we'll start on the kitchen!'

And it was then, while the three of us were scrubbing the walls, that we found out how the story ended . . . I don't remember how we got onto the subject of his father, but for a moment Anouk and I both stopped worrying at our sponges:

'In fact, he needed a partner, but when he realized I wasn't old enough to get paid, it was over, he lost interest . . .'

'Oh, come on . . .' Anouk sighed.

'I swear! He'd screwed up his sums, the idiot. "You're only fifteen? You're only fifteen?" he went, over and over, getting mad, "You're *sure?* You're only fifteen?"'

Since he was laughing about it, we did likewise, but . . . how to put it . . . This washing soda really takes off the surface, doesn't it? No, I just said that because it took us a good while before we got to talking again, busy as we were spitting out those soda crystals . . .

'I've spoiled the mood, I see,' joked Alexis, 'but hey! It's okay, really! I didn't die or anything . . .'

As for Anouk, on the other hand – and no matter how I rework the sums, they don't come out – she didn't survive during his absence. That whole time she never let me see her again. I'd knock on the door in vain, and go away again, worried, as I went down their rotting staircase four steps at a time.

I'd got it all wrong. That spot would never be vacant.

But I got a letter . . . The only letter I ever had during four years at boarding school.

Sorry if I didn't open the door for you yesterday. I think about you a lot. I miss you two. I love you both.

I was a bit annoyed at first, then I tried to imagine she hadn't written 'two' or 'both'. I burned the letter, since I'd read it. She missed me, that was all I wanted to know.

Why am I stirring all this up, anyway? Oh, yes . . . the cemetery.

It's true you're no longer a minor. Your betrayals are legal.

She was never the same again after your little escapade in the Italian sports car. Was it her abstinence that made her more . . . moderate? That prevented her from that point on from taking us and holding us, from devouring us and giving us everything? I don't think so.

It was wariness. The certainty of solitude. And how careful she was, all of a sudden, with that strange sort of gentleness, a change of voltage: it was a tourniquet, a clamp on the vena cava. She didn't tease us any more, she no longer chuckled, 'Uh, there's a certain Julie on the phone . . .' when in fact it was that cretin Pierre who'd forgotten his geography book yet again, and she'd go to her room and shut the door when you were playing particularly well.

She was afraid.

★

After the Gare Saint-Lazare the traffic was lighter. Charles changed direction, left the herd behind, taking back routes worthy of a clever street kid, and began looking at the details on facades again whenever a red light stopped him. That one in particular, along the Square Louis XVI, with the art deco animals: a particular favourite.

That was how he'd charmed Laurence.

He was broke, she was sublime, what could he offer her? Paris.

He'd shown her things other people never see. He'd pushed open the heavy porte-cochères, climbed over little walls, held her hand, and torn off a bit of vine before her eyes. He'd taught her the finer points of mascarons, and atlantes, and carved pediments. He'd arranged to meet her at the Passage du Désir, and he'd declared his love on Rue Gît-le-Coeur. He must have thought he was being bloody clever; in fact he was silly.

He was in love.

She'd inspect her heels while he showed his student card to slippered concierges straight out of a photo by Doisneau; he held her around her waist, raised his index finger, and kissed her neck when she was looking for the face of Madame Lavirotte along the Avenue Rapp, or the rats in Saint-Germain-l'Auxerrois.

'I can't see them,' she said with despair.

Not surprising. He'd deliberately pointed to the wrong gargoyle, to make the high from the line of her *Nº5* last longer.

His best notebooks were from that era, when all the caryatids in Paris owed her something: the curve of her shoulder, her pretty nose, the shape of her breast.

A bloke cut in front of him, shaking his fist.

Once he'd crossed the Seine, he calmed down. He remembered

that he was driving in her direction, and it made him happy. Laurence, and Mathilde, his two shrews . . .

Who frequently ran rings round him.

Huh, he didn't mind, their ring-running . . . Could be a bit dizzying now and again, but it was more cheerful, at least.

5

He decided to surprise them with a good dinner. He thought over the menu while he waited in the queue at the butcher's, bought some flowers, and went to the wine merchant's.

He put on some music, rolled up his sleeves, looked for a tea towel and finely chopped everything for the dinner: garlic, shallots, his weakness and his wandering. Truce, tonight: he was there to listen to them.

He'd get her drunk, and caress her as long as possible. While undressing her, he'd take off his phantom skin, and while he licked her, he'd forget the bitterness of these last days. He'd bury Anouk, forget Alexis, call Claire back to tell her that life was beautiful and that Alexis's tart had a shrill voice. He'd go to meet Mathilde at her school the next day and would give her another voice to discover, one that cracked in a different register – Nina Simone.

I sing just to know that I'm alive.

Yes.

He was alive.

He lowered the flame, set the table, took a shower, shaved, poured himself a glass of wine, and sat closer to the speakers, thinking back on fat Voernoodt and the printing press.

Well, after all, it wasn't so bad . . . For once he could work without an estimate, without jet lag, and without drama. That was luxury . . . He recalled an expression that angry typographers used in the old days, and which he found irresistible: to pack it all in, they'd threaten to 'shit in the apostrophe type case'. Right, he promised to keep his aim less precise.

Maybe he'd be able to rescue that light, at least . . .

The wine was perfect, the pressure cooker was hissing nicely, and he was listening to Sibelius while waiting for two pretty Parisiennes to come home. Everything was fine.

Soon the finale of *Symphony No. 2*. Silence.
Silence inside his skull.

★

It was the chill that woke him up. He groaned – his back – and
took a few seconds to recover his wits. The night was burned, no,
the dinner was . . . shit, what time was it?

Ten thirty. What on –

He called Laurence: voicemail.

He got hold of Mathilde: 'Where are you, girls?'

'Charles? But . . . Aren't you in Canada?'

'Where are you?'

'Well, it's the school holidays, I'm at my Dad's . . .'

'Oh?'

'Mum's not there?'

Ooh, he did not like that little voice . . .

'Hold on, that's the door to the lift I can hear,' he lied, 'I'll ring
off now. I'll call you tomorrow.'

'Hey?'

'Yes.'

'Can you tell her it's all right for Saturday? She'll know what I
mean.'

'Okay.'

'One more thing . . . You know, I listen to your song all the
time . . .'

'Which one?'

'You know – the Leonard Cohen one.'

'Oh?'

'I love it.'

'Brilliant. So I can adopt you now, at last?'

And he hung up, guessing her smile.

What came next is a lot sadder.

He put Sibelius back in his case, pulled on a jumper, headed for
the kitchen, lifted up the saucepan lids, began by sorting the over-
cooked from the charred, sighed, and finally tossed the whole lot
into the rubbish. Had just enough gallantry left to put the saucepans
in to soak, grabbed hold of the bottle, and glanced one last time
at those ridiculous candlesticks.

He switched off the light, locked the door and . . . didn't know what else to do.

So he did nothing.

He waited.

And drank.

And, as in his hotel room on the previous 'night', he kept looking at the second hand.

He tried to read.

And couldn't.

What about an opera?

Too noisy.

At around midnight he rallied. Laurence wasn't the type to take the risk of losing a lovely slipper on the pavement . . .

Or was she?

No fairy godmother tonight . . .

So he aimed for two a.m. A dinner in good company and the time it would take to find a taxi, two a.m. was reasonable.

Or was it?

He opened the second bottle.

The clock struck three, the mouse fell down.

It was dead.

An expression of Mathilde's that meant strictly nothing.

What was dead?

Nothing.

Everything.

Sat drinking in the dark.

Good for him.

That would teach him to come home without warning . . .

He went to fetch the envelope with the photos.

The way things stood, he may as well rub some more salt in the wound.

Alexis and him. Children. Friends. Brothers. In the park. In the garden. In the schoolyard. By the sea. The day there was the Tour de France. At his grandmother's. Feeding the rabbits on the farm and behind Monsieur Canut's tractor.

Alexis and him. Arm in arm. Always. And for ever. They'd become blood brothers, they'd saved a baby bird and stolen a copy of *Playboy* from the café-tabac in Brécy. They'd read it behind the wash house, and had giggled a lot, but they still preferred *Astérix*. They'd swapped it with fat Didier for a ride on his moped.

Alexis before an audition. Serious, his shirt buttoned, the tie that Henri gave him, and his trumpet held tight against his heart.

Anouk after the same audition. Proud. Moved. Her index finger under her eye, and her eyelashes washed pale of make-up.

Finally, there was Nana, with Claire on his knees. Claire with her head down; she must have been playing with his rings.

His father. The photo with a piece cut out. No comment.

Charles as a student with a lot of hair. Waving his hand to the camera lens, making a face.

Anouk dancing at his parents'.

White dress, hair pulled back, the exact same smile as on the first photograph, beneath the cherry tree, almost fifteen years earlier.

And yet, in a few hours she –

Never mind.

Charles fell back against the cushions. What the hell is going on? he grumbled. Here you are, wallowing in the past like a pig in its sty, when it's the present which should be troubling you. It's the present that's running off the rails, mate. Don't you realize that your woman is in someone else's arms, while you sit here whinging with your short trousers on?

React, damn it! Get up. Scream. Hit the wall. Hate her. Bleed.

I beg you . . .

Cry, at least.

I cried all I could in the plane.

Well, say at least that you're unhappy!

Unhappy? He shook his head. But . . . What does that mean, unhappy?

You've had too much to drink, you'll find out in a few hours.

No. I've never been as clear-headed in my life. Quite the reverse.

Charles . . .

Now what? he said, annoyed.

Unhappy is the opposite of happy.

What does that mean, hap—

No, nothing. He closed his eyes.

And it was as he finally decided to pull himself out of his slump, to go back to work, that he heard the sound of a key in the lock.

She walked by him without seeing him, and headed for the bathroom.

Rinsed off the other man's cum.

Went into their room, got dressed, and came back to put her make-up on.

She opened the door to the kitchen.

She may not have shown any dismay, but he could sense her irritation. Yet she stood fast and made herself a coffee before she came to confront him.

What sang-froid, mused Charles; what bloody sang-froid.

She came over, blowing on her cup, sat on the armchair opposite him and steadily met his gaze in the semi-darkness.

'What can I say?' she asked, folding her legs under her.

'Nothing.'

'Did you remember to collect your luggage this time, at least?'

'Yes. Thanks. By the way . . .'

He reached out and picked up the plastic bag next to his briefcase.

'Look what I found for Mathilde.'

On his head he placed a cap stamped *I ♥ Canada* with big sheepskin caribou's antlers on either side.

'It's funny, no? I think I should keep it . . .'

'Charles . . .'

'Quiet,' he interrupted, 'I just told you I didn't want to hear what you have to say.'

'That is not what you –'

He got up and went to put his cup in the kitchen.

'What are all these photos?'

He came back and took them from her hands and put them back in the envelope.

'Take off that ridiculous cap,' she sighed.

'What are we doing?'

'Sorry?'

'What are we doing together?'

'We're doing the same as everyone else. We're doing what we can. We're making headway.'

'Without me.'

'I know. You haven't been around in a while, in case you hadn't noticed.'

156

'C'mon,' he replied, with a tender smile, 'this is your scene. Don't reverse the roles, my tacky little Madame Bovary, tell me, rather, what . . .'

'What?'

'No. Nothing.'

She swayed her hips and scratched at something on her skirt: 'Hey . . . you've lost weight, haven't you?'

He gathered up his things, changed his shirt, and closed the door on the second-rate vaudeville sketch.

'Charles!'

She'd followed him out into the stairway.

'Stop . . . It was nothing . . . You know very well it was nothing . . .'

'Of course. That's why I'm asking you what we're doing together.'

'No, but I meant tonight . . .'

'Oh, really?' he said sympathetically, 'you mean it wasn't even any good? Poor darling . . . When I think I'd opened a nice bottle of Pomerol for you . . . You have to admit that life is cruel.'

He went down a few more steps before announcing: 'Don't expect me this evening. I've got a networking thing at the Arsenal and I –'

She caught him by the sleeve of his jacket.

'Stop it,' she murmured.

He stood still.

'Stop it.'

Then he turned around.

'Mathilde?'

'What about Mathilde?'

'You won't stop me from seeing her, will you?'

A big first: he saw something like panic on her lovely face.

'Why are you saying that?'

'I haven't got the strength to clear the table, Laurence. I . . . I needed you, I think, and –'

'But what – but what is going on? Where are you going? What are you doing?'

'I'm tired.'

'That, I know. Thanks. You've already told me a hundred times. But what's it all about, this being tired? What exactly do you mean?'

'I don't know. I'm searching.'

'Come,' she pleaded in a low voice.

'No.'

'Why?'

'It's too sad, what we've become. We can't go on just for her sake. It won't . . . Do you remember . . . And it was on the stairs that time, too . . . Do you remember what you told me . . . The first day . . .'

'What did I tell you, then?' she exclaimed, exasperated.

'"She deserves better."'

Silence.

'If she weren't there,' continued Charles, 'you're the one who'd've left. A long time ago, as well.'

He could feel her nails closing on his shoulder: 'Who's that dark-haired woman in the photos? Is she the woman, the one who died, that you were talking about the other day? The mother of someone or other? Is she the one who's been fucking up our life for weeks? Who is she? What is this – some sort of *Mrs Robinson* thing?'

'You wouldn't understand.'

'Oh no? Well then try me,' she fumed, 'just try. You tell me, since I'm so stupid.'

Charles hesitated. There was indeed a word which – but he didn't dare say it.

Not because of her. Because of Anouk. A word he'd never been sure about. A word that had been stuck in the gears all these years and which had ended up ruining the fine machinery.

So he chose another one instead. Less definitive, more cowardly. 'Tenderness.'

'I didn't realize we were at that point,' she rejoined.

'Oh? You're lucky.'

She was silent.

'Laurence . . .'

But she'd already turned around and started back up the stairs.

For a split second he thought about catching up with her, but then he heard her humming *God bless you please, Mrs Robinson, na na nani nana nana na* and he realized that she hadn't understood a thing.

That she would never even want to understand.

Holding on to the banister, he continued down the stairs.

*

Why not, after all. May God bless her.

That would be the least He could do, after having put her through the mill like that.

Laurence's car was parked a few metres farther along. He walked by it, stopped, came back, scribbled a few words on a sheet from his notebook and slid it under one of the windscreen wipers.

What did he put? Remorse? Second thoughts? A declaration? A farewell?

No. He put . . .

'Mathilde told me to tell you that it was okay for Saturday.'

That was him.

All over.

Charles Balanda. Our man. About to turn forty-seven years old, in a week, a cuckolded partner with no rights over the child he'd raised, and that he knew. No rights, but a great deal more than that. His insurance, that little note torn out in haste, or the proof that the machinery wasn't completely wrecked. As for Mathilde, she'd make it all right.

He walked on, feeling his pockets for a tissue.

Wrong, yet again.

He hadn't let it all out in the plane.

6

He greeted them briefly. He went back to his worn armrests. He had trouble concentrating. He began by milking the computer: 58 messages. Sigh. He separated the wheat from the bullshit with a few abrupt shakes of his head to clear it of his domestic woes. By error he opened a spam which said: *greeting charles.balanda did you ever ask yourself is my penis big enough?* He gave a forced smile, listened to everyone's grievances, handed out advice and encouragement, checked on young Favre's work, frowned, took his pad and blackened it with unbelievable speed, changed screens, thought, thought for a long time, chased L.'s face away, tried to understand, refused several calls so he wouldn't lose his train of thought, corrected a few errors, made others, checked his notes, leafed through his bibles, worked, thought some more, sent something to the printer and stood up with a stretch.

He realized it was already three o'clock, waited a long time next to the printer, finally twigged and looked in vain for a ream of paper.

And flew into an inordinate rage.

He struck the machine, bent one of the paper trays out of shape by giving it a kick, cursed, bellowed, rained insults upon poor Marc who had the misguided idea of coming to help out, and made all of them suffer the absurdity of these last months and the weight of his cuckold's horns.

'Paper! Paper!' he said, over and over like a madman.

He refused to go and have some lunch. He went down to the courtyard to have a smoke and bumped into the downstairs neighbour who began to tell him about his problems with leaks.

'Why are you telling me all this? Do you think I'm a plumber or something?'

He mumbled some apologies that no one heard. He almost blew

his fuse for the second time when he saw the 'expenses' folder from the PRAT site in Valenciennes, but thought better of it and went back to his desk full of experience and wisdom, to spend the rest of his life among his blueprints.

At the end of the afternoon, he had his lawyer on the telephone.

'I've come with news of your lawsuits!' joked the man.

'Have mercy, no!' replied Charles, using the same tone, 'I pay you a fortune precisely so that you won't give me any news.'

And after a conversation which lasted over an hour during which the other man's meter never stopped running, Charles said these words which he immediately regretted: 'And do . . . do you also do family law?'

'Heavens, no! Why do you ask?'

'No, nothing. Right. Back to my duties . . . Time to create other opportunities for you to fleece me.'

'I've already told you, Balanda, one's duties are the corollary of professional competence.'

'Listen . . . I have a confession to make . . . Find something else to say next time, because I cannot stand that sentence any more . . .'

'Ha, ha! I haven't forgotten that I owe you a lunch at L'Ambroisie, if I'm not mistaken?'

'Quite . . . If I haven't been locked up by then.'

'Oh, but I can't imagine anything better for our Republic, my friend! To give someone like you the opportunity to show an interest in our prisons . . .'

Charles looked at his hand on the receiver for a long time.

Why do you ask? the man had said.

Why, indeed? It was ridiculous. He obviously didn't have a family.

*

A rare occurrence, he was not the last one to leave the agency, and he decided to go to the Pavillon de l'Arsenal on foot.

On the Place de la Bastille he listened to his messages.

'We have to talk,' said the machine.

Talk.

What a strange idea . . .

It was not so much how far apart the river banks were that puzzled him, but rather their . . . *friability*.

161

And yet . . . Perhaps. If he cancelled a few appointments, went far away, drew the curtains on a hotel room in broad daylight, if . . . But whatever Charles might have been fantasizing as he walked along Boulevard Bourdon, the architect in him demolished it right away: the terrain, wherever you looked, had become far too unstable, and it was time to accept that that particular future could not be built.

The edifice had withstood eleven years.

And it was the architect who was sniggering as he crossed the street. This was one instance where no one could come pestering him about his ten-year buildings liability.

He did what was expected of him, shook the right hands, and sent his regards to the right people. At eleven o'clock, standing in the night in front of that statue of Rimbaud that he despised, and hesitating a moment, he took the wrong direction.

Or the right one, as it happened.

7

'And what time d'you call this?' she said, mock-aggressively, with her fist bunched on her hip.

He pretended to shove her against the wall and headed for the kitchen.

'Hey, you've got a nerve . . . Why didn't you ring? What if I'd been here with some gallant company?'

He took a look at her pouting face and began to laugh.

'Right, okay, I said "what if", didn't I? *What if . . .*'

He gave her a kiss.

'Go on then, make yourself at home,' she said, 'besides you *are* at home, in fact . . . Welcome home, darling, what brings you here? Have you come to raise my rent? Uh-oh, something's wrong, isn't it? Is it those Russians making your life miserable again?'

He didn't know where to begin, or even whether he'd have the courage to find the words, so he opted for the simplest formula: 'I'm cold, and hungry, and I want some love.'

'Oh, fuck . . . You're in a bad way, aren't you. C'mon, follow me. I can make you an omelette with some eggs that aren't fresh and some rancid butter, how does that sound?'

She watched him eat, opened a beer for the two of them, pulled off her patch and pinched a cigarette from him.

He pushed back his plate and looked at her in silence.

She stood up, lit the small light above the stove, switched off all the other lights and came back, moving her stool so that she could lean against the wall.

'Where shall we begin?' she murmured.

He closed his eyes.

'I don't know.'

'Of course you do, you know . . . You always know everything.'

'No. Not any more.'

'Do you . . .'

'Do I what?'

'Did you find out how Anouk died?'

'No.'

'You didn't call Alexis?'

'I did, but I forgot to ask him.'

'Oh?'

'He pissed me off and I hung up.'

'I see . . . Want some dessert?'

'No.'

'Good, because I haven't got any. Would you like –'

'Laurence is cheating on me,' he interrupted.

'Well, what do you know,' she scoffed. 'Oh, sorry –'

'Was it that obvious?'

'Noooo, course not, I was just joking . . . Want a coffee?'

'So it was that obvious.'

'I also have some "flat stomach" herbal tea, if you prefer.'

'Am I the one who's changed, Claire?'

'Or "Sleepytime" . . . that's a nice one, too . . . It relaxes you . . . You were saying?'

'I can't hack it any more. I just can't hack it.'

'Hey . . . you wouldn't be warming up for a little mid-life crisis, would you?'

'Do you think so?'

'Well, it looks that way to me . . .'

'God, how dreadful. I would have liked to be a bit more original. I think I'm disappointing myself,' he managed to joke.

'It's not as bad as all that, is it?'

'Getting old?'

'No, Laurence . . . For her, it's just like a trip to the Spa . . . It's . . . I don't know . . . some sort of beauty mask . . . Little bit on the side, discreetly, it's surely less dangerous than Botox . . .'

Charles didn't know what to say.

'And besides . . .'

'Yes?'

'You're never there. You work like an idiot, you're always worrying about something, try to put yourself in her shoes . . .'

'You're right.'

'Of course I'm right! And you know why? Because I'm the same.

I use my profession so that I won't have to think. The more shit cases I get, the more I rub my hands. Brilliant, I go, look at all these hours I've saved and . . . And you know why I work?'

'Why?'

'To forget that my butter dish stinks.'

Charles was silent.

'How do you expect anyone to remain faithful to people like us? Faithful to what, to who? How could they be faithful . . . But . . . You like your profession, don't you?'

'I'm not sure any more.'

'Yes, you like it. And don't you go getting picky about it. That's a privilege we can't afford . . . And then you've got Mathilde.'

'I *had* Mathilde.'

Silence.

'Stop it,' she said, irritated now, 'you cannot make that kid part of your post-nuptial property in common or something . . . And besides, you haven't left.'

He said nothing.

'Have you left?'

'I don't know.'

'No. Don't leave.'

'Why not?'

'It's too hard to live alone.'

'You manage quite well.'

She got up, opened all her cupboards and the door to the refrigerator – wasteland – and looked him straight in the eye.

'You call this living?'

He handed her his plate.

'I have no rights over her, do I? From a legal standpoint, I mean.'

'Of course you do. The law has changed. You can very well put a case together, provide affidavits and . . . But you don't need to do that, you know that perfectly well.'

'Why not?'

'Because she loves you, you fool. Right,' she said, stretching, 'you're not going to believe me but I have work to do now . . .'

'Can I stay?'

'As long as you like. It's still the same old pre-war sofa bed, should bring back a few memories . . .'

She moved her mountains of junk and handed him a set of clean sheets.

As in their heyday, they took turns in the tiny bathroom, and shared the same toothbrush, but . . . the atmosphere was gone.

So many years had passed, and the only important promises that they'd made to each other had not been kept. The only difference was that both of them now paid ten times, a hundred times more in taxes.

He stretched, complaining about his back, and lapsed into the sound that had so often provided the background rhythm to his sleepless nights as a student: the elevated railway.

He could not help but smile at the thought of it.

'Charles?'

Her figure appeared, a shadow puppet against the wall.

'Can I ask you a question?'

'You don't need to. Of course I'll leave again, you needn't worry.'

'No. It wasn't that.'

'I'm listening.'

'You and Anouk?'

'Yes?' he went, changing position.

'You . . . No. Forget it.'

'We what?'

She said nothing.

'You want to know whether we ever slept together?'

'No. Well, no, that isn't what I wanted to know. My question was less . . . more sentimental, I think.'

Charles didn't know what to say.

'Sorry.'

She had turned away.

'Good night,' she added.

'Claire?'

'Forget I ever said anything. Go to sleep.'

And in the dark came this confession: 'No.'

She held the door handle and put her palm flat against the door to close it as discreetly as possible.

But after the fifth noisy passage of the number 6 line, he re-adjusted his reply: 'Yes.'

And later still, contributed to the racket as he threw down his weapons: 'No.'

★

'White dress, hair pulled back, the exact same smile as on the first photograph, beneath the cherry –'

White dress. Hair pulled back. The exact same smile.

A huge reception. They'd been celebrating everything, that night: Mado and Henri's thirty-fifth wedding anniversary, Claire's first year at law school, Edith's engagement, and Charles's successful results.

Which results? He couldn't remember. Some major exam . . . And for the first time, he'd brought a 'girlfriend' to his parents' place. Who was it? He could try and remember, but it was of no importance. A young woman who was like him . . . Serious, from a good family, nice-looking, ankles somewhat thick . . . A first year student; he must have initiated her in the room next door, in fact . . .

Come on, Charles . . . You've accustomed us to something a bit classier than that . . . She must have had a first name, that girl . . .

Laure, I think. Yes, that's it, Laure. She wasn't much fun underneath her fringe, she always wanted the room to be dark, and chatted about kinetic energy after making love. Laure Dippel . . .

He held her round the waist, spoke in a loud voice, raised his glass, said stupid things, said he had not seen daylight in days, let off steam, and trampled on his own hard-earned laurels by dancing like a crazy thing.

He was already three sheets to the wind when Anouk put in her appearance.

'Will you introduce us?' she smiled, glancing quickly at the other woman's revealing top.

Charles did as she requested, and used it as an excuse to extricate himself.

'Who's that?' asked the little genius, still under observation.

'The next door neighbour . . .'

'And why is her hair wet?'

(That was exactly the type of question this girl could not refrain from asking.)

'Why? How the hell should I know? Because she just had a shower, I suppose.'

'And why did she only get here now?'

167

(See . . . She must have two columns' worth in the *Who's Who* by now . . .)

'Because she was at work.'

'What –'

'She's a nurse,' he interrupted, 'a nurse. And if you want to know where and in which ward and how long she's been there and her hip measurements and how much she's got put aside for her retirement, you'll have to ask her yourself.'

She made a face; he walked away.

'Well, young man? Are you ready to devote yourself to the cause of giving old age pensioners a whirl on the dance floor?' he heard behind him, as he was trying to fish his lighter from the bottom of a huge bowl of punch.

His smile turned around before he did.

'Go and put your cane down, Grandma. I'm all yours.'

White dress, funny, beautiful, and devilishly kinetic.

Which means, resulting from motion.

Unleashed in the arms of her prize-winning graduate. She'd had a rough day, had struggled against opportunistic infections and lost. She was always losing, these days. She wanted to dance.

Dance, and touch him, with his millions of white blood cells and his oh so very efficient immune system. He was so modest, he was so careful to keep a safe distance from her dress, she pulled him closer with a laugh. Who gives a fuck, Charles, who gives a fuck, growled her expression. We're alive, you understand? A-live.

And he let her do as she liked, beneath the appalled gaze of his girlfriend. But in the end he was reasonable, oh yes, such a reasonable sort, alas, and eventually he gave her back her arm and the energy proportionate to her mass, before going outside to get some fresh air under the stars.

'Hey, she's hot, your neighbour.'

Shut up.

'Nah, I just mean for her age . . .'

Bitch.

'I have to go home.'

'Already?' he asked, forcing himself.

'You know I have an oral exam on Monday,' sighed his sweetheart.

He had forgotten.

'Are you coming?'

'No.'

'Sorry?'

Right, let's spare ourselves the rest of this deadly conversation. In the end he called her a taxi and she went off to revise what she probably already knew by heart.

When he came back towards the house after a vague kiss and some strong encouragement, the gravel crunched beneath the mock orange.

'So, it would seem you're in love?'

About to answer no, he came out with the opposite.

'Oh? That's nice . . .'

He said nothing.

'And you've . . . How long have you known her?'

Charles raised his head, looked at her, smiled at her, and looked down again.

Then went back into the noise.

For a long time . . .

He was restless, sought her with his gaze now and again, didn't see her, drank, forgot himself, forgot her.

But when his sisters asked everyone to be silent, when the music stopped and the lights went out, when an enormous cake was brought in, and his mother clasped her hands, and his father pulled a speech from his pocket while others were whispering ssh and oh and ssh again, a hand took hold of his and pulled him away from the circle.

He followed her, climbed the steps behind her, hearing snatches of bravura on the way, 'so many years . . . dear children . . . hard-ship . . . trust . . . helped . . . always . . .' then she opened a door at random and turned round.

They went no farther, stood there in the dark, and all he knew about life in that moment of her life, was that her hair was no longer wet.

She shoved him so hard that the door handle dug into his back. He did not have the presence of mind to find it painful, however. She was already kissing him.

Devouring her face, his face, devouring each other.

They had never been so far apart.

Charles struggled with the hairpins in her chignon, while she battled with his belt buckle; he spread her hair, she opened his trousers, he tried to keep her head straight while she kept looking down, he was hunting for words, words he'd said over and over a thousand times and which had changed when his voice did, whereas she was begging for him to be quiet, he was forcing her to look at him while she moved to one side to bite his ear, he nuzzled into her neck while she was biting him until he bled, he hadn't even begun to touch her and already she had wrapped herself around his leg and was pressing herself against him, moaning.

Between his hands he was holding the love of his life, the Madonna of his childhood, the most beautiful of all, the obsession of so many nights and the reason for all his prizes, whereas she was holding . . . something else altogether . . .

The taste of blood, the buzz of alcohol, the smell of her sweat, her whimpers against his skin, the pain in his back, her violence, her orders, her fingernails – none of that could affect his courtly love. He was stronger, managed to hold her still, and she had no choice but to listen to him murmuring her name. But headlamps passed in the distance and he glimpsed her smile.

So he gave up. Restored her arms to her, her twisted bracelets, bent his knees and closed his eyes.

She touched him, stroked him, slipped her fingers into his mouth, licked his eyelids, whispered inaudible words into his ear, pulled on his jaw to make him cry out while obliging him to remain silent, grasped his hand, spat in it, guided it, undulated, moved back and forth on him, hooked him to her, almost broke him –

May he be damned. Damn who he was, damn his feelings. Damn her. Damn this fraud. He pushed her away.

He *didn't want* this.

And yet he had dreamt it all. The worst debauchery, the most unbelievable phantasms, his clothes torn from him, his pain, his pleasure, his pleas, their saliva, his cum and their kisses, the . . . All of it. He had imagined all of it, but not this. He loved her too much.

Too well, too badly, too inappropriately, perhaps, but always too much.

'I can't,' he moaned. 'Not like this.'

She froze for a moment, dumbfounded, before slumping forward, her head against his chest.

'Sorry,' he continued, 'sorr—'

She moved her hips one last time to let her skirt slip down. She dressed him in silence, tightened his belt, smoothed his shirt, smiled as she saw the number of orphaned buttonholes and then, her skin softer, her arms by her side, she came back to him and let him put his arms around her at last.

Sorry. Sorry. That was all he knew how to say. Without even knowing if he was talking to her or to himself.

To her beautiful soul, or his crotch.

Sorry.

He held her tight, breathed in her nape, caressed her hair, making up for twenty years and ten lost minutes. Heard his heart pounding, managed the disaster while applause filtered through the floor-boards, and he hunted for . . . other words.

Other words.

'Sorry.'

'No. It's me,' whispered a little voice, 'I —' and broke. 'I thought you'd grown up.'

Someone was shouting his name. They were looking for him in the garden. Charles! The photo!

'Go. Go and join the others. Leave me, I'll come down later.'

'Anouk . . .'

'Leave me, I said.'

I *have* grown up, he wanted to retort, but the tone of her last words dissuaded him. So he did as he was told and went to pose, between his sisters, for his parents, like the good little boy that he was.

★

Claire had just switched the light off.

Then had her abortion.

And Alexis went on fucking himself up.

But played like a god, so they said.

Charles went away. Portugal to begin with, then the United States.

He left the Massachusetts Institute of Technology with a fine medal, enough vocabulary to translate love songs, and an Australian fiancée.

Her he lost on the way home.

He suffered. A great deal. He worked for other people. Eventually got his final diploma. Joined the order. Put up his brass plate. For some obscure reason he won the competition for a job he never thought he'd get, and bit off more than he could chew. It turned out to be a rough slog. Eventually he learned, most often at his own expense, that the 'responsibility of the liberal architect is unlimited, and that he must be insured for everything he says, does, or writes.' Henceforth he required a receipt every time he sharpened his pencil. He associated himself with a lad who was much more talented than he was, but less ingenious. He left him the glory, the bright, luminous moments, and the interviews. He played the eminence grise, which was a relief, took care of the dirty work, and it was thanks to him that all the aforementioned held together.

He saw Anouk again. They had good-natured lunches together where they talked about nothing more than good nature. He found her as beautiful as ever, but he no longer gave her the opportunity to read his thoughts. He buried his grandmother. He fell out with Alexis for good. During those years he lost a first burst of hair and acquired, beneath his high forehead, a sort of reputation. A label of quality, *traceability*, as stockbreeders would say. He held her hand one last time. He no longer had the courage to witness her going downhill. He cancelled one lunch, too much work, then a second one, then a third.

He cancelled everything.

He filled in title blocks, bought walls, had affairs, stopped going to jazz clubs, which only gave him the blues, and then, during one of his 'little' projects on the side, met a man who liked his marble and had a pretty wife.

He built a doll's house.

And moved in.

And ended up falling asleep at floor level, in a worn-out sofa bed, between the very walls that had witnessed all of this.

Which means, not a great deal.

He'd come back to square one, he'd lost first one woman then another, and perhaps even a third, and a few hours from now he'd have a wretched backache.

8

Charles went home at the same time as Mathilde and granted Laurence the famous 'conversation' she so insisted upon, one Saturday afternoon when they were alone in the flat.

It wasn't really a conversation, either. More like a long litany of complaints. The umpteenth trial. In the end, she even wept. It was the first time, and he was moved. He took her hand. She sidestepped, saying it was probably just her oestrogen levels and her hormones. She added that he couldn't possibly understand, and withdrew her hand. He sidestepped by opening a bottle of champagne.

'Is it my vaginal dryness we're celebrating?' she scoffed, taking the glass he handed to her.

'No. My birthday.'

She struck her forehead, and went over to give him a kiss.

Mathilde arrived shortly thereafter. She'd been at the flea market with her girlfriends, and she went straight to her room and closed the door, leaving in her wake a hurried, 'Evening,' and a pair of misshapen ballet slippers.

Laurence sighed, annoyed, and also probably somewhat relieved to know that she was not entirely alone in her negligence.

It was just then that Miss Draughty Doors breezed in with a huge package sloppily tied up in newspaper.

'I had one, er, bleep of a time to find this, y'know.'

And handed him the box with a big smile.

'I spent every Saturday on it!'

'I thought you were with Camille revising for your exams!' exclaimed her mother.

'Yeah, well, she was helping me find it, wasn't she! Any bubbly left?'

Charles adored this kid.

'Aren't you going to open it?'

'Yes of course,' he smiled, 'but it . . . uh smells odd, don't you think?'

'Hah,' she went, with a shrug of her shoulders, 'that's normal . . . It smells old.'

Charles clapped his hands.

'Right then, girls, shall we do the usual? Shall I take you to dinner at Mario's?'

'You aren't going to go out looking like that, are you?' choked Laurence.

He didn't hear her. He admired his reflection in the shop windows and in the enchanted gaze of his stepdaughter.

'Now I've seen it all,' they heard Laurence grumble, walking behind them.

Hanging from his arm was his reassurance: 'Well, I think you look super classy.'

He replied that he thought so too.

It was a Renoma from the 1970s. A groovy mac with cake-slice lapels and sleeves that stopped at his elbows. The belt was missing, alas, and a few buttons.

And it was torn here and there.

And it stank.

Really.

But . . .

It was blue.

*

There was no trough running down the middle of the frilly duvet that night, and in lieu of a last minute present he found its stand-in, wrapped in a gorgeous nightgown.

To put an end to an awkward situation, Charles rolled over on his side.

The silence which followed this . . . pantomime, was fairly painful. To lighten things up, he joked, bittersweet, 'It must be a sense of solidarity . . . my hormones are no more biddable than yours, it would seem . . .'

She found it funny, or at least he hoped she did, and eventually went off to sleep.

He didn't.

It was his first mechanical failure.

Last week, however, he'd got up the nerve to ask for advice about his bloody hair, which was now falling out in handfuls, and the reply they gave him was that there was nothing that could be done: it was due to too much testosterone.

'Take it as a sign of virility . . .' concluded the chemist with an adorable smile. (He was completely bald.)

Oh really?

Another mystery that defied his fine logic.

One mystery too many. Or too humiliating at any rate.

Stop right there, he mused. Stop. He had to get rid of all these trifles, give his nagging conscience the boot, and get back on his feet.

Failing to keep his appointments, playing hooky from conventions halfway round the world, wasting the agency's money, frittering away his time at ruined abbeys, speaking to ghosts, bringing them back to life for the morbid pleasure of asking their forgiveness, ruining his lungs, breaking the office equipment and throwing his back out between the sheets of his youth – all that might be well and good, but not getting it up? It wasn't on, it simply was not on.

'You got that? Stop it,' he said again, out loud, to be sure it was perfectly clear.

And to prove his good faith, he switched the light back on. He reached out and grabbed the decree of 22 March 2004 *pertaining to the fire-resistance of construction products, elements, and projects.*

Directives, decisions, codes, decrees, laws, opinions of the committee, propositions from the director of Civil Safety, the 25 articles *and* their appendices.

After that, he fell asleep stroking his cock.

Oh. Just barely.

The modest fist-thumping of a routed general at his most faithful trooper. Time to head home, lad, time to head home.

The crows will take care of the rest . . .

9

And he did just what he said he would do: he got rid of them all.

Romeo, Abelard, little Marcel Proust, and the entire bunch of cretins.

He didn't notice the coming of spring. He worked harder than ever. Rummaged in Laurence's things and stole some sleeping tablets. Lay like a zombie on the sofa, only went to the bedroom when any danger of improbable intimacy had passed, started growing some sort of beard that initially incited the mockery of his two housemates, then their threats, and finally their indifference.

He was there. And he was no longer there.

He was overextending himself, pretending to go along with things, but only vaguely. He would act as if he were concentrating on every word whenever anyone was speaking to him, and would go on to ask for the details the moment they were out of earshot.

He didn't notice that people were whispering behind his back.

And he couldn't understand why so many projects were suspended. The elections, they told him. Oh, right . . . the elections.

He untangled snarled skeins, spent hours on the telephone with people, and in endless meetings with men and women who were forever bandying about new acronyms. Verification offices, defence committees, coordination missions, study centres, technical controllers, Socotec and the Veritas office up to your ears, new articles modifying the CCH by imposing a mandatory CT on the ERP of the first four categories, the IGH and class C buildings. Nincompoops at the Chamber of Commerce, megalomaniacal mayors, incompetent assistants, insane legislators, furious entrepreneurs, alarmist forecasters and people prepared to file a report on absolutely anything.

One morning, a voice reminded him that his various construction sites were producing 310 million tonnes of waste a year. One evening, another voice, less aggressive, and for a project that promised to be infernal, finally submitted the figures for an estimation of the vulnerability of existing inventory.

He was exhausted, and didn't listen to anyone any more, but on a page in his notebook he had jotted down the words: The vulnerability of existing inventory.

'Have a nice weekend!'

Young Marc, a huge bag on his shoulder, had come to say goodbye and, as the boss didn't react, went on to add, 'Hey . . . Do you remember what that means?'

'Sorry?' Charles swung his chair round to look at him out of politeness, and to shake himself out of his lethargy.

'Weekend, you know? Those two really weird days at the end of the week?'

Charles allowed a weary smile onto his face. He liked this boy. Recognized in him a few traits from his own past . . .

His somewhat clumsy enthusiasm, his insatiable curiosity, his need to find his Masters and suck them to the bone. To read everything about them, absolutely everything, in particular the most abstruse. The most woolly-minded theories, speeches long disappeared, facsimiles of sketches, comprehensive surveys translated into English and praised to the skies, or published in the back of beyond, surveys that no one had ever understood. (And here he could thank his stars in passing, if he had had the Internet and all its temptations at that age, what an abyss that would have been . . .)

And then the extraordinary capacity for work, the courteous discretion, the way he hovered between formal and casual, the self-confidence that had nothing to do with pawing at the dust of ambition, but still allowed him to believe that the Pritzker Prize was an adventure in life that was actually *conceivable*; and then there was even that long mop of hair that would begin to thin before too long . . .

'Where are you off to with all that gear?' he asked. 'To the ends of the earth?'

'Yes, more or less. Out to the country . . . My parents' place.'

Charles would have liked to prolong this unexpected moment of complicity – keep the conversation going, ask him, for example, 'Oh, really? Whereabouts?' or 'I've always wondered which year you finished?' or even 'How did you end up here, actually?' but he was too tired, sadly, to take the opportunity. And it was only when the brilliant young beanpole was hurrying towards the door that Charles saw the book sticking out of his bag.

An original edition of *Delirious New York*.

'I see you're still in your Dutch period.'

Marc began to stammer like a little kid with his fingers in the biscuit tin. 'Oh, yes, I admit . . . Really fascinating bloke, I, and –'

'Oh, I completely understand! That was the book that sealed his reputation and earned him respect, and he hadn't even built a single skyscraper . . . Hold on, I'll head out with you.'

As he was punching in the alarm code, he added, 'I was very curious at your age, and I was lucky to be present at some particularly hair-raising workshop sessions, but if there is one thing that really bowled me over, you know, it was when he presented his project for the library at Jussieu in 1989 . . .'

'The cut-outs session?'

'Yes.'

'Oh! I would have loved to see that . . .'

'It was really . . . how to explain . . . Intelligent. Yes, there's no other word for it, intelligent.'

'But I heard it's old hat now. That he did it every time.'

'I don't know.'

They were walking down the stairs side by side.

'. . . but I do know he did it at least one more time, because I was there.'

'No!' The younger man stood still, grabbing his bag as it fell from his shoulder.

They stopped at the first bistro they happened upon, and that night Charles, for the first time in months, in years, thought back on his profession.

He told his story.

In 1999, or ten years after the 'shock of Jussieu', because he knew a bloke who was in the Arup engineering group, he was given a ticket to the Benaroya Hall in Seattle to see one of the best shows of his life. (Nana's escapades notwithstanding . . .) There was not a single soloist in the spanking new auditorium, but anyone in the city who was a rich donor or a solid citizen or simply a powerful one was there that night. All along Third Avenue there were nervous exchanges on walkie-talkies and ribbons of limousines.

A few months earlier bidding had opened for the construction of a huge library. Pei and Foster had submitted their tenders, but the two projects that were selected were Steven Holl's, and Koolhaas's. Holl's work was fairly banal, but he was a local lad and that could work in his favour. *Buy American*, so the thinking went.

Charles wasn't telling the story so much as reliving it. He got up, spread his arms, sat back down, shoved their beers out of the way, scribbled in his notebook and explained to Marc how that genius, fifty-five years old at the time, in other words hardly much older than he was now, had managed, by presenting his project in a very theatrical way, with only a sheet of paper, a pencil, and a pair of scissors for a weapon – at times Charles would mime him, at times he would fold and display his paper cut-outs – to walk away with the trophy and a contract for a construction site that would end up costing over 270 million dollars.

'With a simple sheet of A4, huh!'

'Yes, I see, I see . . . 270 million for 5 grams . . .'

They ordered some omelettes, more beer, and Charles, encouraged by his student's questions, continued to dissect the great man. Or rather to dissect how his turn of phrase, his art of concision, his taste for diagrams, his sense of humour, his vivacious wit – mockery, even – had enabled him, in less than two hours, to present a clear, intelligible vision of something extremely complex.

'It's the building with the irregular platforms, right?'

'Exactly. An entire play on horizontal lines in a country that swears by the sky alone . . . You have to admit he's got a nerve . . . Not to mention the seismic constraints and absolutely unbelievable specifications. The bloke I was telling you about, from Arup, told me they nearly went mad . . .'

'And have you seen it finished?'

'No. Never. But it's not my favourite design of his anyway . . .'

'Tell me.'

'Sorry?'

'Which is your favourite?'

Several hours later they were finally forced to leave, and they stood for a long while leaning on the bonnet of Marc's car, comparing their tastes, their opinions, confronting the twenty years between them.

'Right, I'd better get going . . . I missed dinner, but at least I can be there for breakfast . . .'

He tossed his bag in the rear and offered Charles a lift. Charles took the opportunity to ask him where his parents lived, and how far along he was in his studies, and how he had ended up in their office.

'Because of you . . .'

'Why because of me?'

'I decided to do my internship there because of you.'

'What a strange idea.'

'Hmm. Who knows what it takes, things like this . . . I suppose I needed to learn how to repair a printer,' quipped the shadow of his youth with a smile.

He tripped over Mathilde's backpack in the hallway.

'SOS dear stepdad whom I adore with all my heart, I can't do this exercise and it's for tomorrow (and I have to hand it in, and they mark it, and it counts towards my average) (if you see what I mean . . .)

'ps: pleeeze, HAVE MERCY, no explanations! Just answers.

'pss: I know, I'm asking too much but if just this once you could make an effort with your handwriting that would really be a big help.

'psss: thanks

'pssss: good night

'psssss: Love ya.'

A chord of a circle is the hypotenuse of an isosceles right-angled triangle whose legs are radii of the circle. The radius of the circle is 6 times the square root of 2. What is the length of the minor arc subtended by the chord?

Easy as pissing.

And Charles, once again, sat down alone in a phantom kitchen. He opened a famished pencil case, cursed on discovering a chewed-up pencil, took out his own propelling pencil and set about his task, careful to loop his letters nicely.

In so doing, measuring the arc, subtending the chord, cutting out some tracing-paper and saving face for a very lazy young woman, he could not help but measure the abyss separating him at that moment from Rem Koolhaas . . .

He found consolation in the fact – and this went towards his mark – that he was, if nothing else, *love ya'd.*

He slept for a few hours, drank a coffee standing up, reread her note distractedly and added at the bottom, 'you are too much', without specifying whether this was in response to her last P.S. or to her outrageous behaviour.

To help her determine which of the two, he took his Staedtler out of his pocket again and placed it in among the empty ink cartridges, chewed-up biros, and little notes full of spelling mistakes.

What would become of her if I left? he wondered, pulling on his jacket.

And me? What . . .

A taxi was waiting to take him to his other duties.

'Which terminal, did you say?'

Any one, I really couldn't care less.

'Sir?'

'C,' he replied.

And again,

And again,

The meter ticking.

10

The traffic jams were Dantean . . . Dostoyevskian. It took them nearly four hours to cover thirty-odd kilometres; they witnessed two serious accidents and took part in a festival of fender-bending.

They set off into the oncoming traffic, insulting whoever had a problem with that; they drove along the verge with the windows rolled up because of the dust; they bounced out of spectacular potholes and shoved the smaller vehicles out of the way by giving them a taste of Western manufactured bumpers.

They'd even have driven over the injured if they could have.

His driver pointed first to the pavement and then to the windscreen wiper lever, and his joke seemed to amuse him so highly that Charles made an effort to understand his jargon. It is for blood, he guffawed, understand? Blood! *Krov!* Ha, ha. Good joke.

The air was stifling, the pollution extreme, and Charles's migraine kept him from concentrating on the appointments lined up for the following day. He gulped down his packets of powder, running his tongue over his gums to accelerate the effect of the aspirin. In the end he let his files slip to his feet.

Come on . . . Let him switch on his bloody wipers and let's get this over with . . .

When at last Viktor wished him a good night in front of the hotel's bouncers Charles was incapable of reacting.

'*Bla bla chto zhaluytyess?*'

His passenger looked down.

'*Bla bla bla galodyen?*'

He let go of the door handle.

'*Myi staboy bla bla bla vodki!*' he decreed, pulling away from the kerb.

His smile illuminated the rear view mirror.

*

They set off later into streets that grew ever darker, and when their limo began to seem too provocative, they entrusted it to a gang of delighted kids. Viktor gave his instructions, waved his big hand as if to spank them, showed them a wad of notes that he hastily restored to his pocket, and left them with a pack of cigarettes to buy their patience.

Charles drank one glass, then a second one, began to relax, time for a third . . . and woke up at dawn not far from the portable site office. There was a total black hole between 'third' and the snoring on the headrest next to him.

Never had his own breath given him such cause for . . . consternation.

The light was pounding his skull. He staggered to the pump, rinsed off, let his hangover swell up and explode, vomited as he stood up straight, then started all over.

No need to leaf through his phrasebook to understand that Totor was taking the piss.

Finally Viktor took pity on him and handed him a bottle.

'Drink, my friend! Drink!' he said, in French.

Well, well . . . His first words in French. It would seem the night had been merrily multilingual.

Charles obeyed and . . .

'*Spasiba daragoy! Vkusna!*'

That perked him up, all right.

A few hours later he was calling Pavlovich a rotten bastard in the original before taking him in his arms for a bear hug.

He'd made it, he was Russian now.

He began to sober up at the airport while he was trying to reread his, er, notes and recovered the rest of his wits when Philippe called to give him hell.

'Hey, I've just had Becker's informer on the line . . . What's this bloody mess with the shoring towers over at the B-1? Good lord, don't you realize how much money we're losing every day with this? Don't you realize –'

Charles held the receiver away from his ear and looked at it warily. Mathilde, who in other respects didn't care a fig, was forever harping on about how the thing was full of carcinogenic dangers. 'I swear! It's as bad as the microwave!' Oh God, he thought, closing his fist to protect himself from his partner's sputtering, she might be right . . .

He opened the book at random, without ado bought seventeen stallions from a retired cavalry officer who had splendid animals, a carpet-making workshop, liqueurs that were over a century old, and vintage Tokay; and then he accompanied Nikolay Rostov to the ball held by the governor of Voronezh.

Together with Nikolay he waylaid a plump and pretty blonde, and showered her with 'mythological' compliments.

When her husband started walking towards them, he got to his feet abruptly. Obeyed orders, showed his boarding pass, took off his belt, his boots, his sabre, and his frock coat, and piled them in the plastic tray.

He set off the alarm for no reason, and was taken to one side to be frisked.

Ah, these Frenchmen, grumbled Nikita Ivanich, pinching the nape of his wife's neck, they're really all the same . . .

11

No matter how much he fasted, refrained from drinking, dissolved his liver in effervescent tablets, rubbed his temples, massaged his eyelids, closed the shutters and aimed the lamp the other way, the effects of his unforgettable bender refused to dissipate.

Getting dressed, eating, drinking, sleeping, talking, remaining silent, thinking – all of it felt like a huge burden.

From time to time a nasty word crossed his mind. Three syllables. Three syllables taking him in their grip and . . . No. Quiet. You can do better than that. Lose some more weight and you'll wriggle your way out of this shit. It's not your style. You haven't the time, anyway. Get a move on.

Swim, or sink if you have to, but get a move on.

Soon it would be summer; the days had never seemed so long, and the aforementioned list of activities continued, a constant litany to the rhythm of verbs in the simple past tense. (Simple past, remember, is used to describe a one-time action, without taking continuous action or duration into account; expression of actions in succession.) He was, he could, he had to. He did, he said, he came clean. He went, watched, decided.

He withstood, he got.

He got, from a doctor's surgery, an appointment outside normal consulting hours.

He undressed, they weighed him. They checked his throat, his pulse, his lungs. They asked him about his hearing, his eyesight. They asked him to be more specific. Was it local, frontal, occipital, spinal, congenital, viral, dental, matinal, general? Was it . . .

'Enough to have me climbing the walls,' interrupted Charles.

They wrote out a prescription with a sigh: 'I can't find anything. Stress, perhaps?' Then, looking up, 'Tell me, Sir, do you have any worries at the moment?'

Danger. Danger, flashed his last remaining defences. Keep going, I said.

'No.'

'Insomnia?'

'Rarely.'

'Right. I've prescribed some anti-inflammatory medication but if you don't feel better in a few weeks, you should come back for a scan.'

Charles didn't budge. He merely wondered, while hunting for his cheque book, whether a scan would know how to detect a lie.

And fatigue . . . and memories . . .

Friendship betrayed, old ladies emasculated in public toilets, cemeteries by railway lines, the humiliating tenderness of a woman to whom he had not known how to give pleasure, kind words in exchange for good marks, or even those thousands of tonnes of steel framework in the Moscow oblast that would probably never support a single thing.

Worries? Not him. An excess of lucidity, at best.

At home, the atmosphere was highly charged. Laurence was preparing for the sale season (or a new week of fashion shows, he hadn't heard properly), and Mathilde was packing her bags. She was flying off to Scotland the following week, 'to *improve*', she said in English, and then she would go to join her cousins on the coast in the Basque country.

'And your diploma?'

'I'm working on it, all right?' she retorted, inscribing long arabesques in the margins of her workbook. 'I'm revising my stylistic devices, here.'

'I can see that. Art nouveau style, I'd say, no?'

They were supposed to meet up with Mathilde at the beginning of August and spend a week together before dropping her off at her father's. After that, he didn't know. There had been talk of Tuscany, but Laurence had not mentioned it again, and Charles no longer dared bring up the subject of Siena and cypress trees.

The idea of sharing a villa with some people he had only met a few weeks earlier, during an interminable dinner at his sister-in-law's gilt and marble henhouse, was anything but tempting.

'Well? What do you think of them?' Laurence had asked on the way home.

'Predictable.'

'Naturally . . .'

Her 'naturally' was very weary, but what else was he supposed to say?

Vulgar?

No. He couldn't . . . It was too late, his bed was still too far away and this discussion was too . . . no.

Perhaps he should have said 'provident' instead? They had spent a lot of time talking about tax exemption . . . Yes . . . Perhaps . . . The silence in the car would not have been so heavy.

Charles didn't like the summer holidays.

Going away, yet again, shirts off the hangers, close the suitcase, choose, count, sacrifice some books, eat up the miles, find oneself forced to live in hideous holiday rentals, or yet again in hotel corridors with towels that smelled of industrial laundries, bask in the sun for a few days, then say, aah, at last, try to believe in it, and then . . . get bored.

What he liked were the escapades, the things you did on the spur of the moment, the week suddenly broken up. The pretext of an appointment outside Paris, getting lost miles off the motorways.

The *Cheval Blanc* inns where the chef's talents made up for the hideousness of the décor. World capitals. Their stations, markets, rivers, history, architecture. Deserted museums between two meetings, villages barely on the map, embankments without views and cafés without terraces. To see it all without ever being a tourist. And never masquerade as one again, that would be something.

The word 'holidays' had meant something when Mathilde was little and together they would win the prize for best sand castle in the entire world. How many Babylons had he built between two tides in those days . . . How many Taj Mahals for baby crabs . . . All the sunburn on the back of his neck, the comments, the seashells and frosted chips of glass . . . How many plates shoved back so a drawing could take shape on the paper tablecloth, how many tricks to get the mum to sleep without waking the daughter, and indolent breakfasts where all he wanted to do was to sketch the two of them without leaving any crumbs in his sketchbook.

187

And all those watercolours . . . how well the paint used to mix beneath his fingers.

Such a long time ago.

★

'There's a Madame Béramiand who's been trying to get hold of you.'

Charles was sorting the day's mail. Their tender for the headquarters of Borgen & Finker in Lausanne had not been selected.

A lead weight came down upon his shoulders.

Two lines. No rhyme, no reason. Nothing to justify the disgrace. The closing salutation was longer than their dismissal.

He dropped the letter onto his assistant's desk: 'To be filed.'

'Shall I make copies for the others?'

'If you're up for it, Barbara, if you're up for it . . . But I must confess that in this case . . .'

Hundreds, thousands of hours of work had just gone up in smoke. And beneath the ashes, investments, losses, funds, banks, financial arrangements, upcoming negotiations, rates to calculate, energy.

The sort of energy he no longer had.

He'd already walked away when she added, 'And what shall I do about this woman, then?'

'Sorry?'

'Béram—'

'Why's she calling?'

'I didn't quite understand . . . Something personal.'

Charles scoffed at her last word with an irritated gesture.

'Same. File it.'

He didn't go down for lunch.

When one project fell through, a new one had to start up right away: the ultimate conviction of a profession that had undermined all other convictions. Anything, anything at all. A temple, a zoo, his own cage if nothing else turned up, but one idea, one stroke of the pencil, and you were saved.

So that is where he was, lost in the study of an extremely complicated spec sheet, his palms flat against his temples, as if he were trying to stick back together a skull that was cracking on every side, taking notes with his teeth clenched, and then his assistant was there again in the door, clearing her throat. (He had left the phone off the hook.)

'It's her again . . .'

'The lady from the Borgen Bank?'

'No . . . the personal call I told you about this morning . . . What shall I say?'

A sigh.

'It's about a woman that you both knew.'

Ever polite in his despair, Charles owed her at least a smile.

'Goodness! I've known so many women! Tell me everything, what's her voice like? Husky?'

But Barbara wasn't smiling.

'A certain Anouk, I think.'

12

'The paint on her headstone, that was you, wasn't it?'

'Sorry? Yes, but . . . who's speaking?'

'I knew it. It's Sylvie, Charles . . . You don't remember me? I worked with her at the Pitié-Salpêtrière. I was there for your first communion and –'

'Sylvie. Of course . . . Sylvie.'

'I don't want to keep you, it was just to –'

Her voice had grown thick.

'– to thank you.'

Charles closed his eyes, let his hand slide down his face, abandoned his pain, pinched his nose, tried to gag himself once again.

Stop. Stop that right now. It's nothing, it's her emotion, not yours. It's the medication that's got you out of kilter without providing any relief, and all those perfect blueprints that are already taking up too much room in your archives. Get a grip, for God's sake.

'Are you still there?'

'Sylvie . . .'

'Yes?'

'Wh–how,' he fumbled, 'how did she die?'

Silence on the line.

'Hello?'

'Alexis didn't tell you?'

'No.'

'She killed herself.'

Silence.

'Charles?'

'Where do you live? I'd like to see you, Madame Béramiand.'

'Don't be so formal, Charles . . . And yes in fact, I have something for –'

'Now? This evening? When?'

Ten o'clock the following morning. He made her repeat her address one more time, and then he got straight back to work.

Sideration. A state of sideration. Anouk had taught him the word. When the pain is so extreme that the brain just gives up, for a while, ceases to transmit.

That stupor between the tragedy and the first screams of pain.

'So it's like what happens with Monsieur Canut's ducks when he chops off their heads and they keep running around like crazy?'

'No,' she replied, rolling her eyes skyward, 'that's just a joke in very poor taste that they invented in the country to frighten people from Paris. It's utterly stupid, anyway . . . We're not afraid of anything, are we?'

Where had it taken place, that conversation? In the car, surely. It was in the car that she said the silliest things.

Like all children, we were terribly sadistic and, on the pretext that we were revising our biology lessons, we always tried to get her to talk about the goriest side of her profession. We loved wounds, pus, and amputations. Detailed descriptions of leprosy, cholera, rabies. People foaming at the mouth, fits of lockjaw, fingertips left stuck in mittens. Did she believe us? Of course not. She knew our minds were warped, so on occasion she'd lay it on thick and, when she thought that we were well up on the matter, she'd slip in something with a casual air: 'Well, actually, pain is a good thing, you know . . . It's a good thing it exists . . . Pain is survival, boys . . . It is! Without pain, we'd lose our hands in the fire, and it's because you swear when you miss the head of the nail that you still have all ten fingers! Which just goes to show that . . . What's the matter with that idiot, flashing his headlights at me like that? Just overtake, wanker! Now . . . where was I?'

'Nails,' sighed Alexis.

'Ah, yes. Which all goes to show that . . . DIY and barbecues, they're all very well, you know what I mean, there . . . But later on in life you'll find out that there are things that will make you suffer.

I say "things" but I really mean people. People, situations, feelings, and . . .'

On the rear seat Alexis signalled to me that she was utterly off her rocker.

'Hey, if I can see people flashing headlamps at me, I can see you too, you little cretin! C'mon! I'm telling you something important. Anything that looks like it might make you suffer in life, get out of there fast, my little darlings. Run as far away as you can, as quick as you can. You promise?'

'Okay, okay, we'll do just like the ducks, don't worry.'

'Charles?'

'Yes?'

'How do you manage to put up with him?'

I was smiling. I had a good time with them.

'Charles?'

'Yes?'

'Did you understand what I said just now?'

'Yes.'

'What did I say?'

'That pain is good because it means we'll survive but you have to run away from it even if you've lost your head . . .'

'What an arse-licker . . .' moaned my neighbour.

How did you destroy yourself, Anouk Le Men?

With a very big hammer?

13

Sylvie lived in the 19th arrondissement, near the Robert-Debré hospital. Charles arrived more than an hour early. He wandered along the Maréchaux remembering the very upright gentleman who had built the hospital in the 1980s. Pierre Riboulet, his professor of urban composition at engineering school.

Very upright, very handsome, very intelligent. He spoke little. But so well. To Charles he seemed the most accessible of all his professors, but he never dared approach him. Riboulet had been born in an airless, sunless, squalid building, and had never forgotten it. He often said that the creation of beauty served an 'obvious social purpose'. He inspired them to shun competitions and opt rather for the healthy atmosphere of rivalry among studios. He'd introduced them to the *Goldberg Variations*, the *Ode to Charles Fourier*, the texts of Friedrich Engels and, most important of all, the writer Henri Calet. He created on a human scale, on a scale of the soul – hospitals, universities, libraries, and, on the ruins of council estates, housing that had greater dignity. He had died a few years earlier, at the age of 75, and he left behind a number of orphaned building sites.

Exactly the trajectory that Anouk must have dreamt of . . .

He turned round and went looking for the Rue Haxo.

He walked right by the house he was looking for, grimaced as he shoved open the door of a café, ordered a coffee that he had no intention of drinking, and headed for the back of the room. His guts were playing up again.

Fastened his belt: he was now at the last notch.

He got a shock when he walked up to the sink. The bloke standing there really had a nasty look about him – but that's you, you wretch. That's you.

He hadn't eaten for two days. He'd spent all his time at the agency, where he unfolded the emergency bunk, in other words a sort of huge foam armchair that smelled of stale smoke; he had not got much sleep, nor had he shaved.

His hair (ah, ah) was long, the shadows under his eyes were blackish-brown, and his voice was full of mockery: 'Go on, Jesus . . . this is the last station coming up. Two hours from now and it will all be over.'

He left a coin on the counter and went back the way he'd come.

★

She was as moved as he was, didn't know what to do with her hands, brought him into an immaculate room while she apologized for the mess, and offered him something to drink.

'Have you got any Coca-Cola?'

'Oh, I'd thought of everything but I didn't expect that . . . Wait a moment . . .'

She went out into the corridor and opened a closet that smelled of old trainers.

'You're in luck . . . I think the grandchildren have left you some . . .'

Charles did not dare ask for ice, and imbibed his lukewarm panacea, asking her in an almost affable voice how many grandchildren she had.

He heard her answer, did not register the number, and assured her that that was wonderful.

He would not have recognized her if he had passed her in the street. He remembered a perpetually cheerful little brunette, on the plump side. He remembered her buttocks, a great topic of conversation back in those days, and that she had given them a record, a 45 rpm of *Le Bal des Laze*. Anouk was mad about Michel Polnareff in those days, and they eventually grew to hate the song.

'Be quiet, be quiet. Can't you hear how beautiful it is?'

'Fuck, haven't they strung him up yet, that bloke? We can't take it any more, Mum, we just can't take it . . .'

What a strange filing cabinet memory could be . . . Jane and her fiancé – so went the song – and Anouk . . . It had all just come back to him.

Sylvie's hair was an astonishing colour now; she wore glasses with incredibly glitzy frames, and seemed to Charles to be wearing too much make-up. Her foundation had left a tidemark beneath her chin, and her eyebrows had been redrawn with a crayon. At that point in time he felt too wobbly in his guts to really pay attention, but later he would think back on that morning – and God knows he would think back on it – and he would understand. A woman who is lively and still cares about her looks, and who is expecting a visit from a man she has not seen in over thirty years – that was the least she could do. Honestly.

Charles sat down on a leather sofa that was slippery as oilcloth and set his glass on the coaster she had placed before him, between a Sudoku magazine and an enormous remote control.

They looked at each other. They smiled. Charles, who was the most courteous of men, hunted for a compliment, a pleasantry, a little phrase without consequence to lighten the weight of all the doilies, but no. That was just too much to ask.

She lowered her gaze, fiddled with her rings one after the other, and asked, 'So you're an architect now?'

He sat up, opened his mouth, was about to answer that . . . and then went, 'Tell me what happened.'

She seemed relieved. She couldn't care less whether he was an architect or a butcher and she couldn't bear it any longer, keeping everything she was about to tell him all bottled up inside. Moreover, that was why she'd felt it was all right to harass that stuck-up secretary . . . She needed to find someone who'd known Anouk, so she could tell the story, relieve herself of her burden, get it off her chest, pass on her weary load, and move on to something else.

'What happened – starting when?'

Charles grew thoughtful.

'The last time I saw her was in the early 90s . . . As a rule I'm more precise than that, but . . .' He shook his head with a smile. 'I've made great efforts not to be that way any more, I think . . . She had invited me to lunch on my birthday, as she did every year, and . . .'

His hostess encouraged him to continue. A kindly little nod of the head, but so cruel. A little gesture which said, Don't worry, take your time, there's no hurry, you know . . . No, there's no hurry, *now*.

'. . . it was the saddest of all my birthdays . . . In the space of one year, she'd grown terribly old. Her face had got puffy, her hands were trembling . . . She didn't want me to order any wine and she smoked one cigarette after the other to make it through. She asked me questions, but couldn't care less about my replies. She was lying, she said that Alexis was fine and sent his regards, whereas I knew perfectly well that wasn't true. And she knew that I knew . . . She was wearing a cardigan that was covered with stains and smelled of . . . I don't know what . . . sorrow . . . A mixture of cold ashtrays and eau de Cologne . . . the only time there was a spark in her eye was when I offered to go with her some day to Nana's grave, she'd never been back. Oh yes! What a good idea! she said, suddenly cheerful. You remember him? You remember how nice he was? You . . . and then huge tears drowned it all.

'Her hand was icy. When I took it into my own, I suddenly realized that that old fellow, who could have been her father, and who didn't even like women – he'd been her only love story . . .

'She insisted I talk about him. Tell her my memories, over and over, even the ones she knew by heart. It was a bit of an effort, but I had an important appointment that afternoon, and I was doing a lot of sleeve-adjusting to keep an eye on my watch without it being obvious. And to be honest I really didn't feel like reminiscing any more . . . Or at least not with her. Sitting opposite that ravaged face – it spoiled everything . . .'

Silence.

'I didn't suggest any dessert. What was the point? She hadn't eaten anything anyway. I ordered two coffees and called the waiter back to signal to him to bring the bill at the same time, and then I went with her to her metro station and . . .'

Sylvie must have felt that the time had come to help him a bit: 'And then?'

'I never took her to Normandy. I never called her. Out of cowardice. So that I wouldn't have to see how she was going downhill, so that I could keep her in the museum of my memories and stop her from giving me a guilty conscience. Because it was too much . . . And yet my guilty conscience did trouble me, and I'd lighten the load every year when it came time to send greetings cards. From the agency, of course . . . Impersonal, commercial, stupid, and acting the fine gentleman I'd add a few words by hand and "hugs and kisses", like a rubber stamp. I called her two or three times after that; in particular, I recall one time when my niece had swallowed some medicine or other . . . And then one day my parents, who hadn't seen her in a long time, told me that she had moved away and that she'd gone . . . to Brittany, I think –'

'No.'

'Pardon?'

'She wasn't in Brittany.'

'Oh really?'

'She was not far from here.'

'Where?'

'In a housing estate, near Bobigny.'

Charles closed his eyes.

'But how?' he murmured, 'I mean, why? That was the one thing she was determined never to – I remember, the only promise she ever made, never to – How can that be? What happened?'

She raised her head, looked him straight in the eye, let her arm drop alongside the armchair and let it all out.

'In the early 90s . . . Well, I suppose it was then, I'm not good at dates . . . You must be the last person she went to have lunch with in those days . . . Where to begin? I'm lost, now . . . I'll start with Alexis, I guess. Since it was because of him that everything started to go to pieces. She hadn't had any news from him for years. I think you were one of their only links as well, weren't you?'

Charles nodded.

'It was hard for her. So as a result she was working an enormous amount, piling on shifts and overtime, never taking any holiday, living for the hospital alone. I think she was already drinking quite a bit, too, what have you . . . It didn't prevent her from becoming head nurse, and she was always in the toughest departments . . . After immunology she went to neurology and that's when I started working with her. I liked working with her . . . And she was a lousy head nurse by the way . . . She preferred care-giving to organizing people's shifts. She would forbid the patients to die, I remember . . . She'd shout at them, make them cry, make them laugh . . . In short, all sorts of things that weren't allowed . . .'

A smile.

'But she was untouchable because she was the best. Whatever

197

she was lacking in the way of medical knowledge she made up for with the way she cared for people.

'Not only was she the first one to notice if there'd been any change, even the faintest symptom, but in addition she had an extraordinary instinct . . . A nose . . . You can't imagine . . . The doctors had understood as much, and they always arranged it so that they could do their rounds when she was on duty . . . Of course they'd listen to the patients but when she added something, believe me, it did not fall on deaf ears. I've always thought that if her childhood had been different, if she'd been able to go to university, she'd have made a truly great doctor. One of those who do honour to the profession, without ever forgetting the first and last name or the face or the concerns on the chart . . .'

She sighed.

'She was great. And it was because she had no more life of her own that she gave them so much, I suppose . . . Not only did she look after her patients, but their families as well . . . And her youngest co-workers, too, the little auxiliaries who would go into certain patients' rooms dragging their feet, it was so hard for them to put a bedpan under a body that was so . . . She would touch people, take them in her arms, caress them, come back after she'd put in so many hours already, out of uniform, with a bit of make-up, to fill in for the visits they hadn't got, or more. She'd tell them stories, talked a lot about you, I recall . . . Said you were the most intelligent boy on earth . . . She was so proud . . . This was at a time when you were still having lunch together now and again, and lunch with you was sacred. Good Lord, no messing around with the schedule, there, and the entire hospital could go hang! And then she'd talk about Alexis, and music . . . She invented all sorts of stuff, concerts, standing room only, fantastic contracts . . . In the evening . . . and we'd all be staggering with fatigue and you could hear her voice in the corridor . . . Her lies, her fantasies. She was comforting herself, then, she didn't fool anyone. And then one morning, a call from the emergency services was like a bucket of cold water on her head: her so-called virtuoso was dying from an overdose . . .

'And that's when she began to go downhill. For a start, she didn't expect this at all – which will never cease to surprise me in fact – the old story about the shoemaker's children. She thought he

198

was smoking a joint or two from time to time because that helped him to "play better". A likely story . . . And here's this woman, the most professional person I've ever worked with – I've been talking about her gentle ways, but she also knew how to be tough, she could keep them all at a distance: the Grim Reaper, the doctors who were always overwhelmed, the snooty little interns, her blasé colleagues, the administrative stuffed shirts, the invasive families, the complacent patients – No one, you hear? *No one* could resist her. They called her *La Men*, they said, *Amen*. It was her mixture of gentleness and professionalism that was so astonishing, so exceptional, and which earned her their respect . . . Wait, I've forgotten what I was going to say . . .'

'The emergency services –'

'Ah yes. Well, she utterly panicked. I think she'd been traumatized, I mean medically traumatized, "damage and injury to the structure or the functioning of the body", by the early years of the Aids epidemic. I think she never got over it . . . And the knowledge that there was a strong chance, no, that's the wrong word, a strong probability that her son would end up like all those poor wretches, it . . . I don't know . . . It broke her in two. Snap. Like a stick. After that it got harder for her to hide her drinking problem. She hadn't changed, but it wasn't her any more. A ghost. A robot. A machine for smiling and bandaging; a machine you obeyed. A name and a number on a badge on a blouse that stank of booze . . . First she quit her position as head nurse, said she'd had enough of dealing with all the bloody paperwork, then she wanted to go half-time so she could look after Alexis. She went to great lengths to get him out of there and get him admitted into a better centre. It became her reason for living and, in a way, it saved her, too . . . You might say it was a good splint . . . But as a respite it was short-lived because . . .'

She removed her glasses and pinched the bridge of her nose, for a long time, then continued, 'Because that . . . that bastard, forgive me, I know he's your friend, but I can't think of any better word –'

'No. He . . .'

'Pardon?'

'Nothing. I'm listening.'

'He sent her packing. When he'd got enough strength back to

be able to string two words together, he calmly announced to her that, as a result of the work he'd done with the "support team", he mustn't see her any more. He announced it very kindly, too . . . You understand, Mum, it's for my own good, you mustn't be my mother any more. Then he kissed her, something he hadn't done for years and years, and he went off to join the others in his lovely garden surrounded by a tall iron fence . . .

'And she requested sick leave for the very first time in her life. Four days, I recall. After the four days were over she came back and asked to work the night shift. I don't know what reasons she gave them, but I know why she did it: it's easier to tipple when the hospital's quiet . . . The entire team was great with her. She had been our rock, our point of reference, and now she became our biggest convalescent. I remember this marvellous old man, Jean Guillemard, a doctor who'd spent his life working on multiple sclerosis. He wrote her a wonderful letter, full of detail, reminding her of the many cases they'd worked on together, and he concluded by saying that if life had given him more opportunities to work with first-class people like her, he'd probably know more than he knew now, and he'd be leaving for his retirement a happier man.

'Are you all right? Another Coke, perhaps?'

Charles started. 'No, no, I . . . thanks.'

'I think I will have something, myself, if you don't mind . . . Talking about all this, you've no idea how it upsets me. Such a waste . . . Such a monstrous waste. An entire life, do you understand?'

Silence.

'No, how could you . . . Hospitals are another world, and people who don't belong can't possibly understand. People like Anouk and me have spent more time with sick people than with our loved ones . . . It was a life that was very hard and very sheltered at the same time . . . A life spent in uniform . . . I don't know how they manage, nurses who don't have that thing that's considered a bit old hat nowadays – a vocation. No matter how I try I just can't imagine . . . It's impossible to last if you don't have it. And I'm not talking about death, no, I'm talking about something that's even more difficult. About . . . about faith in life, I think. Yes, that's the hardest thing when you work in such a difficult industry, not to lose sight of the fact that life is more . . .

I don't know . . . *legitimate* than death. There are some evenings, I swear, when the fatigue is absolutely vicious. And you feel this dizziness, this sort of pull towards . . . and you . . . Well, listen to me,' she chuckled, 'I've gone quite philosophical all of a sudden! Ah, doesn't it seem a long time ago that we were in your parents' garden having those battles with the candied almonds!'

She got up and went into the kitchen. He followed her.

She poured a large glass of sparkling water. Charles stood with his back against the railing of the balcony, on the twelfth floor, above the void. Silent. Unwell.

'Of course, all those kind things people said were very important to her, but what helped her the most, at the time – helped only in a manner of speaking, though, because of what came afterwards – was what one man alone, Paul Ducat, said to her. He was a psychologist who didn't belong to any particular service, but who came several times a week to the bedside of the patients who asked for him.

'He was very good, I have to admit. It's daft but I really got the impression, I mean physically the impression, that he was doing the same job as the cleaning crew. He'd go into those rooms full of putrid fumes, close the door behind him, stay there sometimes ten minutes, sometimes two hours, never asked us a thing about our cases, never said a word to us and scarcely said hello, but when we'd come in after he'd gone, it was . . . how can I explain . . . the light had changed. It was as if the chap had opened the window. One of those huge windows without a handle and which are never opened otherwise, for the simple reason that they have been sealed shut.

'One evening, late, he came into the office, something he'd never done before, but he needed a sheet of paper, I think, and . . . She was there, with a mirror in her hand, putting her make-up on in the half-light.

'"Sorry," he said, "may I switch on the light?" And he saw her. And what she was holding in her other hand, it wasn't an eye pencil or a lipstick, but the blade of a surgical knife.'

Sylvie took a long swig of water.

'He knelt down next to her, cleaned her wounds, that evening and for months afterwards . . . He listened to her for a long time, and assured her that Alexis's reaction was perfectly normal. Better than that, even – vital, healthy. That he would come back, that he had always come back, hadn't he? And no, she hadn't been a bad mother. Never in her life. He had worked with a lot of addicts, and those who had been well loved made it through more easily than the others. And God knows he'd been loved, hadn't he! Yes, he laughed, yes, God knew! And he was even jealous! He said that her son was well taken care of where he was, and that he'd ask around, he'd keep her up to date and she should go on behaving the way she'd always behaved. Which meant she should simply be there for him and, above all, more than anything, be herself, because it was up to Alexis to find his way now, and it could be that that way might lead him away from her . . . At least for a time . . . Do you believe me, Anouk? And she believed him and . . . You don't look well. Are you all right? You've gone all white . . .'

'I think I'd better eat something but I . . .' He tried to smile. 'Well, I . . . Do you have a bit of bread?'

'Sylvie?' he said, between two mouthfuls.

'Yes?'

'You're a good storyteller . . .'

Her eyes misted over.

'For good reason. Since she died, that's all I think about . . . Night and day, little fragments of memories come back to me, all the time . . . I'm not sleeping well, I talk to myself, I ask her questions, I try to understand . . . She's the one who taught me my profession, and it's to her I owe the most important moments of my career, as well as the craziest laughs. She was always there if I needed her, she always found the right words to give people strength, make them more tolerant . . . She's my eldest daughter's godmother, and when my husband got cancer she was marvellous, as usual . . . With me, with him, with our little girls . . .'

'Did he, uh –'

'No, no,' she said, her face lighting up, 'he's still around! But you won't see him, he thought it was better to leave us alone . . . Shall I go on? Do you want something more to eat?'

'No, no . . . I'm listening.'

'So, she believed this man, as I was saying, and after that I saw, really *saw* with my own eyes, d'you hear? what people call "the

202

power of love". She pulled herself together, stopped drinking, lost weight, looked younger again, and from under that layer of . . . sorrow, as you called it earlier, out came her old face. The same features, the same smile, the same cheerfulness in her expression. You remember how she used to behave if there was an opportunity for mischief? She was lively, irresistible, crazy. Like a saucy schoolgirl who ends up in the wrong dormitory and doesn't get caught . . . And she was lovely, Charles, so lovely . . .'

Charles remembered.

'Well, it was him. That Paul. You cannot imagine how happy I was to see her like that. I said to myself, Right. Life has finally understood what it owes her. Life is thanking her at last . . . It was at about that time that I quit the profession. Because of my husband, in fact. He'd had a really close call, and if we tightened our belts, we could do without my salary. And then our daughter was expecting a baby, and Anouk had come back, so . . . It was time to retire, and look after my own loved ones. The baby was born, little Guillaume, and I went back to living the way normal people do. No stress, no shifts, no need to go hunting for a calendar whenever anyone suggested a day off, and I could forget all those smells . . . The meal trays, the disinfectant, the coffee brewing, the blood platelets . . . I swapped all that for afternoons in the park and packets of biscuits . . . At that point I lost sight of Anouk a bit, but we called each other from time to time. Everything was fine.

'And then one day, one night rather, she called and I couldn't understand what on earth she was on about. The only thing I did know was that she'd been drinking. So I went to see her the next day.

'He'd written her a letter that she couldn't understand. I was the one who had to read it to her, now, and explain it. What was he saying? What was he driving at? Was he leaving her or wasn't he? She was . . . devastated. So I read it, that . . .'

She shook her head.

'. . . that piece of shit, full of bullshit psychobabble . . . Oh, it was eloquent enough and all tangled up with lovely words. It was meant to be dignified and generous, but all it amounted to was . . . the most cowardly thing you've ever seen . . .

'"Well, well?" she was pleading. "What does it mean, do you think? What does it mean for me?"

'What was I supposed to say? That it meant she was nowhere? Look . . . You no longer even exist. He despises you so much that he can't even be bothered to explain himself clearly . . . No. I couldn't say that. Instead, I took her in my arms, and then, of course, she understood.

'You see, Charles, it's something I've often seen with my own eyes, something I'll never manage to understand . . . why people who are so exceptional in their profession, people who, objectively, are able to do good on earth, turn out to be despicable bastards in real life? Huh? How can such a thing be possible? In the end, where did it go, all their fine humanity?

'So I stayed with her all day. I was afraid to leave her. I was sure that at best she would drown herself in booze, and at worst . . . I begged her to come and stay a few days at our place; she could have the girls' room, we'd keep out of her way and . . . She blew her nose, tied her hair back, rubbed her eyelids, lifted her chin and smiled. The most heartbreaking smile I've ever seen on her face.

'Oh, and God knows that . . . Well. Never mind. She tried to make it last as long as possible, big show-off that she was, and she assured me, as she was walking me to the door, that I could leave now, that she wouldn't *do* anything, that she'd been through rougher times than this and so, thanks to that, she had a thick skin.

'I agreed, on condition I could ring her any time of the day or night. She laughed. She said okay. She added that one hassle more or less would hardly make any difference. And in fact, she held up. I couldn't get over it. I saw her a bit more often at that point, and try as I might to find warning signs – scrutinizing the whites of her eyes, or sniffing her coat when I went to hang it up – there . . . no . . . she was sober.'

Silence.

'With hindsight, I can see that, on the contrary, I should have been worried. It's horrid what I'm about to say, but in the end, as long as she was drinking, it was proof that she was alive and, in a certain way, it meant that she was *reacting* . . . Well . . . all these thoughts come to me nowadays . . . And then one day she told me that she was going to hand in her resignation. I was utterly flabbergasted. I remember it very well, we'd just come out of a tea room and were walking along the Tuileries. The weather was fine, we were arm in arm, and that's when she told me: it's over. I'm quitting. I slowed down and didn't say anything for a long time, hoping there'd be some explanation: I'm quitting because . . . or this is why I'm quitting . . . No. Nothing. I eventually managed to say, Why, Anouk, why? You're only fifty-five . . . How will you live? What will you live on? What I was really thinking was *who* or *what* will you live for, but I didn't dare put it to her like that. She didn't reply. Okay.

'And then she murmured, "All of them. They all abandoned me. One after the other . . . But *not the hospital*, do you understand? That's why I have to leave first, otherwise I know I'd never get over it. This way, at least one thing in my bitch of a life won't leave me stranded . . . Can you imagine me on the day of my farewell party?" she scoffed, "thanks for the present, kiss on the cheek to everybody, and then? Where do I go from there? What do I do? When is it time to die?"

'I didn't know what to say but it didn't really matter: she was already climbing onto her bus, waving goodbye through the window.'

She put her glass down and didn't say anything.

'And then?' ventured Charles. 'Is . . . is that it?'

'No. Well yes, in fact. Yes . . .'

She apologized, removed her glasses, tore off a paper towel and ruined her make-up.

Charles got up, went over to the window, and with his back to her this time, held onto the railing of the balcony as if he were on board a ship.

He wanted a smoke. Didn't dare. There'd been cancer in this house . . . Perhaps it had had nothing to do with tobacco but how could he know? He looked at the tower blocks in the distance and thought about that family of hers . . .

The ones who had never loved her. Who had never called her by her real name. Who had filled her blood with addiction and affliction and alcoholism. Who had never held their hand out to her other than to take her money. The money she earned by forbidding her patients to die, while Alexis buckled his schoolbag all on his own and put the key around his neck. But to give them their due, those people were the ones who – one evening when they were all a bit down – had given Nana the chance to improvise a marvellous illusionist's act.

'Stop it, treasure, stop wasting your time with those useless dregs . . . What is it you want from them, anyway? Tell me?'

Digging around here and there in the kitchen to find his props, he had imitated them all.

Incarnated, rather.

The scolding dad. The consoling mum. The needling brother. The stammering little sister. The waffling granddad. And the old aunt who prickled beneath her suction-cup kisses. And the farting great-uncle. And the dog, and the cat, and the postman, and the priest, and even the gamekeeper, for whom he borrowed Alexis's trumpet . . . And it was as cheery as any real family dinner, and . . .

Charles inhaled a good lungful of ring road air and – God knows what an ugly word this is – *verbalized* what it was that had been haunting him these last six months. No, twenty years:

'I – I'm one of them.'

'One what?'

'One of those who abandoned her . . .'

'Yes, but you cared for her very much . . .'

He turned around and she added, with a mocking dimple, 'No, I don't think *care for* is the right expression now, is it?'

'Was it that obvious?' asked the old little boy, anxiously.

'No, no, don't worry. You could hardly tell. It was every bit as discreet as . . . Nana's outfits . . .'

Charles looked down. Her smile was tickling his ears.

'You know, I didn't want to interrupt you earlier on when you were saying that he had been her only love story, but when I went to the cemetery the other day and I saw those orange letters going off like a huge fireworks display in the middle of all that . . . desolation, well, there I was, and I'd sworn to myself no more crying, but I confess that . . . And then this horrid woman from the next plot came over to me going tsk tsk. She had seen him, too, the shameless fool who'd done that, and wasn't it a crime . . . I didn't say anything. How could you expect an old bag like her to understand anything? But I did think to myself, that shameless fool you're referring to was the love of Anouk's life.

'Don't look at me like that, Charles, I just told you I didn't want any more crying. I'm up to here with it, really I am. And besides, she wouldn't want to see us like this, it's . . .'

Paper towel.

'She had a photo of you in her wallet, she talked about you all the time, she never said a single unkind thing about you. She said that you were the only man in the world – and this means that poor Nana wasn't even in the running – who ever behaved like a gentleman with her . . .

'She said, Good job I met him, he absolved all the others . . . She said too that if Alexis had made it in the end, it was thanks to you, because when you were little you used to look after him better than she did . . . She said you'd always helped him with his homework and his auditions, and that without you he'd have turned out a lot worse . . . She said that you had been the backbone of a house full of crazy people . . .

'The only thing that . . .' she added.

'That what?'

'That really made her lose hope, was the fact that you two had fallen out . . .'

Silence.

'Come on, now, Sylvie,' he finally managed to say, 'let's get it over with . . .'

'You're right. It won't take long. So she left the hospital, discreetly. She'd fixed it with management so that the others would think that she was leaving on holiday, and she never came back. They were all terribly disappointed not to have been able to show her their admiration and affection, but since that's the way she'd chosen to do things, then . . . She got letters from them, instead. The first ones she read, and then after that she confessed to me that she couldn't read any more. If you could have seen . . . It was impressive. After that our phone calls were further and further apart, and didn't last as long . . . First of all because she no longer had much to tell me, and then my daughter had twins and I was *very* busy! And finally because she told me that she and Alexis had had a reconciliation and at that point, subconsciously I suppose, I assumed Alexis had taken over from me. That it was his turn now. You know how it is with people you've worried about a lot . . . When the situation seems to improve a bit, you're really pleased just to be able to have a break. So I did the same as you. Sort of the bare minimum for politeness. Her birthday, holiday greetings, birth announcements, postcards. Time went by and gradually she became a memory from my former life. A wonderful memory.

'And then one day one of my letters was returned. I wanted to ring her but the line had been disconnected. Right. She must have gone to join her son somewhere outside Paris and she surely had masses of grandchildren on her lap . . . She'd call some day or other and we'd exchange all our senile old lady chit-chat . . .

'She never called. Huh. That's life. And then . . . it must have been about three years ago, I think, I was in the train and there was a very upright old lady at the end of the carriage. I remember my first reflex was to think, I'd like to be like her when I'm that age. You know, the way you say to yourself, "A fine-looking old person." A lovely mass of white hair, no make-up, skin like a nun's, very wrinkly but still fresh, a slender shape and . . . she moved over, a bit closer to me, to let someone get off and that's when I got such a shock.

'She recognized me too and gave me a gentle smile as if we'd met only the day before. I suggested we get out at the next station and go for a coffee. I could sense she wasn't terribly keen on the idea but, oh well . . . if it would please me . . .

'She used to be so talkative, so voluble in the old days, but now I had to worm it out of her to get her to tell me the least little thing about herself. Yes, her rent had gone up and she'd had to move. Yes, it was a tough estate she was living in, but there was a sense of solidarity she'd never encountered elsewhere. She was working in an infirmary in the morning and doing volunteer work the rest of the time. People came to her place or she'd go to their homes . . . She didn't really need much money, anyway . . . Everyone used the barter system: a bandage for a dish of couscous or a shot for some plumbing work . . . She seemed strangely calm but not unhappy either. She said she'd never done a better job at her profession. She had the feeling she was still useful, and she got mad whenever anyone called her "doctor", and she nicked prescription drugs on the sly from the dispensary. The medication that had expired . . . Yes, she was living alone and . . . And you? she asked. And you?

'So I told her my boring little life, but at a certain point I could see she wasn't listening. She had to go. They were expecting her.

'And Alexis? Oh . . . There she seemed to cloud over . . . He lived far away and she could tell her daughter-in-law didn't like her very much . . . She always felt like she was in the way . . . But anyway he had two lovely children, a big girl and a little boy who was three, and that was the main thing . . . They were all fine . . .

'We were on the platform again when I asked her if she'd heard from you. And what about your Charles? So she smiled. Yes. Of course . . . You were working a lot, travelling all over the world, you had a big agency near the Gare du Nord, you were living with a superb woman. A real Parisian. The most elegant of all. And you had a girl, too . . . Who was your spitting image, by the way . . .'

Charles was startled.

'But . . . how did she know?'

'I don't know. I suppose she never lost sight of you.'

His face was reduced to a cramp.

'I got off at the next stop, all confused and upset, and the last time I ever had any news was the announcement that she was to be buried two days later.

'And it wasn't Alexis who got in touch with me, it was a neighbour she'd been friendly with and who had looked for my number in her things.'

She pulled her cardigan closer.

'So here we are at the final act . . . Bitter cold, a few days before Christmas in a God-awful cemetery. No service, no speech, nothing. Even the chaps from the funeral director's were embarrassed. They kept making these anxious little movements with their heads to see if someone was about to make a speech, but nothing. So after a short while they moved closer to her and pretended to meditate for five minutes or so, their hands crossed in front of their flies, and then what, well they lowered their ropes, that's what they were paid for after all.

'I was surprised not to see you there, but since she had told me that you were travelling a lot . . .

'There was almost no one in front of me. One of her sisters, I think, who seemed to be fearfully bored and never stopped fiddling with her mobile. Alexis, his wife, another couple and an older man who wore some sort of Red Cross uniform and who was weeping like a big baby, and . . . that's all.

'But behind me, Charles, behind me . . . Fifty or sixty people . . .

perhaps even more . . . A lot of women, masses of kids, toddlers, teenagers, big tall gangly youths who didn't know what to do with their arms, old women, old men, people in their Sunday best, bouquets of flowers, superb jewellery and trinkets on designer jackets, old people hobbling along, others all patched up, some . . . All walks of life, all ages, all sorts . . . All the people she must have taken care of one day, I suppose . . .

'What a motley crew. And yet they didn't make a sound, no wailing, an unbelievable silence, but when the gravediggers stepped back, they all began to applaud. For a long, long time . . .

'That was the first time I'd ever heard applause in a cemetery and at that point I finally let myself cry: she had had her tribute . . . and I can't imagine what a priest or any other appropriate blah blah might have said about her that would have been more fitting.

'Alexis recognized me and collapsed in my arms. He was sobbing so hard that I couldn't understand what he was saying. Basically that he was a bad son and that right up to the end he hadn't done what he should have. I put my hands back in my pockets, it was cold, so there was no way to hug him. His wife gave me a pinched little smile and came to peel him away from my coat. Then I went off again because . . . I had nothing more to do there . . . But in the car park a woman called out to me by name. It was her, the one who'd called me . . . She said, why don't we go and get something hot to drink. Well, one quick closer look told me that it wasn't really the hot drinks that she was into . . . For that matter, she ordered a pastis . . .

'She's the one who told me about Anouk's last years. Everything she'd done for so many people, and then some. They hadn't all been able to come to the funeral . . . there was no more room in Sandy's son's bus! Well, besides, it wasn't actually his bus . . .

'I won't go on and on about Anouk, you knew her like I did . . . you can imagine the scene . . . this woman had some, shall we say, elocution problems, but at one point she said something really sweet: "That there lady, and let me tell you, well she wore a heart of gold on her sleeve, if you want my opinion . . ."'

Smiles.

'"How did she die?" I asked. But the woman couldn't tell me any more. It all made her feel just too down . . . And then suddenly there was a draught of air in my back and she cried out, "Jeannot! Come and say hello to the lady! She's a friend of Anouk's!"

'It was the man who'd been crying his eyes out earlier on, and he had a handkerchief as big as a tea towel and a cape from the Red Cross – Great War vintage. He gave me a lop-sided smile and I figured straight away that he must have been her last blue-eyed boy . . . A chap who looked as unpredictable as Nana. As well disguised, at any rate. Pleased to meet you . . . He sat down across from me and the other woman went to drown her sorrows a bit closer to the bar. I sensed that he too really wanted to open his heart, but I was tired. I wanted to leave, to be alone at last. So I went straight to the point: what happened *at the end?* And that is when I learned – pinball machine and telly blasting away – that our lovely Anouk, the same woman who'd spent her entire life telling death where to get off, had finally made peace with it.

'Why? He didn't know. But there could be several reasons.

'Twice a week she worked at the Friendship Bakery, a charity grocery reserved for people who were hard-up and where they sold food for next to nothing. A "customer" had come in with all her brats and she didn't want any meat because it wasn't halal, nor any bananas because they'd got black spots on them, nor any yoghurts because they'd be past their sell-by date the next day, and in the midst of all that she'd go, to her kids, Are you looking for a smack on the bottom or what, and Anouk, who's normally so kind, started to shout at her.

'It wasn't surprising that poor people stayed poor because they really were bloody idiots. Who gave a damn what they did over at the abattoir, when your kids are that pale and already under-nourished? And if you smack that child one more time, you horrible cow, just one more time, *I will kill you.* And how did she get off having a spanking new mobile phone and smoking ten euros' worth of fags every day when her kids didn't even have socks in the middle of winter! And where did that bruise come from, there? How old was he, anyway, three? What did you hit him with, you piece of scum, for him to have a bruise like that? Huh?

'The woman left the shop screaming insults at Anouk, and Anouk took off her apron. She said she'd had enough. She wouldn't be coming back. She couldn't take it any more.

'And the other thing, murmured this fat Jeannot, was that it was

211

the 15th of the month, and her son hadn't invited her for Christmas yet, so she didn't know whether she ought to hang on to the presents for her grandchildren or send them by post. It was trivial, but it really upset her, this business. And then there was that kid, I can't recall her name, she'd helped her a lot with school and so on, she'd even found her an internship at the town hall, and the kid came and told her she'd got pregnant. Seventeen years old. So Anouk told her there was no point in her coming back to see her if she didn't get an abortion and . . .

'You want me to tell you what Anouk died of? She died because she'd lost heart. That is why she died. Jeannot gestured with his chin towards Joëlle, Madame Hot Drink, and said that she was the one who found her. The flat was completely empty. Not a stick of furniture. Nowt, as he put it. Seems she'd given it all to the Sally Army, so they told him afterwards. There was just an armchair and that thingammy with flowing water . . . A water fountain? No, a hospital thing, you know, with a sort of tube. A drip? That's it. The police said she'd committed suicide and the doctor replied no, that wasn't quite it, she'd put herself to sleep more like . . . And when he saw Joëlle crying he told her that she hadn't suffered, she'd just gone to sleep. But still, all the same . . . It's all right.

'"You were a friend of hers?" I asked him.

'"Oh, you might put it like that, but I was mainly her assistant, you see . . . I went round people's homes with her, carried her bag, that sort of thing."'

Silence.

'"Now it'll cost us even dearer . . ."

'"What will?"

'"The doctor . . ."'

Sylvie stood up. She glanced at the clock, put a pan of water onto the gas and then, staring off into the distance, continued in a low voice: 'On the way home, caught in the traffic, I remembered something she had said millions of years earlier, one day when we were moaning in the changing-room after a particularly trying day: "You want to know something, lovey . . . there's only one good thing about this job: when the day comes, we'll be able to depart this world without disturbing a soul . . ."'

She raised her eyes.

'There you are, Charles my boy. You know as much as I do, now.'

She began to grow restless and he could tell it was time to leave. He didn't dare give her a kiss.

She caught up with him on the landing.

'Wait! I've got something for you.'

And she handed him a box held together with thick Sellotape, where his name had been written in capital letters.

'The old fellow, again . . . He asked me if I knew a certain Charles, and he pulled this thing out from under his coat. At her house, he said, there was just a big bag for her son with the children's presents, and then this thing . . .'

Charles wedged the box under his arm and walked out in a daze. Straight ahead. Rue de Belleville, Faubourg du Temple, Place de la République, Turbigo, Sébasto, les Halles, Châtelet, across the Seine, going on to Saint-Jacques like a zombie and Port-Royal at random, and when he felt the right moment had come, that simple physical fatigue was winning over the somersaults of his emotions, without slowing down he pulled out his key ring, and used the smallest key to tear through the Sellotape.

It was a children's shoe box. He put his key ring back in his pocket, bumped into a column, apologized, and lifted the lid.

Dust, moths, or simply time had done their dirty work well, but he recognized her all the same. It was Mistinguett, the stuffed dove belonging to Na—

But what —

There was only one thing he could think of, only one thing to do: pull the box closer, and hold it as tight as possible against his chest. After that, nothing.

Nothing more could reach him.

So much the better. He was too weary to carry on, in any case.

14

Something warm on his cheek. He closed his eyes, it felt good.

Oh no, who was this bothering him already. People all round him.

I didn't see him! I didn't see him! It's those bloody new bus lanes they've put in! How many dead do those wankers need? I didn't see him, I swear! Besides, he wasn't on the crossing, either, was he! Ah, fuck . . . I didn't see him . . .

Sir? Sir?

Are you all right?

He was smiling.

Fuck off, all of you, why don't you . . .

Call the ambulance, he heard someone say. No, not that. He decided to get to his feet.

Not the hospital.

He'd had his fill of hospitals.

He stretched out his hand, leaned against someone's arm, then a second one, let himself be lifted to his feet, gestured towards his shoe box, nodded thanks and, with the box for sole support, trotted over to the other shore.

Move your arm, let's see . . . The other one . . . And your legs . . . It's your face that's all messed up . . . Yes, but with the shock, you never know . . . You don't always see them right away, the after-effects . . . Is he vomiting, or not? Don't touch him too much, you just don't know . . . Don't you want me to call an ambulance? I can take you to casualty . . . why not, we're not far from Cochin, here! Are you sure? We shouldn't leave him like this, huh. What's he saying?

He's saying that he's sure.

The crowd dispersed. A dead man who doesn't die isn't so very interesting after all.

And then . . . if there's no fuss, there's no fun. A good citizen did however offer to write down the driver's number plate for him and act as a witness, for the insurance . . .

Charles hugged his box against his heart and moved his head from right to left.

No. Thank you. He was just a bit stunned. It would pass. No problem.

The only one who stayed with him on the bench was some sort of tramp. No merit in that; the man was just bored.

Charles asked him for a cigarette.

Leaning over for the light, he thought he was going to pass out. He straightened up as slowly as possible, ran his tongue over his lips so he wouldn't soil the filter and breathed in a long puff of calm.

After a very long while, perhaps an hour, his guardian angel reached out an arm.

He pointed to the shop front of a chemist's.

The little assistant, Géraldine, it said so on her breast, let out a cry when she saw him. Her boss ran over, begged him to sit down on a chair, and made him suffer a thousand exquisite little tortures.

She was a wannabe doctor, giddy with this rare opportunity to perform . . .

His new friend was waiting for him on the other side of the window, and raised his thumb to give him courage.

His new friend was quite taken with Géraldine . . .

Charles winced a great deal. His face, or what was left of it, was scraped, cleaned, disinfected, studied, commented upon, then covered with little postoperative dressings.

He stood up, holding onto a display case, hobbled up to the till, allowed them to palm off a stack of ointments on him in exchange for a promise to see a doctor, lied in response, thanked them, paid, and went off to confront the world once again.

His former friend had vanished. He dragged himself to a café-tabac, astonished to be attracting so many fleeting glances.

The proprietor was not so sensitive. He'd seen his share . . .

'Well then,' he jested, 'run over by the bus this morning?'

Charles smiled as much as the pain would allow: 'Delivery van.'

'Huh. Better luck next time.'

This from a shopkeeper. A *Parisian* shopkeeper, with a sense of humour, no less. This was marvellous.

He ordered a beer, to celebrate.

'There you go! I've given you a straw . . . What's that? Hungry? Nicole! Bring a plate of mashed potatoes for the young man!'

Charles, with one buttock on the bar stool, gingerly sought sustenance while listening to Monsieur Nicole rattle off the list of all the injured, run over, crippled, lame, dead and other amputees that his excellent location (corner of a major crossroads, just what is required for a business) had allowed him to tally up over twenty-five years of keeping a look-out.

'I think I've got a petition somewhere against their latest bloody idea of having the buses come down the wrong way; are you interested?'

'No.'

He made painful progress, holding his box with one hand and his leg with the other. He was lost.

Not here in the Rue Monge, of course, but . . .

He dialled Laurence's number as if he were removing five bullets from a barrel, pointed the thing at his temple, and waited.

Voicemail.

He headed back the other way and pushed open the door of a car rental service he'd walked by five minutes earlier while lost deep in thought.

He assured the salesman that it was nothing, a glass door. Ah . . . went the man, relieved, my colleague did exactly the same thing . . . Three stitches. Charles shrugged. What a wimp, his colleague.

At the last moment, his swollen knee conjured him to change his mind: 'Hold it! Give me an automatic, instead . . .'

Holding back his little tears of pain, he wriggled himself in behind the wheel of a tiny category A city car, checked his diary, put it back on the right page, then as he adjusted his mirrors he suddenly realized that the Elephant Man was coming along for the ride.

He was grateful for his . . . unexpected company, turned left, and headed for the Porte d'Orléans.

The light had just turned green. He accelerated with a quick glance at the dashboard. With any luck, he'd be at Alexis's place in time for dinner.

He wouldn't allow himself to smile because it already hurt too much, but his heart was in it.

III

1

In the beginning it was easy: he'd made his decision.

He left the city behind and drove fast, and to hell with keeping a safe distance.

He had no idea what to expect but he wasn't afraid. Nothing frightened him any more. Neither his reflection (or what took the place of his face); nor his fatigue; nor what he saw there before him: that conscientious woman, looking for the vein, sticking the long needle in, fixing it carefully, opening her fist for the last time, loosening the tourniquet and checking on the flow of her death before sitting back down in the only armchair in an empty flat . . . What . . . No. He was immune, now.

He managed to reach his assistant between two crash barriers.

'Fine, I'll cancel. Oh, and about Monday evening . . . Take-off is at 19.45. I think I've managed to get you an upgrade . . . I have the code for the ticket, do you have something to write with?' asked his assistant.

Then he left a message for Laurence. 'I got your message,' she replied, eventually; 'look, that's fine because as you know I'm stuck with the Koreans this weekend . . . (No, he didn't know.) And while I've got you on the line, don't forget Mathilde, will you? You'd promised to go with her to the airport on Monday . . . I think it's early afternoon, I'll let you know . . . (The Air France lounge, his second home . . .) And what about her spending money? Do you have any pounds left?'

No. No. He hadn't forgotten. Neither his kiddo, nor Howard.

Charles never forgot anything. That was actually his Achilles' heel. What was it Anouk used to say? That he was intelligent? Not at all. He'd often had the opportunity of working with people who had extraordinary minds, so he did not nurture any illusions about his own. If he'd been able to put on a good show all these years, and fool them all, it was precisely because of his good memory . . . Whatever he read or saw or heard, he remembered.

And now he was a man with a burden – he was *loaded*, as the English would say, like dice. Yes, loaded dice. And those dreadful migraines – which, for the time being, seemed to be giving him some respite, buried beneath a screed of more . . . urgent suffering – well, there was nothing physiological about them. It was more in the nature of a computer glitch. The letter from Alexis and the tidal wave it brought with it, his childhood, his memories, Anouk, the little we know about her, and everything that he hasn't told us, everything he prefers to keep to himself, to protect her for a while yet, and because he is so modest, the whole overload of unexpected emotions: all of this had, in a way, saturated his memory. Chemistry, molecules, perhaps a scan? Oh, feel free, go ahead, but it would have no effect. It was up to him to restore his files.

'Where are you?' asked Laurence.

'Saint-Arnoult . . . Motorway . . .'

'What's that? A new site?'

'Yes,' he lied.

It was the truth.

But as the horizon gradually opened, the journey began to seem less certain. He'd dropped back from the fast lane and sat brooding in the shadow of an enormous lorry.

Instinctively, whenever he passed a sign indicating a new exit, his fingertips sought the indicator lever.

The fault of his memory, that he knew. Tut, tut. False modesty . . . a sun visor is damned useful when you're headed south . . . Let's talk about him for a while, and give this twice-shy man his due.

It was purely by chance that Charles became an architect, as a tribute, or out of a sense of allegiance, and because he was remarkably good at drawing. Of course he retained what he saw, and what he understood, but he also represented it. Easily. Naturally. On the drawing sheet, in space, and with any sort of clientele. Even the most discouraging critics eventually came round. But talent of that sort was not enough. What he was so good at sketching was his reasoning, his clear-sightedness.

He was calm and patient, and the mere act of thinking, in his presence, was a privilege. Better than that, even; it was a game.

For lack of time he had always turned down the teaching positions he was offered, but at the agency he enjoyed being surrounded
by young people. Marc and Pauline, this year, or before that the
brilliant Giuseppe or even the son of his friend O'Brien. They had
been welcomed with open arms in the spacious premises on the
Rue La Fayette.

He was tough on them, gave them an enormous work load, but
treated them as equals. You're younger, therefore you're quicker
than I am, he would assert, so prove it to me. What would you do
in this case?

He took the time to listen to them, and scuppered their more
inept projects without ever humiliating them. He encouraged them
to copy and draw as much as they could, however poorly; they
should travel, read, listen to music, learn to read music again, visit
museums, churches, gardens, and . . .

He was dismayed by their crass ignorance and eventually he would
look at his watch, startled when he saw the time. But . . . ? Aren't you
hungry? Well yes, they were hungry. So? Why are you letting me
pontificate like an imbecile, then? Haven't they told you that the days
of the old waffling professors at the Art and Architecture Schools are
over? Come on . . . To buy their forgiveness, he told them to head
straight for the Brasserie Terminus Nord. Seafood platter, on him! But
no sooner had they sat down, he couldn't help himself: they put down
their menus and he implored them to take a look all around them.
School of Nancy, art deco, new simplifications, reaction against art
nouveau, streamlining, sober geometric lines, Bakelite, chromed steel,
rarefied essences, and . . . by then the waiter had returned.

Sighs of relief in the ranks.

In their small world, it was easy to belittle him. They reproached
him for being . . . how to put it . . . a bit *classical*, no? As a young
man, that had hurt. But he'd listened. It was why he had hitched
his wagon to Philippe, the lad was more . . . subjective, and he had
no fear, did Philippe, of having an emotional response to a given
situation; Charles admired his intransigency, his talent, his creativity.
Professionally, they worked well as a pair, but it was Charles whom
the students sought out.

Even the most brilliant ones. The feverish visionaries, the ones
who were ready to die of hunger at the foot of their own Sagrada
Família.

Yes, it was Charles.

His common sense, his moderation . . . For a long time, this left him feeling confused. On a bad day he mused that he was the son of his father and that he had indeed not gone – nor would he go – very far. But there were other days, like that winter morning a few months earlier when, although he was already late and had climbed out of his taxi in the middle of a traffic jam, he'd suddenly found himself alone in the middle of the Cour Carrée at the Louvre, somewhere he had not been for absolutely ages: he decided to skip his appointment; he stopped running; he caught his breath.

The frost, the light, the absolutely perfect proportions, the sensation of something so powerful, yet utterly devoid of any overpowering intentions, a trace of the divine in human hands . . . He'd spun on his heel, calling out to the pigeons, 'Hey! Fucking classical, no?'

But that absurd fountain . . . He set off at a run, again, and hoped that Lescot, Lemercier and all the others, from their perches up on high, were having a thoroughly good time spitting into it now and again.

To avoid any misunderstanding: the criticism – mainly of a very typically French kind – was restricted to, or focused upon, a moral attitude, a disposition, and under no circumstances the nature of his work. Given his background as an engineer (a weakness, a handicap, or so he came to believe, on the odd evening), his attention to detail, and his perfect knowledge of structures, materials, and other physical phenomena, Charles's reputation remained, as it had done for a considerable length of time, completely above suspicion.

It was simply that he could see traces of himself in the theory put forward by inspired Irish engineer Peter Rice, and by Auden before him, according to which, in the course of a project, someone had to take on the dirty job of playing Iago and systematically impose reason upon other people's disorderly flights of passion.

Classical? Huh. So be it. But conservative, no. No. And to prove it, he had to convince the industry, the promoters, the political circles and the public that his ideas were a hundred times, a thousand times superior to all those buildings that were ordinary but decked out in pretty post-modern or pseudo-historical flounces, and this had become the most trying aspect of his profession.

So he was given a rough time, and found himself – to get back to Othello – to be *Perplex'd in the extreme*. Fortunately, as it happened, fortunately. That role was somewhat shorter, but . . .

Hey? Where you off to, old man? He shook himself as he steered back into the middle lane, what are you waffling on about this time? Why are you talking about Rice and the Moor all of a sudden?

Sorry, sorry. It's just this business of my memory not holding the road.

Well, what's new.

Anouk was right . . .

Remember.

One last time.

When she got here earlier and she saw all that maths you were stuck with, just as she was hugging you she was feeling sorry for you at the same time. She thought to herself that for your age, you were spending far too much time trying to fold the world up into neat little squares. She knew, she knew! You were going to say that this was for your studies and all that, but . . .

But?

What was there to say? He no longer tried to argue, he was tired. The next exit would be the right one.

No.

Please.

Come back.

We haven't followed you this far just to turn round at Rambouillet.

Why do you always have to *think* about everything? Living as a project manager, drawing up plans, models, scaffolding, calculating, anticipating, foreseeing? Why so many constraints? You said just now that you weren't afraid of anything, any more . . .

I was lying.

What are you afraid of?

I would like . . .

Yes?

Right. You want to play clever. Let's look elsewhere. The shape of clouds, the first cows, the latest Audi, the rest area at La Briganderie, that buzzard taking flight, the price of unleaded, 17 kilometres further along, the –

223

When we were children, continued his inner voice in an under-
tone, and we used to pick on each other – and that happened a
lot, because we both had a filthy temperament and I imagine we
were fighting for the love and attention of one and the same woman
– Nana, who'd used up all his patience and threats trying to recon-
cile us, always ended up going to fetch his little stuffed bird which
was gathering dust on top of the refrigerator, and into its beak
he'd cram whatever he happened to have on hand – most often a
sprig of parsley – and then he'd come to wave it under our grumpy
little noses.

'Rruu, rruu . . . The dove of peace, my loves . . . Rrruuuu . . .'

And we'd burst out laughing. And bursting out laughing together,
that meant we weren't angry with one another, any more, and . . .
And now he had that shoe box, there, in the passenger seat, and . . .

Who cares about unleaded petrol. Rental cars always run on
diesel, no? What? Sorry? You were saying?

He sat up straight, tugged on his seatbelt, couldn't . . . Couldn't
there have been just a little bit of hope, too, in that bloody IV?
Maybe she was actually overestimating us, there, *testing* us yet again?

Would she never leave us in peace with her fucking over-
abundance of love that had already . . .

Ah-hah. One euro twenty-two, look at that . . . Hey, Balanda, you're
starting to try my patience with all your gobbledygook, you know
that? You think you're so bloody clever, with your quotations from
Shakespeare et al. in the original, your rigour, your students dumb
with admiration, your culture, your ingenuity and all that crap, you
know we'd gladly swap all that gibberish for one single solid sentence
that really went somewhere?

He frowned, lit a cigarette, waited for the nicotine to free his
grey matter from the wreckage and eventually confessed his misery
to himself: 'I would like to think she didn't die for nothing.'

Ah, at last, there we are! Right, it's okay now. Deep breath. There
you are. You've conceptualized the thing.

Hey? You've got your project now, no? So drive. Drive, keep
your mouth shut and, sorry, don't breathe quite so hard. You may
not realize it, but you've got a cracked rib.

Yes but if things don't go –

Shut up, we said. Disconnect.

Because he could not trust himself, at least on that level, he reached his arm out, ouch, to switch on the FM.

Between two idiotic adverts, a pop singer with a squeaky voice began to bleat, *Relax, take it easy* at least a dozen times.

Eeeeeeeeeeeaaaaaa-sy.

Okay, okay, I got it.

He looked for his sunglasses, immediately took them back off, too heavy, too many injuries, slammed the glove compartment shut and turned off the sound.

His mobile began to vibrate. It suffered the same fate.

A moth-eaten dove and a disfigured cripple in a tiny Japanese car, not exactly the greatest Noah's ark imaginable, and yet, and yet . . . Beneath his sticking plasters he was secretly disintegrating.

After him, the deluge . . .

*

He left the motorway for the main road, then the secondary roads.

And then he realized, for the very first time in months, that the Earth turned around the Sun – well what d'you know – and that he lived in a country that was subject to the rhythm of the seasons.

His own sluggishness, and the lamps and neon lights, and the flicker of computer screens and the changing time zones had all conspired to make him forget. It was the end of June, the beginning of summer; he opened the windows wide, and brought in his first hay.

Another revelation, France.

So many landscapes for such a small country. And so much colour. An extraordinary palette with variations and contrasts and specificities according to region and building material . . . Bricks, brown flat tiles, the warm hues of the Sologne. Stones with a patina, or a coating, the ochre sand of the riverbeds. Then the Loire, clay and tufa. The endless play of grey and chalky white on the facades . . . Ivory and greyish beige in this late afternoon light . . . Bluish roofs highlighted by the red brick of the chimney stacks . . . The woodwork was often pale, or darker, depending on the owner's fantasy or what was left at the bottom of the tin of paint.

And before long, another region, other quarries, other stones . . .

Shale, thackstone, sandstone, lava, even granite here and there. Other rubble stones, other bondings, other facings, other coverings. Here gutter-bearing walls have replaced gables, there winters will be harsher and the dwellings built closer together. Or there, the door and window frames or the lintels are not as finely wrought, and the tones are more . . .

This was a once-in-a-lifetime chance for Charles to invoke the remarkable work of Jean-Philippe Lenclos and his Atelier, but, well . . . He'd been asked not to keep on about it, so . . . So he kept it to himself, all his paraphernalia, his contacts, his *references*, and he was driving ever more slowly. He turned his head, made a face, ran onto the embankment, jerked the steering wheel suddenly, scraped the kerb and went through tiny villages attracting everyone's gaze.

The soup was on the stove. It was time to nip out the geraniums and sit on benches and pull chairs outdoors in front of facades still drenched with sunlight. People shook their heads as he drove through and commented on it until the next turn of events.

As for the dogs, they hardly raised an ear. Let sleeping fleas and Parisians lie.

Charles was useless where nature was concerned. Groves, hedges, forests, moors, prairies, pastureland, hillsides, copses, woods, arbours – all words he was familiar with, but he wouldn't have known where to put them, on a topographical chart. He had never built anything far from a town, and he could not recall any books to which he might have referred, as the likes of Lenclos confined themselves to housing, for example.

In any case, for him the countryside meant one thing: a place to read. By a fireplace in the winter, against a tree trunk in the spring, and in the shade in the summer. It was not for lack of opportunity, however. When he was little, at his grandparents', during the grand epoch of Monsieur Canut, with Alexis; then, later on, when Laurence had dragged him off to stay with one friend or another, at their *country home*.

Memories of weekends where he felt a bit lost, where people were constantly begging him for an opinion, an estimate, advice on whether to knock down a wall. He would clench his teeth as he surveyed hideous bay windows, criminal apertures, incongruous swimming pools, padlocked cellars, and country folk in their Sunday

226

best, their wellingtons skilfully muddied, their cashmere in matching tones.

He'd given vague answers – it was hard to say, he'd have to see, he didn't know the region – and then, once he had scrupulously disappointed all these fine folk, he'd go off with a book in his hand, looking for a nice little hidey-hole where he could take a nap.

Talk about holes, he was in one now – no more signposts, no indication, ghostly hamlets, pavement colonized by wild grasses and, for sole escort, a squad of rabbits out for a good time.

What was Miles Davis's heir doing in this hole?

And where was he, anyway?

His diary was useless as a GPS. Where was the D73? And why hadn't he gone through the dump of a village whose name he couldn't even read any more?

Anouk . . .

Where are you taking me this time?

Can you see me now? The petrol gauge and my stomach on empty, completely lost at a fork in the road telling me nothing other than that I'll find firewood eight kilometres from here, or how to get to some long-extinguished summer solstice bonfires?

Where would you go, in my place?

Straight ahead, right?

Right.

In the next village, he rolled down his window.

He was lost. Marcy? Manery? Maybe it was Margery? Did that ring a bell?

No.

And the D73?

Oh, yes, in that case. It was the road over there, to the left on your way out of town, cross the river and immediately after the sawmill, take the first right.

One woman said, 'Maybe it's Les Marzeray the gentleman from the Oise is looking for?'

And there, he had to admit it, Charles felt a moment of over-whelming solitude. What on . . .

To his poor brain he granted the respite of a stupid smile, to give it time to untangle the whole mess.

First of all, as for the Oise, it must have been his number plate, he hadn't noticed when he'd picked up the car but that must be why; and then how did you write, and pronounce, Les Marzeray? Did it end in a 'y'? An 'M' and a 'y' that he'd scribbled any old how on the page of 9 August, that was all he had to go on. He tried to read it again but there was nothing for it: apart from the name of that day's saint, nothing was clear. As for the saint in question, hah hah, St Hilarious indeed.

The villagers put their heads together, argued for a fairly long time, and came to an agreement. Must be a 'y'.

They sure asked some funny questions, that lot from the Oise . . .

'But . . . is it still a long way?'

'Well . . . twenty-odd kilometres . . .'

Twenty kilometres, far enough for his steering wheel to get very slippery and his ribcage increasingly rough. Twenty very slow kilometres which confirmed one thing to him: he really did look like a fool.

When the steeple of Les Marzeray appeared in the distance, he pulled over onto the verge.

He was limping, he took a piss in the brambles, then a deep breath, felt the pain, let out his breath, loosened his shirt, lifted it by the tips of the collar and shook it to make it dry. Then he wiped his brow on his arm. His scratches were hurting him. He breathed in again, God what a pong, buttoned himself, put his jacket back on, and breathed out one last time.

His stomach began to rumble. He was grateful for the reminder but told it off, on principle. Shit, things were pretty serious here! A what? A steak? But there's no more room, you idiot. You're all skin and bone, now, can't you see?

Yes, that's it . . . A nice big steak with Alexis . . . To make him happy . . . *Eat, boys, eat, the rest will follow* . . .

His only problem (what, more? Starting to have his fill of all this!), was his stomach.

Which was beginning to heave.

So he lit up a fag.

To quieten it.

He sat on the warm bonnet, took his time, increased his risk of impotence, and covered a swarm of little bugs in a cloud of smoke.

He could remember the rough time he'd had of it, however. He'd been a real cynic back then: he said that giving up smoking was the only great adventure left to overfed little Westerners like themselves. The only one.

No longer a cynic.

He felt old, haunted by death, dependent.

He switched his mobile back on just to check. Nothing. No more coverage.

2

Outside the town hall he turned to the page for 10 August: Alexis lived on the Clos des Ormes. He searched for a long time and eventually had to switch once again to Radio Gossipy Neighbours:

'Oh, that's way further along . . . In the new houses, past the cooperative.'

'New houses': at the time it hadn't registered, but what was meant was the housing estate, in its fancy parade. Off to a good start, then . . . Everything he loved . . . Crap construction, crap roughcast, sliding shutters, letter boxes all in a row and ornate pseudo streetlamps.

And the worst of it is that eyesores like that don't come cheap.

Right, enough. So where is number 8?

Thuyas, a pretentious fence and a gate with DIY medieval iron-work. All that was missing were the little lions at the top of each pillar. Charles smoothed his jacket pockets and, open sesame, pressed the buzzer.

A little blond genie appeared in the window in the door.

A pair of arms moved it to one side.

Okay . . .

He pressed the bloody buzzer again.

A woman's voice answered, 'Yes?'

No? Could it be? There was an entry phone? He hadn't noticed. An entry phone? Here? In one of the most deserted regions in France? Classified a national park and all that? Fourth house in a botch-up of a development that hardly had more than a dozen, and there was an entry phone? But . . . what could it possibly mean?

'Who are you?' repeated the . . . device.

Charles answered fuck off but articulated it somewhat differently: 'Charles. A fr— – an old friend of Alexis's.'

Silence.

230

It was not hard to imagine their astonishment: action stations at Dunroamin', calls of 'Are you sure?' and 'Did you hear properly?' He squared his shoulders, made himself a sort of sublime garment worthy of a gladiator, and waited for the (automatic) gate to open and splatter Moses.

Missed.

'He's not here.'

Right . . . slowly, slowly catchee monkey, etc. Seems he had a surly client at the other end of the wire, time to get on with it, get out the heavy artillery.

'You must be Corinne,' he simpered. 'I've heard a lot about you . . . My name is Balanda, Charles Balanda . . .'

The front door (exotic wood, a Cheverny model, or was it Chambord, comes ready to install, lattice work with lead-look strips set into the double glazing and peripheral waterproofing seals on the frame) opened onto a face that was . . . not quite as stylishly put together.

She reached out her arm, her hand, her battering ram, and because he was trying to smile in order to mollify her, he finally understood what it was that was making her so tense: it was his face. His own bloody face.

But still, all the same . . . He'd forgotten about it. His trousers had a hole in them, his jacket was torn, and his shirt was covered in blood and antiseptic.

'Hello . . . Sorry . . . It's . . . Just . . . I fell down this morning. I'm not disturbing you?'

She didn't reply.

'Am I disturbing you?'

'No, no . . . He should be back any minute.' Then, turning to the little boy, 'You get back in the house!'

'Fine . . . I'll wait for him, then.'

She was supposed to say, 'Well, do come in, please', or 'Would you like something to drink while you're waiting?' or . . . but all she said was, 'Fine,' very curtly, and went back into her little builder's house.

The genuine article.

Quality stuff, too.

So Charles indulged in a bit of anthropology.

Wandering down Clos des Ormes.

Compared the hollow, embossed granite-style rough-hewn pillars, the balusters costing less than ten euros the linear metre, the factory-aged cobblestones, the concrete flagstones dyed to look like stone, the grandiose barbecue equipment, the epoxy resin garden furniture, the fluorescent children's slides, the polyester arbours, the garage doors as wide as the so-called 'living' area, the . . .

God what taste.

True enough, no longer a cynic. He was a snob.

Turned around and walked back. Another car was parked behind his. He slowed, felt his leg grow even stiffer, and the same little blond boy bounced out of the garden, followed by a man who must have been his daddy.

And at that point – it's bloody pathetic when you think of it, but you're not thinking, you're merely stating a fact – the first thought to enter Charles's mind after so much shock was: 'Bastard. He's still got all his hair.'

Shattering.

And then. What could possibly happen next?

Violins? Slow motion? Soft focus?

'And what's this? You walk like a little old man, now?'

What did you expect . . .

Charles didn't know what to say. He must be getting soft.

Alexis hurt him when he slapped him on the shoulder.

'What brings you here?'

Stupid jerk.

'This your son?'

'Lucas, get over here! Come and say hello to your uncle Charles!'

Charles leaned over to give the boy a kiss. And took his time. He'd forgotten the fresh perfume of a child's skin . . .

He asked him whether he wasn't fed up with Spider-Man clinging to his T-shirt, he touched his hair, his neck; what? Even on your socks? Well, well . . . and your pants, too? He learned how to place his fingers to make the 'sticky' web, tried it himself, got it wrong, promised he'd practise then stood up straight and saw that Alexis Le Men was weeping.

He forgot all his good resolutions and ruined the chemist's good work.

All the cuts and scrapes and bumps and stitches and barriers and plasters in life – they all gave way.

Their hands closed over each other and it was Anouk that they were embracing.

Charles stepped back first. Pain, bruises. Alexis lifted up his kid, made him laugh by nibbling his tummy, but actually it was so that he could hide, and blow his nose; then he lifted him onto his shoulders.

'What happened to you? Did you fall off some scaffolding?'

'Yes.'

'Did you see Corinne?'

'Yes.'

'You were just passing through?'

'That's right.'

Charles stood still. Three steps along, Alexis finally turned around. Put on his arrogant air of landed gentry and pulled on his son's legs to balance his load. That load, at any rate.

'Did you come here to lecture me, is that it?'

'No.'

They looked at each other for a long time.

'Are you still going on about cemeteries?'

'No,' said Charles, 'no. I've finished with that.'

'So where are you then?'

'Are you going to invite me for dinner?'

Relieved, Alexis granted him a fine smile, from the old days, but it was too late. Charles had just taken back all his marbles.

One Mistinguett in exchange for dinner at the Clos des Ormes, for the price of bad taste, petrol, and time wasted: it seemed like a fair bargain.

The sky was clear, my darling. Did you see her, did you get your olive branch, then?

Of course it was short-lived, more of a withdrawal than a surge, I'll grant you that, and of course it's not enough for you. But nothing ever was enough for you, so ·. .

And to feel his pockets full again, to have that certainty that the game was over, that he wouldn't play any more, and so he wouldn't lose any more, because this course, however hellish, was now too short for him to measure up against such a mediocre opponent, and this was an immense relief.

He had a jolly lilt to his limp now, tickled the knees of the super hero, opened his hand, curled back his index and ring finger, took aim and pow! snared a little bird that was dancing on the telegraph wires:

'You didn't really!' countered little Lucas. 'Where is it, then?'

'I put it in my car.'

'I don't believe you.'

'You ought to.'

'Pfff . . . know what, I'd've seen you if you truly did.'

'I'll have you know that that would really surprise me, because you were looking at the neighbours' dog.'

And while Alexis was unloading the weekly shop, going to and fro between the boot of his car and his perfect garage, Charles silenced a very suspicious little boy.

'Yes, but why is he already stuck onto a piece of wood, then?'

'Uh . . . May I remind you that spiderwebs are sticky . . .'

'Shall we show Daddy?'

'No. It's still a bit shaken up, now . . . We should leave it alone for a while . . .'

'Is he dead?'

'No, he isn't! Of course not! He's a bit shaken up, I said. We'll let him go a bit later on.'

Lucas nodded gravely then looked up, Light bulb!, and asked, 'What's your name?'

'Charles.' He smiled.

'And why d'you have all those plasters on your head?'

'Guess.'

''Cause you're not as strong as Spider-Man?'

'Yup. Sometimes I miss . . .'

'Want me to show you my room?'

His mother disturbed their arachnoid complicity. First they had to go through the garage and remove their shoes. (Charles raised an eyebrow, he'd never yet had to remove his shoes on entering a house.) (Except in Japan, naturally . . .) (Quite. What a snob he was . . .) Then she raised her index finger. No making a mess, all right? Finally she turned to this individual who seemed to be imposing on them.

'Will you . . . will you stay for dinner?'

Alexis had just appeared behind his handful of Champion shopping bags. (This would please his brother-in-law no end . . . What a delightful vignette . . . If he dared, if he could get reception what a fine MMS he could send to Claire . . .)

'Of course he's staying! What . . . ? What's the matter?'

'Nothing,' she retorted in a voice that meant quite the opposite, 'it's just that I've got nothing ready. Tomorrow is the school fair and in case you'd forgotten I still haven't finished Marion's costume. I'm not a seamstress, you know!'

Alexis, feverish and naïve, all wrapped up in the emotion of reconciliation, put down his stuff and brushed aside her arguments: 'No problem. Don't worry. I'll do the cooking.'

He turned around: 'And where is Marion, anyway? Isn't she here? Where is she?'

Another sigh emerged from the woman in her cloth pad floor-polishing slippers: 'Where is she, where is she . . . You know perfectly well where she is.'

'At Alice's place?'

'Obviously.'

'I'll call them.'

'Good luck. They never pick up over there. I don't know why they even have a phone.'

Alexis closed his eyes, reminded himself that he felt cheerful, and headed for the kitchen.

Charles and Lucas did not dare move.

'She's asking if she can sleep over!' shouted Alexis.

'No. We have a guest.'

Charles gestured, no, no, no, he refused to act as a poor alibi.

'She says they're rehearsing their choreography for tomorrow –'

'No. She has to come home.'

'She's begging you,' insisted her father, 'she says, "on her knees", even.'

Running out of arguments, Corinne the life and soul of the party used the meanest one of all: 'Out of the question. She hasn't got her dental brace with her.'

'Well hang on, if that's the only reason, I can take it over to her.'

'Oh, really? I thought you were the one doing the dinner.'

What an atmosphere . . . Charles suddenly felt that he needed a bit of air, so he stuck his nose into something that wasn't his business: 'I can be the messenger boy if that's of any help . . .'

The look she shot him confirmed his suspicion: this was ab-so-lute-ly none of his business.

'You don't even know where it is.'

'But I know!' exclaimed Lucas. 'I can show him the way!'

A sudden silence; an angel passing, hugging the walls.

The master of the house felt that it was time to show his mate, his comrade, his former army pal, just *who* laid down the law here. There are limits, after all.

'Okay, you can stay, but you come back straight after breakfast, all right?'

Charles put him in the back seat, turned the car round and hightailed it out of Noddy Close.

He raised his eyes to the rear view mirror: 'Right, where do we go from here?'

An enooooormous smile informed him that the tooth fairy had been by twice already.

'We're going to the wickedest house in the whole wide world!'

'Oh, really? And where is it, this wicked house?'

'Well, uh . . .'

Lucas removed his seat belt, moved forward, looked at the road, thought for two seconds and trumpeted, 'Straight ahead!'

His driver rolled his eyes heavenward.

Straight ahead.

Of course.

How stupid could he be.

To heaven . . .

Which had taken on a pink hue.

And powdered its nose to accompany them . . .

'You look like you're crying?' said his companion anxiously.

'No, no, it's just that I'm very tired . . .'

'Why're you tired?'

'Because I didn't get much sleep.'

'Did you take a very long trip to come and see me?'

'Oh, if you only knew!'

'And did you fight a lot of monsters?'

'Hey,' said Charles cheekily, thrusting his thumb towards his brawler's face: 'You don't think I did this myself, now, do you?'

Respectful silence.

'And what's that? Is that blood?'

'What d'you think?'

'Why are there some spots that are dark brown and other ones that are light brown?'

The age of why and then why and then why. He'd forgotten . . .

'Well . . . it depends on the monsters.'

'And which ones were the meanest?'

They were out in the sticks now, chattering away . . .

'Hey, is your wicked house much further?'

Lucas peered at the windscreen, made a face, turned round: 'Oh, we just drove past.'

'Oh, well done!' groaned Charles, pretending, 'well done, co-pilot! I don't know if I can take you along on any future expeditions, now!'

Contrite silence.

'Hey . . . Of course I'll take you. Why don't you come and sit on my knee in the front here? You'll be able to see better to show me the way.'

This time, it was clear, and there would be no regrets: he had just made himself a friend in the Le Men clan, and for life.

But oh Lord, he was aching all over.

They stopped so that Lucas could change places. Then they did a fine manoeuvre on a brown cow pasture, slalomed along the warm tarmac, turned in front of a sign that said *Les Vesperies*, had a job locating the rut that would take them on to the dirt road, then finally found themselves headed down a magnificent avenue lined with oak trees.

Charles, who had forgotten neither the way he smelled nor the way he looked, began to panic.

'Does she live in a château, your friend Alice?'

'Well, yes.'

'But er . . . how well do you know these people?'

'Well . . . I mainly know the baroness and Victoria . . . Victoria, you'll see, she's the oldest and fattest.'

Oh, fuck. The beggar and his scruffy urchin dropping in on the local toffs . . . That's all he needed . . .

What a day, can you believe what a day.

'And, uh, are they nice?'

'No. Not the baroness. She's a bee-eye-tee-see-aitch.'

Right, okay, uh-huh . . . After the stucco and pebbledash, bring on the crenellations and machicolations.

France, land of contrasts . . .

Because they were tickling him and it felt good, his navigator's unruly locks get him back on course: 'Zounds, m'lad! Charge! Straight to the dungeon!'

Yes, but the problem was, that there was no château . . . The centuries-old avenue ended in the middle of a huge meadow, only partially mown.

'You have to turn that way . . .'

They followed a little stream (the former moat?) for a hundred metres or more, then a cluster of roofs, more or less collapsed (but mostly more) came into view among the trees.

So we're headed for the former outbuildings, then . . .

He felt better.

'And now you stop here, because that bridge, it might fall down . . .'

'Oh?'

'Yeah, and it's really really dangerous,' he added, with relish.

'I see . . .'

He pulled over next to an ageless Volvo estate car splattered with mud. The tailgate was open and two mutts were snoozing in the boot.

'That one's called "Ergli" and that one's "Eedyuss".'

Tails began to wag, stirring up dustclouds from hay.

'They are really ugly, aren't they?'

'Yes but it's on purpose,' his mini-guide assured him, 'every year they go to the pound and they ask the man there to give them the ugliest dog of all . . .'

'Oh, really? Whatever for?'

'Well, um . . . to get it out of there, that's why!'

'Yes, but . . . How many do they have altogether?'

'I don't know . . .'

I see, thought Charles ironically, so we're nowhere near the residence of Godefroy de Bouillon, but in some refuge for neo-hippies of the back to Nature variety.

God help us.

'And do they have goats, too?'

'Yes.'

'I knew it! And the baroness, does she smoke grass?'

'Hey . . . you're really silly, y'know. She eats grass, you mean.'

'She's a cow?'

'A pony.'

'And what about fat Victoria?'

'No. She used to be a queen, I think.'

Help.

After that Charles kept quiet. Stuffed his snide thoughts in his pocket and placed his disgusting handkerchief on top of them.

The place was beautiful . . .

Yet this was something he already knew: that the people who lived in outbuildings – the 'common folk' if you like – were always more touching than their masters . . . He could think of dozens of examples . . . But he wasn't trying any more, he wasn't even thinking, he was admiring.

The bridge should have made him realize right away. The way the stones were arranged, the elegant approach, the pebbles, the guardrail, the pillars.

And the courtyard beyond . . . it was called a 'closed' courtyard but it was full of grace . . . These buildings . . . Their proportions . . . The impression of safety, invulnerability, even though everything was crumbling . . .

A dozen or so bicycles had been abandoned along the way and hens were pecking between the sprockets. There were even some geese and, above all, an astonishing duck. How could he describe it . . . almost vertical . . . As if it were standing on the tips of its . . . feet.

'You coming?' urged Lucas.

'What an odd duck, eh?'

'Which one? Him? And he can run really fast, you'll see.'

'But what is it? Is he some sort of cross with a penguin?'

'I don't know . . . they call him the Indian . . . And when he's with the rest of his family, they always walk one behind the other, it's really funny . . .'

'In Indian file, you mean?'

'Are you coming?'

Charles was startled once again: 'And what's that thing, there?'

'That's the lawnmower.'

'But it's — it's a llama!'

'Don't start petting it because if you do it will follow you every-where and you won't be able to get rid of it.'

'Does he spit?'

'Sometimes . . . And his spit doesn't come from his mouth but from his stomach, and it stiiiinks . . .'

'Tell me something, Lucas, this place . . . What is it exactly? Is it some sort of circus?'

'Oh, yes!' he laughed, 'you c'n say that again! That's why Mummy, well, she —'

'She doesn't like you coming here.'

'Not every day, no. Are you coming?'

The door was collapsing beneath a riot of . . . vegetation (Charles knew nothing about botany either), vines and roses, right, that much he knew, but also some sort of bright orange climbing things shaped like little trumpets and other incredible purple flowers with a very ornate heart and some . . . stamens (is that what they were?) the likes of which he had never seen, three-dimensional, impossible to draw, and then a profusion of flower pots . . . Everywhere . . . On the windowsills, along the base of the house, crowding in on an old pump or set on wrought iron tables and pedestals.

Cramped and squeezed and piled together, some with labels, even. In every size, from every era, from cast iron Medici pots to old tin cans, by way of buckets that used to house *highly digestible* granules and huge glass jars where long pale roots were visible beneath the *Le Parfait* label.

And then there was pottery . . . Probably made by the chil-dren . . . Ugly, rough, funny; then other pieces, older, unbelievable, an 18th-century basket covered with lichen, or that statue of a faun who was missing a hand (the one for the flute?) but whose other arm was still long enough to hold an entire collection of skipping ropes . . .

Cat bowls, dog bowls, a pressure cooker that had lost its handle, a broken weathervane, a plastic barometer singing the praises of *Sensas* fishing supplies, a bald Barbie doll, some wooden skittles, watering cans from a bygone era, a child's schoolbag covered in dust, a half-eaten bone, an old whip hanging from a rusty nail, a rope with a bell on the end, birds' nests, an empty cage, a shovel, some threadbare brooms, a fire truck, a . . . And in the middle of all this bric-a-brac, two cats.

Imperturbable.

The inner chambers of Ferdinand Cheval's *Palais idéal* . . .

'What are you looking at? Are you coming?'

'Alice's parents . . . do they run a flea market?'

'No they're dead.'

Charles didn't know what to say.

'Are you coming?'

The front door was half open. Charles knocked, then placed his palm against the expanse of warm wood.

No reply.

Lucas had slipped inside. The door handle was warmer still, and Charles held it for a moment before daring to follow.

In the time it took for his pupils to adjust to the change in the light, his senses were dazzled.

The return to Combray.

That smell . . . which he'd forgotten. A smell he thought he had lost. Or couldn't care less about. That he would have scorned; and that was causing him to melt once again. The smell of a chocolate cake cooking in a real kitchen in a real house . . .

No chance to let his mouth water for long, because, as on the threshold a few moments earlier, he could not contain his astonishment.

It was a *substantial* mess, but it left a strange impression. An impression of gentleness, and cheer. Of order . . .

Wellingtons lined up in decreasing size along several metres of terracotta tiles, another profusion of seedlings (cuttings?) in every window in polystyrene boxes or sprouting from former vanilla ice cream tubs, a gigantic fireplace built into the stone itself and topped by a very dark, almost black, wooden mantelpiece, on which lay the bow to a violin, some candles, some walnuts, more nests, a crucifix, an old spotted mirror, some photos, and an astonishing procession of creatures made out of things from the forest: bark, leaves, twigs, acorns, acorn cups, moss, feathers, pine cones, chestnuts, dried berries, tiny bones, shells, burrs, little wings, catkins . . .

Charles was fascinated. *Who* has done all this? he asked into the empty room.

There was an impressive Aga, in sky blue enamel, with its two large domed lids on top and five little doors on the front. Round, soft, warm, inviting you to stroke it . . . A dog lying in front of the stove on a blanket, a sort of old wolf that began to whimper when he saw them, and tried to get to his feet to greet them, or impress them, but then gave up and collapsed on his blanket again with a whine.

And a huge farmhouse table (or was it from a refectory?), lined with chairs no two alike, and the remains of dinner not yet cleared away. Silver cutlery, plates wiped clean, mustard glasses copyright Walt Disney, and ivory napkin rings.

The dishes were a glorious well-used, delicate collection of every imaginable sort of earthenware vessel – bowls, plates and chipped cups. In a recess in the wall was a stone sink, surely not very practical, where a pile of saucepans teetered in a yellowed plastic bowl. Up near the ceiling were baskets, a meat safe with holes in the fly screen, a shelf covered with jam jars, a sort of box almost as long as the table, concave and filled with openings and notches where the history of the spoon through the ages was tranquilly swinging, a fly paper from another century, with its flies who, ignoring their ancestors' sacrifice, were already rubbing their legs together in anticipation of all those delicious cake crumbs . . .

On the walls, which must have been whitewashed at the time of the Hundred Years War, were numerous cracks, a still life, a silent cuckoo clock, the dates and names of children along an invisible height gauge, and shelves which valiantly attempted to restore some order . . . They attested to a life that was more or less contemporary with our own, straining under the weight of packets of spaghetti, rice, cereal, flour, jars of mustard and other familiar brands, in what were known as family sizes.

And then . . . But . . . It was the density, more than anything. The last rays of sunlight on one of the longest days of the year, through a windowpane festooned with spiders' webs.

Like the light of an acacia tree, amber, silent. Full of wax, dust, animal fur and ash . . .

Charles turned around: 'Lucas!'

'Out the way, I have to get her out otherwise she'll pooh everywhere.'

'And what on earth is that?'

'You've never seen a goat?'

'But she's tiny!'

'Yes, but she still does a lot of pooh. Pleeaase get out of the doorway . . .'

'And where's Alice?'

'She's not up there . . . C'mon, let's go and look for them outside. Drat, she got away!'

The pooh-monger had just climbed onto the table and Lucas shrugged never mind, it was no big deal, Yacine would collect the droppings and put them in a sweet tin and take them to school.

'Are you sure? The big dog doesn't seem to like it . . .'

'Yes but he's got no teeth. Are you coming?'

'Don't walk so fast, Lucas, my leg hurts . . .'

'Oh, right, I forgot. Sorry.'

The little lad was truly a marvel. Charles was dying to ask him if he'd known his grandmother, but didn't dare. He didn't dare ask any more questions. He was afraid of spoiling something, of being vulgar, of feeling even more of a dolt on such a disarming planet, out of this world, a place you reached by crossing a bridge on the verge of collapsing, where parents were dead, ducks were vertical, and goats could fit inside bread baskets.

He placed his hand on Lucas's shoulder and followed him towards the setting sun.

They went round the house, and through a meadow of very tall grasses where a narrow path had been mown; the dogs from the boot of the car came to join them, and they could smell the odour of a brushwood fire (something else he had forgotten . . .), and finally could see them in the distance, at the edge of the woods, in a circle, calling to one another, laughing and leaping around the flames.

'Drat, look who's following us.'

'Who?'

'Captain Haddock.'

Charles didn't need to turn around, he knew which beast it must be this time . . .

He chuckled.

Who could he share this with?

Who would believe him?

He'd come as a rat exterminator, to grapple with his childhood and sell it off at last so that he could start getting old without a fuss, and here he was plummeting right back into it, dragging his peg leg behind him, no way round it, ouch . . . llamas are temperamental, aren't they? Yes, he was chuckling, and he would have liked so much for Mathilde to be here . . . Oh fuck . . . It's going to spit, now . . . It's going to spit. I can tell.

'Is it still following us?'

But Lucas wasn't listening any more.

A light show with shadows . . .

A first silhouette turned round, a second waved to them, an umpteenth dog came to greet them, a third figure pointed at them, a fourth, tiny, began running towards the trees, a fifth leapt over the fire, a sixth and seventh applauded, an eighth got ready to follow, and finally a ninth turned round.

Lucas had told the truth: no matter how he squinted and shaped his eyes, Charles could not see a single adult. This worried him . . . There was a smell of burning rubber . . . Wasn't it dangerous, all these trainers skidding over the embers?

Then he stumbled. His little walking stick had just dodged away from him. The last silhouette had turned round, the one with a ponytail, and she leaned over just as Lucas jumped into her open arms.

Ding.

Like a pinball hitting home.

'Hellooo, Mister Spider-Man . . .'

'Why are you always saying Spy-de-Man,' he asked, annoyed, 'in the film it's Spy-*derrr*-Man, I already told you lots of times.'

'Okay, okay . . . Sorry, hello Mister Spy-*derrr*-Man, how's life? Have you come to join in our leap of death contest?'

And she stood up to let him run off again.

I've got it, thought Charles, eureka! Little Lucas had been pulling his leg. The parents weren't dead at all, they'd just gone off somewhere, and the au pair was letting them get up to all sorts of mischief.

This au pair, whom he couldn't see clearly against the light, was clearly not a very sensible creature, but she did have a glorious smile. With a small imperfection. One of her incisors slightly crossing its neighbour.

He slipped into her shadow in order to say hello without being bothered by the light . . . but he was, anyway.

She had lived too much for an au pair, and everything within radius of her smile confirmed as much, made it fact.

Everything.

She blew on a lock of hair to have a better look at him and, pulling a thick leather glove from her hand which she then rubbed against her trousers, she reached out to Charles and filled his palm with sawdust and tiny bits of wood.

'Good evening.'

'Good evening,' he replied, 'I . . . Charles –'

'Delighted, Charles.'

She'd pronounced his name in the English way, rather than the French *Shaarrl*, and hearing his name like that, with such a different emphasis, left him feeling pleasantly flustered.

As if he were someone else. Lighter, more pronounced.

'I'm Kate,' she added.

'I . . . I came with Lucas to –'

He pulled a little sponge bag from his pocket.

'I see,' she said, with a different smile, even more incisive, 'the instrument of torture. So, you're a friend of the Le Mens?'

Charles hesitated. He knew what was customary, but felt it would be pointless trying to give a girl like this the usual chit-chat.

'No.'

'Oh?'

'I used to be . . . of Alexis, I mean, and . . . No, nothing . . . It's an old story.'

'Did you know him when he was a musician?'

'Yes.'

'Right, then I see what you mean . . . When he plays, he's my friend as well . . .'

'Does he play often?'

'No, sadly.'

Silence.

Back to the customary stuff.

'Where are you from? The land of Her Gracious Majesty?'

'Well . . . yes and no. I . . .' She went on, extending her arm, 'I'm from here.'

In her gesture she included the fire, the children, their laughter, the dogs, the horses, the meadows, the woods, the river, Captain Haddock, her hamlet of crumbling roofs, the first diaphanous stars, and even the swallows, which were having a grand time putting the entire heavens between brackets.

'It's a lovely part of the country,' he murmured.

Her smile became dreamy, distant: 'This evening, yes . . .'

Then back to earth: 'Jeff! Roll up your tracksuit bottoms or you'll catch fire!'

'It already smells like roast pork!' someone chimed in.

'Jeff! The *mechoui*! The *mechoui*!' came a loud shout from across the way.

And Jeff, before sprinting off again, knelt to roll up his tracksuit bottoms.

Hey . . . 'lovely part of the country', that was sucking up, thought Charles, but it was her arm you were looking at . . .

Obviously. Have you seen how she's put together? All those muscles along such a slender arm, it's quite astonishing, you have to admit.

Yeah, yeah . . .

Uh . . . Excuse me, but lines and curves are part of my profession, after all . . .

Well, now . . .

A magnificent laugh suddenly knocked Mr Jiminy Crap-Talk straight off his perch.

A flutter beneath a broken rib. Charles turned around very slowly, located the source of the wild chimes and knew that he hadn't come all this way in vain.

'Anouk,' he murmured.

'Sorry?'

'She . . . over there . . .'

'Yes?'

'Is that her?'

'Who, her?'

'The little girl . . . Alexis's daughter . . .'

'Yes.'

It was she. The one who leapt highest, shouted loudest, and whose laugh carried furthest.

The same gaze, same mouth, same forehead, same rakish air.

Same gunpowder. Same wick.

246

'She's beautiful, isn't she?'

Charles nodded. He was overjoyed, in seventh heaven.

For once the rush of emotion made him feel immeasurably happy.

'Yes, beautiful . . . but a right little monkey,' Kate confirmed. 'It isn't over for our friend Alexis yet. For someone who has always been extremely careful to put things back in their case whenever they were falling out, he's going to have a right old time of it . . .'

'Why do you say that?'

'About the case?'

'Yes.'

'I don't know . . . An impression . . .'

'He really never plays any more?'

'He does . . . When he's a bit drunk . . .'

'And does that happen often?'

'Never.'

The famous Jeff went by them again, rubbing his calves. This time it did indeed smell of something charred.

'How did you recognize her? She doesn't really look like him . . .'

'Her grandmother.'

'Granouk?'

'Yes. You – you knew her?'

'No . . . hardly. She came here once with Alexis.'

Charles said nothing.

'I remember . . . We were drinking coffee in the kitchen and at a certain point, on the pretext of putting her cup in the sink, she came and stood behind me and stroked my neck.'

Charles didn't know what to say.

'It's ridiculous but it made me burst into tears. But why am I telling you all this?' She took hold of herself. 'Forgive me.'

'Oh no, please.'

'It was rather a rough time. I expect she knew about . . . *my predicament* . . . You don't really have such a word in French, do you, the shit I was in I suppose you'd say. Then they left, but after they'd gone a few metres the car stopped and she came back up to me.

'"Did you forget something?" I asked.

'"Kate," she murmured, "just don't drink alone."'

Charles was watching the fire.

'Yes . . . Anouk. I remember. Hey! Let the little ones have a go now! Lucas, why don't you come over this way . . . It's not as wide . . . Jeez, if I send him roasted back to his mum, I'll be for the high jump, won't I . . .'

'Speaking of which,' said Charles, 'we'd better get going. They must be waiting for us to start dinner.'

'You're *already* late,' she joked, 'there are people who, even when you're on time, give you the impression that you've kept them waiting . . . I'll walk you back.'

'No, no.'

'Yes, yes!'

Then, calling out to the older children, 'Sam! Jeff! I'm going back to my cakes! Who wants to come and help? You stay by the fire until the end and no more jumping, all right?'

'Yeah, yeah,' bleated the echo.

'I'll come with you,' announced a rather round little boy with olive skin and a head full of curls.

'But . . . you said you wanted to jump, too. Go on. I'll watch you.'

'Um . . .'

'He's scared stiff!' shouted someone to their right. 'Go, Yaya! Go! Work off some of your fat, c'mon!'

The little boy shrugged his shoulders and turned round: 'D'you know Aeschylus?'

'Uh . . .' went Charles, opening his eyes wide, 'is that . . . is that one of the dogs?'

'No, he was a Greek who wrote tragedies.'

'Ah! That shows how much I know . . .' laughed Charles, 'well, I know him vaguely, sort of . . .'

'And do you know how he died?'

Silence.

'Well, eagles, when they want to eat a tortoise, they have to drop it from very high up to break it open, and since Aeschylus was bald, the eagle thought he was a rock and boom! dropped its tortoise on his head and that was that.'

Why is he telling me this story? I've got a little bit of the stuff left on my head, haven't I?

'Charles,' she said, coming to his rescue, 'let me introduce Yacine . . . commonly known as Wiki. For Wikipedia. If you need

248

some information, or someone's biography, or you're curious to know how many baths Louis XVI took in his life, he's your man.'

'How many?' asked Charles, squeezing the little outstretched hand.

'Hello, forty, when's your birthday? November 4th?'

'Do you know the entire calendar by heart?'

'No, but November 4th is a *very* important date.'

'Your birthday?'

Slight. A child's very slight disdain.

'Rather that of metres and kilos, I'd say. 4 November 1800, official date of the transition in France to the decimal system of weights and measures.'

Charles looked at Kate.

'Yes . . . It's a bit wearing at times, but you eventually get used to it. Right. Let's get going. And Nedra? Has she disappeared?'

He pointed in the direction of the trees: 'I think that . . .'

'Oh no,' she went, woeful. 'Poor thing. Hattie! Come over here a minute!'

She walked away with another girl and murmured something in her ear before sending her into the foliage.

Charles glanced at Yacine questioningly, but the boy pretended not to understand.

She came back and bent down to pick up –

'Leave it, leave it,' said Charles, bending down in turn.

Okay. He was *almost* bald, and *almost* an ignoramus but never, ever would he let a woman walk by his side carrying a heavy load.

Nor would he ever have suspected this thing could be so heavy. He stood up straight, turned his head to one side to hide his wincing, and walked on with a, um, casual stride, gritting his teeth.

Oh, fuck . . . Yet he'd done his share of schlepping girls' things around in his life. Handbags, shopping bags, coats, boxes, suitcases, blueprints, even files, but a chainsaw, that . . .

He felt his cracked rib spreading, expanding.

He lengthened his stride and made one last effort to appear, er, virile: 'And what's that there behind the wall?'

'A vegetable garden,' she replied.

'That big?'

'It was the kitchen garden for the château.'

'And do you – are you the one who looks after it?'

'Of course. Though it's really René's private kingdom . . . He used to be the farmer.'

Charles could not go on, he was in too much pain. It wasn't so much the weight of the gear, it was his back, his leg, his restless nights . . .

He stole sidelong glances at the woman walking next to him.

Her tanned complexion, her short fingernails, the bits of twig in her hair, her shoulder courtesy of Michelangelo, the cardigan she'd wrapped around her waist, her worn T-shirt, the traces of sweat on her chest and back – and he felt absolutely pathetic.

'You smell like freshly cut wood . . .'

Smile.

'Really?' she went, bringing her arms back alongside her body, 'you're very gallant.'

'Actually . . . You know why he is called René?'

Phew . . . Trivial Pursuit Junior was aiming his question at her this time.

'No, but you're going to tell me.'

'Because his mother had another boy before him who died almost right away, so he was Re-né, Re-born. Same root as in Renaissance and renascent and –'

Charles had got ahead of them, to be able to offload his burden more quickly, but he could hear her murmur, 'And you, Yacine? Do you know why I adore you?'

A sound of birds.

'Because you know things that even the Internet will never know . . .'

He thought he would not make it, changed hands, that was even worse, felt huge drops of sweat pouring off him, scrambled the last few yards and ended up leaving the thing outside the door of the first barn he saw.

'Perfect. I have to take the chain off, anyway.'

Oh?

Blimey.

He pulled out his handkerchief to hide his agony.

Fucking hell, what he had just done, he'd be willing to swear that not even Hercules could have done it. Right . . . and now where was Lucas?

She walked with them back to the other side.

Charles would have had a ton of things to say to her, but the bridge was too fragile. Something like, 'I was very happy to make your acquaintance' seemed out of place. He was not really acquainted with anything other than her smile and her calloused hand. Yes, but . . . What else could you say in circumstances like these? He was hunting round desperately, and found . . . his keys.

He opened the rear door and turned round.

'I would have been very happy to make your acquaintance,' she said, simply.

'I . . .'

'You're all messed up.'

'Sorry?'

'Your face.'

'Oh, I . . . I wasn't concentrating.'

'Oh?'

'Me too. I mean, I would have been happy . . .'

By the time they'd passed the fourth oak tree, he managed to come out with a sentence that made sense, after a fashion.

'Lucas?'

'Yes?'

'Is Kate married?'

3

'Well? You took your time!'

'It's 'cause they were right down the other end of the meadow,' explained the little boy.

'What did I tell you,' she scowled, 'come on then . . . let's have dinner . . . I've still got three buttons to sew on.'

The terrace was tiled, the tablecloth was the kind with protect-ive spot-proofing, and the barbecue ran on gas. Charles was shown to a white plastic chair, and sat down on a flowered cushion.

In short, it was bucolic.

The first quarter of an hour lasted an age.

'Penelope' was in a mood, Alexis didn't know what to do, and our hero was lost in thought.

He was looking at this face that he had grown up with; he had watched it play, suffer, love, promise, and lie, he had seen it grow handsome then gaunt, then finally twist and vanish, and he was fascinated.

'Why are you looking at me like that? Have I aged that much?'

'No . . . I was telling myself the opposite, in fact. You haven't changed.'

Alexis reached over with the wine bottle: 'I don't know whether I ought to take that as a compliment . . .'

She sighed. 'Oh, please. You're not going to start with the old comrades-in-arms routine, are you?'

'Yes,' replied Charles, looking her straight in the eye, 'you can take it as a compliment.' Then, turning to Lucas, 'You know that your dad was smaller than you are when I met him?'

'Is that true, Daddy?'

'It's true . . .'

'Alex, it's burning, you know.'

She was perfect. Charles wondered if he'd tell Claire about

252

this evening. No, probably not. Although . . . Alexis in Quechua shorts with his well-starched 'I'm the Chef' apron: it might help her to swallow the myth.

'And he was the greatest marbles champion of all time.'

'Is that right, Daddy?'

'I don't remember.'

Charles winked at Lucas to confirm that it was true.

'And did you have the same teacher?'

'Of course.'

'So, you knew Granouk, too –'

'Lucas,' she interrupted, 'eat your dinner, now! It's getting cold.'

'Yes, I knew her very well. And I thought that my friend Alexis was very lucky to have her for a mother. I thought she was beautiful, and kind, and we always seemed to be laughing when we were with her.'

As he said these words, Charles knew he had said all he would say, that he would go no further. To let her know as much, and reassure her, he turned to the lady of the house, gave her a charming smile, and switched to two-faced bastard mode: 'There . . . That's enough talk about the past. The salad is delicious. And so you, Corinne . . . what do you do in life?'

She hesitated for a second and then decided to leave her pincushion behind. It was actually rather nice to be questioned in this way by an elegant man, who didn't roll up his shirtsleeves, who had a nice watch, and who lived in Paris.

She talked about herself, and he went along with it by drinking more than was strictly necessary.

To stay the course.

He didn't hear all of it, but gathered she worked in human resources (as she said these last two words, she probably misjudged the nature of her guest's smile), in a branch office of France Telecom, and her parents lived in the area, and her father had a small business in cold rooms and cold storage for industrial catering, and times were hard, there was a chill in the air, and there were a lot of Chinese about.

'And you, Alexis?'

'Me? I've been working a lot with the father-in-law! Commercial stuff . . . What's wrong? Did I say something?'

Silence.

'It's the wine? It's corked, is that it?'

'No, but I . . . You . . . I thought you were a music teacher or, uh . . . I don't know . . .'

At that very moment, because of his slight grimace, his hand swatting at a – shall we say – mosquito, and because of the 'Chef' on his apron that had disappeared under the table, Charles saw at last, on the forehead of the local rep in fast freezing units, the twenty-five years of distance between them.

'Oh,' he said, 'music . . .'

Implying what an easy lay *that* had been; just a passing fling.

A nasty bout of acne.

'What did I say?' he asked again anxiously. 'Did I say something stupid?'

Charles put down his glass, forgot the roller for the awning above his head, and the tabletop rubbish bin that matched the tablecloth, and the scold who matched the tabletop rubbish bin: 'Of course you did. And you know it perfectly well. In all those years we spent together, every time you had something important to say, I remember, *every time*, you would use music . . . And when you didn't have an instrument you'd invent one, when you started at the Conservatory you finally became a good student, whenever you auditioned, you blew them away, when you were sad you'd play happy stuff, when you were happy you made us all cry, when Anouk sang it was Broadway numbers, when my mother made crêpes for us, you'd get out your bloody *Ave Maria*, when Nana was down you'd –'

He didn't manage to finish his sentence.

'It's past, Balanda. Everything you've just said there is in the past tense.'

'Exactly,' said Charles in a still more neutral voice, 'yes. You're right. That's the best way to put it. Thanks for the grammar lesson.'

'Look. Why don't you wait until Lucas and I have gone to bed before you start showing each other your scars, all right?'

Charles lit a cigarette.

She stood up at once and started clearing their plates. 'And who is this Nana, anyway?'

'He never told you about Nana?' asked Charles, startled.

'No, but he told me a lot of other things, you know . . . And your crêpes and your so-called happiness, well, excuse me, but I –'

'Stop,' said Alexis curtly, 'that's enough, now. Charles . . .' His voice grew softer. 'You're missing a few episodes, you realize that, don't you . . . and I hardly have to explain to you that you're on shaky ground with a theory that's missing some basic calculations.'

'No, of course not. Sorry.'

Silence.

He put together a sort of ashtray with a piece of aluminium foil and added, 'So what about the fridges, then? How're tricks?'

'What a jerk you can be . . .'

Said with a lovely smile, which Charles gladly returned to him.

Then they talked about other things. Alexis complained about a crack in the stairwell, and the expert promised to go and take a look.

Lucas came to kiss them goodnight.

'And the bird?'

'He's still sleeping.'

'When will he wake up?'

Charles turned up his palms to show his ignorance.

'And will you still be here tomorrow?'

'Of course he'll still be here,' insisted his father. 'Right . . . off to bed now. Mummy's waiting.'

'Will you come and see me in my show at school then?'

'You have lovely children.'

'Yes . . . And Marion? Did you see her?'

'Absolutely . . . I saw her,' murmured Charles.

Silence.

'Alexis . . .'

'No. Don't say anything. You know, if Corinne behaves that way with you, you mustn't hold it against her. She's the one who's had to do all the dirty work, and . . . And I expect that everything from my past frightens her. Do – d'you understand?'

'Yes,' replied Charles, who didn't understand at all.

'Without her, I'd never have made it out of there and . . .'

'And?'

'It's hard to explain, but I got the impression that in order to get out of hell, I had to leave the music behind. A sort of pact, or something.'

'So you never play any more?'

'I do . . . Bits of rubbish now and again . . . For their show, tomorrow, for example, I'll accompany them on the guitar, but as for really playing . . . No.'

'I can't believe it.'

'It's . . . It makes me fragile. I don't want that feeling of withdrawal, ever again, and music gives me that feeling . . . It sucks me in . . .'

'Any news from your father?'

'Never. And you? Tell me . . . Do you have kids?'

'No.'

'Are you married?'

'No.'

Silence.

'And Claire?'

'Claire isn't either.'

Corinne had just come back in with the pudding.

★

'Will this be okay?'

'It's perfect,' replied Charles. 'Are you sure I'm not a nuisance?'

'Hey, c'mon on . . .'

'I'll be leaving really early, anyway. May I take a shower?'

'It's through there.'

'You wouldn't have a T-shirt you could lend me?'

'Even better.'

Alexis came back holding out an old Lacoste polo shirt.

'You remember?'

'No.'

'And yet I nicked it from you.'

Among other things . . . mused Charles, thanking him.

He was careful not to pull off his plasters and then he felt himself liquefy. And let the water run.

He wiped the mirror with the corner of his towel so he could see himself more clearly.

He pushed his lips forward.

He thought he looked a bit like a llama.

All messed up.

That's what she'd said.

Leaning outside to close the shutters he saw that Alexis was sitting alone with a glass in his hand on one of the steps to the terrace. He pulled his trousers back on and grabbed his packet of cigarettes.

And the bottle, in passing.

Alexis moved over to make room: 'Have you seen the sky? All these stars . . .'

Charles didn't know what to say.

'And in a few hours, it will be daylight again.'

Silence.

'Why did you come, Charles?'

'Grief work.'

'What was it I used to play for Nana? I don't remember . . .'

'It used to depend on how he was disguised . . . When he put on his ridiculous raincoat . . .'

'I know! *The Pink Panther* . . . Mancini . . .'

'When he was taking his shower and you saw him bare his hairy chest, you'd play some sort of arrival of the gladiators in the arena thing.'

'Do . . . Do-soh,' trumpeted Alexis.

'When he wore his lederhosen . . . The ones with the acorns embroidered on the flap in front, God what a laugh, you did this little Bavarian polka.'

'Lohman.'

'When he tried to force us to do our homework, you'd get out *Bridge on the River Kwai*.'

'He loved that one. He'd put his stick under his arm, and there he'd be, in it completely.'

'When he managed to tweak a hair out of his ear on the first go, it was *Aida* . . .'

'Exactly. The *Triumphal March*.'

'When he'd piss us off you'd do an ambulance siren as if to take him off to the hospice. When we'd done something stupid and to punish us he'd lock us in your room until Anouk got home, then you'd wail something by Miles Davis through the keyhole . . .'

'*Elevator to the Gallows*?'

'Exactly. When he chased us into the bath, you'd climb onto the table and it was the *Sabre Dance*.'

'That one used to kill me, I remember. Fuck, the number of times I almost passed out . . .'

'When we wanted some sweets, you'd flog him your Gounod bonbons . . .'

'Or Schubert . . . It depended on how many sweets we wanted. When he'd do his rotten little act on us, I'd give him the *Radetsky March*.'

'I don't remember that one.'

'Yes, go on –'

He umpah-pahed some Strauss.

Charles smiled.

'But the thing he liked best of all –'

'Was this –' continued Alexis, whistling.

'Yes! Then we could get whatever we wanted. He'd even imitate my dad's signature.'

'*La Strada*.'

'You remember . . . He took us to see it, on the Rue de Rennes.'

'And we were in a foul mood all day long.'

'That's right. We didn't get it. The way he'd described it, it should have been *Rookies Run Amok*.'

'We were so disappointed.'

'We were so clueless.'

'You seemed surprised earlier on . . . but who else can I talk to about him? Who have you talked to about him?'

'No one.'

'You see . . . Someone like Nana . . . it's not something you can begin to describe,' added Alexis, clearing his throat, 'you had to – you had to be there.'

An owl protested. What's going on? We can't hear ourselves out here in the dark!

'You know why I didn't let you know?'

Charles said nothing.

'The funeral . . .'

'Because you're a piece of shit.'

'No. Yes . . . No. Because I wanted to have her all to myself for once.'

Charles was silent.

'From day one, Charles, I . . . I was so jealous I thought I'd die . . . And in fact I —'

'Go on, tell me. I'd be interested to know why you became such a fucked-up junkie because of me. Good excuses based on bad faith have always fascinated me.'

'That's just how I remember you. You and your high-sounding words.'

'That's funny, I'd always got the impression that you didn't really see all that much of your mother . . . That she'd felt somewhat alone towards the end . . .'

'I phoned her.'

'Great. Right . . . I'm going to bed. I'm so tired I'm not even sure I'll be able to fall asleep.'

'You only saw her good side. When we were kids, she used to make you laugh, but I'm the one who had to clean the bog and carry her to bed . . .'

'Sometimes we cleaned it together . . .' murmured Charles.

'She was always on about you. How you were so clever, so talented, so interesting . . .'

Charles stood up.

'See what a good mate I am, Alexis Le Men . . . What a marvellous little boy I was — and I'm going to the trouble to remind you, so that some day you'll move up a gear and tell your kids how an old trannie made us piss our pants laughing when he'd imitate Fred Astaire drunk in the gutters at school — this marvellous little boy dropped her a hell of a lot sooner than you did, dropped her like a piece of shit, without a *single* telephone call, not one . . . And he probably wouldn't have come to her funeral even if you'd been magnanimous enough to let him know, because all that cleverness and talent and hard work made him very very busy and bloody fucking stupid. On that note, goodnight.'

Alexis followed him in: 'So you know what it's like.'

'What what's like?'

'To leave things behind when you hit bottom.'

Charles looked at him questioningly.

'To sacrifice bits of people's lives so you can climb back up again.'

'Sacrifice . . . bits of people's lives . . . You're not too bad at rhetoric for an ice-lolly vendor,' scoffed Charles, 'but we didn't sacrifice a thing! We were just cowards . . . Oh, I know, it doesn't sound as smart, does it, coward? Not as high-sounding, is it?' He placed his thumb close to his index finger: 'A really narrow mouthpiece, is that it? Teeny, tiny, narrow . . .'

Alexis shook his head.

'Flagellation. You've always gone in for that stuff. Well, you did spend time with the Brothers, didn't you. I'd forgotten about that. You know the big difference between the two of us?'

'Yes,' said Charles emphatically, 'I do know. It's Ssssufffering. With a capital S as in syringe, make a note, it could come in handy. What do you expect me to say to that?'

'The difference is that you were brought up by people who believed in a whole lot of things, whereas I grew up with a woman who believed in nothing.'

'She believe in li—'

Charles immediately regretted what he'd been about to say. Too late:

'Sure. Just look what she made of it.'

'Alex. I understand. I understand that you need to talk about it. And for sure, the scene's been rehearsed over and over. I even wonder if that isn't why you sent me that friendly announcement last winter . . . To offload on me everything you can't go and leave in the basement any more . . .

'But I'm the wrong person, don't you see? I have . . . I've got too much invested in this business. I can't help you. It's not that I don't want to, it's that I *can't*. At least you've had kids, at least – whereas I, I . . . I'm going to bed. Please give my regards to madame your redeemer.'

He opened the door to his room. 'One last thing . . . Why didn't you donate her body to science the way she made you promise you would?'

'That bloody hospital? Don't you think she gave them –'

The machine jammed.

Alexis fell backwards and slid to the floor.

'What have I done, Charlie?' He burst into tears. 'Tell me what I've done.'

Charles couldn't bend over, let alone get down on his knees.

He touched his shoulder.

'Stop it . . . I'm full of shit too . . . If she had really wanted to, she would have left you a letter.'

'She did.'

Pain, signal, survival, promise. Charles withdrew his hand.

Alexis moved to one side, dug around for his wallet, took out a white sheet folded in four, shook it out, and cleared his throat: '*My love*,' he began.

He had started weeping again, and handed the letter to Charles.

Charles, who didn't have his glasses, took a step back into the light from the bedroom.

It was pointless.

There was nothing else.

He let out a very long, very deep sigh.

To shift his pain.

'You see, she did believe in something . . . You know,' he said in a more cheerful tone of voice, 'I'd like to be able to give you my hand to pull you up, but the thing is, I got run over this morning, would you believe.'

'Bloody idiot,' said Alexis with a smile, 'you've always got to be better than everyone else.' He caught hold of Charles's jacket and hoisted himself up, folded his letter and went off imitating Nana's shrill voice: '*C'mon, ducks! Shoo! Bedtime!*'

Charles staggered to his bed, fell onto it in a heap, ouch, and thought that he had just lived the longest day of his . . .

And was already asleep.

4

Now where was he?

Whose sheets were these? Which hotel?

The truly scary leafy design of the curtains roused him with a start. Ah, yes. The Clos des Ormes . . .

Not a sound. He looked at his watch and at first he thought he was holding it upside down.

Eleven fifteen.

The first lie-in of the century.

There was a note outside the bedroom door: 'We didn't dare wake you. If you don't have time to come by the school (opposite the church), leave the key with the neighbour (green gate). Hugs.'

He admired the wallpaper in the bathroom and the loo paper which matched the flowers on the Liberty print, heated up some coffee, and groaned at his reflection in the bathroom mirror.

The llama had taken on some colour during the night . . . A pretty shade of mauve tending towards a greenish hue . . . He didn't have the courage to spit in his own face, and he borrowed some blades from Alexis.

He shaved what could be shaved, and instantly regretted it. He'd made it even worse.

His shirt stank of rotting flesh. So he put back on his young man's old crocodile and it made him feel oddly happy. Even though it had lost its shape and was very worn, not to mention the fact that the croc's tail had come unstitched and was fairly washed-out, no, not to mention it, he had recognized his shirt. It had been a gift from Edith. From a time when they still gave each other gifts. She had said, I got you a white one, you are *so* conventional, and, almost thirty years later, he was grateful for her bloody-minded principles. The way he looked today, any other colour would have been . . . less becoming.

*

He rang several times at the neighbour's, the one with the green gate, no answer. He didn't dare leave the set of keys with anyone else (fearing Corinne's wrath), so he resigned himself to making a detour past the school.

He was actually somewhat sorry to see Alexis in broad daylight. He would have preferred to leave things on the parting note of the night before, and carry on his way without him . . . But he took consolation in the fact that he'd be able to give Lucas a hug, and little maid Marion too, before losing sight of them altogether.

Opposite the church, well, perhaps, but it was the most secular school you've ever seen.

A typical country school, probably built in the 1930s, the boys symmetrical to the girls, or so it was decreed and carved in stone under the intertwined letters R and F of the République Française with a real covered playground whose walls had been repainted wagon green to the height any scuff marks might reach, the height of the white chalk marks round the chestnut trees. Permanent hopscotch grids (surely not nearly as much fun) and bulges in the asphalt, which must have been the delight of kids shooting marbles . . .

A very fine building, with brick trim: tall, stern, and *républicain*, despite all the balloons and other lanterns with which it had been decked out that day.

Charles elbowed his way through the crowd, arms raised to avoid the swarms of children running every which way. After the chocolate cake and the smell of a wood fire, he was rediscovering the atmosphere of Mathilde's school fairs. With a rather more rural touch . . . Little old grandpas in caps and grannies in thick stockings had replaced the elegant ladies of Paris's 5th arrondissement, and gone was the organic sandwich stand, replaced by a real suckling pig roasting on a spit.

The weather was fine, he had slept over ten hours, the music was lively and his mobile battery was dead. He put it back into his pocket, leaned against a wall and, snuggled between the aroma of candy floss and roasting piglet, he let himself be dazzled by the show.

It was Tati's *Jour de fête* . . .

All that was missing was the postman.

A woman was handing him a cup. He thanked her with a simple nod of his head, as if he were a stranger, too disoriented to recall the very basics of the language; he took a swallow of the potion . . . hard to say what it was, a dry, rough drink; he turned his sores towards the sun, closed his eyes, and silently thanked Alexis's neighbour for having vanished the way she did.

The heat, the alcohol, the sugar, the local accent, the children's cries, his head beginning to nod gent—

'Are you asleep *again?*'

No need to open his eyes to recognize the voice of his superpower team mate.

'No. I'm getting a suntan.'

'Well, if y'ask me you'd better stop, because you're all red already!'

He looked down: 'What's this? You're disguised as a pirate?'

A nod from beneath the black headband.

'And you haven't got a parrot on your shoulder?'

Lucas lowered his hook: 'Uh, no . . .'

'Would you like us to go and get my bird?'

'But what if it wakes up?'

Although he owed part of his upbringing to Nana – or perhaps for that very reason – Charles had always thought it was simpler to tell children the truth. He didn't have many principles where child-raising was concerned, but where the truth was concerned, he did. Telling the truth had never restrained the imagination. Quite the opposite.

'You know something. He can't wake up, because he's stuffed.'

Lucas's moustache stretched from one earring to the other. 'I knew it! But I didn't want to tell you. I was afraid you might be sad . . .'

Whose great idea was it to invent children? Whose? He melted, wedging his cup behind a tile.

'C'mon. Let's go and find it.'

'Okay, but . . .' said the little boy hesitantly, 'he's not really a parrot.'

'Yes, but . . .' proclaimed the grown-up boldly, 'you're not really a pirate, either.'

On the way back they stopped off at the Rendez-vous des Chasseurs, which was also a grocery, a gunsmith's, a branch of the Crédit Agricole and, on Thursday afternoons, a hairdresser's, and there they bought a ball of string. Charles, gingerly bending outside the church, moored Mistinguett tightly to her new perch before sending her back out on stage.

'And where are your parents?'

'I don't know.'

Lucas was enchanted, and went back to join his classmates, as though walking on eggs.

He was talking to her already: 'Polly? Can you say, Polly want a cracker?'

Charles went back to his wall. He'd wait until after Lucas had finished his sketch before heading back to Paris . . .

A little girl brought him a plateful of something piping hot.

'Oh, thank you . . . That's sweet of you . . .'

Farther along, behind a huge table, the same woman as before, the one with the imposing bosom, was sending a volley of polite banter his way.

Oops. He'd made a hit . . . As quickly as he could he went back to his plastic knife and fork and with a laugh turned all his concentration upon his piece of grilled ham.

He had just remembered Madame Canut's washing line.

'I swear it's her bra,' Alexis had said, for the umpteenth time.

'How can you be so sure?'

'Well . . . you can see it.'

It was . . . fascinating.

On stage there was some commotion. Grandmothers were being led one tiny step at a time to the best seats, while the sound system blared, One, two, can you hear me? There's feedback, Jean-Pierre, please, we need a technician, put your glass down now, one two, is everyone here? Hello everybody, take your seats, let me remind you that the draw for the tombola . . . feedback, Jean-Pierre! For Chri— click.

Right.

Mums on their knees checked the children's hair and make-up, while dads fiddled with their videocams. Charles came upon Corinne deep in conversation with two other ladies, a problem about a jacket that had apparently been stolen, and he handed her the key ring.

'Did you remember to close the gate as well?'

Yes. He had remembered. He praised her marvellous hospitality, and moved on. As far away as possible.

He found a place in the sun, pulled a chair over on the court-yard side so that he could slip away discreetly between two sketches, stretched out his legs and, his break almost over, turned his thoughts once again to his work. He pulled out his diary, checked his appoint-ments for the week, decided which files he'd take with him to Roissy and began to draw up a . . .

A sudden commotion to the left made him lose his concentration for a second. If that. A graceful to and fro between retina and cortex. Just time enough to realize that there were also some very sexy mums at the Les Marzeray primary school . . . list of phone calls to make, need to check with Philippe about this business with the –

He looked up again.

She was smiling at him.

'Hullo,' she said, in English.

Charles dropped his diary, stepped on it as he extended his hand and, in the time it took for him to pick it up, she'd moved over to sit next to him. Well, not quite, she'd left one empty chair between the two of them.

As a sort of chaperone?

'Sorry. I didn't recognize you.'

'It's because I'm not wearing my wellies . . .' she joked.

'Yes. That must be it.'

She was wearing a wraparound dress that criss-crossed her heart, cinched her waist, and gave her thighs a lovely shape, as well as revealing her knees whenever she crossed or uncrossed her legs and pulled on the grey-blue fabric flecked with hosts of little turquoise arabesques.

Charles liked fashion. The cut, the material, design, finishings – he had always found that architects and clothing designers performed the same work, more or less, and now he observed the way in which the arabesques went about following the curve of the sleeve without losing the thread of their scrolling pattern.

She could sense he was looking at her. She winced:

'I know . . . I oughtn't to have worn it . . . I've put on a lot of weight since . . .'

'No, not at all!' he protested, 'not at all. I was thinking about your –'

'My what?' She still had him on the grill; now she turned him over.

'Your . . . your *motif.*'

'My *motif.* My God . . . well, so long as you can't see my motives.'

Charles looked down with a smile. A woman who knew how to dismantle a chainsaw, could let you get a glimpse of a pale pink bra when she leaned forward, and knew how to play with two languages – no point him even trying to compete.

He felt, oh woe, that it was now her turn to scrutinize him.

'Did you sleep under a rainbow?'

'Yes . . . with Judy Garland.'

What a smile she had . . .

'You see, that's what I miss the most, living here . . .' she sighed.

'Musical comedies?'

'No . . . This sort of idiotic repartee . . . Because,' she added, more solemnly, 'that's what solitude is all about . . . It's not the getting dark at five o'clock, or the animals to feed and the children squabbling all day long, it's . . . Judy Garland.'

'Well,' he said, and continued in English, 'to tell you the truth, I feel more like the Tin Man right now . . .'

'I knew you must speak English,' she said.

'Not well enough to "see your . . . motives", unfortunately . . .'

Her turn to say sharply, 'So much the better.'

'But you?' he added, 'which is your mother tongue?'

'Mother tongue? French, because my mother was born in Nantes. Native language? English. On my father's side.'

'And where did you grow up?'

He could not hear her reply because Super DJ was once again in charge: 'Hello to everyone then, and thank you all for such a good turn-out. The show is about to begin. Yes, indeed . . . The children are all wound up and ready to go . . . Let me remind you, you still have time to buy your tickets for our big tombola. Lots of fa-bu-lous prizes to win this year!

'First prize, a romantic weekend for two in a three-star self-catering cottage on Lake Charmièges with . . . Wait for it . . . pedalos, a playground for boules, and a giant karaoke!

'Second prize, a Toshiba DVD player graciously offered by Duddle and Company, and we'd like to take this opportunity to thank them – with Duddle, no muddle! And let's not forget –'

Charles had put his finger on the uppermost sticking plaster. He could tell it would come off if he went on laughing like an idiot.

'– the numerous gift baskets offered by Graton and Sons, located at 3, Rue du Lavoir in Saint-Gobertin, a butcher's shop specializing in pig's trotters and blood pudding, weddings, funerals, and communions, over a dozen consolation prizes because not everyone has the good fortune to be a cuckold, isn't that right, Jean-Pierre? Ha, ha! All right, all right . . . Time for our performers now, so please let's have a big hand – louder than that, come on! Jacqueline, you're wanted at the welcome booth . . . Have a nice day, every—' And again, click.

Jean-Pierre had no sense of humour.

Alexis, accompanied by one of the best pupils in the class, with her ribbons and her clarinet, took his seat to the rear of the stage, while the teachers placed the tiny tots disguised as fish in the midst of the cardboard waves. The music set them to swaying, and the kids all fell out of step. They were far too busy waving to their mummies to keep the rhythm of the waves.

Charles glanced at Kate's thi— – no, sorry, the programme on her lap: *The Revenge of the Pirate of the Caribbean.*

Well, well.

He saw, too, that she was no longer trying to be clever, that her eyes were shining more than was reasonable, so he looked up at the stage to see which of those little sardines could be getting her into such a state.

'Is one of yours up there?'

'Not even,' she said, choking on her laughter, 'but I always find it so moving, these little sketches they put together on a shoe-string . . . It's silly, isn't it?'

She had placed her hands together on either side of her nose to hide from him and, when she realized he was still staring at her, she grew even more confused.

'Oh . . . don't look at my hands. They're all –'

'I'm not. I was admiring your signet ring.'

'Oh?' She took a deep breath and turned her palm over, as if astonished to see it was still there.

'It's magnificent.'

'Isn't it? And very old. A gift from my . . . Right,' she whispered, pointing to the waves, 'I'll tell you the rest later on.'

'I'm counting on it,' murmured Charles, even more quietly.

He watched the rest of the show reflected on Alexis's face.

Lucas and his band of pirates had just come aboard, singing their disillusioned air:

> 'We're as fierce and as cruel as they come
> So why are we here on this leaky drum?
> We swab the decks and wash the dishes
> Enough now captain, we're off with the fishes!
> Scrubbing copper and dumping rubbish
> Captain, do ye hear us there below?
> Find us a frigate or a good cargo,
> Captain, that's why we signed up
> Give us our rum and a good punch-up!'

Alexis, concentrating on his guitar, didn't notice a thing at first.

Then he sat up, smiled at the audience, located his son, and went back to his chords.

No.

And looked again.

Squinted, missed two or three chords, looked again, opened his eyes wider, and played whatever he could manage. But it didn't matter. Who would hear, anyway, beneath the raging of the freebooters? Rum and a good punch-up-up-up! they shouted in every imaginable key, before disappearing behind the mains'l.

A cannon thundered, and they reappeared armed to the teeth. Another song, other notes, Mistinguett was having a grand old time and Alexis was all over the place.

Finally he relaxed his visual grip on his son's shoulder and swivelled his eyes to look for the explanation elsewhere, in the audience.

After much diligent searching he eventually lighted upon his old comrade's mocking smile. The one who'd finally understood that it was not as hard as it looked, to read a person's lips if you're hard of hearing . . .

He pointed to Lucas with his chin: *Is that her?*

Charles nodded.

But . . . how did you . . .

With a smile, he pointed heavenward with his index finger.

Alexis shook his head, looked down, and didn't look up again until the booty was being divvied up.

Charles took advantage of the applause to slip away. He had no desire to hear the plangent sobbing of violins.

Mission accomplished.

Time to go back to real life.

He was heading out of the school gates when a very English '*Hey!*' caught up with him. He put his cigarette back in his pocket and turned round.

'Hey, you bloody liar!' She was shaking her left first at him, 'Why did you say, I'm counting on it, if you don't give a shit?'

She didn't wait for his face to give him away before adding in a more affable voice, 'No . . . sorry. That is really not *at all* what I meant . . . Actually, I wanted to invite you to . . . no . . . forget it . . .' She looked in his eyes and said, even more quietly, 'Are you – are you leaving already?'

Charles did not try to return her gaze.

'Yes, I . . .' he stammered, 'I should have said goodbye, but I didn't want to . . . I didn't want to disturb you.'

'Oh?'

'I hadn't planned on coming. I've been, how can I put it, of a truant disposition, and now I really do need to head back.'

'I see . . .'

With a final smile, one he had not seen before, she loaded, without any real conviction, her most pathetic shot: 'And what about the tombola draw, then?'

'I didn't buy a ticket.'

'Oh, right. Well then. Goodbye . . .'

She reached out her hand. Her ring had slipped round; the stone was cold.

Invite me to what? recalled Charles, but it was too late. She was already beyond reach.

He sighed and watched: fading into the distance, the swing of her arabesques.

★

Looking for his own car, he recognized hers, parked sideways beneath the plane trees opposite the post office.

The boot was still open and the same dogs that had been there the night before greeted him with the same good-natured wagging and panting.

He opened his diary, found the page for 9 August and went over the list of names of towns he'd be driving through.

He drove for half an hour, literally miles away. He looked for a petrol station, found one behind a supermarket, and took absolutely ages to find the bloody fucking piece of shit of a button to release the cover of the fuel tank. He opened the glove compartment, hunted for the instruction manual, got even more noisily angry, found it, filled the tank, used the wrong card, then the wrong pin, gave up, paid cash and went three times round the roundabout before he could read the spidery scrawl in his diary.

He switched on the radio, then switched it off. He lit a cigarette, then crushed it. Shook his head, and regretted it: it merely brought on one of his headaches. He finally found the signpost he'd been waiting for. He stopped at the white line, looked to the left, looked to the right, looked straight ahead and . . .

. . . indulged in some verb conjugation:

'I am one bleeding idiot. You are one bleeding idiot. He is one bleeding idiot!'

5

She was busy fumbling for something in her apron pocket.

'Yes?'

'Hello, uh . . . I'd like a slice of that chocolate cake that was cooking in your oven last night at around quarter to nine . . .'

She raised her head.

'Well, yes,' he continued, shaking a handful of tombola counter-foils, 'after all . . . The playground for boules *and* the giant karaoke . . . I had second thoughts . . .'

It took her several seconds to react: she frowned and bit her lip to keep from smiling.

'There were three.'

'Sorry?'

'Cakes . . . in the oven.'

'Oh?'

'Yes,' she retorted, still just as tight-lipped, 'as it happens, we don't do things by halves in my house.'

'I was under the impression . . .'

'So?'

'Well, uh . . . Perhaps you could give me a little bit of each?'

Without further ado she sliced three tiny portions and handed him a plate: 'Two euros. You can pay the young girl next door.'

'What did you want to invite me to, Kate?'

'Dinner, I think. But I've changed my mind.'

'Oh?'

She was already helping someone else.

'And what if I invite you?'

She stood up straight and gently sent him packing: 'I promised to help them with the tidying up, I have half a dozen kids to keep an eye on, and there's not a restaurant within fifty kilometres, so, apart from that, is it good?'

'Sorry?'

'The cake?'

Uh . . . Charles no longer really felt like it. He was hunting for a heartfelt reply when a fellow came up out of breath and visibly very out of sorts and stole the scene. 'Hey? Wasn't your son supposed to be looking after the Tin Can Alley this afternoon?'

'Yes, but then you asked him to look after the drinks stand.'

'Oh yes, of course. Never mind, I'll ask –'

'Wait a second,' she interrupted, turning to Charles, 'didn't Alexis tell me you're an architect, is that right?'

'Uh . . . yes . . .'

'Right then, that's the perfect stand for you. Making piles of tin cans, that should be right up your alley, no?' Then, calling to the other fellow, 'Gerard! No need to look further!'

In the time it took Charles to devour a mouthful of cake he found himself being led to the far side of the schoolyard.

'Hey!'

Now what . . .

He turned around, wondering what *bloody* thing she could reproach him with this time.

But, it was nothing.

Just a little wink above a huge knife.

★

'For each game, the kids have to give you a blue ticket, they know where to buy them . . . and the winners get to choose a prize from this box over here . . . One of the parents will drop by in the afternoon to fill in for you for a few minutes if you have to take a break,' explained the man, herding to one side the children who were already clustered round. 'Will that be okay? Do you have any questions?'

'No questions.'

'Good luck, then. I always have trouble finding a kind soul to take over this stand – well, you'll see,' and he mimed covering his ears, 'it's a bit noisy . . .'

For the first ten minutes, Charles was quite content to pocket the tickets, hand out the rolled-up socks filled with sand, and put the cans back in place, and then he began to feel more confident,

273

so he did what he had always done: improved the site under construction.

He placed his jacket on a stool and announced the new land use plan:

'Right. Be quiet a minute here, I can't hear a thing. Okay, you – go and fetch me a piece of chalk . . . First of all, no more of this mess here, you're going to make a proper queue and stand one behind the other. The first one who tries to cheat, I'll put him in the middle of the tin cans, is that clear? Thank you.'

He took the piece of chalk, drew two distinct lines on the ground, then a mark on the wooden pole: 'This is the height gauge. Anyone shorter than this mark has the right to step up to the first line, and the others have to stand behind the second one, got it?'

They got it.

'Now then. The little ones have the right to toss the sock at these tins here (pointing to the larger ones, that the cook had given them and that must have once contained ten good kilos of mixed vegetables or peeled tomatoes), and the bigger kids have to knock down these ones here (smaller and far more numerous). You're allowed four socks each, and to win a prize you've got to knock down the whole lot . . . Are you still with me?'

Respectful nodding of heads.

'Finally, I don't want to spend my Saturday picking up your mess, so I need an assistant. Who'd like to be my assistant number one? And don't forget, an assistant is allowed a few free shots . . .'

A struggle was waged to provide him with a second.

'Perfect,' exulted General Balanda, 'perfect. And now . . . may the best one win!'

Now all he had to do was count the points, encouraging the younger kids and provoking the teenagers. Guiding the arms of the little ones, and pretending to lend his glasses to the teenagers if any of them got too big for their boots – maaan! This Tin Can Alley, dead easy – and hit the wall more often than they should have . . .

Fairly quickly a crowd gathered and, with the resulting echo chamber, Charles reckoned that while he may have saved his back, and his honour, by nightfall he would probably be deaf . . .

Speaking of his honour . . . From time to time he looked up and scanned the crowd for her. He would have liked her to see him like this, triumphant among his sharpshooters, but no such luck. She was still among her cakes, chattering, laughing, leaning over to throngs of children who came to hug her and . . . she couldn't care less. About him, so to speak.

If he could even hear himself speak by the day's end . . .

Never mind. He was happy. For the first time in his life he felt he was enjoying his role as project manager, and as for overseeing aluminium buildings, well, that was a first, too.

Jean Prouvé would have been proud of him.

Naturally, no one ever came to fill in for him; naturally, he wanted to have a piss and a smoke and, naturally, he eventually gave up the whole business of blue tickets.

'You've run out?'

'Well, yeah . . .'

'Go on, have a go anyway . . .'

No ticket? The news spread so quickly that he had to abandon any vague desire he might have had for an escape from the stand. He was the Tin Can King, he had made his decision and, for the first time in years, he regretted not having his sketch-book with him. There were a few smiles, a few acts of bravado, a few poses that would have been well worth catching for eternity . . .

Lucas came to see him.

'I gave my parrot to Daddy.'

'That was a good idea.'

'It wasn't a parrot. It was a white pigeon.'

Well, well. Yacine must have been there, too.

He was saved by the tombola. The loudspeaker announced that it was time for the draw, and all the kids vanished as if by magic. Ungrateful wretches, he thought, sighing with relief. He handed his notebook to the boys, collected the socks scattered all over the schoolyard, gathered all the tins into a canvas bag and picked up all the sweet wrappers, wincing each time he had to bend over.

He held his sides.

Why did it hurt so much?

Why?

He grabbed his jacket and looked for a place where he could have a smoke without being caught by the supervisor.

He made a detour via the toilets and found himself . . . in difficulty. The bowl was so low to the ground . . . He took aim as best he could and rediscovered the odour of carbolic soap, the kind that never produced any lather and never went away, clinging in a dry shrivelled lump to its chromed brass knob.

The irresistible pull of nostalgia . . . He hid behind the old building to have a smoke.

Aah . . . That was good.

Even the graffiti had not changed much . . . The same hearts, the same Thingammy + Whatsit = Eternal Luv, the same tits, the same willies and the same enraged lines crossing out the same revealed secrets . . .

He flicked his cigarette butt over the wall and headed back towards the loudspeakers.

He was walking slowly. He didn't really know where to go. He didn't feel like seeing Alexis again. He could hear the rubbish that Jean-Pierre's mate was spouting, and did a mental countdown of the number of hours until he'd reach the outskirts of Paris.

Right. I ought to go and say goodbye to her all the same, this time. *Goodbye, Farewell, So long*: it was not so much the vocabulary that was lacking . . . there was even *Adieu*, which, like many of the loveliest words, was elegant enough to travel without a passport.

Yes, *adieu*, to God . . . not bad, for a woman who –

And he had reached this point in his ruminations when Lucas suddenly jumped on him: 'Charles! You won!'

'The pedalos?'

'No! A huge basket of pâté and sausages!'

Oh dear Lord.

'Aren't you happy?'

'Yes, yes . . . Wickedly happy.'

'I'll go and fetch it for you. Don't budge, okay?'

'That's great. You'll be able to invite me to my place, then.'

He turned around.

She was untying her apron.

'I don't have any flowers,' he smiled.

'It doesn't matter . . . I'll lend you a few.'

One of the boys he'd glimpsed the evening before greeted him before interrupting their little gallantries: 'Can Jeff, Fanny, Mickaël and Leo come and sleep over at the house tonight?'

'Charles,' she said, 'I'd like to introduce Samuel. My big boy.'

It's true that he was big . . . He was almost as tall as Charles himself . . . Long hair, teenage skin, a wrinkled but very elegant white shirt, which must have belonged to someone from an earlier generation, monogrammed with the letters L.R. in sans serif, jeans with holes in them, a straight nose, a frank gaze, very thin and, in a few years, very handsome.

They shook hands.

'Hey, have you been drinking?' She frowned.

'Well . . . I wasn't exactly at the cake stall, I can tell you.'

'Well then, don't go home on your scooter.'

'I won't . . . It's just I spilled the last of a barrel onto my kecks . . . Look . . . Right, and about tonight?'

'If their parents are okay with it, I'm okay. But you've got to help us put everything away, all right?'

'Sam!' She called him back. 'Tell them to bring their sleeping bags, okay?'

He raised his thumb to show that he'd heard.

To Charles: 'You see what I mean . . . I told you there'd be half a dozen kids but I'm always a bit pessimistic . . . And I've got nothing to eat . . . Good job you bought some tickets.'

'I'll say.'

'And the Tin Can Alley? How did –'

They were interrupted yet again, this time by the little girl she'd called Hattie the evening before, or so he recalled.

'Kate?'

'And now here comes Miss Harriet, our number three . . .'

'Good evening.'

Charles gave her a kiss.

'Can Camille come and sleep over at the house? Yes, I know, sleeping bag . . .'

'So, if you know, that's perfect,' replied Kate. 'And Alice? Has she got someone for us as well?'

'I don't know, but wait till you see everything she found at the junk sale! You'll have to bring the car closer . . .'

'Good Lord, no! Don't you think we already have enough bloody stuff as it is?'

'But wait, it's really terrific! There's even an armchair for Nelson!'

'I see . . . Hang on a sec,' she said, running to catch up with her and handing her a wallet, 'run to the bakery and buy all the bread that's left.'

'Yes, Ma'am.'

'You're so organized!' said Charles, impressed.

'Oh? You call this organized? I would have said it was quite the opposite . . . Are you – are you coming anyway?'

'And how!'

'So, who's Nelson?'

'A very snooty dog . . .'

'And L.R.?'

Kate stopped in her tracks. 'Why are you asking me that?'

'Samuel's shirt.'

'Oh yes. Sorry. Louis Ravennes, his grandfather. You don't miss a thing, I see.'

'Yes I do, a lot of things, but monogrammed teenagers are not that common.'

Silence.

'Right.' She gave a little shiver. 'Let's clear all this away and go home. The animals are hungry and I'm tired.'

She pulled her hair back into an elastic band.

'And Nedra?' she asked Yacine, 'where has she got to this time?'

'She won a goldfish.'

'Well, that's not about to make her any more talkative . . . C'mon, let's get to work.'

Charles and Yacine piled up chairs and dismantled canopies for over an hour. Well . . . mainly Charles . . . Yacine was not particularly efficient, because he was forever telling him stories:

'See, for example, you just stuck out your tongue while you were untying that knot. D'you know why?'

'Because it's hard and you're not helping me?'

'Not at all. It's because when you concentrate on something, you use the side of your brain that's also in charge of your motor activity, so by blocking one thing in your body *on purpose*, you can concentrate better . . . That's why people, when they walk, they slow down when they start thinking about a complicated problem . . . D'you understand?'

Charles stood up straight, holding his lower back: 'Hey, Mr Encyclopaedist . . . Wouldn't you care to stick out your tongue a bit now, too? We'd go a lot faster . . .'

'And the most powerful muscle in your body, d'you know which one it is?'

'Yes. It's my biceps when I use it to throttle you.'

'Wrong! It's your tongue!'

'I should have known . . . C'mon, take the other end of the table, there . . .'

He seized the chance while Yacine was struggling with the sides of his brain to ask him his own question:

'Is Kate your mum?'

'Oh,' he replied, in that fluty little voice that children use when they want to wind us up, 'she said she isn't, but I know that she is . . . at least a little bit, that is.'

'How old is she?'

'She says she's twenty-five but we don't believe her.'

'No? And why not?'

'Because if she were really twenty-five she wouldn't be able to climb trees any more . . .'

'No, of course not . . .'

Stop, thought Charles, stop right there. The more you try to find out the less you understand. Put the operating instructions to one side. Play the game yourself, too . . .

'Well, I can tell you that she really is only twenty-five . . .'

'How do you know?'

'You can tell.'

When they'd finished sweeping everywhere, Kate asked if he could drive the two youngest back.

While he was settling them on the rear seat, a tall girl came up to him: 'Are you going over to the Vesp'?'

'Pardon?'

'Kate's place, that is . . . Can you drive us over there, with my friend?' She pointed to another tall girl.

'Uh . . . sure.'

Everyone squeezed into the tiny rental car and, with a smile on his face, Charles listened to them chattering.

He hadn't felt this useful in years.

The hitchhikers were talking about a night club where they

weren't allowed to go yet, and Yacine was saying to Nedra, the mysterious little girl who looked like a Balinese princess:

'Your fish . . . You'll never see him asleep because he doesn't have any eyelids and you'll think he can't hear you because he doesn't have any ears . . . But in fact, he'll be resting, you know . . . And goldfish are the ones who have the best hearing because water is a very good conductor and they have a bone structure that reflects all the sounds to their invisible ear, so, uh . . .'

Charles, fascinated, was trying hard to focus on what he was saying above the giggling of the two girls.

'. . . so you'll be able to talk to him all the same, you see?'

In the rear view mirror, he could see her nodding her head, gravely.

Yacine caught his eye in the mirror, leaned forward and murmured, 'She almost never speaks . . .'

'And what about you? How do you know all that you know?'

'I don't know . . .'

'So you're a good pupil?'

A little scowl.

And a big smile from Nedra in the mirror, shaking her head.

He tried to remember what Mathilde was like at that age. But couldn't . . . didn't remember at all. For someone who never forgot a thing, this was something he'd lost along the way. The childhood of children . . .

Then he thought about Claire.

About the mother she would have –

Yacine, who didn't miss a thing, put his chin on Charles's shoulder (ah, he'd found his own parrot . . .) and said, to help him think about something else, 'Still, you're glad you won them, aren't you, your sausages?'

'Yes,' he answered, 'you've no idea how glad I am . . .'

'Actually I'm not supposed to eat any . . . Because of my religion, y'know . . . But Kate said God doesn't care . . . He's not Madame Varon after all . . . D'you think she's right?'

'Who is Madame Varon?'

'The dinner lady, at the cafeteria . . . You think she's right?'

'Yes.'

He'd just recalled the story that Sylvie had told him the day before about the charity grocery, and he felt a sudden twinge of distress.

'Hey! Watch out! This is where you have to turn!'

6

'Well then! I can see you haven't been wasting your time! You've already found the two prettiest girls in the county!'

Who giggled all the more, asked where the others had got to, and vanished into thin air.

Kate had her wellies on.

'I was about to go on my rounds, are you coming?'

They crossed the courtyard.

'Normally, the children are supposed to feed the menagerie, but oh well . . . It's their party today . . . And this way, I can show you round.'

She turned to him: 'Are you all right, Charles?'

He was aching all over. His head, his face, his back, his arm, his torso, his legs, his feet, his diary, his accumulation of late arrivals, his guilty conscience, Laurence, and all the phone calls he hadn't made.

'I'm fine, thank you.'

She had the entire henhouse following in her wake. And three mutts. And a llama.

'Don't pet him, otherwise he'll –'

'Yes, Lucas warned me . . . Then he won't go away . . .'

'It's the same with me.' She laughed, bending down to pick up a bucket.

No, no. She didn't say that.

'Why the smile?' he asked anxiously.

'Nothing . . . *Saturday Night Fever* . . . So. Over there you have the former pigsty, but now it's the pantry. Mind the nests, there . . . Here, and in all the other buildings, it rains bird droppings all summer long . . . That's where we store the bags of seed and grain, and when I say "pantry" it's more like one for the mice and the dormice, unfortunately . . .' She stopped to address a cat who was snoozing

281

on an old duvet: 'All right, little old guy? Life not too hard for you now, is it?' She lifted a plank and used a tin can to fill up her bucket. 'Here . . . Can you take that watering can, over there?'

They went back across the courtyard in the opposite direction. She turned around: 'Are you coming?'

'I'm afraid I might squash a chick.'

'A chick? No fear. Those are ducklings. Just keep going, don't worry about them. Here . . . the tap's right there.'

Charles didn't fill the watering can up to the top. He was afraid he mightn't be able to lift it . . .

'This is the henhouse. One of my favourite spots. René's grand-father had very modern ideas where the farmyard was concerned, and nothing could be too good for his little hens. Which was appar-ently the cause of no end of rows with his wife, so I've heard.'

Charles was repelled by the smell at first, then he was amazed by – how to put it – the care, the attention which had been given to planning the place. The ladders, roosts, nest boxes, all in straight rows, prepared, bevelled, even sculpted . . .

'Look at that . . . opposite this beam he even put in a window so that these little ladies could enjoy the view whilst relieving themselves . . . And here, follow me . . . A chicken run for them to romp about in, a rock garden, a pond, watering troughs, a little bit of dust to discourage the vermin and . . . Do have a look at the view, really . . . Look how beautiful it is . . .'

While he was emptying the contents of his watering can, she added: 'One day when . . . I don't know . . . I must have been quite desperate, I suppose –' She was laughing. '– I got the ludicrous notion to take the children to one of those holiday park complexes, you know the ones?'

'Vaguely . . .'

'I think it was the stupidest idea I've ever had . . . To put all these wild creatures in a jar . . . They were impossible. Okay, nowadays we all laugh about it a lot, but at the time . . . and when I think how much it cost . . . anyway, forget it . . . My point is that on the first evening, after he'd had a walk around that . . . place, Samuel made this solemn declaration: our hens are treated better. Then they spent the entire week watching television . . . Morning and night . . . Real zombies. I just let them. After all, for them that was exotic . . .'

'You don't have a telly?'

'No.'

'But you have the Internet?'

'Yes. I can't deprive them of the entire world, after all . . .'

'And do they use it a lot?'

'Mostly Yacine. For his research,' she smiled.

'That kid is amazing.'

'You said it.'

'Tell me, Kate, is —'

'Later. Careful, it's spilling. Okay . . . we'll leave the eggs, that's Nedra's special treat.'

'What about Nedra, then —'

She turned around: 'Do you like really good whisky?'

'Uh . . . Yes.'

'Okay, later. Now . . . This is the old bakehouse. Which we use as a doghouse. Careful, the smell is unbearable . . . and here's the storeroom . . . This was a stable. Transformed into a garage for bicycles . . . There's the wine cellar . . . Don't look at all this rubbish . . . That's René's studio.'

Charles had never seen anything like it. How many centuries were accumulated here? How many skips, how many arms, and how many weeks would it take to get rid of it all?

'Have you seen all these tools?' he exclaimed. 'It's like the Museum of Folk Art and Tradition, it's extraordinary . . .'

'You think so?' she grimaced.

'They may not have the telly but they can't ever be bored, not for a second.'

'Not *one* second, alas.'

'And that? What's that?'

'That's the famous motorbike that René has been fixing up ever since . . . the war, I imagine.'

'And that?'

'Not a clue.'

'It's incredible.'

'Wait . . . there's better, if you'll follow me into the shop . . .'

They went back out into the daylight.

'Here you have the rabbit hutches — empty. I have my limits . . . This here is a first barn for the hay, the fennel . . . Over there, for straw . . . What are you looking at?'

'The roof framework . . . It's amazing . . . You cannot imagine the theoretical knowledge you need to create something like this . . . No,' he said again, thoughtful, 'you cannot imagine . . . Even me, even when it's my own field, I . . . How did they do it? It's a mystery. When I get old I'll take classes in carpentry . . .'

'Mind the cat –'

'Another one! How many do you have?'

'Oh . . . there's a big turnover . . . One dies and another kitten takes its place . . . Mainly because of the stream. Those idiots swallow hooks that still have the bait on them and they don't make it . . .'

'And how do the kids take it?'

'A tragedy. Until the next litter . . .'

Silence.

'How do you do it, Kate?'

'I don't do it, Charles. I don't do it. But occasionally I do give English lessons to the vet's daughter in exchange for a few visits . . .'

'No, I meant – I was referring to everything else.'

'I'm like the kids: I wait until the next litter. That's one thing life has taught me. One day' – she turned the lock – 'after another. That's more than enough.'

'You're locking the cats in?'

'Cats never go through doors, don't you know that?'

They turned round and saw . . . the rogues' gallery.

Five mongrels, each one more battered than the next, were waiting for their dinner.

'C'mon, me beauties . . . Your turn now.'

She walked back through to the pantry and filled their bowls.

'That one, there –'

'Yes?'

'He only has three paws?'

'And he's missing an eye . . . That's why we call him Nelson. Here's where we store the wood . . . That's another barn over there, with the old granary . . . For the grain, obviously . . . Nothing special. What a mess. Another museum, as you say . . . This one is even more tumbledown than the others . . . But look at those lovely double doors . . . that's because this is where they kept the horse-drawn carriages. There are two left, in appalling condition, though – come and see.'

284

After they had disturbed the swallows, Charles said, 'But this one still looks fine . . .'

'The little trap? Sam restored it. For Ramon . . .'

'Who's Ramon?'

'His donkey,' she explained, rolling her eyes skyward. 'His bloody ass of a donkey . . .'

'Why the look?'

'Because he's got it in his head to take part this summer in a local harness race.'

'And? Isn't he ready?'

'Oh, yes, he's ready! He's so ready that he's had to stay down a year at school. But let's not go into that, I don't feel like being in a bad mood.'

She was leaning against a shaft: 'You can tell, can't you . . . Everything's a mess here . . . all wonky, coming apart, falling down . . . The children go around barefoot in their boots all day long – that is, if they even have any boots. I have to worm them twice a year, they run around everywhere, they come up with a million idiot things a minute, and they invite all the friends they like whenever they want, but there's one thing that still really really matters: school. If you could see us in the evening, all round the kitchen table, it's no joke. Dr Jekyll transformed into Mr Hyde! So with Samuel, now, this is the first time I've failed . . . I know, I shouldn't say that I'm the one who failed, but there you are . . . It's complicated . . .'

'It's not that serious, is it?'

'No, I suppose not . . . But . . .'

'Go on, Kate, go on, tell me . . .'

'He started at the lycée last September, so I had to send him to boarding school. I had no choice. The school here isn't great . . . So this has been a disaster. I didn't expect it at all, because I've got really fantastic memories of my years at boarding school, but, I don't know, perhaps it's different in France. He was so relieved to get home at weekends that I didn't have the heart to make him work. So this is the result . . .'

She gave a crooked smile.

'I might have a champion of France in donkey harness racing instead . . . C'mon, let's go, we're frightening the mothers . . .'

True, there was some serious cheeping in the nests above their heads.

'Do you have children?' she asked.

'No. Yes. I've got a Mathilde . . . she's fourteen . . . I didn't make her myself, but . . .'

'But that doesn't change much.'

'No.'

'I know. Look . . . I'm going to show you a place you'll really like.'

She knocked on the door of the umpteenth building:

'Yes?'

'I'm with Charles, can I show him round?'

Nedra opened the door to them.

If Charles thought he'd reached the limits of his capacity for amazement, he was wrong.

He stood in silence for a long while.

'Alice's studio,' Kate whispered.

He was still speechless.

There was so much to see . . . Paintings, drawings, frescoes, masks, puppets made of feathers and bark, furniture made of bits of wood, garlands, and foliage, models, and lots of extraordinary animals . . .

'So she's the one . . . the mantelpiece?'

'That's Alice.'

Alice sat with her back to them at a table beneath the window; now she turned and handed them a box.

'Look at all the buttons I found at the fair! Look at that one, isn't it gorgeous? It's mosaic. And that one . . . a fish in mother-of-pearl. It's for Nedra. I'm going to make her a necklace with it to celebrate the arrival of Monsieur Blop.'

'And who, may we ask, is Monsieur Blop?'

Charles was pleased that he was no longer the only one asking stupid questions.

Nedra pointed to the end of the table.

'But . . .' said Kate, 'you've put him in Granny's lovely vase?'

'Well, yeah . . . That's what we wanted to tell you . . . We couldn't find an aquarium . . .'

'That's because you didn't look properly. You've already won dozens of goldfish, and you've never been able to keep them alive longer than a summer, I might remind you, and I've *already* bought loads of bowls. So . . . figure it out yourselves.'

'Yes, but they're so tiny . . .'

286

'Well then, just build an aquarium! Like Gaston!'

She closed the door and turned to Charles with a moan: 'I should never have said that, "just build one", it's always a sign that there will be exhausting consequences . . . C'mon. We'll finish with a visit to the stables and the museum shop is on the left. Follow me.'

They headed towards another courtyard.

'Kate? May I ask one last question?'

'Go ahead.'

'Who is Gaston?'

'You don't know Gaston Lagaffe?' she deplored. 'Gaston and his fish Bubulle?'

'Yes, yes, of course.'

'It was in order to understand Gaston that I really worked at learning French when I was ten. And I had a really tough time of it . . . because of all the onomatopoeia . . .'

'But . . . How old are you? If that's not indiscreet . . . Rest assured that I insisted to Yacine that you are in fact twenty-five, but . . .'

'I thought we already had the last question,' she said with a smile.

'I was wrong. There will never be a last question. It's not my fault, you're the one who –'

'Who what?'

'I feel really stupid, but . . . it's like discovering the New World . . . so, it's unavoidable, there are lots of questions.'

'Oh, honestly . . . you've never been to the country?'

'It's not the place I find so impressive, it's what you've done with it.'

'Oh, really? And what am I supposed to have done with it, in your opinion?'

'I don't know . . . made it into a sort of paradise, perhaps?'

'You're just saying that because it's summer, and the light is lovely, and school is over . . .'

'No. I'm saying that because I've seen children who are funny, and intelligent, and happy.'

She stopped in her tracks.

'You – you really mean what you've just said?'

Her voice had become so serious . . .

'I don't mean it, I'm convinced of it.'

She leaned on his arm to remove a pebble from her boot: 'Thank you,' she said, making a terrible face, 'I . . . shall we go?'

Stupid: the word wasn't strong enough. Charles felt like a complete and utter idiot, that was it.

Why had he just made this adorable girl cry?

She walked ahead a few steps, then said, more cheerfully: 'That's right . . . almost twenty-five . . . Not quite . . . Thirty-six, to be exact . . .

'Well then, as you see, the long avenue of oak trees wasn't for this modest farm, but for a château which belonged to two brothers . . . And, can you imagine, they burnt it down themselves, during the Terror . . . They had only just finished building it, they'd put all their heart into it, all their savings, well, all their ancestors' . . . and when they started stringing them up in the region, according to legend – but the legend is enchanting – the brothers conscientiously took their time and emptied out the wine cellar before setting the place on fire and stringing themselves up all on their own.

'I heard the story from a real nutter who showed up at the house one day because he was looking for . . . No . . . it's too long a story . . . I'll tell you some other time. So, to get back to the brothers . . . they were old bachelors and all they lived for was hunting . . . By hunting I mean fox hunting, horses therefore, and nothing was too good for their horses. Judge for yourself . . .'

They had just come round the corner of the last barn:

'Look at this, isn't it wonderful?'

'Sorry?'

'Nothing. I was just grumbling because I didn't bring my sketchpad.'

'Huh . . . you'll be back. It's even lovelier in the morning.'

'You should live in here.'

'The children live here during the summer. There are all these little rooms for the grooms, you'll see.'

His hands on his hips, breathless, Charles admired the labours of his long-ago colleague.

A rectangular building with a faded ochre coating that revealed the cornerstones and the cut-stone window arches, with mansard roofs covered in fine, flat tiles, a rigorous alternation between dormer windows decorated with volutes and oeils-de-boeuf, and a large arched door framed by two very long watering troughs . . .

288

A simple, elegant stable, built in the middle of nowhere for the sole pleasure of two petty noblemen who did not have the patience to wait their turn at the tribunal: this in itself was eloquent testimony to the spirit of the Ancien Régime.

'These guys had delusions of grandeur . . .'

'It would seem they didn't. According to the same nutter, it would seem that the design of the château was actually rather disappointing. It was horses they were mad about. And now,' she said with a guffaw, 'it's fat old Ramon who gets to enjoy it. Come along . . . look at the floor . . . These are pebbles from the stream.'

'Like on the bridge.'

'Yes. So that the horses' hooves wouldn't slip.'

It was very dark inside the stable. Here, more than anywhere else, the beams and joists had been colonized by dozens of swallows' nests. The space must have measured roughly ten metres by thirty, and consisted of six stalls separated by very dark wooden partitions that were fixed to columns topped by small brass globes.

Pegasus, Valiant, Hungarian . . . Two centuries, three wars, and five republics had not sufficed to efface their names . . .

The coolness of stone, the numerous antlers covered with cobwebs, the light piercing in round circles through the oeils-de-boeuf projecting long beams of phosphorescent dust; and the silence, suddenly, disturbed only by the echo of their hesitant steps against the uneven surface of the pebbled floor – it was . . . Charles, who had always been horribly frightened by horses, felt as if he had entered a religious edifice, and dared go no farther than the nave.

Kate roused him from his torpor, swearing: 'Look at this jumper . . . Too late . . . The mice have eaten it. Fuck. This way, Charles . . . I'm going to tell you everything the gentleman from Historical Monuments told me the time he came . . . It may not seem so, but we are in an ultra-modern stable here. The stone of the mangers was polished, for the comfort of the horses' chests – breasts?'

'Breasts sounds good,' he smiled.

'. . . for the comfort of the nags, then, and carved into individual troughs so that they could keep an eye on their daily rations. The racks seem to be worthy of Versailles. All in turned oak wood and mounted at either end with little sculpted vases . . .'

'Acroters.'

'If you say so . . . But that's not the height of refinement . . . Look . . . Each bar turns on itself in order to – how did he put it? – "so that the fodder could be pulled out without meeting any resistance". The fodder was always getting soiled with dust and mouse droppings that could cause disease, and that's why these racks, unlike the ones in the other hicks' stables, are not inclined but almost vertical, with a little hatch, here at the bottom, to collect the bloody dust . . . And since the horses were facing a blind wall, they put grilles between each stall so that they wouldn't get bored, and could have a chat with their neighbour: *Hello dear, did you see the fox today?* Look, aren't they lovely? Like a wave, breaking against the column . . . Above your head there are several openings to bring the hay down from the loft and –'

She pulled on his sleeve to make him follow: 'This is the only box stall. Very large, with panelling . . . They would put the pregnant mares here, and their foals . . . Look up . . . That oeil-de-boeuf up there was so that the stable boy could keep an eye on the birthing from his bed . . .'

She stretched out her arm: 'You cannot fail to admire these three lanterns on the ceiling. They gave practically no light, and were incredibly complicated to manoeuvre, but far less dangerous than hand-held lamps set on windowsills and . . . What is it? What's so funny?'

'Nothing. I'm amazed. I feel as if I've got a special guide all to myself.'

'Huh.' She shrugged her shoulders. 'I'm making an effort, because you're an architect, but if I'm boring you, just tell me to stop.'

'Tell me one thing, Kate –'

'Yes?' She turned around.

'You wouldn't by any chance have a bloody bad temper?'

'Oh yes,' she eventually conceded, after a series of little pouts that were very much in keeping with the era, very 18th century, 'it is quite possible . . . Shall we carry on?'

'I'm coming.'

He put his hands behind his back, and his smile on standby.

'Here,' she continued, learnedly, 'look at this stairway, for example: isn't it *sublime?*'

'Indeed.'

There was nothing extraordinary about it, however. A winding flight of steps which, as it was not intended for the darling nags, had been constructed in a very ordinary type of wood. It had gradually taken on the colour of the stones and been worn down by boots, but its proportions – and wasn't this what it always boiled down to – were absolutely perfect. To such a degree that it did not even occur to Charles to appreciate the proportions of his pretty guide as she went up the steps just ahead of him, holding onto the banister; he was too busy defining the height of the risers in comparison with the width of the steps.

What idiots, these intellectuals, with their big heads . . .

'Here are the rooms, four of them, well, three actually, the last one's been condemned.'

'Is it collapsing?'

'No, it's expecting baby owls. What's the proper word, anyway, owlets?'

'I don't know . . .'

'You don't know a great deal, do you?!' she teased, walking right by him to open the second door.

The furniture was fairly basic. Little iron beds with worn, gaping mattresses, wobbly chairs, mouldy leather straps hanging on hooks. Here was a blocked-off fireplace, and there, well, it might have been a beehive, then a little farther along was an engine all taken to bits, and some fishing rods, and piles of books read and reread by generations of enthralled rodents, then whole sections of peeling plaster walls, another cat, boots, old issues of *Agricultural Life*, empty bottles, a radiator grille from a Citroën, a hunting rifle, boxes of cartridges, a . . . On the walls, cheap naïve prints being led astray by naughty posters, a Playmate pulling on the knot of her bikini and eyeing a crucifix that was already hanging rather crookedly, a calendar for 1972 courtesy of Derome fertilizers and, wherever you looked, everywhere, the same wall-to-wall carpeting, dark and thick and patiently woven by tens of thousands of dead flies . . .

'When René's parents were alive, this is where they housed the farm workers.'

'And is this where your children sleep?'

'No,' she said reassuringly, 'I forgot to show you the last room

below the stairs . . . But wait, you like seeing how things are built
– come and see the attic, watch your he—'

'Too late,' moaned Charles, who had stopped counting his
bruises.

But he soon removed his palm from his forehead, 'Can you
imagine, Kate? All the work, the intelligence those men must
have put into building a structure like this? Have you seen the
size of those struts? Or the length of that ridge purlin? That's the
main roof beam up there. Just the thought of chopping down
and sizing and manipulating a trunk of that size, can you imagine
how tricky it must have been? And it's all perfectly pegged . . .
And the queen post wasn't even reinforced with metal.' He showed
her the spot where it all seemed to hold together. 'This is known
as a mansard roof, it allows you to gain a lot of height under the
roof, and that's why there are such beautiful dormer windows.'

'Right. I guess you do know something, after all.'

'No. I'm useless where rural construction is concerned. I have
never – to use the jargon of my colleagues – had any inclination
for *heritage* work, the patrimonial stuff. I like to invent, not restore.
But naturally when I see something like this, because I'm always
looking for ways to experiment with new materials and new tech-
niques with the help of calculations from ever more sophisticated
software, I feel – how can I put it – out of my depth . . .'

'And the matrimonial stuff?' she said suddenly, when they were
again in the stairway.

'Pardon?'

'You just said you weren't into patrimonial stuff, but what about
the other, I mean, what about *marriage*?'

Charles stopped, holding onto the worm-eaten banister.

'No.'

'And you . . . do you live with her – your – Mathilde's mother?'

'No.'

Ouch.

It was nothing. A nasty splinter that had it in for fibs.

Had he fibbed?

Yes.

But was he *living* with Laurence?

'Look . . . they've already brought all their stuff.'

A mountain of cushions and sleeping bags had been piled in

the middle of the room. There was also a guitar, some packets of sweets, a bottle of Coke, a tarot deck and a few six-packs of beer.

'Well, this looks promising,' she sighed. 'So, this is the tack room. The only comfortable room in our so-called "Vesperies" . . . The only place with a beautiful hardwood floor and well-kept woodwork. The only place that had a stove worthy of the name. And why do you think that is?'

'For the steward?'

'For the leather, old boy! To protect it from the humidity. So that the saddles and bridles of their lordships would be perfectly kept at a perfectly regulated temperature! Everyone else was freezing their arse off but the riding crops were warm and toasty. Isn't that great? I've always thought that it was this room that decided the fate of the dovecote.'

'What dovecote?'

'The one the local people tore down stone by stone to make up for the fact they'd missed out on the château . . . This is more your history than mine, but dovecotes were despised symbols of the Ancien Régime . . . The more the lord wanted to show off, the bigger the dovecote, and the bigger the dovecote, the more pigeons there were to eat up all the peasants' seed. One pigeon can gobble up almost fifty kilos of grain a year – not to mention all the new shoots in the kitchen garden that they were so crazy about . . .'

'You're as knowledgeable about things as Yacine . . .'

'Oh! Well, he's the one who taught me all that.'

She laughed.

That smell . . . Mathilde when she was a little girl . . . Why had she stopped her horse riding, in the end? She'd loved it so much.

Yes, why? And why didn't he know? What had he let slip by, yet again? He must have been in the throes of some meeting that day . . . one morning she had come to him and said, There's no point taking me to the pony club any more, and he hadn't even tried to find out why she was giving it up. How could he . . .

'What are you thinking?'

'My blinkers . . .' he murmured.

He turned his back to her and let his gaze wander over the hooks and saddle-holders, the broken bridles, the bench that also served as a chest, the little marble corner sink, the jar filled with – was it tar? the tub full of extra-strength Fly-Be-Gone, the mouse-traps, the mouse droppings, the boot-pulls under the window, an incredibly well-kept harness – must belong to the donkey – the horseshoes in a row along the shelf, the brushes and hoofpicks and children's riding caps, the ponies' blankets, the stove that had lost its pipe but gained a six-pack of Kronenbourg, and that odd thing hanging from a hook that was very intriguing . . .

'What's that thing?' he asked.

'It's for the martingales.'

Right.

He could look it up . . .

'And over there?' asked Charles, his face up against the windowpane.

'The kennels . . . Or what's left of them.'

'They were huge.'

'Yes. And what's left makes you think the dogs were treated every bit as well as the horses. I don't know if you can see them from here but there are two sculpted medallions with the profiles of the dogs above each door. No, you can't see them any more. I'll have to clear away all that growth. We'll wait just long enough for the blackberries . . . Look, even the railings are lovely. When the children were small and I wanted some peace and quiet I'd bring them here. For them it was like a playpen and it allowed me to get a few things done without having to worry about the river . . . One day one of – I think it was Alice's – teachers called me in and said, "I'm sorry, it's very awkward to have to ask you this, but your little girl has been telling everyone in the class that you lock her up in a kennel with her brothers, is it true?"'

'And what happened?' asked Charles, delighted.

'So I asked her if Alice had told her about the whips as well. In short, after that, my reputation . . .'

'How wonderful.'

'Whipping children?'

'No . . . all these stories you have to tell.'

'Hmm. And what about you? You haven't said a thing.'

'No. I – I like to listen.'

'Yes, I know, I'm a chatterbox. But it's so rare to actually have a civilized human being come this far . . .'

She opened the other window, and informed the sudden draught of air, 'So so rare . . .'

They walked back the way they'd come. 'I'm dying of hunger, what about you?'

Charles shrugged his shoulders.

It wasn't an answer but he didn't know what to say.

He no longer knew how to keep to the blueprint. No longer knew how to read the scale. Didn't know if he should stay or go. Continue listening or flee. Wait and hear the real story, or drop the car keys into the agency's letterbox as indicated on the contract.

He wasn't a calculating sort, but this was his life, to wait and see what happened, and . . .

'Me too,' he asserted, to drive away everything Cartesian, logistician, initials in the margin, I the undersigned, everything that was firmly rooted in a life filled with provisos, clauses, and guarantees. Me too.

After all, he'd come all this way to look for Anouk, and he sensed she was not all that far away.

She had even touched that nape, just there.

Just there.

'Well, let's go and see what the snails have left us.'

She looked for a basket, which he immediately took from her hands. And as on the evening before, under the same vast wash of pale sky, they left the yard and melted into the tall grasses.

Shepherd's purse, daisies, yarrow with slender sunshades, greater and lesser celandine, stitchwort, Charles hadn't a clue about the names of all these flowers, but he wanted to suck up to her, just a bit.

'What's that . . . with the white stalk, over there?'

'Where?'

'Right in front.'

'A dog's tail.'

'Oh?'

Her smile, even mocking, blended well with the landscape.

The wall of the kitchen garden was in poor repair but the gate, framed by a column on either side, was still impressive. Charles ran his hand over the stone as they went through, felt the rough prickle of lichen.

The shed door squeaked as Kate opened it to hunt for a knife; Charles followed her in among the vegetables. Every row was straight as a die, impeccably kept, and on either side there were paths arranged in a criss-cross pattern. There was a well in the centre, and flowers everywhere you looked.

No, he wasn't sucking up to her, he liked learning.

'And those little trees, the crooked ones along the path, what are they?'

'Crooked?' she said, indignant, 'you mean pruned! Those are apple trees . . . they've been espaliered, if you please.'

'And that magnificent blue colour on the wall?'

'You mean the Bordeaux mixture? It's for the vine . . .'

'You make wine here?'

'No. We don't even eat the grapes. They taste horrible.'

'And that big yellow corolla?'

'Dill.'

'And over there, those feathery things?'

'Asparagus stalks.'

'And those big round things?'

'Garlic.'

Turning around, 'Is this the first time you've ever seen a kitchen garden, Charles?'

'This close up, yes.'

'Really?' she exclaimed, as if she were truly sorry, 'how have you managed to survive this long?'

'I sometimes wonder myself.'

'You've never eaten tomatoes or raspberries that have just been picked?'

'Perhaps when I was a kid . . .'

'You've never rolled a fresh gooseberry over your lip? You've never eaten a wild strawberry still warm from the sun? You've never broken a tooth or burned your tongue on a bitter hazelnut?'

'I'm afraid not. And what are those huge red leaves on the left, there?'

'You know . . . you should be asking all these questions of old René, you'd make him so happy. And he can tell you much better than I can. I scarcely have the right to come here. Anyway, look –' She bent down. 'Let's just take some lettuce to go along with your feast and then we'll put the knife back, and no one'll be any the wiser.'

Which is what they did.

Charles inspected the contents of his basket.

'Is something bothering you?'

'Under a leaf . . . there's a huge slug . . .'

She bent over. The nape of her neck . . . She grabbed the beast and dropped it into a bucket near the gate.

'Used to be, René would crush them all, but Yacine went on about it so much that he didn't dare touch them any more. Now he tosses them into the neighbour's vegetable garden . . .'

'Why the neighbour's?'

'Because he killed his rooster.'

'And why does Yacine have a thing about slugs?'

'Only those fat ones . . . Because he read somewhere that they can live between eight and ten years.'

'And so?'

'My goodness! You're as dogged as he is! I don't know . . . He thinks that if Nature, or God, or whatever, created such a small creature *on purpose*, something so repulsive and yet so sturdy, well then there must be a reason for it, and that smashing a shovel onto them to get rid of them is an insult to all of creation. He has a lot of theories like that, actually . . . He watches René at work, and talks to him for hours, and tells him about the origins of the world from the first potato until the present day.

'So he's happy, he's got an audience, and the old man is over the moon – he confessed to me one day that he'll finally have his diploma before he dies, and the giant slugs are delighted. A night on the town . . . At any rate, everyone is happy. Follow me, I'll take you back the other way, for the view, and then we'll check and see what mischief they've been up to . . . It's always worrying when you don't hear anything.'

They walked along what was left of the wall, and took a dirt path which led them to the top of a hill.

Undulating meadows enclosed by hedges as far as the eye could see, haystacks, woods, an immense sky and, down below, a bunch of kids, most of them in their swimsuits, most of them straddling hairy beasts, laughing, shouting, screaming, and running along the banks of a dark stream that wound its way until it disappeared behind yet another copse . . .

'Right. Everything's okay,' she sighed. 'We can sit and relax now, too.'

Charles didn't move.

'Are you coming?'

'Do you ever get used to it?'

'To what?'

'To this . . .'

'No. Every day it's something different.'

'Yesterday,' he said, thinking out loud, 'the sky was pink and the clouds were blue, and this evening it's the other way round, it's the clouds that are . . . Have you – have you been living here for long?'

'Nine years. Come on, Charles, I'm tired . . . I got up really early, I'm hungry, and I'm feeling a little chilly . . .'

He took off his jacket.

It was an old trick. He'd done it thousands of times.

Yes, it was an old trick, putting one's jacket on the shoulders of a pretty woman on the way home, but what was new in this case was that the evening before he'd been carrying a chainsaw, and today it was a basket full of slugs.

And tomorrow?

'You look tired yourself,' she told him.

'I work a lot.'

'I can imagine. And what are you building at the moment?'

Nothing.

He let his arm drop.

A huge wave of the blues had just washed over him.

He hadn't answered her question.

Kate bowed her head. Mused that she too was barefoot in her boots . . .

And there were stains on her dress, her nails were chipped, and her hands a mess. She wasn't twenty-five any more. And she had spent the afternoon selling home-made cakes in the courtyard of a little country school that survived on borrowed time. And she had lied to him. There was a restaurant fifteen kilometres from there. She must have seemed utterly ridiculous, giving him the tour of her pile of stones as if it were a magnificent palace. To someone like him, moreover. A man who must have toured them all, at some point. And she must have bored him senseless with all her stories about horses and hens and boorish kids . . .

Yes, but . . . what else could she have talked to him about? What else was there now in her life?

To start with, she put her hands back in her pockets.

The rest would be harder to hide.

They walked down the hill, shoulder to shoulder, silent and very distant from each other.

Behind them, the sun went down, and their shadows stretched ahead, endless.

'I –' she murmured in English, very slowly,

'And I will show you something different from either
Your shadow at morning striding behind you
Or your shadow at evening rising to meet you;
I will show you fear in a handful of dust.'

As he had stopped, and was looking at her in a way that made her ill at ease, she felt obliged to explain: 'T.S. Eliot.'

But Charles couldn't give a toss about the poet's name, it was the rest which . . . that . . . how had she guessed?

She reigned over a world full of ghosts and children; she had such beautiful hands and could recite transparent verse at nightfall: who was she?

'Kate?'

'Hmm.'

'Who are you?'

'How funny, that's exactly what I was just wondering myself. Well . . . From a distance, just like that, you might say I'm a big farm girl wearing grubby wellingtons who's trying to sound interesting by quoting bits of a gloomy poem to a man who's covered in sticking plasters . . .'

And her laughter knocked their shadows over.

'Come along, Charles! Let's go and make some huge sandwiches! We've earned them.'

7

They were greeted by the old dog, whimpering on his mean pallet. Kate knelt down, took his head on her lap and rubbed his ears as she murmured tender words to him. And then — and this is where Charles *hallucinated*, to use Mathilde's favourite expression — she spread her arms, grabbed the dog from underneath and lifted him off the floor (biting her tongue as she did so) to take him for a piss in the courtyard.

He was hallucinating so severely that he did not even dare to follow her.

How much would a creature like that weigh? Thirty kilos? Forty?

This girl would never cease to . . . to what? To amaze him. To leave him gobsmacked. Seriously gobsmacked, as his fourteen and a half year old dictionary would say.

Her smile, the nape of her neck, her ponytail, her little 1970s dress, her hips, her ballet flats and wellies, her merry band of outdoorsy kids, her plans to clear away all the foliage, her gift for repartee, her tears when you least expected them, and now the way she had winched that monster hound into her arms in less than four and a half seconds, it was just . . .

It was just too much for him.

She came back, arms empty.

'What's wrong?' she asked, dusting off her thighs, 'you look as if you'd just seen the Virgin Mary in a pair of Bermuda shorts. That's what the local kids say. I love that expression . . . "Hey, Mickaël! You just seen the Virgin in shorts or what?" Want a beer?'

She was inspecting the refrigerator door.

He must have looked like a halfwit, because she reached out to show him what a beer was.

'You still here?'

Then, when she realized that his silent confusion must not have anything to do with her own prosaic self, she found the logical explanation:

'He's paralysed in his hindquarters. He's the only one who doesn't have a name. We call him the Big Dog and he is the last gentleman in this house . . . Without him we would probably not even be here tonight . . . Well, at least I wouldn't be here . . .'

'Why not?'

'Hey . . . Haven't you had enough?'

'Of what?'

'Of my little home-grown novellas?'

'No.'

And as she was busying herself at the sink, he picked up a chair and came over to her side.

'Washing lettuce is something I do know how to do,' he assured her. 'Here . . . you sit down there. Take your beer and tell me your story.'

She hesitated.

The architect frowned and raised his index finger as if he were trying out a bit of dog training: 'Sit!' he barked, in English.

So she sat down, pulled off her boots, arranged her dress over her lap, and leaned back.

'Oh,' she moaned, 'this is the first time I've sat down since yesterday evening. I'll never get up again . . .'

'I *cannot* imagine,' added Charles, 'how you can cook for so many people with such an impractical sink. This isn't even rustic design, it's . . . it's masochism! Or some kind of snobbery, perhaps?'

With the neck of her bottle she pointed to a door next to the fireplace: 'The rear pantry. There's no kitchen maid, but you'll find a huge sink and even a dishwasher if you look hard enough . . .'

Then she burped, long and loud.

As befits a *Lady* like herself.

'Perfect . . . but, uh . . . never mind. I'll stay here with you. I'll manage.'

He disappeared, came back, got busy, opened cupboards, found things, and made do with them.

Before her bemused gaze.

While he was struggling with the slugs, he added, 'I'm still waiting for the next instalment.'

She turned towards the window: 'We got here in . . . October,

I think it was . . . I'll tell you the circumstances later on, I'm too hungry just now to start scrounging around in my subconscious . . . After we had been here a few weeks, and it was getting dark earlier and earlier, I began to be frightened . . . And that was something new for me, being frightened.

'I was all alone with the little ones and every evening you could see headlights in the distance . . . First at the end of the lane, and then closer and closer . . . Nothing more than that. Just the lights of a stationary car . . . But that was the worst thing about it – this nothing happening. As if a pair of yellow eyes were watching us . . . I spoke to René about it. He gave me his father's hunting rifle but uh . . . that didn't get me very far. So one morning, after I'd dropped the kids off at school, I went to the animal shelter which is about twenty kilometres from here. It's not a proper shelter, really, just a sort of animal refuge where they have scrap metal, too. A really, er, friendly place, with a fairly . . . *picturesque* sort of bloke running it. Now he's a friend, who wouldn't be, given all the wretched mutts he's flogged us since then, but that day, believe me, my heart was in my mouth. I thought I was going to end up strangled and raped, and then they'd put me through the crushing machine.'

She was laughing.

'I said to myself, "Damn, who'll pick up the kids at four o'clock, then?"

'I'd got it wrong. His white eye, the hole in his head, missing fingers, crazy tattoos – that was all just . . . a look. I told him my problem, he was silent for a long time and then he waved to me to follow him. "With this one here, you won't have no problems with no one buggin' ya under your balcony, ya have my word on that." I was absolutely terrified: in this cage that stank of shit was this sort of wolf that was hurling itself like a madman against the bars, trying to get at us. Then the bloke said, between two gobs of spit, "Have ya got a leash?"

'"Uh . . ."'

Charles, who had put down his lettuce hearts, turned around with a laugh, 'Did you have a leash, Kate?'

'Not only did I not have a leash, but above all I wondered how I'd ever get into the car with that thing. I'd be eaten alive, for sure! But anyway . . . I managed not to lose my cool . . . He took a strap,

302

opened the cage, screaming at the beast, came back out with this monster foaming at the mouth, and then he handed him to me as if it were a radiator or a chrome wheel trim. "Usually I ask people to pay a little somethin' just for the principle but I was gonna do this one in, anyhow . . . Well, uh, I'll be off, then, I got work to do . . ." And he just left me there. Well, left me is a manner of speaking, because I got tugged away in no time. I ought to point out that in those days I was still somewhat feminine, I hadn't yet morphed into Charles Ingalls!'

Our Charles was having too much fun to even dream of contradicting her.

'In the end I managed to manoeuvre the dog as far as the boot, and then . . .'

'And then?'

'And then I chickened out.'

'So you took him back to the bloke?'

'No. I decided to walk home. I let him tug me along another hundred metres or so and then I ended up letting the crazy thing go. I told him, "Either you follow me and you'll live the life of a pasha, and when you're old, I'll grind your meat up for you and carry you out into the yard every night, or you go back where you came from and you end up as a foot rug in some rotten Renault. Take your pick." Of course, he headed straight for the fields and I thought I'd never see him again. Yeah, right. From time to time there he'd be . . . I saw him chasing the crows, and then he'd go into the undergrowth and run huge circles round me. Huge circles that started getting smaller and smaller . . . And three hours later, when we went through the village, he was following me quite peacefully, his tongue hanging out. I gave him some water and I wanted to put him in the kennels just long enough for René to take me back to the car on his moped, but then he started acting crazy again, so I just told him to wait there for us, and we left him.'

She took a breath along with a big gulp of beer.

'When we got back, I really had the willies . . .'

'You thought he'd run away?'

'No, that he'd eat the kids! I'll never forget the scene . . . In those days, I still parked in the courtyard. I didn't know that the bridge was collapsing . . . The dog was lying in front of the door, and he raised his head, I switched off the engine and turned round to face the kids: "We've got a new dog, he looks mean but I think it's just an impression he gives. We'll soon find out, okay?"

'I got out first, took Hattie in my arms, and I went round to open for the other two. The dog had just got to his feet. I tried to walk towards him but Sam and Alice were clinging to my coat. He came towards us, growling, and I said, "Stop that, stupid, you can see these are my puppies, no . . ." and we went for a walk. I confess my legs were like jelly and the kids weren't about to make a fuss, either . . . And then eventually they let go of me. We went over to the swing, and the big dog lay down in the lane. Then we went back to the house and had supper, and he went and found a spot by the fireplace . . . It was later that the problems started. He killed a sheep, then two sheep, three sheep . . . A hen, then a second hen, then ten hens . . . I would reimburse everyone but it started to become clear to me, from one of the little grumbling acts that René is so talented at, that the hunters were talking about the dog at the café, a lot. That they were getting up a battue . . . So one evening I went over to the dog and said, "If you carry on like this, they're going to kill you, you know . . ."'

Charles was fiddling with a salad spinner that must have dated from the early Beatles era.

'And then?'

'Well, he did his usual thing. He obeyed. It's true that it was about then that we got a puppy and, I don't know, perhaps he wanted to set a good example. Whatever the reason, he stopped his nonsense.

'Before coming here I'd never had any animals and I used to think people were pathetic the way they'd go on with their little doggies, but this one here, you see . . .

'He's trained me well.

'A real lord, as I was saying. Without him, I'd never have managed. He's been my guardian angel, my nanny, my lifeguard, my confidant, my messenger, my antidepressant, my . . . a lot of things. If the children wandered out of sight, he'd round them up, and when I had the blues, he'd come up with some stupid prank to distract me. A little hen that was just happening by, a ball, the postman's leg, the succulent Sunday roast . . . Oh, yes! He went to a lot of trouble to get me to keep my chin up! That's why I . . . I'll carry him into the yard to the end.'

'And those evening visitors?'

'The morning after I brought him here, the headlamps were there again. I was in my nightgown behind the kitchen window and I think that the dog *felt* my fear. He stood behind the door and began to bark like a thing possessed. No sooner had I opened the door than he was already at the end of the lane. I think he must have woken everyone for miles around . . . After that, I slept soundly. That night, and all the ones that followed.

'In the beginning, people round here called me the wolf woman . . . Right,' she said, stretching, 'is it ready?'

'Just doing the vinaigrette.'

'Excellent. Thank you, Jeeves.'

*

'And this,' she was saying, 'is my garden.'

They were on the other side of the house, and Charles had never seen so many flowers in his life.

It was as wild and messy and astonishing as all the rest.

There were no paths or rockeries, or flowerbeds, or lawn. Just flowers.

Everywhere.

'In the early days, it was magnificent. It was my mother who designed it but then . . . I don't know . . . over the years, it's gone all topsy-turvy . . . Well, to be honest, I don't look after it a great deal. There's not enough time. And every time my mother comes to visit she's devastated and spends her entire holiday on her knees trying to find her little labels . . . From that point of view she's far more English than my father . . . She's a very, very serious gardener. She's mad keen on Vita Sackville-West, she's a member of the Royal Horticultural Society and the National Rose Society and the British Clematis Society, and . . . Well, you get the picture.'

Charles thought that roses were curly flowers, generally pink, or white, or red, the sort of thing you'd ask the florist about when you needed a hand to charm an impressionable woman, so he was astonished to learn that all these bushes and creepers and large corollas, and those climbing things and these very simple little petals – all these were *also* roses.

In the middle of the flowers there was a large table surrounded by chairs even more ill-matched than those in the kitchen, all set out beneath an arbour where anything that had leaves and liked to climb had taken hold. Kate cheerfully provided him with the inventory:

'Wisteria . . . Clematis . . . Honeysuckle . . . Bignonia . . . Akebia . . . Jasmine . . . But it's in August that it's the most beautiful. When you sit here in August, at the end of the day, and you're pleasantly tired and suddenly all the perfumes are there, on the breeze: it's . . . wonderful.'

On the tablecloth they set down their piles of plates, the basket full of charcuterie, four long loaves, a bottle of wine, napkins, jars of pickles, pitchers of water, a dozen mustard glasses, two wine glasses, and the big salad bowl.

'Right. I think it's time to ring the bell.'

'You've got something on your mind,' she said, once they were back in the house.

'May I use your telephone?'

Their eyes met.

Kate lowered her head.

She'd just seen some headlights in the distance.

'Of . . . of course,' she stammered, waving her hands around her in search of an invisible apron, 'the . . . down there, at the end of the hallway.'

But Charles didn't move. He waited for her to come back to his senses.

Which she did, with a little nibbled smile.

'I have to notify the agency. About the car, you see . . .'

She nodded nervously. In a way that said, No, I don't want to know. And while he headed for Paris, she went out and crouched down by the pump.

You knew it was a bad idea, she thought, cursing herself as she drowned herself beneath an ever colder stream of water.

What were you thinking, you silly old fool – that he had come to take pictures of the bridges of Madison County?

It was an old telephone, with a rotary dial. And it takes forever to dial a number on a rotary phone. So he began with Mathilde, to give himself courage.

Voicemail.

He sent her a kiss and assured her she could count on him on Monday morning.

306

Then the agency.

Answerphone.

He said hello, explained the situation, said that he would understand if they charged him extra.

And finally Laurence.

He counted five rings, wondering what he would –

Voicemail.

What else?

'Please be so kind as to leave me a message,' she begged everyone, in a very haute couture voice.

Kind? That, Charles was. He went into a muddled explanation, used the word 'hitch' and scarcely had the time to send his . . . before he was cut off by the beep.

He put the receiver down.

He noticed the traces of saltpetre and the cracks along the wall. He touched the leprous surface and stood for a long time flaking away into space.

He joined Kate in the yard.

She was sitting on the third step of a stone stairway, and had put her ballet flats back on, along with a thick jumper.

'Come and watch the show!' she exclaimed. 'I'll do the voiceover.'

He was hesitant to sit at her feet. She'd see his bald spot.

Right . . . never mind.

'Yacine will go first. Because he's the greediest and because he's never in the middle of *doing* anything . . . Yacine never takes part in any of the games. He's fearful and clumsy . . . The others say it's because his head is too heavy. He will be accompanied by Hideous and Ugly, our ravishing Thomson and Thompson of the canine order . . . Look . . . here they come . . . And then Nelson, accompanied by his mistress, followed by Nedra, who worships Alice to a similar degree . . .'

The door to the studio opened a crack.

'What did I say . . . Then it's the teenagers . . . Ambulating stomachs who never hear a thing except the bell when it's time for a meal. Three full shopping trolleys every fortnight, Charles . . . *Three* trolleys filled to overflowing! Not counting, of course, Ramon, Captain Haddock, and the goat, who always brings up the rear of the procession . . . All our little friends for the evening carrot. Yes, indeed, the carrot . . .' she sighed, 'we're in a house full of silly rituals like that. It took me a while but I finally understood that silly rituals help you live . . .

'And to conclude, a few odd dogs who are still roaming around here and there: the puppy I mentioned earlier and who is now a magnificent, uh, sort of basset hound, given the astonishing length of his ears . . . last but not least, our dear Freaky, who must have been Frankenstein's muff in a former life – you see the one I mean?'

'No,' said Charles from his loge, with his hand to his forehead and his smile firmly in place, 'I don't think so . . .'

'You'll see, he's the fat little dog covered in scars with one badly stitched ear and protruding eyes . . .'

Silence.

'Why?' he asked.

'Why what?'

'So many animals?'

'They help me.'

She pointed towards the hill: 'There they are, my God, there are even more of them than I thought there'd be . . . And all the way over there, by the fir trees, I don't know if you can see them . . . Our fine horsewomen, Harriet and her friend Camille on their little ponies, riding flat out for once. Will there be any carrots left?'

The major procession which ensued showed that she had been right in every respect. The courtyard was soon filled with cries, dust, and cackling.

Kate followed her guest's reactions out of the corner of her eye: 'I've been trying to put myself in your shoes since you arrived,' she eventually confessed, 'and I say to myself, "What on earth will he be thinking about all this?" You must imagine you've landed in a houseful of nutters, no?'

No. He was thinking about the contrast between the excitement in this house and his laborious rotary-dial goose chase down at the end of the corridor.

Lately, he'd been getting the feeling that he spent his life talking to machines . . .

'You haven't answered.'

'Don't try to put yourself in my shoes,' he jested, bittersweet, 'it is much more . . .'

'More what?'

With the tip of his shoe he was tracing semi-circles in the gravel.

'Less alive.'

Suddenly he felt like talking to her about Anouk.

'Time to eat!' she cried, getting up.

He took advantage of her departure to ask Yacine, 'Tell me, what do you call a baby owl?'

'A now-let's-hoot.' Alice smiled.

Yacine looked troubled.

'Hey! It doesn't matter, if you don't know,' he said reassuringly.

But it did.

It mattered a lot.

'I know you say "fledglings" for birds that aren't adults yet, but as for owls, um . . .'

'And baby camels?' added Charles at random, to get him out of his sticky moment.

Big smile.

'Chameleons.'

Sigh of relief.

Well, sigh of relief, after a fashion . . . The boy went on about it for a good part of the dinner. Hatchling, gosling, yearling, duckling, fingerling, nestling, darling, spiderling, and crockling.

No. Sorry. Crocklet.

Sitting across from them, she watched as he nodded conscientiously, and she was having a grand time.

There were twelve of them under the arbour. Everybody was talking at once. The bread and the pickles went back and forth a great deal, and stories about country fairs were told.

Who had won what, how the teacher's son had cheated, and how many drinks it took for old man Jalet to slide from the counter at the drink stand.

The big kids wanted to sleep out under the stars, and the little kids asserted that they too were big kids. With one hand Charles refilled Kate's glass; with the other he pushed away the snout of something that was drooling on his shoulder, and she scolded, 'For Christ's sake! Stop feeding the dogs!' while no one listened because she was speaking Chinese. Finally she sighed and fed slices smeared with rillettes to her Big Dog on the sly.

For dessert they lit torches and candles. Samuel and his gang cleared the table and went to fetch all the unsold cakes. There was a bit of a fight; no one wanted to eat Madame Whosiwhatsit's apple pie because Madame Whosiwhatsit smelled bad. The teenagers, polishing the screens of their mobiles with their sleeve all the while, talked about where the best fishing holes were, about calving problems, and about the Gagnoux's new forage harvester. There was a lovely specimen wearing a white tank top, with a black dot printed right on her left nipple, next to an arrow which warned: 'slap distributor'; the machine seemed to work rather well.

Yacine wondered out loud if for a beaver you said a kitten or a pup, Nedra stared into the candle flame, and Charles stared at Nedra.

A portrait Georges de la Tour might have painted . . .

The hitchhikers had set off in search of a spot where they could get reception, and Alice was manufacturing ladybirds with candle wax and pepper grains from the salami.

Between two bursts of conversation you could hear the wind in the trees, and the cries of the young people in the distance.

Charles, attentive, was concentrating hard, for later.

Their goofiness, their laughter, their faces.

This harbour in the night.

He didn't want to forget a thing.

She stopped him, placing her hand on his sleeve, 'No, don't get up. Let the children work for once. Would you like a coffee?'

Alice said she would go and make it for him, Nedra brought the sugar, and the others unearthed a torch so that they could lead the animals back to the meadow.

The mayflies were in attendance: it was a joyous, ephemeral dinner.

8

They were alone.

Kate had picked up her glass and turned her chair to face the darkness. Charles came to sit in Alice's place.

He wanted to look at her little ladybirds . . .

Then he lifted one hip, dug around for his cigarettes, and offered her one: 'Shock horror,' she moaned, 'I'd love to join you but I had *such* trouble giving it up . . .'

'Look, I only have two left. Let's smoke these last two together and that will be it.'

Kate looked worriedly all around her: 'Are any of the kids around?'

'I don't see any.'

'Okay . . . great.'

She took a puff and closed her eyes.

'I'd forgotten . . .'

They smiled at each other and poisoned themselves religiously.

'It's because of Alice,' she declared.

She looked down and continued, lowering her voice, 'I was in the kitchen. The kids had been asleep for a long time. I was chain-smoking and I . . . was *drinking alone* – to use Alexis's mum's expression . . .

'Alice came into the room, crying. She had a stomach ache. It was at a time when we all had a stomach ache of sorts, I think . . . She wanted someone to hold her, some affection, words of comfort, all those things that I wasn't able to give them any more . . . And she managed somehow to climb up on my lap.

'She put her thumb in her mouth and no matter how I tried I couldn't think of what to say to calm her down or help her to get back to sleep. I . . . never mind.

'So instead, we watched the fire.

'After a very long while, she asked, "What does 'prematurely' mean?"

'"Earlier than expected," I replied. She was silent for a moment and then she added, "Who's going to look after us if you die prematurely?"

'I leaned over her and saw that I'd left my Craven As on her lap.

'And that she had just learned how to read . . .

'How was I supposed to answer such a question?

'"Toss it in the fire."

'I watched as the packet twisted and disappeared, and then I began to cry.

'It really felt as if I'd just lost my last crutch . . . Much later, I carried her through to her bed and came back at a run. Why the rush? To rake through the ashes, what else!

'I was already feeling very down, and going cold turkey like that made it even worse . . . At that point in time, I loathed this cold, sad house that had already taken everything from me, but I had to admit it did have one redeeming feature: the nearest tobacconist was six kilometres away and he closed at six in the evening . . .'

She crushed the butt in the earth, then placed it on the table and poured herself a glass of water.

Charles was silent.

They had the night ahead of them.

'They're my sister's ch—' Her voice broke. 'Sorry. My sister's children and . . . oh,' she said, cursing herself, 'that's why I didn't want to invite you to dinner.'

He was startled.

'Because when you got here with Lucas last night I could see, even behind your injuries, or perhaps because of your injuries, I could see the way you were looking around you —'

'And?' he urged, somewhat anxiously.

'And I knew what would happen. I knew that we'd have dinner around this table, that the children would run off, that I'd be here alone with you and that I'd tell you what I've never told a soul . . . I feel a bit sheepish to admit it, Mr Charles the Stranger, but I *knew* that you'd be the lucky one . . . That's what I told you earlier on in the saddle room . . . There have been plenty of expeditions passing through here, but you are the first civilized man who's ventured as far as the henhouse and, to be honest . . . I was no longer expecting you.'

A rather botched attempt at a smile.

Always the same old problem with words, damn it. Charles never had them available when he needed them. If at least the tablecloth had been made of paper, he could have sketched something for her. A vanishing line or a horizon, the idea of a perspective or even a question mark – but to speak, dear lord, what . . . What could you say with words?

'You still have time to get up, you know!' she added.

This time the smile was a success.

'Your sister,' he murmured.

'My sister was . . . Well, listen,' she continued more cheerfully, 'I may as well start crying straight away, that way it's done.'

She pulled on the sleeve of her jumper as if unfolding a hand-kerchief:

'My sister, my only sister, was called Ellen. She was five years older than me and she was a . . . wonderful girl. Lovely, funny, radiant . . . I'm not just saying that because she was my sister; I'm saying it because of who she was. She was my friend, my only friend I think, and much more than that . . . She looked after me a lot when we were children. She wrote to me when I was at boarding school and even after she got married we'd ring each other nearly every day. Rarely for more than twenty seconds, because there was always an ocean or two continents between us, but twenty seconds, that we could manage.

'And yet we were very different. Like in Jane Austen novels, you know . . . The sensible big sister and the sensitive little one . . . She was my Jane and my Elinor, she was calm, I was turbulent. She was sweet, I was a pain. She wanted a family, I wanted a mission. She was waiting to have children while I was waiting for visas. She was generous, I was ambitious. She listened to people; I never did. Like with you, this evening . . . And because she was perfect, that gave me the right not to be . . . She was the pillar, and the pillar was solid, so I could go and gad about, the family would survive . . .

'She always supported me, encouraged me, helped me and loved me. We had adorable parents, but they were utterly clueless, and she's the one who brought me up.

'Ellen . . .

'I haven't said her name out loud for so long . . .'

Silence.

'Cynical as I was at the time,' she continued, 'I did have to acknowledge that happy ends were not the exclusive domain of Victorian novels . . . She married her first love and her first love was worthy of her . . . Pierre Ravennes . . . A Frenchman. An adorable man. As generous as she was. *Beau-frère* came to mean a lot more than brother-in-law. I loved him dearly, and the law didn't have anything to do with it. He was an only son and he'd suffered a lot as a result. In fact, he'd become an obstetrician . . . Yes, he was that type of man. Who knew what he wanted . . . I think he would have been delighted to see everyone round the table like we were this evening . . . He used to say he wanted seven children and you never knew if he was joking. Samuel was born; I'm his godmother. Then Alice, then Harriet. I didn't see them very often but I was always surprised by the atmosphere at their place, it was . . . Did you ever read Roald Dahl?'

He nodded.

'I adore that man. At the end of *Danny the Champion of the World*, there's a message addressed to the young reader which says, more or less, When you grow up, please do not forget that children want and *deserve* parents who are *sparky*.

'I don't know how you'd say that in French, *sparky* . . . It's like . . . brilliant? Funny? Dazzling? Dynamite? Champagne, perhaps . . . But what I do know is that their home was . . . *sparkyssimo*. I was filled with wonder and also a bit confused, and I said to myself that I'd never know how to do that . . . I thought I didn't have the generosity, or the cheerfulness, or the patience required to make children as happy as their children were . . .

'I remember it very clearly, I used to say to myself, jokingly and at the same time to reassure myself, If ever I have kids some day, I'll leave them with Ellen, she'll look after them . . . And then.'

A sad face.

Charles would have liked to touch her shoulder, her arm.

But he didn't dare.

'And there we are, now I'm the one reading them Roald Dahl stories . . .'

He took her glass out of her hand, filled it, and handed it back.

314

'Thanks.'

A long silence.

Laughter and the sounds of the guitar in the distance gave her the courage to continue.

'One day, I came to visit, unexpectedly. For my godson's birthday, actually. At the time I was living in the US, working a great deal, and I had never even seen their youngest . . . I had been with them for a few days when Pierre's father arrived. The famous Louis, the one on the shirt . . . He was a mad sort, funny, larger than life. Pure concentrate of sparky, absolutely. He was a wine merchant who loved to drink, eat, laugh, toss the kids up to the ceiling then hang them upside down by their feet, and crush his loved ones against his big belly.

'He was a widower, he adored Ellen and I think she married him as much as she married his son . . . You have to bear in mind that our own father was already an elderly gentleman when we were born. A professor of Latin and Greek, at university. Very kind, but fairly . . . vague. More at ease with Pliny the Elder than with his own daughters. When Louis heard that I was staying and that I could look after the kids, he begged Pierre and Ellen to go with him to visit a cellar or some such thing in Burgundy. Oh come on, he insisted, it will do you good. You haven't been away for such a long time! Oh go on . . . We'll be visiting a fine estate, we'll have a grand feast, stay in a sublime hotel and tomorrow after-noon you'll be home again. Pierre! For Ellen's sake! Time to get her away from the baby bottles!

'Ellen was hesitating. I think she really didn't want to leave me . . . And that's where life really is a bitch, Charles, because *I'm* the one who insisted she go. I got the feeling that this little outing would be such a treat for Pierre and his father . . . Go on, I told her, go and have a grand feast and sleep in a fourposter bed with a canopy, we'll be fine.

'She said, all right, but I knew she was forcing herself. That once again she was putting the others first, before herself.

'It all happened very quickly. We had decided not to say anything to the children, who were in the middle of watching a cartoon, to avoid any risk of a pointless scene. When Mowgli got back to his village, Mummy would come home tomorrow and that was that.

'Auntie Kate felt she was up to the task. Auntie Kate hadn't even taken all the pressies out of her travel bag . . .'

Silence.

'It's just that . . . Mummy never came home. Nor did Daddy. Or Grandpa.'

'The phone rang during the night, a voice rolling his "r"s asking me whether I was related to Rrravennes Louis, Rrravennes Pierre, or Shay-rrrang-tonne Ay-lenn. I'm her sister, I replied, so they put someone else on the line, higher rank, and it's this someone else who had to do the dirty work.

'Had the driver drunk too much? Fallen asleep? The inquest would determine that, but what was certain was that he was driving far too fast, and the other driver, in a truck transporting farm equipment, should have pulled farther over to the side and switched on the hazard flashers before going off to take a piss.

'By the time he buttoned his flies and turned around, there was nothing sparky left.'

Kate had got up. She moved her chair over by her dog, took off her shoes, and slipped her bare feet under the dog's unmoving body.

Up to that point Charles had held up fairly well, but when he saw that huge animal, who could no longer even wag his tail, raise his eyes solemnly to look at her and convey the happiness he felt, to be of use to her still, Charles felt his surface cracking completely.

And he was out of cigarettes.

He placed his hand on his swollen cheek.

Why was life so careless with those who served it most loyally? Why?

Why those very people?

He was lucky. It had taken him forty-seven years to understand what Anouk was celebrating when, on the pretext that she was alive, she said fuck-it to everything else.

Fuck-it to parking tickets, bad marks, disconnected phones, broken down cars, hideous problems with money, and the insane state of the world.

At the time, he'd found it all a bit too easy, cowardly even, as if one simple word could suffice to excuse all her failings.

'Alive.'

Of course. What else could they be?

It was obvious.

Besides, it didn't even count.

Frankly, she went on about it all too much.

'Ellen and her father-in-law died instantly. Pierre, who was sitting in the rear, waited until he was in hospital in Dijon in order to bow out in the presence of his colleagues . . . I've often had the opportunity to . . .' Here she winced: '*relate the facts*, as you might imagine. But in fact, I've never really said a thing . . .

'Are you still there, Charles?'

'Yes.'

'Can I tell you?'

He nodded. He was too upset to risk letting her hear his voice again.

Several minutes went by. He thought she'd changed her mind.

'In fact, you don't believe it when people tell you, it makes *no sense whatsoever*, it's all a bad dream. So you say, go back to bed.

'Of course you can't, and you spend the rest of the night in an absolute state, staring at the telephone while you wait for Captain Whatsit to call back and apologize. Look, there was an errrror in identifying the bodies . . . No. The earth keeps turning. The furniture in the living room is all where it belongs and a new day has arrived, ready to insult you.

'It's almost six o'clock and you tour the flat to gauge the extent of the tragedy. Samuel in a little blue room, he turned six just the day before, his forehead against his teddy bear and his palms wide open. Alice, in her little pink room, three and a half years old and already riveted to her thumb. And next to her parents' bed, Harriet, eight months old, and she opens her big eyes when you lean over her cradle and you can tell she is *already* a bit disappointed to see your uncertain face rather than her mother's.

'You pick the baby up, and close the doors to the other rooms because she has started to babble and, to tell the truth, you're not in a great hurry for them to wake up . . . You congratulate yourself for remembering how many spoonfuls of powder you have to put in the baby's bottle, you settle into an armchair by the window because in any case you're going to have to face this fucking new

317

day, so you may as well do it lost in the eyes of a baby who's feeding, and you . . . you don't cry, you're in a state of . . .'

'Sideration,' murmured Charles.

'Right. Numb. You hold the baby against your shoulder for the burp and you actually hurt her, you're clinging to her so hard, as if that little burp was the most important thing in the world. The last thing you think you can actually hang on to. Sorry, you say to her, sorry. And you lull yourself, against the back of her neck.

'You suddenly remember that your flight is leaving the next day, that you've just been awarded the grant you've been waiting for for so long, and you have a fiancé who has just gone to sleep, thousands of kilometres from there, and you'd planned to go to the Millers' garden party the following weekend, and your father is about to turn seventy-three, and your mother, that little bird-like creature, has never been able to look after herself, and . . . there's no one on the horizon. But above all – and this is what you haven't realized yet – you will never see Ellen again.

'You know that you have to ring your parents, if only because someone has to go there. To answer questions, and wait while body bags are unzipped, and sign papers. You say to yourself, I cannot send *Dad* there, he is . . . unequipped for this type of situation, and as for Mummy . . . You look at people going by in the street with their great long strides and you are angry at them for their selfishness. Where do they think they're going? Why are they acting as if nothing has happened? Then it is Alice who rouses you from your torpor, and the first thing she asks is, Did Mummy come back?

'You make up a second baby bottle, you sit her in front of the telly and you bless Tweety Bird and Puddy Tat. And, you even watch them with her. Samuel comes in, he curls up next to you and says, It's stupid, Tweety always wins. You agree. It really is utterly stupid . . . You stay with them in front of the television as long as possible but then there comes a time when there's nothing left to watch . . . And the night before you had promised to take them to the Jardins du Luxembourg, so it's time to get dressed, right?

'Samuel shows you where to take the rubbish bins and how to lift the back of the pushchair. You watch him while he does it and you sense that this little boy has only just started teaching you how to live . . .

318

'You walk along the street and you don't recognize a thing, you really should ring your parents but you don't have the courage. Not for their sake, for your own. As long as you don't say anything, they are not dead. The policeman can still send his apologies.

'It was Sunday. And Sunday doesn't count. Sunday is a day when nothing ever happens. When people are with their family.

'Sailing boats on the pond, slides, swings, puppet shows, it's all there for the asking. A tall lad puts Samuel on the back of a donkey, and his smile gives you a wonderful moment of reprieve. You had no way of knowing, but this was the beginning of an enduring passion that would lead to the harness race at Meyrieux-sur-Lance nearly two years later . . .'

She was smiling.

Charles wasn't.

'And then you take them to eat chips at the Quick Burger, and you let them play all afternoon in the ball pit.

'You sit there. You haven't even touched the food on your tray. You watch them.

'Two children having a lot of fun in the play area of a fast-food restaurant on an April day in Paris – and the rest isn't important.

'On the way home, Samuel asks if his parents will be there when you get back, and since you're a coward, you say you don't know. No, that's not it, you're not a coward, it really is that you *do not know*. You've never had children, you don't know if you should break the news to them point-blank or create some sort of . . . dramatic progression to give them time to get used to the worst case scenario. Say, to begin with, that they've had a car accident, give them their tea, then say that they're in hospital, give them their bath, then add that it's really serious and . . . If it were you, you'd tell them right away, but alas it's not you. Suddenly you're sorry you're not in the States, it would be easy there to find some sort of Helpline and a shrink who'd be certain sure of herself, on the other end of the line, to advise you. But you're lost and you spend a long time staring into the window of the toy store on the corner of the Rue de Rennes, to gain some time . . .

'When you push open the door of the flat, Samuel rushes to the flashing light on the answerphone. You haven't realized, because you're in the process of struggling with Harriet's tiny little coat,

319

and then, above Alice's chirping as she unwraps her tea set in the entrance, you recognize the Captain's voice.

'He isn't apologizing at all. He's actually telling you off. He cannot understand why you didn't call him back and he asks you to write down the number of the police station and the address of the hospital where the bodies are. He says an awkward goodbye, and offers his condolences once again.

'Samuel looks at you and you . . . you look away. With Harriet firmly wedged on your hip you help her sister to carry all her stuff, and while you're settling the little one in her playpen, a little voice behind your back murmurs, What bodies?

'So you go into the bedroom with him and you answer his question. He listens to you gravely and you are blown away by his . . . self-control, and then he too goes back to playing with his little cars.

'You can't get over it, you're relieved, but you find it somehow rather . . . fishy. Okay, there's a time for everything. Let him play for now, let him play. But when you leave his room, he asks you again, between two vrooms vrooms: Okay, they're never coming back but how long are they never coming back?

'So you go and seek refuge on the balcony and you wonder where in this house they keep the strong spirits. You take the telephone from its socket and, still on the balcony, you start off by calling your boyfriend. You get the impression you've woken him up, you explain the situation coolly, and after a silence as long as the Atlantic Ocean is wide, his voice leaves you with the same desperation as the children's: "Oh honey . . . I feel so terribly sorry for you, but . . . when are you coming back?" You hang up, and there, finally, you begin to cry.

'You have never felt so alone in your entire life and, of course, it's only just beginning.

'Precisely the sort of situation where you would have wanted to ring Ellen . . .

'Charles?'

'Yes?'

'Am I boring you?'

'No.'

'Strong spirits, I was saying . . . Do you like whisky? Hang on a sec.'

She showed him the bottle:

'Did you know that one of the finest whiskies in the world is called Port Ellen?'

'No. You may have noticed, I don't know a great deal . . .'

'It's very hard to find. The distillery closed, over twenty years ago, I think.'

'Then keep it!' he protested.

'No. I'm very happy to drink it with you here tonight. You'll see, it's extraordinary. A gift from Louis, in fact. One of the rare things that managed to make it here with us. He'd have been better than I am at telling you about the notes of citrus, peat, chocolate, wood, coffee, hazelnut and I don't know what all, but for me it's just . . . Port Ellen. What's amazing is that there actually is some left! There was a time when I had to drink myself to sleep, and I wasn't very careful about checking the labels. But this bottle – I'd never have dared use it to knock myself out. I was waiting for you.

'Just joking,' she amended, handing him a glass, 'don't listen to me. What will you think? I'm being ridiculous.'

Once again, the words escaped him. She was not ridiculous at all, she was . . . He didn't know . . . A woman with notes of wood, salt, perhaps some chocolate . . .

'Right, let me finish my story. I think I'm past the worst of it . . . After that we had to live, and whatever people may say, it's always easier when you've *got to* live. I called my parents. My father retreated into silence, as usual, and my mother became hysterical. I left the children with the concierge's daughter and I borrowed my sister's car to join her in hell. It was all very complicated. I never knew that dying could be so complicated. I stayed there two days . . . In a depressing hotel. I'm sure that's where I started my apprenticeship with the bottle . . . Near the station in Dijon, after midnight, it's easier to find a bottle of J&B than sleeping tablets . . . I went to the funeral director's and arranged everything so that the bodies could be cremated in Paris. Why cremated? Because I didn't know where the children would end up living, I suppose . . . It's stupid, but I didn't want to bury them far away from their chi—'

'It's not stupid at all,' interrupted Charles.

She was surprised by the tone of his voice.

'Louis was buried with his wife in the Bordeaux region. Where else?' she smiled, 'but Pierre and Ellen's urns are here.'

Charles was startled.

'In one of the barns. In the middle of all the junk. I think the children have already seen the urns a million times without ever imagining for an instant that . . . Well, anyway, we'll talk about it when they're grown up . . . That's another thing I've discovered . . . What do you do with your dead? In the absolute, it's so simple . . . You think that their memory is far more important than the way they are buried, and obviously you'd be right, but in practice, especially when the dead in question are not really your dead, what are you supposed to do? For me, it was particularly complicated because I . . . The mourning period was much longer for me than for them . . . It's not there any more but for a long time there was this enormous photograph in the kitchen. I wanted Pierre and Ellen to be present at all our meals. And not only in the kitchen, either. I'd put their photos all over the place. I was obsessed by the idea that the children might forget their parents. How I must have tormented them with all that, now that I think about it . . . In the living room there was a shelf where we would place, religiously, all the presents they made at school for Mother's Day. One year Alice brought home a . . . I can't remember what it was now . . . a jewellery box, something like that . . . and of course, like everything Alice makes, it was absolutely splendid. I congratulated her and went to put it on the altar with the others. She didn't say anything, but when I'd gone out she took it and threw it with all her strength against the wall. "I made it for you!" she shouted, "for *you*! Not for a dead woman!" I picked up the pieces and went to remove the photo in the kitchen. Yet again, the children had taught me a lesson and I think that was the day that I stopped wearing black . . . It's good stuff, isn't it?'

'Divine,' answered Charles, between swallows.

'And for the same reason I've always refused to let them call me Mummy, and with hindsight, I think it cost them a great deal. Not so much for Sam, but for the girls, yes. Above all at school. In the yard, during break . . . But I'm not your mother, I said, over and over, your mother was much better than I am. I talked about her a lot, to them, and about Pierre, too. I didn't really know him all that well, in the end . . . And then one day

322

I realized they weren't listening any more. I had thought I was helping them but it was just . . . morbid. It was me I was trying to help. As a result there was always this sort of shadow over this "mummy", as if it were a bad word. Which is really too much, when you think . . . And yet I can't blame myself, can I . . . I adored my sister.

'Even today, not a day goes by without me talking to her. I think I was doing all that in order to . . . I don't know . . . pay tribute to her. Listen,' she said, looking up, 'what an atmosphere . . .'

From the valley came the sounds of splashing and laughter.

'Sounds like midnight swims . . . To get back to my story, it was Yacine, the wise Yacine, who got us out of that situation. He'd just arrived, the night before, wasn't saying a thing, listened to all our conversations and then, at dinner, he struck his forehead: "Aaah, now I see, I get it . . . In fact, Kate means Mum in English." And we all looked at each other with a smile: he'd figured it out.'

'But that bloke who hired me for the Tin Can Alley, for example . . . he said "your son" when he referred to Samuel . . .'

'Well, yes. How could he know that "your son" means "your nephew" in the French we speak at Les Vesperies? Shall we go and see what they're up to?'

As usual, they were accompanied by a herd of mongrels who'd escaped the knacker's yard.

Kate, who was barefoot, made her way carefully. Charles offered her his arm.

He forgot about all his sores, and stood tall and proud.

And felt like he was escorting a queen through the night.

'Won't we disturb them?' he said anxiously.

'Hardly . . . they'll be delighted.'

The older children were clowning around by the stream, and the little ones were amusing themselves melting sweets over the fire.

Charles accepted a little half-melted crocodile that looked rather like the badge he had on his heart.

It was revolting.

'Mmmm . . . delicious.'

'You want another one?'

'No, really, thanks.'

'You coming for a swim?'

'Um . . .'

The girls were chatting in one corner, and Nedra was leaning against Alice's shoulder.

This child spoke only to the flames . . .

Kate requested a serenade. The resident musician was most pleased to comply.

They were all sitting cross-legged on the ground, and Charles felt as if he were fifteen years old again.

With lots of hair . . .

He thought about Mathilde. If she had been there, she could have taught the guy a few songs that would have been more interesting than this laborious pling pling. He thought about Anouk, all alone in her shit cemetery hundreds of kilometres from her grandchildren. And Alexis, who had consigned his soul to the left-luggage office and had to 'meet his objectives' flogging cold storage to municipal cafeterias. And Sylvie's face. The gentleness and generosity with which she had related an entire life so deprived of either . . . And Anouk again, whom he had followed to this place, and who would have been so happy to play the fool with Ellen's children . . . She would have eaten kilos of revolting sweets and performed a gipsy dance around the fire, clapping her hands.

She would, surely, even have been in the water by now . . .

'I need to lean against a tree,' he confessed, wincing, his hand against his chest.

'Of course. Let's go over there.' She grabbed a torch on the way. 'Is it painful, is that it?'

'I've never felt so good in my life, Kate.'

'But . . . what happened to you, exactly?'

'I got run over yesterday morning. Nothing serious.'

She pointed to a pair of plush tree-bark armchairs, and set their chandelier down among the stars.

'Why?'

'Why what?'

'Why did you get run over?'

'Because . . . It's a long story. I'd like to hear the end of yours, first. I'll tell you mine next time.'

'There won't be a next time, you know that perfectly well.'

Charles turned to her and . . .

'Well then, where were we?' is what he preferred to say, rather than some sort of melted gummy-bear declaration.

He heard her sigh.

'I'll tell you what happened because I . . . I'm just like you. I . . .'

Shit. The next bit was already sticking to his fingers.

He could hardly tell her that he'd practically given up hope of ever finding her. She'd said that as a kind of joke – the henhouse, the conquistadors and all that, whereas he . . . it wasn't . . .

It wasn't just some sort of cheap trinket.

'You, what?'

'Never mind. I'll wait my turn.'

Silence.

'Kate?'

'Yes?'

'I'm very happy to have met you. Very, *very* happy.'

She said nothing.

'Now tell me what happened, between your mother's cries and today's fair . . .'

'Oh, my. Yacine! Come over here a sec, love! Can you go and fetch us the bottle and the two glasses that are on the table, please?' Then, turning to Charles, 'Please, whatever you do, don't go imagining things. I did listen to her.'

'Listen to who?'

'Granouk. I never drink alone any more. It's just that I need my Port Ellen to get us that far . . . Why are you looking at me like that?'

'Nothing. You must be the only person on earth who actually trusted her.'

Yacine, out of breath, handed them their glasses and went back to his grub.

'So. Back to hell. My parents arrived the next day. If the children hadn't yet realized that their life was in ruins, the wretched expression on their Granny's face left them in no doubt. Through one of Ellen's friends I found an au pair girl to help out, and I went back to my campus in Ithaca.'

'You were still a student?'

'No, I had . . . well, I was an agricultural engineer. What's bred in the bone . . .' she joked, 'my mother had learned to be a gardener,

325

but I wanted to save mankind! It wasn't some medal at the Chelsea Flower Show that I wanted; I wanted, once and for all, to solve the problem of hunger on the planet! Ha, ha,' she added, not laughing, 'nothing more, nothing less. I'd done research into a lot of diseases and . . . I'll tell you all that later on . . . But at that point I had just got a grant to study black spots in papayas.'

'Really?' asked Charles, amused.

'Really. Ring spot virus. But anyway . . . They solved that problem without me. Although I didn't show it to you earlier, I do have a little laboratory over there.'

'Really!'

'I do, yes. Now I'm not saving the planet, I fiddle with plants to help rich people live better and longer . . . Let's just say I dabble in comfort pharmacopoeia. I'm really into yew trees at the moment. Have you ever heard of yew taxol in cancer treatment? No? Well, that's another topic for debate. But back then, there I was, in my little service flat, with my fiancé asking me if I'd make a pasta salad for the Millers' barbecue.

'The situation was totally insane. What the fuck was I supposed to be doing at the Millers' barbecue, when I had two urns in the bottom of a wardrobe, three orphans on my hands, and two parents to console? The night that followed was very long. I understood, I could hear what he was saying, but it was already too late. I was the one who had urged Ellen to go off and have a good time, and it seemed to me that I had . . . how can I put it . . . my share of *responsibility* in what had happened.'

Gulp of peat to get the word down.

'The worst was that we were in love, Matthew and I . . . We had even planned to get married, I seem to recall . . . In short, there are nights like that when an entire life disappears in the space of a few hours. I ought to know. The next morning I did the rounds of all the administrative offices and I very conscientiously *deleted* myself. In the eyes of most of my colleagues I was cancelled, crossed off, removed, and on all the papers they handed me to sign as well, and they glowered at me as if I were being a selfish little girl who broke her toys and didn't keep her promises.

'I had worked like a dog to get that far, and there I was leaving with my tail between my legs, I think I even felt guilty. I even had to ask them to forgive me. In the space of a few hours I abandoned everything I had: the man I loved, ten years' worth of studies, my friends, my adoptive country, my weak strains, my DNA, my papayas and even my cat . . .

'Matt came with me to the airport. It was awful. I said to him, I'm sure there are plenty of fascinating projects in Europe, too . . . We were in the same field . . . He shook his head and said something that haunted me for the longest time: "You only think about yourself."

'I was crying as I went through the gate. Imagine, someone like me who's been all over the place, to plantations the world over, I have never been on a plane since that day.

'I still think about him sometimes. When I'm here, lost in this godforsaken place, in my wellies, half-frozen, watching Sam train his donkey, with my decrepit dogs and old René and his incomprehensible patois and all the village kids perched on the fences, cheering me on while I'm baking the latest cake, I think about Matt, and what he said, and a magnificent *fuck you* warms my heart a whole lot better than my old friend in the kitchen . . .'

'Who's that?'

'The cooker, my Aga . . . The first thing I bought when I arrived here. That was madness, too.

'All my savings went into her. But my nanny had one in England and I knew I wouldn't manage without . . . It's funny, I had a French friend, whose English was a bit wobbly, who used to say "cooker" when she meant "cook", and her confusion always seemed especially apt to me. For me, for all of us, my Aga *is* the cook, a real person. A sort of fairy godmother, warm, kindly, always there for you, and we're always cuddling up to her. The bottom oven on the left is particularly useful, for example . . .

'When the children are in bed and I've had it up to there, I sit down in front of the Aga and put my feet inside that little oven. It's lovely . . . Fortunately no one ever comes here! The wolf lady with her feet in the oven, they would dine out on that for years! We may have had a really crap car back then, but we did have a Wedgwood blue Aga that must have cost me the equivalent of a Jaguar . . .

'Anyway . . . where were we? My parents went back to England, the au pair made it clear that my mother had been the hardest one to deal with and . . . And then . . .

'It was a very tough time.

'Samuel began wetting the bed again. Alice had nightmares and kept asking me every day when her Mummy wouldn't be dead any more.

'I took them to a child psychiatrist who said, Ask them questions, engage them constantly, force them to verbalize their angst and, above all, never let them sleep with you. I said, Yes, fine, and dropped everything after three sessions.

'I never asked them any questions but I became the world's greatest expert on Playmobil, Lego and coloured sticky labels. I closed the door to Pierre and Ellen's room, and we slept all three together in Sam's room. Three mattresses on the floor . . . Apparently that's a criminal thing to do, but I found it terribly efficient. No more nightmares, no more bed-wetting and lots of stories before lights out. I knew that Ellen spoke to them in French but read them Enid Blyton, Beatrix Potter and all the books we grew up with in English, and so I picked up where she'd left off.

'I didn't force them to "verbalize their angst" but Samuel often stopped to correct me and explain how Mummy used to read that particular passage and also that she would imitate Mr McGregor's gruff voice, or Winnie the Pooh's, much better than I did. Even now, with Yacine and Nedra, we're reading *Oliver Twist* in the original. But that doesn't stop them having dreadful marks at school, I can tell you.

'And then came the first Mother's Day, the first of a long series that always leaves us a bit shaken. I had to go and see their teachers, to ask them to stop going on about their bloody Mothers' Hour. Something Alice told me one evening. That it made her cry all the time. "And now, children, put on your coats because it's time for Mothers' Hour!" I asked them if they couldn't add "and Aunties" but it never really caught on.

'Teachers . . . they really are my bêtes noires. Do you realize that Yacine is bottom of his class? Yacine? The most brilliant, the most curious little boy you've ever seen? And all because he can't hold a pencil properly. I suppose no one ever showed him how to write. I did try, but there was nothing for it, no matter how he tries it's illegible. A few months ago he had to put together a presentation on Pompeii. He spent ages on it, and it was amazing. Alice had done all the illustrations and we even made some plaster models on the kitchen table. Everybody pitched in. Well, they only gave him 10 out of 20, because she said the captions had to be hand-written. I went to see her to assure her that he'd typed it all himself, but she answered that it was "only fair to the others" . . .

'"Only fair to the others."

'I hate that expression.

'I despise it.

'Only fair to the others – what has our life been about for the last nine years, huh?

'A shipwreck?

'A jolly shipwreck.

'For the moment, I'm keeping a lid on it because Nedra is coming up behind him, but when we're done with primary school I'm going to go and see that woman and say, "Madame Christèle P., you are a fucking stupid bitch." Yes, I may be vulgar, but I don't regret it, because being vulgar earned me a very nice reward . . .

'I was telling this anecdote to someone, I don't remember who, how I would go and insult that stupid cow one of these days, and Samuel was there with his mates and he said with a big sigh, "My real mother would never have dared do that . . ." For me that's a reward because things have been pretty rough with him lately. Typical adolescent crisis I suppose, but much more complicated in our case. Never has he missed his parents more than now. All he ever wears now are his father's and grandfather's clothes and, obviously, Auntie Kate with her cakes and carrots in the window box, all that has become a bit lightweight as role models go . . . Fortunately, those little words, which he said *tenderly*, reminded me that the ungrateful good-for-nothing spotty glutton still has a sense of humour. But I won't let that deter me for a moment, I've got her number, that bitch.'

Laughter.

'And how on earth did you end up here?'

'I'm getting there. Pass me your glass.'

Charles was drunk. On her stories.

'So I did what I could . . . Often I was utterly useless, but the kids showed me exemplary kindness and patience. Like their mum. Their mum, whom I missed so much. Because in fact, *I* was the one who was crying at night. When they were unhappy, I wanted so badly for her to be there, and when they were happy, it was even worse. I was living in her flat in the middle of her things, I used her hairbrush and borrowed her jumpers. I read her books, her little notes on the door of the fridge, and even her love letters, one horribly distressing night. There was no one I could talk to about her. My dearest friends were only just getting up when I was on my way to bed, and there was no Internet or Skype in those days, or all those amazing satellites that have transformed our big planet into a little chat room . . .

'I wanted her to teach me to do Pooh's voice. And Tigger's. And Rabbit's too. I wanted her to send me signs from up there to tell me what she thought of all my hare-brained schemes, and whether it really was so bad for us to sleep all hugger-mugger in our un-happiness. I wanted her to confirm that my boyfriend hadn't been worth it and that I'd been right not to give him a chance to get back together with me. I wanted her to hold me in her arms and make big bowls of hot milk with orange blossom, for me as well.

'I wanted to ring her and tell her how hard it was to be raising children who belonged to a sister who had disappeared, a sister who had been so careful not to say goodbye in order not to make them sad. I wanted to rewind the whole thing and say, Let them go off the two of them to drink their wine, let's stay here and finish the sherry and I'll tell you stories about papayas and sex on campus.

'She would have *loved* for me to talk to her like that. Was expecting it, really . . .

'I think I was going a bit barmy, and it would have made more sense to move, but I couldn't force that on them along with everything else. Besides, it wasn't that simple. I've forgotten to tell you the whole . . . *technical* side of the matter. The Family Court, the summons to the judge about guardianship, the lawyers and all the hassles to get the wherewithal to bring them up . . . Are you interested in this, too, Charles, or shall we head straight for the country?'

'I'm very interested, but . . .'

'But?'

'Aren't they going to get cold, splashing about this late?'

'Nah . . . They're indestructible, those creatures. In two minutes the boys are going to chase the girls and everyone will get quite warm again, I assure you.'

Silence.

'You're the attentive sort, aren't you,' she said.

He blushed in the dark.

The slap distributor had just rushed past, shrieking, followed in close pursuit by Bob Dylan.

'What did I tell you . . . By the way . . . would you put condoms in the saddle room, if you were me?'

Charles closed his eyes.

What a roller-coaster ride with this girl . . .

'I put a few . . . by the box of sugar for the horses. When I told Sam, he looked at me completely horrified as if I were some sort of dreadful perv, but in the meantime the dreadful perv has her peace of mind!'

Charles refrained from adding to the discussion. Their shoulders touched from time to time, and the topic was rather . . . well . . .

'Yes. I am interested in the technical side,' he smiled, contemplating the bottom of his glass.

In the dark it was hard to tell, but he thought he could hear her smile.

'It will take a while,' she warned.

'I have as long as it takes . . .'

'The accident happened on 18 April, and I filled in as guardian up to the month of May, but then they had to constitute what they call a Board of Guardians, in other words three people from each side of the family. On our side, it was straightforward: Dad, Mum, and me; on Pierre's side, things were a lot more complicated. This wasn't a family, it was a nest of vipers, so to speak, and by the time they could agree, we'd already had to cancel a first meeting.

'I saw them coming and I felt a huge rush of tenderness for Louis and his son. I understood why Louis had no longer wanted to see them and why Pierre had fallen madly in love with my sister. They were . . . how can I describe them . . . very well-armed people . . . Yes, that's it . . . Well-armed against life. There was Louis' older sister, her husband, and Édouard, Pierre's uncle on his mother's side . . . um . . . are you still following?'

'I'm still following.'

'Uncle Édouard had a nice smile and presents for the children;

the other two – let's call them the "chartered accountants", since that was his profession, and her obsession, accounts that is – began by asking me if I spoke French. Off to a really splendid start!'

She laughed.

'I think I've never spoken French as well as . . . as on that particular day! I got out all my Chateaubriand and my finest subjunctive imperfects for those two hicks from the *provinces*!

'So, first issue: who would be appointed guardian? Right . . . no one was exactly queuing up. The judge looked at me and I smiled. The matter was closed. Second issue, who would be appointed surrogate guardian? In other words, who would police me? Who would "supervise my guardianship"? Oh, my! Right away, agitation in the cashmere camp. If the children had earaches or nightmares, or made drawings of people without arms, that was no big deal, but their inheritance, watch out!'

As she mimed their behaviour, Kate gave him frequent gentle nudges with her elbow . . .

'What would you have me do against such formidable opponents? Suffer the slings and arrows of outrageous fortune or . . . ? I looked at my old dad's face as he took notes, while my mother wrung her handkerchief and moaned, and I listened to the other two making their pitch to the judge. Poor Eddy was worth nothing, it was on Louis' side that there was some cash . . . A flat in Cannes and another one in Bordeaux, not to mention Pierre and Ellen's place. Well, Pierre's place, principally . . . The chartered lady was more familiar with the deed of sale than I was . . . The problem was that Louis and his sister had been embroiled in a lawsuit for ten years or more over some plot of land or I don't know what and . . . in short, I'll spare you the details.

'Good Lord, I could tell we were in for a bumpy ride, all this business . . . In the end it was Louis' brother-in-law who went away with the title. *Civil Code article 420 and following*, quoted the judge, *the role of the surrogate guardian is to represent legally incompetent minors when their interests are in opposition with those of the guardian.* We all came to an agreement while the clerk did her clerking, but I remember that I was already miles away. I was thinking:

'Seventeen years.

'Seventeen years and two months with that lot watching over me . . .

'Help.'

'On the way out of the courthouse, my father finally opened his mouth: "*Alea jacta est*."

'Well, brilliant. That was a big help. And because he could see that I was upset, he added that I had nothing to fear, according to Virgil: "*Numero deus impare gaudet*."'

'Which means?' asked Charles.

'That there were three children, and that Divinity favours odd numbers.'

She looked at him and chuckled: 'And here I was, telling you I felt alone! After that there were numerous meetings with the lawyer to draw up a financial support schedule, with a sum that would be paid me every three months, and that also included the assurance that the children would be able to go to university if I looked after them properly in the meantime . . . Which was, I won't hide the fact, an enormous relief. Seventeen years and two months, even with such a small income, I could manage, and unless they went off with the dough at the age of 18 to blow it all at the casino, they would have a good start in life . . .

'Anyway. We shall see. As I was saying, earlier on: one day at a time. Right, last glass each, just enough to get us as far as the stream . . .

'In the middle of all those appointments and hundreds of phone calls, life went on.

'I lost their vaccination booklets, bought shoes for the summer, met the other mums, heard a lot about Ellen, smiled vaguely, opened her mail and sent death announcements or photocopies of death certificates; I started cooking, I learned to convert pounds and ounces, cups and tablespoons, feet, inches, and all the rest, I took part in my first school fête, I began to do a good job with Tigger's ludicrous voice, I held up, I cracked, I called Matthew in the middle of the night, I disturbed him during some important manoeuvre in the lab, he couldn't talk, he'd call me back. I cried until dawn and had the number changed for fear he really would call me back and find some more convincing arguments to lure me back there . . .

'Then it was summer. We went to my parents' cottage near

Oxford. Dreadful weeks, terribly sad. My father was devastated with grief and my mother continually mixed up Alice and Hattie. I never knew that the school holidays were so long in France . . . I felt as if I had aged twenty years. I wanted to put my lab coat back on and shut myself away with my germs . . . I didn't read them as many stories, but I helped Harriet take her first steps and . . . I had trouble keeping up with her . . .

'It was the backlash, I suppose. As long as we were still in the scaffold – scaffolding?'

'Of what?'

'Of our new life . . .'

'Try scaffolding, it's less hard on the neck and it's even used for cathedrals . . .'

'Oh? As long as we had had that scaffolding, I was active, fighting, but now that was over. There was nothing left to do but hold out for seventeen years and one month. I had five people on my hands, and I cut short the holidays, they were really getting me down. Because I'd lost a lot of weight and left everything back there, I was wearing Ellen's clothes more and more often and . . . I wasn't doing well at all.

'In Paris it was stifling, the children were going round in circles and I gave Samuel his first spanking. Then, on a whim, I decided to rent a self-catering flat just outside a tiny village in the middle of nowhere. The village was called Les Marzeray and we walked every day with the pushchair to get our supplies and have a drink opposite the church.

'I learned how to play pétanque and I started reading books that were again full of sad stories, but at least they were invented ones. The woman who had the grocery-café told me about a farm where I could find fresh eggs and even a chicken. The man wasn't the friendly type but I could always try . . .

'The children had colour in their cheeks, we walked a lot, we picnicked and had siestas in the meadows, Samuel went into raptures over a donkey and her foal, and Alice started a magnificent herbarium. It's in the blood . . .'

Smile.

'I was like her, and I discovered, or rediscovered, nature in a different form, other than through the microscope. I bought a disposable camera and asked a tourist to take a picture of me with the children. The first one . . . It's on the mantelpiece in the kitchen and it's my most precious possession . . . The four of us, in front of the fountain next to the bakery in Les Marzeray, that summer. Recovering, sitting precariously on the edge of the fountain, hardly daring to smile at this stranger but . . . alive.'

Tears.

'Sorry,' she said, wiping her nose against her sleeve, 'it's the whisky . . . What time is it? Almost one . . . I've got to get them to bed.'

Charles, who felt buoyed up after all these stories, offered to carry Nedra.

She refused.

Yacine was walking next to him, silent. He felt sick. Harriet and Camille followed, dragging their sleeping bags behind them.

It was too cold under the stars . . .

★

Kate carried her dog back into the kitchen and disappeared upstairs after asking Charles if he would light the fire.

He had a moment of panic, but no, he wasn't that useless . . . He went to fetch the logs beneath the awning, and rinsed out their glasses, and then he too came to rub up against their cast-iron nanny. He knelt down, caressed the dog, touched the enamel, opened all the oven doors and lifted up the two lids.

Each temperature was totally different to the touch.

All the things he was discovering . . .

He went and found the photo she'd been telling him about, and winced.

They were so little.

'It's a lovely picture, isn't it?' she said over his shoulder.

No. That's not what he would have said.

'I didn't realize they were so young.'

'Less than eighty kilos,' she replied.

'Sorry?'

'That's what we weighed at the time. All four of us, on the scales at the bus terminal. Well, anyway . . . Jumping on the thing with all our books and our parkas, and we managed to get told off by the bloke at the ticket office. Madame! Mind your children, please! You'll bugger up the mechanism with your nonsense!

'Good.

'That was precisely my intention.'

She'd pulled over a cane armchair that was missing an armrest. Charles was sitting lower down, his arms round his knees, on a tiny footrest tapestried with rosebuds and moth holes.

They sat in silence for a moment.

'The awkward old man, that was René, right?'

'Yes,' she smiled. 'Oh, there's something I'd like to do, just for fun. I'll take my time. But I'm worried that you're not sitting comfortably?'

He turned around so that he could lean against the mantelpiece.

For the first time, she sat directly opposite him.

He looked at her face, lit only by the fire he had built and would maintain, and he sketched her in his mind.

Beginning with her eyebrows, that were very straight, and then . . .

So many shadows.

'Take your time,' he murmured.

'It was on the 12th of August. Harriet's birthday . . . Her first candle. A sad day, or a happy one, it was up to us. We decided to make her a cake and we went looking for those famous fresh eggs. But that was a pretext. I'd already noticed the farm beyond the village during our earlier walks, and I wanted to see it closer up.

'It was very warm, I remember, and already, beneath the long avenue of oak trees, we felt better . . . Some of the trees were diseased and I thought about all those mushroom genomes that others in my place were probably in the middle of sequencing . . .

'Samuel, on his little bicycle, was riding ahead of us, counting the trees. Alice was looking for acorns "with holes in them", and Hattie was asleep in her pushchair.

'Even with the prospect of that birthday candle, I felt rather down. I couldn't really see where we were headed. I felt as if I too were afflicted with a sort of scabies or some other parasite . . . *Solitudina vulgaris* perhaps? The kids were intoxicated with our long walks and the fresh air, and fell asleep very early, and that left me with long evenings to ruminate on my fate. I'd started smoking again, I lied to you earlier on . . . I didn't read all those

336

novels I'd taken with me . . . But I did read haikus. A little book I'd stolen from Ellen's night table . . .

'I turned down the corner on pages that read:

> *Covered with butterflies*
> *the dead tree*
> *is in bloom!*

Or:

> *Without a care*
> *on my pillow of herbs*
> *I am absent.*

'But the only one that really obsessed me at the time is something I'd read on the door of the toilets, on campus:

> *Life's a bitch*
> *and then*
> *you die.*

'Yes, that one had a good ring to it.'

'And yet you still remember them, the Japanese ones, I mean,' countered Charles.

'No particular merit in that. The anthology is in the loo, now,' she answered with a smile.

'To continue . . . We crossed the bridge and the children were in a trance. Frogs! Water boatmen! Fireflies! They didn't know where to begin to look.

'Samuel dropped his bike on the spot and Alice handed me her sandals. I let them play for a moment while I gathered some rushes and water crowfoot . . . *ranunculus aquatilis* . . . for her . . . And then Harriet, whom I'd left in her pushchair up on the road, called for us and we went back up with our treasures. And then . . . I don't know what you thought, yesterday evening when you arrived here with Lucas, but for me, these little walls, and the courtyard, and the little house hidden under the vines and all the buildings round here . . . they're worn but still so valiant – well, it was love at first sight. We knocked on the door: no one, and because it was so hot we went to have our picnic in one of the barns. Samuel immediately ran to look at the tractors and was fascinated by the old carts. "Are there horses, do you reckon?" The girls made a mess with their biscuits, laughing among all the hens, and I was absolutely desperate that I'd forgotten my camera. This was the first time I'd ever seen them like that . . . Neither older nor younger than their real age . . .

'A dog came up to us. Some sort of little fox terrier who also liked BN Choco biscuits and who could jump as high as Samuel's shoulder. His master soon followed. I waited until he'd put his buckets down and rinsed off at the pump before I dared bother him.

'Because he was looking for his dog he soon saw the four of us and came slowly over to greet us. I scarcely had time to say hello before the kids were bombarding him with questions.

'"Oh my!" he went, raising his hands, "I can tell you lot are from the city then, ain't ya!"

'He told them the dog's name, Filou, and made him perform all sorts of funny little tricks.

'A regular little drill sergeant . . .

'I told him we'd come to buy some eggs. "Ah, I reckon I must have a few in the kitchen now, but the little lad and lass will be wanting to fetch 'em theirsels, won't they?" and he led us to his henhouse. For a bloke who wasn't the friendly type I found him very amiable . . .

'Then we followed him into his kitchen to look for a box for the eggs and I realized he must have been living there on his own for a very long time . . . It was absolutely filthy . . . Not to mention the smell . . . He offered us something to drink and we all sat down round his table with the oilcloth that stuck to our elbows. It was a very weird syrup drink and there were dead flies in the sugar bowl but the children behaved perfectly. I didn't dare take Hattie out of her pushchair. The floor was as sticky as the rest . . . At one point I couldn't take it any more and I got up and went to open the window. He watched me without saying a thing, and I think that was the beginning of our friendship, when I turned round and said, "Aah, that's better now, isn't it?"

'He was an old bachelor, all awkward and embarrassed, and he'd never seen children that close up, and I was a future old maid with seventeen years to go, and who wasn't about to be daunted by a stiff window handle, so he and I smiled at each other in the warm breeze . . .

'Sam explained that the eggs were so that we could make a

338

birthday cake for his little sister. He looked at Hattie now on my lap: "Is it her birthday today?" I nodded, and he added, "Seems to me I must have a cuddly toy for the little lass round here some-where." Oh Lord, I wondered what sort of repulsive sticky thing he was going to put in her hands . . . A pink rabbit he'd won at the shooting range at a county fair in 1912?

"'Follow me,' he declared, helping Alice down from her chair. He led us into another building and began grumbling in the gloom: "And where the divil have they got to now?"

'It was the children who found them, and this time there really was no way I could have kept hold of Hattie . . .'

Charles was becoming an expert on Kate's particular smiles, but this one was even more contagious than the others.

'What was it?'

'Kittens. Four tiny kittens hidden under an old banger of a car . . . The children went wild. They asked him if they could hold them and we all went to play in the grass behind the house.

'While they were playing with the kittens as if they were marsh-mallow paste, he and I went to sit down on a bench. He had his dog on his lap, was rolling a cigarette, smiled as he watched the kids and congratulated me: I'd had a lovely litter, myself. I burst into tears. I had had nowhere near enough sleep, and I hadn't spoken to a kindly adult since . . . Ellen, so I came out with the whole story.

'He sat there silent for a long time with his lighter under his thumb and then he said, "You'll see, they'll be a happy lot, all the same. Well then, which one has she chosen, the little kid?"

'Her brother and sister decided for her and I promised we'd come to fetch the kitten on the day we left. He walked us back as far as the oak trees. The rack under the pushchair was filled with vegetables from his garden and the children turned round to wave to him for a long time.

'Once we were back in our little rental kitchen, I realized I had no oven . . . So I planted a candle in a bought sponge cake, and they went to bed exhausted. Sigh of relief, the bloody day was behind us . . . I'd decided it would be a cheerful time, but I'd never have managed it without that house and its beautiful vesperal name . . .

'I was smoking on the terrace when Sam joined me, dragging

his teddy bear behind him. It was the first time he'd come to find me like that. The first time he put his arms around me . . . And this time it wasn't my cigarette but the stars that served as our smokescreen . . .

"'You know, we mustn't take him, the little kitty," he finally announced, very gravely. "Are you afraid he'll be sad in Paris?" "No, but I don't want him to be taken away from his mummy and his brothers and sisters . . ."

'Oh, Charles, I was an absolute sponge myself, full of tears . . . Everything made me cry, absolutely everything.

"'But we can go and see it again tomorrow," he added.

'Of course we could. And we went back the next day, and the day after that, and finally we spent the rest of our holiday at the farm. The children amused themselves in the barns while I emptied the kitchen out into the courtyard and cleaned it with big buckets of water. Our Monsieur René, with his hens and his cows and the old horse that he boarded, and his little dog and his gigantic mess, had become our new family. For the first time I felt good. Protected. It was as if nothing bad could ever reach us behind those walls, and the rest of the world was out there, beyond the moat . . .

'The day we were due to leave, we were all rather upset and we promised we'd come back to see him during the holidays at All Saint's. "Well, you'll have to see me in town then, 'cause I won't be here on the farm no more." No? And why not? He was too old, he didn't want to go through another winter there on his own. He'd been very sick the year before, and he'd decided to go and live at his sister's place, now that she'd just been widowed. He was going to rent the house out to some young people and he'd only keep the vegetable garden.

"'And the animals?" asked the kids, anxious. Bah . . . he'd take the hens and Filou, but as for the others, well . . .

'In that little "well" there was an echo of the abattoir.

'Right. Well, we'd go to see him in town, then. We took one last long tour before leaving, and I wasn't able to take all the crates he'd so kindly filled for me: the car was too small.'

She got up, lifted the left-hand lid, and filled up a kettle.

'After that the flat seemed really tiny . . . And the pavements . . . And the square . . . And the traffic wardens . . . And the sky . . . And the trees on the Boulevard Raspail . . . And even the Jardin du

340

Luxembourg – I didn't want to go there any more, the lightning swift donkey rides had become far too much of a luxury . . .

'Every evening I thought to myself that I'd fill up some boxes and rearrange the flat, and every morning I'd put off the ordeal until the following day. Through a former colleague, the American Chestnut Foundation offered me the job of translating a huge dissertation on chestnut tree diseases. I signed Hattie up at the day-care centre – there, too, I'll spare you all the administrative hassles, so wretchedly humiliating . . . And while the older children were at school, I struggled with the *Phytophthora cambivora* and other *Endothia parasitica*.

'I hated the work, spent my time staring at the grey sky through the window, and wondered if there were a stove with holes in it for grilling chestnuts in René's kitchen . . .

'And then a day came that was darker than all the others . . . Hattie was ill all the time, blowing her nose and coughing and choking at night in her phlegm. It was hell to get an appointment at the doctor's and the waiting time for a physio to sort her chest was driving me mad. Sam was on the verge of reading on his own already and was bored to death in his first year in primary school, and Alice's teacher, the same one she'd had the year before, was still requiring the signature of both parents on the little notes she would send home. I couldn't really reproach her for it but if I were the one who'd chosen such a profession, I'd've been a bit more attentive towards this little girl who was already so much better at drawing than all the others . . .

'What else happened that day? The concierge had got on my case about the pushchair, that it was cluttering up the entrance; I had just got a letter from the building manager with an estimate for all the work to be done on the lift – it was exorbitant and totally unexpected; the boiler was not working; my computer had just crashed and fourteen pages of chestnut trees had disappeared into thin air . . . and, the icing on the cake, when I did finally manage to get an appointment at the physio's, I found the car had been towed away . . . Anyone else, with a bit more sense, would have simply called a cab, but I burst into tears.

'I was crying so noisily that the children didn't even dare tell me that they were hungry.

'Finally Samuel fixed a bowl of cereal for everyone and . . . the milk was off, it had turned.

'"Don't cry over it," he said, distressed, "we can eat it with yoghurt, you know."

'How sweet they were, when I think of it . . .

'We lay down in our bivouac. I didn't have the heart to read any stories and we made one up in the dark instead. As was often the case, our daydreams took us back to Les Vesperies . . . How big would the kittens be now? Had René taken them with him? And the little donkey? Were other children bringing him apples after school?

'"Wait here," I said.

'It must have been nine o'clock in the evening, I went to make a phone call and when I came back I stepped on Sammy's tummy to make him shout. I got back under my duvet with the three of them and said these words very slowly: "If you'd like to, we'll go and live there forever . . ."

'Long silence and then he whispered, "But . . . can we take our toys?"

'We talked a while longer and when they had finally fallen asleep I got back up and started to fill up the cardboard boxes.'

The kettle was whistling.

Kate put a tray down by the fire. The scent of lime flowers.

'The only thing René had said on the telephone was that the house hadn't been rented yet. The young people who were supposed to move in thought it was too isolated. Perhaps that should have started me thinking – the fact that locals with young children had decided against living there . . . But I was too excited when I heard what he had to say . . . That winter, much later, I would often think back on that moment. There were some nights when it was so cold . . . But anyway, by then we'd got used to camping and we all settled in the living room around the fireplace. Physically, our first years here were the most exhausting in my life but I felt . . . invulnerable . . .

'Then came Big Dog, and then the donkey to thank this little lad who had helped me carry logs every night, and then the cats had more cats, and by then it had become the merry shambles you see today . . . Would you like some honey?'

'No, thanks. But . . . you've lived here alone all these years?'

'Ah!' smiled Kate, hiding behind her mug. 'My love life. I wasn't sure whether I ought to go into that chapter, to be honest . . .'

'Of course you're going to talk about it,' answered Charles, stirring the embers.

'Oh really? And why is that?'

'I need it in order to finish my inventory.'

'I don't know if it's worth it . . .'

'Well, try.'

'And what about yours?'

Silence.

'Right. I see that *yet again* I'm the one who has to pack the cardboard boxes! Here goes but it's nothing to be proud of, you know . . .'

She moved closer to the fire, and Charles turned an invisible page.

Her profile, now . . .

'Hard as they were, those first months flew by. I had so much to do . . . I learned how to fill cracks, and coat surfaces, paint, chop wood, put a drop of bleach in the hens' water so that they wouldn't get sick, sand the shutters, kill rats, wage war against draughts, buy the cuts of meat that were reduced and divide them up before freezing them, and do a ton of things I would never have thought myself capable of and, all the time, there'd be a very curious little girl under my feet . . .

'In those days I went to bed at the same time as the children. After eight in the evening I could have had a sign saying "out of order". It was the best thing that could have happened to me, actually . . . I never regretted my decision. Nowadays it's more complicated because of school and in future it will be even worse, but nine years ago, believe me, this Robinson Crusoe lifestyle saved us all. And then the good weather returned . . . The house was almost comfortable and I began to look in the mirror again to brush my hair. It's daft but it was something I hadn't done in almost a year . . .

'One morning I put on a dress again, and the next day I fell in love.'

She was laughing.

'Obviously at the time the whole business seemed like the most romantic thing imaginable. The unexpected arrow of some Cupid who had got lost in the fields and all that foolishness, but nowadays, with hindsight, and given the way things turned out . . . Well anyway, I've sacked the cherub now.

'It was springtime and *I wanted* to fall in love. I wanted a man to take me in his arms. I was fed up with being this Superwoman who took forever to take off her boots and had had three children in less than nine months. I wanted someone to kiss me and tell me my skin was soft. Even if it wasn't true for a second . . .

'So I put on this dress to go with Samuel's class to visit I can't remember what with the other teacher's pupils and . . . I sat next to that teacher during the return trip.'

Charles gave up on his sketches. Her face was too change-able. Ten minutes ago she was ageless but when she smiled like that, she was in the back of the bus again, and not quite fifteen years old.

'The next day I found an excuse to make him come here, and I raped him.'

She turned towards Charles: 'Um . . . he was consenting, actu-ally! Consenting, kind, a bit younger than me, single, a local man, very good at handiwork, very good with kids, very good on birds, trees, stars, and hikes . . . In short, the ideal man. Wrap him up quick so I can take him home and freeze him!

'No . . . I shouldn't be so cynical. I was in love. I was dying of love and I loved him *well*. Life had become so much simpler. He moved in. René, who'd known him as a wee lad, gave me his blessing, and Big Dog didn't eat him, and he took everything on without making a fuss. It was a gorgeous summer and for her second birthday Hattie had a real cake. And it was a fine autumn as well . . . He taught us how to love Nature, how to look at it and understand it, he got us a subscription to *La Hulotte* – it's a brilliant nature magazine – introduced me to loads of adorable people whom I'd never have known without him . . . He reminded me that I wasn't yet thirty and that I loved to have fun, and that I liked to have my lie-in . . .

'I'd gone completely daft. Over and over I said, "I've found my master! I've found my master!"

'The following spring, I decided I wanted a child. It was prob-ably a bit early, but it meant a lot to me. I must have reckoned that it would be a way to strengthen all the ties – to him, to Ellen, to the house . . . I wanted a child of my own to be sure I would never abandon the other three . . . I don't know if you see what I mean?'

No. Charles was too jealous to try to unravel all that.

I loved him *well*.

The 'well' had bitten him just beneath the crocodile.

He did not even know what it meant . . .

And, besides, it went without saying that a country bumpkin teacher would be good with kids and be able to find the Great Bear.

'Sure, I understand,' he murmured gravely.

'It wasn't working. Perhaps another woman would have had more patience than I did, but at the end of a year, I went into the big city to undergo a whole series of tests. I'd taken on three kids at once without batting an eyelid – so I ought to be entitled to my own child, no?

'I was so obsessed with my belly that I kind of fucked up on the rest . . .

'He wasn't sleeping at home every night? He needed peace and quiet to mark his dictations. He no longer wandered around the back roads with us on Sundays looking for boot sales? Well, he must have been fed up with all our junk. He no longer made love quite so tenderly? But that was my fault, too! All that calculating is a real turn-off . . . He found that the children were always in the way? Well, there were three of them . . . And badly behaved? Indeed . . . I thought that Life owed them that much . . . that in their childhood at least they ought to be able to tell the rest of the world where to get off . . . I spoke to them in English too often? Well, yes . . . when I'm tired, I speak the language that comes to me most easily . . .

'For this reason and that one and this one and that one . . . and he had asked for a new posting for the next school year.

'Ah. There was nothing I could say.

'I really hadn't seen it coming. I thought he was just like me, that the words he'd said and the commitments he'd made even without the judge and his clerk, meant something. Despite the forecast of rough winters, and a rather cumbersome dowry . . .

'They gave him a new posting and I turned into what I was when I told you about my last cigarette . . .

'An abandoned guardian . . .

'I was really miserable, when I think back on it,' she smiled, sheepishly. 'But what the hell was I doing here, anyway? Why on earth had I come to balls up my life in a shithole of a house like this, anyway? Acting like I was Karen Blixen among the dunghills . . . Bringing in the wood every night and going to do my shopping farther and farther away so that no one would comment on the number of bottles I placed discreetly between the packets of biscuits and the tins of cat food . . .

'And to add to the entire world collapsing around me there was something even more pernicious: loss of self-esteem. Right, our affair had come to an abrupt end but . . . that happens to a lot of people. The trouble was the three years' difference in our ages. I didn't say to myself, he left me because he no longer loves me; I said, he left me because I'm too old.

'Too old to be loved. Too ugly, too much baggage. Too kind, too blind, too far behind.

'Hardly very glamorous, either, with my chainsaw and my chapped lips and red hands and my cooker that weighs six hundred kilos . . .

'No. Hardly very glamorous.

'I didn't hold it against him for leaving; I understood.

'I would have done exactly the same thing in his shoes.'

She poured another cup and blew on the lukewarm water for a long time.

'The only good thing to come out of the whole business,' she scoffed, 'is that we still have our subscription to *La Hulotte*! Do you know him, the bloke who puts it together? Pierre Déom?'

Charles shook his head.

'He's brilliant. An absolute genius. I doubt whether he'd want to go there, but he deserves his plot of earth at the Panthéon one day, that man . . . But anyway. I was no longer really in the mood to try to tell a hazelnut nibbled by a squirrel from a hazelnut nibbled by a vole . . . Although . . . I must have been interested in all of that or we wouldn't be here this evening . . .

'The squirrel breaks the nut open into two halves, whereas the vole makes a neat little hole. For further details, see the mantelpiece . . .

'I was more of a vole's nut in all this business. I was still in one piece, but completely emptied out inside. Uterus, heart, future, confidence, courage, cupboards . . . Everything was empty. I was smoking and drinking deeper and deeper into the night and, since

Alice had learned how to read, I could no longer die prematurely, so I suffered from some sort of depression instead . . .

'You asked me earlier on why I have so many animals; well, at that point, I knew why. It was so that I would get up in the morning – feed the cats, open the door for the dogs, take the hay out to the horses and have the children none the wiser. The animals enabled the house to go on living and to keep the children busy, away from me . . .

'The animals reproduced during mating season and the rest of the time all they cared about was eating. It was a glorious example. I didn't read any more bedtime stories, and I gave the kids these ghostly kisses, but every evening, when I closed the door to the their room, I made sure that each one had his or her appointed kitty as a hot water bottle . . .

'I don't know how long it would have lasted nor how far it would have gone . . . I was beginning to lose my grip. Wouldn't they be better off in a real family? With a standard issue mummy and daddy? Wouldn't I do better to just ditch all this and go back to the States with them? Or even without them?

'Wouldn't I . . . I wasn't even talking to Ellen any more, and I kept my eyes down to make sure I never met her gaze . . .

'My mother rang one morning. Apparently I had turned thirty years old.

'Oh?

'Already?

'Only?

'I knocked myself senseless with vodka to celebrate.

'I'd fucked up my life. I was willing to do the minimum, three meals a day and take them to school and back, but that was it.

'In the event of a claim, please refer to the judge.

'That was more or less the stew I was in when I met Anouk and she put her hand on my neck . . .'

Charles was staring at the firedogs.

'And then one day I got a call from the gynaecologist's office where I'd been examined a few weeks earlier. They couldn't tell me anything over the phone, I had to go in. I wrote down the appointment date, fully aware that I wouldn't go. The matter was no longer on the agenda, and probably never would be, ever again.

'But for some reason I did go. To get out, get a different perspective, and because Alice needed some tubes of paint or some other supply that you can't find anywhere around here.

'The doctor called me in. Analysed my X-rays. My uterus and my tubes had completely atrophied. Tiny, blocked, in no condition to procreate. I would have to do another series of more advanced tests, but he'd read in my file that I'd spent long periods of time in Africa, and he thought I must have caught tuberculosis.

'But . . . I have no recollection of ever being sick, I protested. He was very calm, he must have been the top-ranking officer in the barracks and he was used to having to break unpleasant news to people. He went on for a long time but I wasn't listening. Some sort of tuberculosis that you don't even notice and . . . I can't remember what else . . . My brain as necrotic as all the rest.

'What I do remember is that when I was back out on the street, I touched my belly underneath my jumper. Stroked it, even. I'd completely had it.

'Fortunately time was passing. I had to get a move on if I wanted to stop by the big stationer's before going to pick up the kids at school. I bought everything for her. Everything she could have possibly dreamed of. Paint, pastels, a box of watercolours, charcoal, paper, brushes of all sizes, a Chinese calligraphy set, beads . . . Everything.

'Then I went into a toy shop and spoiled the other two rotten as well. It was really daft, I had trouble enough making ends meet, but never mind. Life was *indisputably* a bitch.

'I was very late, nearly had an accident, and arrived outside the gate utterly dishevelled. It was almost night time and I could see them there waiting for me, anxious, all three sitting under the overhang.

'There was no one else in the schoolyard.

'I saw them look up and I saw their smiles. The smiles of children who have just realized that no, they haven't been forgotten. I threw myself at them and took them in my arms. I laughed and cried and begged their forgiveness and told them I loved them and that we'd never be apart, that we were the strongest and that . . . And that the dogs must be expecting us by now, right?

'They opened their presents, and I began to live again.'

*

'There,' she concluded, putting down her cup, 'you know it all. I don't know what sort of report you'll file with whoever sent you on this mission out here, but as far as I'm concerned, I've shown you everything.'

'And the other two? Yacine and Nedra? Where did they come from?'

'Oh, Charles,' she sighed, 'this makes nearly –' She reached out and took his wrist, turned it over to consult his watch – 'nearly seven hours I've been talking about myself without interruption. Haven't you had enough?'

'No. But if you're tired –'

'Are you completely out of cigarettes?'

'Yes.'

'Shit. Well . . . Put on another log, then. I'll be right back.'

She'd put on a pair of jeans underneath her dress.

'To start to live again, with my dead belly, meant opening my home to other children.

'Such a big house, with so many animals, so many hiding places, so many little sheds . . . And I had so much time on my hands, in the end . . . So I submitted an application to the social services to become a foster carer. My idea was to take children in over the holidays. To give them a fabulous holiday camp, with great memories, and . . . Well, I wasn't really sure but it seemed to me that our way of life here might be well adapted to that sort of thing . . . We were all in the same boat, and we had to stick together . . . and then I thought that I could make myself useful, after all. I talked to the kids and they must have answered something like, Well, does this mean we'll have to share our toys, then?

'If that was as traumatic as it could get . . .

'I discovered a new world. Went to get the paperwork at the mother and child care office and filled out every box. My status, my income, my motivations . . . I used a dictionary so I wouldn't make any spelling mistakes and I added photos of the house. I thought they'd forgotten about me but a few weeks later a social worker got in touch so she could come out and see if I could obtain a consent.'

She touched her forehead with a laugh.

'I remember, the night before, we washed all the dogs in the

349

yard. I had to admit that they really reeked! And then I plaited the girls' hair . . . I think I may even have disguised myself as a proper lady . . . We were per-fect!

'The social worker was young and smiling; her co-worker, the nursery nurse was, um, less pleasant. I began by offering to show them round, and we set off with Sam, his sisters, any of the village kids who happened to be hanging about, the dogs, the – no, the llama wasn't here yet . . . well, anyway, you can imagine the parade.'

Charles could imagine it well.

'We were as proud as peacocks. It's the most beautiful house in the world, no? The nursery nurse was spoiling our pleasure asking every three seconds whether this or that wasn't dangerous. And the stream? It's not dangerous? And the moat? It's not dangerous? And the tools? They're not dangerous?

'And the well? And the rat poison in the stables? And . . . that big dog over there?

'And your bloody thick head? was what I felt like replying. Hasn't it caused enough damage already?

'But I played fair. Well, my kids have managed fine up to now, was what I said, jokingly.

'After that I invited them into my lovely living room. You haven't seen it yet but it's very elegant. I call it my Bloomsbury. It wasn't Vanessa Bell and Duncan Grant who designed the frescoes on the walls and above the fireplace, it's my lovely Alice . . . The rest is somewhat the same atmosphere as at Charleston. Piles of things, bric-a-brac, paintings . . . At the time of that visit, it was more civilized. Pierre and Ellen's furniture still had a certain style, and the dogs weren't allowed to climb onto the chintz sofas . . .

'I'd brought out the heavy ammunition. Silver tea set, embroidered napkins, scones, cream, and jam. The girls did the service and I smoothed my skirt before sitting down. The Queen herself would have been . . . enchanted . . .

'With the young social worker, we hit it off straight away. She asked me some very pertinent questions about my "vision" . . . My ideas regarding child-rearing, my ability to question my own judgment, to adapt to difficult children, my patience, my tolerance level . . . Even with the lack of self-esteem that I mentioned earlier, and which has remained my faithful companion ever since, at that point in time I felt untouchable. It seemed to me that I'd proven my worth . . . That this draughty old house radiated tolerance, and that the children's joyful cries in the courtyard were proof if ever any was needed . . .

'The other nanny-goat wasn't listening. She was looking, horrified, at the electric wires, the sockets, the gnawed bone that my eagle eye had missed, the broken windowpane, the spots of damp on the walls . . .

'We were chatting quite calmly when she suddenly let out a cry: a mouse had come to see whether there might be a few crumbs under the coffee table.

'Holy shit!

'"Oh, this one's an old friend," I said, to reassure her, "she's a member of the family, you know. The children feed her cornflakes every morning . . ."

'It was true, but I could tell she didn't believe me . . .

'They left at the end of the afternoon and I prayed to the heavens that the bridge wouldn't collapse under their car. I had forgotten to warn them to park on the other side . . .'

Charles was smiling. He had a front row seat, and the play was truly excellent.

'I didn't get the consent. I can't recall all their blah blah exactly, but roughly it was something to the effect that the electricity wasn't up to standard. Right, at the time I was annoyed as hell, and then I forgot about it. Was it kids I wanted? Well, all I had to do was look out the window! There were kids everywhere.'

'That's what Alexis's wife said,' retorted Charles.

'What?'

'That you were like the Pied Piper of Hamelin . . . That you lured all the children out of the village . . .'

'To drown them, is that it?' she asked, annoyed.

Charles didn't know what to say.

'Pff . . . She's a bloody cow, as well . . . How does he manage, your friend, to live with her?

'I told you, he's not my friend any more.'

'That's your story then, is it?'

'Yes.'

'Is he the reason you came down here?'

'No . . . I came for myself.'

Kate said nothing.

351

'My turn will come, I promise. So tell me about Yacine and Nedra, then.'

'Why are you so interested in all this?'

What could he reply?

To look at you for as long as possible. Because you are the luminous side of the woman who brought me to you. Because, in her way, she would have become what you are, had she been less mutilated by her childhood.

'Because I'm an architect,' he replied.

'What's that got to do with it?'

'I like to understand what keeps things standing.'

'Oh really? And what does that make us, then? A zoo? Some kind of boarding house or . . . a hippy camp?'

'No. You are . . . I don't know quite how to put it, yet . . . I'm looking. I'll tell you. Go on. I'm waiting for Yacine.'

Kate rubbed her neck. She was tired.

'A few weeks later, I got a phone call from the nice one, the one who liked my standards . . . She told me again how sorry she was, and began to rail against the administration and its stupid rules and . . . I interrupted her. No problem. I'd got over it.

'And, by the way. She had a little boy who really needed a holiday. He was living with one of his aunts but things weren't going well at all. Could we, perhaps, do without the blessing of the Board? It would just be for a few days. To give him a chance to see something different. She wouldn't have dared "fiddle" like this if it had been someone else, but this little boy, well, I'd see, he was really something else . . . And she added with a laugh, "I think he deserves to come and see your mice!"

'It was for the Easter holidays, I think . . . One morning, she "smuggled" him over here, so to speak, and . . . You can see what he's like . . . We adored him from the start.

'He was irresistible, asking loads of questions, was interested in everything, was constantly helping out, developed a passion for Hideous, would get up very early in the morning to help René in the garden, knew what my name meant and told all sorts of epic stories to my little bumpkins who'd never been out of their village.

'When she came to fetch him at the end of the holidays, it was . . . awful.

'He was sobbing, tears running down his face . . . I remember I took him by the hand and we went down to the end of the garden. I said, "A few weeks from now it'll be the summer holidays, and then you'll be able to come for two months." But, he hiccupped, he wanted to stay for–for–foreh–eh–ver. I promised him that I'd write often, so there, yes, if I could prove to him that I wouldn't forget him, all right. He'd agree to get back into Nathalie's car . . .

'In the time it took for him to give a big cuddle to his favourite dog, well, Nathalie, a civil servant who served straight from the heart, confessed to me that the boy's father had beaten his mother to death before his eyes.

'I came down with a bump. That would teach me to play the fine charitable society lady, wouldn't it . . . I wanted to open a holiday camp, not find myself with a whole slew of problems staring me in the face all over again . . .

'Anyway. It was already too late. Yacine was gone, but not the images. Not the obsession with a man destroying his children's mother in a corner of the living room . . . I thought I'd got tough . . . but I guess not. Life always has plenty more nasty surprises up its sleeve . . .

'So, I wrote to Yacine. We all wrote to him. I took lots of pictures of the dogs, the hens, René, and I'd include one or two with each letter. And he came back, at the end of June.

'Summer went by. My parents came for a visit. He soon had my mother wound round his little finger, and he'd repeat after her all the Latin names of all the flowers, then he'd ask my father to translate them all for him. My father would be there reading below the tall locust tree, and he'd be declaiming, "*Tityre, tu patulae recubans sub tegmine fagi*," teaching Yacine to sing the name of the lovely Amaryllis.

'I was the only one who knew his story, and it was a marvel to see how a little boy who'd witnessed so much could have such a restful effect on everyone . . .

'The children made fun of him all the time because he was constantly afraid of everything, but he never got cross. He would say, "I'm looking at you because I'm thinking about what you're doing." I myself knew that he didn't want to run the slightest risk of being hurt *ever again*. He let the other kids get on with their

"Indian torture" games, and he went off to see Granny among her roses.

'By mid-August I was beginning to dread his departure.

'Nathalie had planned to come and fetch him on the 28th. On the 27th in the evening, he disappeared.

'The next morning, we organized a huge game of hide and seek. In vain. And Nathalie went away again, rather annoyed. This business could get her into a lot of trouble. I promised her that I'd bring him to her myself as soon as I found him. But by the following evening we still couldn't find him. She was in a panic. We had to call the police. Perhaps he'd drowned? And while I was trying to reassure her, I saw the oddest thing in the kitchen, so I said, Give me a bit more time, I'll call the police, I promise.

'The children were completely stressed out, they ate their dinner in total silence and went to bed, calling his name as they went along the corridors.

'In the middle of the night, I came down to make a cup of tea. I didn't switch on the light, I sat at the end of the table and I spoke to him. "Yacine, I know where you are. You have to come out now. You don't want the police to have to come and get you, now do you?"

'No answer.

'Obviously.

'I would have done the same thing in his place, so I did what I would have wanted someone to do with me, if I had been in his place.

'"Yacine, listen. If you come out now, I'll work something out with your uncle and aunt and I promise you that you'll be able to stay with us."

'Naturally, I was taking a risk, but anyway . . . according to various things Nathalie had let drop, I'd figured that the uncle in question was not all that eager to have an umpteenth mouth to feed . . .

'"Yacine, please. You're going to catch all the fleas on that dog! Have I ever lied to you, ever, even once, since you've known me?"

'And then I heard, "Oh, all right . . . you've no idea how hungry I am!"'

'Where was he?' asked Charles.

Kate turned round: 'That bench over there against the wall, the one that looks like a huge chest . . . I don't know if you can see them, but there are two openings in the front. It's a dog kennel bench I found at an antique shop when we were moving in . . . I thought it was a grand idea, but, naturally, the dogs never used it. They prefer Ellen's sofas. And what a coincidence, suddenly Hideous was in there all the time, and never once came out to drool over our plates during dinner . . .'

'Elementary, my dear Watson,' smiled Charles.

'I fed him, I called the uncle, and I enrolled Yacine in school. That's Yacine's story . . . As for Nedra, she came through the same channel, smuggled in, but her circumstances were far more tragic. No one knew a thing about her except that she'd been found in some sort of squat and her face was broken. That was two years ago, she must have been about three, maybe . . . well, we've never been very sure. And it was another of Nathalie's schemes.

'And in her case, too, it was supposed to be temporary. Just time enough for her jaw to heal – a heavy-handed slap had knocked it out of place – and for her to recover properly while they tried to find some family member somewhere . . .

'And believe me, Charles, when you have all your baby teeth but no papers, life becomes very complicated. We found a doctor who agreed to operate on her on the quiet but everything else was appalling. They wouldn't let me enrol her in school, and I've been teaching her myself. Anyway, I do what I can, since she doesn't speak.'

'Not at all?'

'Yes, well, a little . . . When she's alone with Alice. But she has a dog's life. No. Sorry. Nothing to do with my dogs. She's not stupid at all, and she understands her situation perfectly well. She knows that someone can come and fetch her from one day to the next, and that I won't be able to do a thing for her.'

Now Charles understood why the little girl had run off into the woods the night before.

'She can always hide under the bench . . .'

'No . . . It's not the same . . . Yacine had the right to be here, he's boarding. I simply switched the dates round and I make him go to stay with his family during the holidays. Whereas Nedra . . . I don't know . . . I'm trying to put together an adoption application, but it's absolute hell. Always the same old problem with standards . . . I ought to find myself a nice little husband who

355

works as a civil servant,' she smiled, 'some sort of school teacher or something . . .'

She arched her back and stretched her arms out towards the fire.

'There,' she yawned, 'you know it all.'

'And the three others?'

'What?'

'You could adopt them as well.'

'Yes. I've thought about it. To get my surrogates off my back, for a start, but . . .'

'But?'

'I'd get the feeling I was killing their parents a second time round.'

'Don't they ever talk about it?'

'They do. Of course. It's even become a sort of gimmick. "Yeah, yeah, I'll tidy my room . . . When you adopt me." And that's fine.'

Long silence.

'I didn't know they existed,' murmured Charles.

'Who?'

'People like you.'

'And you're right. They don't exist. Or at least I don't feel like I exist.'

'I don't believe that.'

'Well, still . . . We haven't been out much in nine years. I always try to put a bit of money aside to take them on a long trip, but I can't manage it. Especially as I bought the house last year. It was an obsession. I *wanted* us to be in our own home. I *wanted* the children to have a place that they're from, for later. I'll force them to leave, at some point, but I *wanted* them to have this as a base . . . I bugged René about it every day until finally he gave in. "Oh, I don't know," he whinged, "it's been in my family since the Great War . . ." Why should it change . . . And then there were his nephews in Guéret . . .

'I stopped drinking my morning coffee with him on the way back from the school and, five days later, he relented.

'"You idiot, you know perfectly well that *we're* your nephews," I scolded, gently.

'Of course I had to run it by the judge and my beloved surrogate, and they all began to make a big fuss. What? Is that really wise?

356

And why such a tumbledown place? How will you keep it up, then?

'Oh fuck. They hadn't spent a winter here, had they . . . Eventually I said, it's quite simple, either you let me sell the flat so that I can buy this house, or I'll give the children back to you. The new judge had other fish to fry and the two others are such idiots that they actually thought I was serious.

'So I went to the notary with René and his sister, and I swapped a bloody awful Résidence des Mimosas for this magnificent kingdom. What a party we had, that night . . . I invited the entire village. Even Corinne Le Men . . .

'That's how happy I was . . .'

'Now I live off the rent of two flats with very zealous managing agents . . . There's always some sort of bloody maintenance work to do . . . Well . . . Perhaps it's just as well, the way things are . . . Who'd look after the wild animals if we went away?'

Silence.

'Living? Surviving? Maybe. But *existing*, no. I may have more muscle tone to show for it, but my poor brain has abandoned me along the way. Now I make cakes and sell them at the school fair . . .'

'I still don't believe you.'

'No?'

'No.'

'And you're right again. Of course, from a distance, I look a bit like a saint, right? But you mustn't believe in the kindness of generous people. In reality they're the most selfish . . .

'I confessed as much when I was talking about Ellen, earlier, that I was an ambitious young woman . . .

'Ambitious and *very* proud! I was ridiculous, but I wasn't really joking when I said I wanted to eradicate global hunger. My father brought us up speaking dead languages and my mother thought that Mrs Thatcher had a lovely hairdo or that the Queen Mum's latest hat did not go at all well with her dress. So . . . it was hardly a surprise that I would want something more . . . a somewhat larger life, no?

'Yes, I was ambitious. And here we are. This destiny that I never would have been able to aspire to all on my own, because the people I admired were head and shoulders above me – well, these children have given it to me. It's an itty-bitty sort of destiny,' she winced, 'but at any rate . . . it's entertaining enough to keep you awake until three in the morning . . .'

She had turned around, and was smiling into his eyes.

And at that very moment, Charles knew.

His goose was cooked.

'I know you're in a hurry, but you can't leave now? You can have Samuel's room, if you like . . .'

Because she had crossed her arms and put the matter to him like that, and because he wasn't in a hurry at all any more, he added, 'One last thing . . .'

'Yes?'

'You haven't told me the story behind your ring.'

'Of course! What was I thinking!'

She looked at her hand: 'Well . . .'

She leaned towards him and placed her index finger above her right cheek: 'Do you see that little star, there? In the middle of the crow's feet?'

'Of course I can see it,' Charles assured her, blind as a bat.

'The first and last smack my father ever gave me. I must have been sixteen, and his ring got me. Poor man, he was just sick . . . So sick about it that he never wore it again.'

'But what had you done, to make him . . .' Charles asked, indignant.

'I don't remember . . . I must have told Plutarch to put it up his . . .'

'And why?'

'Plutarch wrote a treatise on the upbringing of children that really got on my nerves, you can imagine! No, I'm joking, I think it must have been something to do with going out on the town . . . It hardly matters . . . I was bleeding. Naturally, I went on and on about it so I never saw the ring again.

'Although I liked it a great deal. As a little girl I used to dream about it. The stone was so blue . . . I can't remember . . . I think it's called a nicolo . . . And the image . . . Well, it's really dirty just now, but look at the young man striding along with a hare on his shoulder . . . I loved him . . . He's got such a lovely derrière . . . I often asked my father what had become of the ring, but he said he couldn't remember. Perhaps he'd sold it . . .

'And then ten years later, when we were leaving the judge's office and the die had been cast, we went to have tea on the Place Saint-Sulpice. My old dad rummaged around pretending to look for his glasses and then out came the ring, wrapped in a handkerchief. "We're proud of you," he said, and gave it to me. "Here, you'll need it too when you're looking for respect . . ." At first it was far too big and would slide around my middle finger, but with all the wood I've been chopping, it stays very nicely on these big paws of mine.

'My father died two years ago. That was another sadness but at least it came about naturally.

'When he used to come, in the summer, I would put him in charge of watching the jam cooking on the stove . . . It was just the right sort of job for him . . . He'd take his book, sit by the Aga, turn the pages with one hand and the wooden spoon with the other . . . It was during one of those long apricot afternoons that he gave me my final lesson in ancient civilization.

'He'd hesitated for a long time, he confessed, before giving me the ring, because according to his friend Herbert Boardman, the little image was part of a recurring theme in the repertory of ancient gemmology, that of the "Rural Sacrifice".

'He went into a long theory on the notion of sacrifice with the *Elegies* of Tibullus and the whole lot of them as background music, but I wasn't listening any more. I was looking at his reflection in the copper cauldron and thinking how lucky I'd been to grow up with such a thoughtful man watching over me.

'Because, you see, that notion of sacrifice is quite relative and . . .

'"Take it easy, Dad," I reassured him, "you know perfectly well that there is no sacrifice at all in all this . . . Go on. Concentrate, or else it will burn."'

Kate got up with a sigh: 'There. That's it. You can do what you like but I'm going to turn in.'

He took the tray from her hands and headed for the pantry.

'What's incredible,' he called out, 'is that with you, everything is a story and all the stories are beautiful . . .'

'But everything *is* a story, Charles. Absolutely everything, and for everyone. The thing is, you usually never find anyone to listen to them . . .'

★

Last room at the end of the corridor, she had said. It was a little garret room, and Charles, as if he were in Mathilde's room, spent a long time gazing at its adolescent walls. One photo in particular held his attention. It was tacked above the bed, in the place where a crucifix would go, and the couple who stood there smiling gently delivered the last deep bruise of the day.

Ellen was exactly as Kate had described her: radiant. Pierre was kissing her on the cheek, and in the crook of his elbow he held a little boy, fast asleep.

Charles sat on the edge of the bed with his head down and his hands together.

What a trip . . .

In his entire life he had not felt so jet-lagged. But this time he wasn't complaining, it was just that he was a bit . . . lost.

Anouk . . .

What in hell's name was the meaning of this mess?

And why did you clear out, when all these people whom you would have loved have gone to so much trouble to carry on?

Why didn't you come to see her more often? You always told us that one's true family are the people one meets along the way.

And so? You were at home here . . . And you'd have found a daughter in this lovely girl. She would have been a consolation to you, for Alexis . . .

And why did I never call you back? I've worked so hard all these years, and yet I won't leave anything behind. The only important foundations, the ones that have led me to this little room and that would have deserved my full attention, well, I filled them with selfishness and ambition. And for the most part, I lost out. No, this isn't self-flagellation, you would have hated that, it's just that . . .

He jumped. A cat was licking his hand.

On the wall of the toilet he found Kate's handwriting. A quotation from E.M. Forster which said,

I believe in aristocracy though − If that is the right word, and a democrat may use it. Not an aristocracy of power, based upon rank and influence, but an aristocracy of the sensitive, the considerate and the plucky. Its members are to be found in all nations and classes, and all through the ages, and there is a secret understanding between them when they meet. They represent the true human tradition, the one permanent victory of our queer race over cruelty and chaos.

Thousands of them perish in obscurity, a few are great names. They are sensitive to others as well as for themselves, they are considerate without being fussy, their pluck is not swankiness, but the power to endure, and they can take a joke.

Well well, sighed Charles, who had already felt himself shrinking as she was telling him her life story, put that in your pipe and smoke it . . . Only a few hours ago he would have read the text, focusing principally on a few translation issues – queer race, swankiness – but now he *heard* the words. He had eaten their cakes, drunk their whisky, had wandered around with them all afternoon, and had seen them become incarnate in a smile that was never far from tears.

The castle may have fallen down, but the nobility endured.

Bent over, his trousers round his ankles, he felt shitty.

While he was hunting for the loo paper, he came across her haiku anthology.

He opened it at random and read:

> *Climb slowly*
> *Little snail –*
> *You are on Fuji!*

He smiled, thanked Kobayashi Issa for his moral support, and fell asleep in a young man's bed.

★

Charles got up at dawn, let the dogs out and, before going to his car, went out of his way to catch the first rays of sunlight on the ochre walls of the stables. He placed his hands against the window, saw a herd of sleeping adolescents, then drove to the bakery and bought the entire oven-load of croissants. Or of, well, what the shop assistant, who was still pasty with sleep, referred to as croissants . . .

A Parisian would have called them, 'your curved brioche thingies'.

When he came back, the kitchen had a smell of coffee, and Kate was in her garden.

He prepared a tray and went to join her.

She put down her shears, walked barefoot through the dew, was even more pasty than the baker's shop assistant, and confessed that she hadn't slept a wink all night.

Too many memories.

She squeezed her mug of coffee to warm herself.

The sun rose in silence. Kate had nothing more to say, and Charles had too much to unravel.

Like cats, the children came to rub against her.

'What are you going to do today?' he asked.

'I don't know . . .' Her voice was sad. 'And you?'

'I have a lot of work.'

'I can imagine . . . We've kept you from the straight and narrow.'

'I wouldn't go that far . . .'

And as the conversation was veering towards the blues, he added, more cheerfully, 'I have to leave for New York tomorrow and for once I'm going as a tourist . . . An evening devoted to an old architect I admire a great deal.'

'Really, you're going to New York?' she said, her voice suddenly lively. 'How lucky! Dare I ask you to –'

'Dare, Kate, dare. Tell me.'

She sent Nedra to fetch something on her night table and then handed it to Charles.

It was a little round tin with a badger on the lid.

Badger Healing Balm. Relief for Hardworking Hands.

'Is it badger grease?' he asked with a chuckle.

'No, beaver, I think. At any rate, I've never found anything better. A friend used to send it to me but she's moved away.'

Charles turned the tin over and read, '"Paul Bunyan once said, 'Give me enough Badger, and I can heal the cracks in the Grand Canyon.'" Indeed. Quite the project. And where can I find this stuff? In a drugstore?'

'Will you be anywhere near Union Square?'

'Of course,' he lied.

'You're lying.'

'Of course not.'

'Liar.'

'Kate, I'll have a few hours to myself and I would be . . . honoured to devote them to you. Is it right on Union Square?'

'Yes, a little shop called the Vitamin Shoppe, I think. Otherwise, Whole Foods might have it . . .'

'Perfect. I'll manage.'

'And . . .'

'And?'

'If you go a bit farther down Broadway, there's the Strand Bookstore. If you have two more minutes to spare, could you just have a quick wander round the stacks for me? I've been dreaming about it for so long . . .'

'Would you like any book in particular?'

'No. Just the atmosphere. You go in, go to the back on the left, where they have the biographies, look at all the books you can and breathe in and think of me . . .'

Breathe in and think of you? Hmm. Do I need to go that far?

As he was searching for the way to the bathroom, he came upon Yacine who was deep in an encyclopedia.

'Tell me, how high is Mount Fuji?'

'Uh, hold on. "Highest point in Japan, an extinct volcano, 3,776 metres."'

Extinct? My foot.

He took his shower and wondered how such a big family managed in such a spartan place. Not a single jar of beauty cream in sight. He stopped off at each bedroom to kiss the children goodbye, and asked them to say goodbye to the older kids for him when they woke up.

He looked everywhere for Kate.

'She went to take some flowers to Totette,' Alice informed him. 'She told me to say 'bye to you for her.'

'But . . . when will she be back?'

'I don't know.'

'Oh?'

'Yes, that's why she told me to tell you goodbye.'

So like Ellen she preferred to avoid a pointless scene . . .

This impossible departure felt very violent.

Beneath the dark arch of the oak trees he thought back on

Ellen's leave-taking, while Baloo was teaching Mowgli to sing, after him, about the bare necessities of life . . .

He breathed out, felt the pain, and turned right, back on to the asphalt.

IV

1

'PARIS 389.'

For the first three hundred and eighty-eight kilometres, Charles thought of nothing else but those hours, still warm, he had just spent. He put himself on automatic pilot and was assailed by a host of images.

Nedra like a wounded bird with her gaping jaw, the names of the horses, Lucas's smile in the rear view mirror, his long gold cardboard sabre, the church steeple, the love letter that Alexis kept in his wallet, the taste of Port Ellen, the shrieks of one of the Amazons when Léo wanted to spray her with 'Lures for Wild Boar, scent of sow in heat', the aroma of strawberry ice lollies melting on the tips of their sticks, the lapping of the stream in the night, the night beneath the stars, the stars that the man she'd wanted a child from claimed to know, the donkeys in the Jardin du Luxembourg, the Quick Burger where he'd so often taken Mathilde, the toy store on the Rue Cassette where they had also stood dreaming and which was called Once Upon a Time, the dead flies in the grooms' quarters, that dork Matthew who hadn't known how to isolate the DNA of happiness, the curve of her knee when she had come to sit next to him, the spark that had followed, Alexis's embarrassment, the case he no longer opened, Big Dog's sad smile, the llama's menacing eye, the purr of the cat that had come to console him, the view from over the rims of their bowls in the morning, the great wall of dreary convention with which Corinne had enclosed her very fragile husband, the laughter of their daughter Marion who would not take long to knock it all down, the way she would blow on a lock of hair even when it was firmly tied behind her head, the children's shouts and the din of tumbling tins in the schoolyard, the *Wedding Day* rosebush that was collapsing beneath the arbour, the vestiges of Pompeii, the whirling of the swallows and the owl banging with his broom handle to complain about the noise when they reminisced about Nino Rota, Nana's voice as he sent them off to bed one last time, the lorry driver's bladder, the old professor of classics who on his youngest daughter's cheek had left the imprint of a handsome ephebe, the utterly new sensation of the taste of warm fruit, the Lacoste T-shirt he'd never wear again, René's prediction, the four of them clowning around on the scales, the mouse in the carpet, the ten children with whom they'd had dinner the night before, homework beneath the lamp, the consent they'd refused to give her, the bridge that would collapse some day and leave them cut off from the world for good, the beauty of the roof beams, the spots of greyish-green lichen on the walls in the stairway, her ankle next to his, the design of the locks, the delicate outline of the cornices, the old banger of a Volvo, her two nights in a hotel near the funeral parlour, Alice's studio, the smell of singed trainers, the beauty spot on the back of her neck which had fascinated him all through her confession – as if Anouk were winking at him every time Kate held her face between her palms with laughter or tears, the resilience of little Yacine, the resilience of them all, the fragrance of honeysuckle, and the dormer windows, the corridor on the first floor and the wall where they had all written their dreams, her own dream, the policeman's condolences, the urns in the barn, the condoms among the sugar lumps, her sister's face, the life she had left behind, the beds she had moved together, the passport which must be expired, her dreams of plenty that had left her sterile, the thickness of the walls, the scent of Samuel's pillow, the death of Aeschylus, the headlamps in the night, their shadows stretched before them, the window she had opened, the . . .

During the last kilometre, where, according to the day's forecast, the air quality was 'fair to good', he realized that he had spent the entire outbound trip obsessed with death, and the entire return trip amazed by life.

One face had been superimposed upon another, and that hard letter of the alphabet that they shared eventually left him completely shaken.

Instruction manuals were a waste of time; as far as the ear was concerned, twists of fate opened and closed with the letter 'k'.

2

He went straight to the office. Nearly threw a fit because some of the lights had been left on. Decided not to (have a fit). Some other day. He plugged his mobile into the charger, looked for his travel bag and finally got changed. While struggling with a trouser leg he saw the pile of mail waiting on his desk.

He fastened his belt, and switched on his computer without letting it get to him. The bad news was behind him, the rest could only be hassles, and hassles would no longer affect him. Their new standards, their environmental regulations, their laws, their estimates, their rates, their interest, their conclusions, their judicial appeals, their reminders and their claims, their hypocritical legal decisions to save a planet that had already been bled dry – froth, froth, nothing but froth. There are, in our midst, people of another caste, who have a secret understanding between them when they meet, and now they had taken him into their trust.

And yet he was not one of them. He was not the courageous sort, and he'd been careful not to 'endure' any heartbreak. Except here was the rub. He could no longer ignore that special caste. Anouk had passed on a dead bird, and he'd ventured into a henhouse . . .

He may have come back disfigured, but his hold was laden with spices and gold.

Do not shower the mapmaker with honours, nor receive him at court; but let him sift through his gold in peace.

Perhaps he would never go back there, perhaps he would never have the chance to say goodbye to her, perhaps he would never hear Nedra's voice, or find out whether Samuel had trained hard enough; but one thing was certain, he would never leave it all behind, either.

Wherever he went, whatever he did from now on, he would be with them, and would move forward, palms outstretched.

Anouk didn't give a damn whether she disintegrated here or else-where. She didn't give a damn about a single thing – except what she had just offered to him, depriving herself of it in turn.

To use Kate's own expression, the people he admired were head and shoulders above him, he had never had children, and he would perish 'in darkness', but in the meantime he would live. He would live.

That was his jackpot, hidden among the terrines and the sausages.

After such eloquently sliced and lyrically peppered thoughts, he read his e-mails and got back to work.

After a few minutes he stood up and went over to the book-shelf.

He was looking for a dictionary of colours.

There was this thing that had been bugging him, since the first bonfire . . .

Venetian: hair colour, with mahogany highlights. The tint known as Venetian blond *contributes to the beauty of the Venetian women.*

Just as he thought . . .

Since he had the dictionary to hand, he looked up 'martingale'.

True enough, mate, you're still back there, aren't you?

He shrugged his shoulders and *really* got back to work. The shit was hitting the fan from every direction. No matter. Around his throat was a 'strap or arrangement of straps fastened at one end to the noseband, bit, or reins of a horse and at the other to its girth, to prevent it from star-gazing or throwing back its head and to strengthen the action of the bit'.

He concentrated until seven, returned the rental car, and went home on foot.

He hoped he would find someone behind the door . . .

The two answerphones he had just checked one after the other were unable to answer his question.

Still somewhat stiff, he headed up the Rue des Patriarches.

He was hungry, and he dreamt he heard a church bell in the distance.

3

'I won't kiss you, I've just put a face pack on,' she warned, speaking out of the corner of her mouth. 'You've no idea how exhausted I am . . . I've spent the entire weekend with this lot of utterly hysterical Korean women . . . I think I'll have a bath and then go to bed.'

'You don't want to have some dinner?'

'No. They dragged us to the Ritz and I ate too much. And you? How did it go?'

She hadn't looked up. She was lounging deep in the sofa, leafing through American *Vogue*.

'Just look at that, how vulgar.'

No. Charles didn't feel like looking at that.

'And Mathilde?'

'She's at her girlfriend's.'

He held onto the knob and experienced a moment of . . . dejection.

It was a made-to-measure kitchen, designed by one of Laurence's friends who was an interior architect, space designer, volume creator, lighting enhancer and holder of other such nonsensical conceptual qualifications.

Door fronts in light maple, wide vertical columns in brushed stainless steel, countertops in Dolomite stone, sliding doors, a seamless one-piece sink, state-of-the-art hobs and cutting-edge cooling devices, Miele appliances, extractor hood, espresso machine, wine cellar, convection oven and all the bells and whistles.

Oh, yes. Undoubtedly beautiful.

Clean, neat, immaculate. As lovely as a morgue.

The problem was that there was nothing to eat. An abundance of jars of cream in the refrigerator door, but not from the pastures of Normandy, renowned for their dairy cream, but rather, alas, from

La Prairie, renowned for their face cream . . . There was some Diet Coke, some non-fat yoghurt, a few microwave dinners and some frozen pizzas.

True, Mathilde was taking off the next day . . . And it was mainly because of her that meals materialized on any sort of regular basis in this house. Laurence cooked for friends, but it would seem that his unpredictable schedules and his trips one after the other had scattered those friends far and wide . . .

Nothing left but meals on expenses these days.

And since he had recently resolved to stop sighing over small things, he grabbed the latest issue of his architects' newsletter from his briefcase and went in to tell her he'd be going down for a bite at the local bistro.

'Goodness . . .' The beauty mask cracked with wrinkles. 'What happened to you?'

He must have looked as surprised as she did because she added, 'Were you in a fight?'

Oh . . . *That?*

It was so long ago . . . In another life . . .

'No, I . . . I ran into a door.'

'It's ghastly.'

'Oh, there are worse things.'

'No, I meant your face!'

'Oh. Sorry . . .'

'Are you sure you're all right? You look very odd.'

'I'm hungry. Are you coming?'

'No. I just told you I was exhausted.'

He leafed through his weekly bible over a rib steak and ordered another beer to wash down the *frites* with Béarnaise sauce. He was enjoying his meal, and pored over the invitations to tender, feeling almost invigorated. Whether it was his all-nighter at Alexis's or the night at Les Vesperies, he wasn't the least bit tired now.

He ordered a coffee and got up to buy a pack of cigarettes.

And halfway to the counter, turned back.

A sense of solidarity.

To stop smoking would be a good way not to be sure exactly what it was he was craving.

He sat back down, fiddled with a sugar lump, pressed his fingernail into the white paper wrapping and wondered what she was doing at that very second . . .

Twenty minutes to ten.

Were they still having dinner? Were they dining outdoors? Was the air as warm as yesterday? Had the girls found a decent aquarium for Monsieur Blop? Had the big kids left the saddle room the way the Blason Brothers would like to find it upon returning from exile? Had they remembered to close the gate to the meadow? Was Big Dog lying at their nanny's enamelled feet again?

And Kate?

Was she by the fireplace? Was she reading? Dreaming? If so, about what? Was she thinking about –

He would not finish the question. He had been wrestling with ghosts for over six months, he had just made his way through a mountain of *pommes frites* to make up for lost time and the lost notches in his belt, and he didn't want to lose sight of his jackpot.

He was no longer tired. He circled a few projects that seemed interesting, and was on to a mission of the utmost importance – to find a badger in New York; he didn't know her name but was almost certain that if he wrote 'Mademoiselle Kate at Les Vesperies' the postman would find her and deliver her healing balm.

He called Claire, told her about Alexis, made her laugh. He had so much to tell her . . .

'I have a very important hearing tomorrow morning, I absolutely must go over everything,' she apologized; 'can we have lunch soon?'

Just as she was about to hang up, he said her name.

'Yes?'

'Why are men such . . . cowards?'

'Um . . . Why are you asking me that all of a sudden?'

'I don't know. I've just run into a lot of blokes like that lately.'

'Why?' she sighed. 'Because they don't give birth, I suppose . . . I'm sorry, that's a real cliché of an answer, but you caught me a bit unawares with your question, and I haven't had time to prepare my defence just yet . . . But . . . Are you asking because of me?'

'Because of all of you.'

'Have you had a bang on the head or something?'

'Yes. Hang on, let me show you . . .'

Claire, puzzled, put her phone down on her pile of hassles.

It vibrated again. There on the tiny screen came her brother's colourfully striped face, and she burst out laughing one last time before returning to her water purification plants.

Alexis in his flip-flops and apron standing over his gas barbecue . . . How good to hear it. And her brother, his voice so cheerful this evening . . .

So he'd found her, his Anouk, mused Claire mistakenly, with a slightly melancholy smile.

★

Melancholy? The word was not strong enough. When Kate returned home that morning she knew that his car would be gone, and yet . . . she could not help but look for it.

She hung about the house all day. Went back without him to the places she'd shown him – the barns, the henhouse, the stables, the vegetable garden, the hill, the stream, the arbour, the bench where they'd had breakfast among the sage bushes, and . . . everything felt deserted.

She told the children more than once that she felt tired.

That she had never been this tired . . .

She cooked up a storm just to stay in the kitchen where they'd spent part of the night with Ellen.

For the first time in years the prospect of the summer holidays was making her very anxious. Two months here, alone with the children . . . Oh God.

'What's wrong?' asked Yacine.

'I feel old.'

Sitting on the floor, leaning up against her ovens with Big Dog's head in her lap.

'But you're not old! Your twenty-sixth birthday is years away!'

'You're right,' she laughed, 'light years away, in fact!'

She kept up appearances until the swallows had departed, but was already in bed by the time Charles ran into Mathilde in the corridor:

'Wow!' she exclaimed, startled, 'what was that door made of?' She stood on tiptoe: 'Right . . . now where do I aim to give you a kiss?'

He followed her and flopped down on her bed while she started packing and told him about her weekend.

'What sort of music would you like to listen to?'

'Something cool . . .'

'Not jazz, though?' she went, horrified.

She had her back to him, counting her socks, when he asked, 'Why did you stop the horse-riding?'

'Why do you ask?'

'Because I just spent two marvellous days among children and horses, and I couldn't stop thinking about you . . .'

'Really?' she smiled.

'All the time. Every minute I was wondering why I hadn't brought you with me.'

'I don't know . . . I stopped because it was far away . . . Because . . .'

'Because what?'

'Because you were always afraid . . .'

'Of the horses?'

'Not just the horses. Afraid that I'd fall off, or that I'd lose, or hurt myself . . . or that I'd be too cold or too hot . . . or that there would be a traffic jam . . . or that Mum would be waiting for us . . . or that I wouldn't have time to finish my homework . . . That . . . I got the feeling I was ruining your weekends.'

'Oh?' he murmured.

'No, that wasn't the only reason . . .'

'What else was it?'

'I don't know . . . Right, I think you'd better let me have my bed, now.'

He closed the door behind him and felt as if he had been banished from paradise.

The rest of the flat was intimidating.

Go on, he urged himself, what's all this play-acting! This is your home! You've been living here for years! This is your furniture, these are your books and clothes and mortgage payments . . . Come *on, Chaaahles* . . .

This last with her lovely English accent.

Come on home.

He wandered round the living room, made a coffee, wiped the countertop, leafed through magazines without even reading the pictures, looked up at his bookshelf, decided it was far too orderly, looked for a CD, but forgot which one, washed his cup, dried it, put it away, wiped the countertop again, pulled over a stool, rubbed his side, decided to polish his shoes, went into the hallway, squatted down, winced, opened a cabinet and polished every single pair of shoes.

He pushed aside the cushions, lit a lamp, placed his briefcase on the coffee table, looked for his glasses, pulled out his files, read the images without even registering the texts, started again from the beginning, flopped back against the sofa and listened to all the sounds from outside. Sat up straight, tried again, pushed his glasses down his nose and rubbed his eyes, closed the file, and placed his hands on it.

All he could see was her face.

If only he were tired.

He brushed his teeth, quietly opened the door of the conjugal bedroom, could just make out Laurence's back in the darkness, placed his clothes on his designated armchair, held his breath, and lifted up his side of the bedclothes.

He recalled his last performance. Could smell her perfume, feel her warmth. His heart was all a jumble. He wanted to love.

He curled against her, stretched out his hand and slid it between her thighs. As always, he reeled with the softness of her skin; he lifted her arm and licked her armpit while he waited for her to turn to him, to open to him altogether. He let his kisses follow the curve of her hips; he held her elbow so that she would not move and . . .

'What's that smell?' she asked.

He did not understand her question, tugged the duvet over him and . . .

'Charles? What is that smell?' she asked again, shoving the feathers aside.

He sighed. Moved away. Answered that he didn't know.

'It's your jacket, is that it? Is that your jacket that smells of wood-smoke?'

'Could be . . .'

'Could you move it off the armchair, please? It's distracting me.'

He left the bed. Picked up his clothes.

Threw them in the bath.

If I don't go back now, I'll never go back.

He returned to the bed and stretched out with his back to her.

'Well?' said her nails, drawing long figure eights on his shoulder.

Well nothing. He had proved to her that he could still get it up. As for the rest, she could go fuck herself.

The figure eights changed into little zeroes and gradually disappeared.

Once again, she fell asleep first.

Easy.

She'd been dragged round the Ritz by hysterical Korean women.

As for Charles, he was counting sheep.

And cows, and hens, and cats, and dogs. And children.

And beauty marks.

And the miles . . .

He got up at dawn, left a note under Mathilde's door. 'Eleven o'clock downstairs. Don't forget your ID card.' And three little crosses, because that's the way they sent kisses where she was going.

He opened the door onto the street.

Took a deep breath.

4

'We have nearly an hour, don't you want to eat something?'

She said nothing.

This was not his usual Mathilde.

'Hey,' he went, grabbing her by the neck, 'are you stressed out or what?'

'I am a bit . . .' she whispered against his chest, 'I don't even know where I'm going.'

'But you showed me the photos, they look very kind, those McThingammies . . .'

'A month is a long time, all the same.'

'No it's not . . . It will fly by. And Scotland is such a beautiful place . . . You're going to love it. Come on, let's go and get some lunch.'

'I'm not hungry.'

'Something to drink, then. Follow me.'

They wove their way through suitcases and baggage carts and found a spot at the very rear of a grungy greasy spoon. Only in Paris were the airports this dirty, he mused. Was it the thirty-five-hour working week, or the renowned offhand *Frenchy* attitude, or the knowledge that one was only a grumpy taxi ride away from the loveliest city on earth? Whatever the reason, he was always dismayed.

She was nibbling on the end of her straw, looking anxiously all around her, checking the time on her mobile, and she hadn't even put her headphones on.

'Don't worry, sweetheart, I've never missed a flight in my life . . .'

'Really! You're coming with me?' she quipped, pretending to mis-*comprendre*.

'No,' he said, shaking his head, 'no. But I'll text you every evening.'

'You promise?'

'Promise.'

'Not in English, though?'

She was making a huge effort to seem offhand.

As was Charles.

It was the first time she was going so far away, and for so long.

The prospect of her absence distressed him terribly. One month in that flat, the two of them, and without this child . . . Oh God.

He took her backpack and went with her as far as the X-ray machines.

Because she was walking very slowly, he was sure she was looking in the shop windows. He offered to get her some newspapers.

She didn't want any.

'Some chewing gum, then?'

'Charles . . .' She stood still.

He had already lived this scene. He'd often gone with her when she left for holiday camp, and he knew how this plucky little lass could lose it altogether, the closer they got to the actual rallying point.

He took her hand, felt flattered to be her support, and began mentally preparing a few firm but reassuring phrases for her to slip into her rear pocket.

'Yes?'

'Mum told me you two are going to split up.'

He stumbled slightly. He'd just got an Airbus right in his temple.

'Oh?'

A squashed little syllable that could mean, 'Oh? So she told you?' or 'Oh, really? That's the first I've heard of it.'

He lacked the strength to play the tough guy: 'I wasn't aware.'

'I know. She's waiting for you to feel better before she tells you.'

It's an enormous model. The A380, perhaps?

He didn't know what to say.

'She says that you haven't been yourself these last few months, but that as soon as you're better you would split up.'

'You . . . You have some odd conversations for your age,' was all he managed to say.

They stood opposite the departures.

'Charles?'

She'd turned round.

'Mathilde?'

'I'll come and live with you.'

'Pardon?'

'If you really do split up, I'm warning you, I'll come with you.'

Since she had the grace to spit out the last words like a cowgirl spitting a wad of tobacco, he answered in kind: 'Oh! I see what you're driving at! You're just saying that so that I'll go on doing your maths and physics homework!'

'Damn. However did you guess?' She forced a smile.

He couldn't keep it up. He had the Airbus's landing gear in his guts now.

'And even if it were true, you know that it really isn't possible . . . I'm never here . . .'

'Exactly . . .' she said, still lightly.

But just as he could no longer keep up, she added, 'It's your business, I don't care, but I will leave with you. You ought to know that . . .'

Her flight was called.

'We haven't got that far yet,' he whispered into her ear, giving her a hug.

She said nothing. She must have thought he was very naïve.

She went through the gate, turned round, and blew him a kiss.

The last of her childhood.

Her flight disappeared off the board.

Charles was still there. He hadn't budged a millimetre, he was waiting for the emergency services. His pocket vibrated: *1 New Message*.

'JE TM.'

His thumbs slipped over the touch pad and he had to wipe his hand on his heart to help it get the message across: 'ME 2.'

He checked his watch, turned round, bashed into hordes of people, stumbled over their bags, dropped his own off at the left luggage, ran to the taxi rank, tried to jump the queue, got told off, saw a motorcyclist with an 'all destinations' sign, and asked him to take him back to where the straw had just broken the proverbial camel's back.

Never again would he take a flight feeling wobbly.

Never again.

5

A hundred metres or so from the lycée where Mathilde would be going back to school in the autumn, he pushed open the door of an estate agent's, told them he was looking for a two-room flat as near to there as possible; they showed him photos, he added that he didn't have time just now, chose the one with the most light, left his card, and signed a big fat cheque so that they'd take him seriously.

He'd be back in two days.

He put his helmet back on and asked his driver to take him to the other side of the Seine.

He left his briefcase with him and said he wouldn't be long.

The famous beige carpet *chez Chanel* . . . As if he'd rewound the clock ten years; as if he were standing there once again in his big shoes, in the angry glare of the doorman on duty.

He had them page her. He added that it was urgent.

His mobile rang.

'Did she miss her flight?' asked Laurence.

'No, but can you come down here, now?'

'I'm in the middle of a meeting . . .'

'Then don't come down. I just wanted to tell you I'm feeling better.'

He could hear the cogs turning beneath the lovely black velvet snood that held back her hair.

'But . . . I thought you had a flight to catch, too?'

'I'm on my way. Don't worry. I'm better, Laurence, I do feel better.'

'Look, I'm delighted,' she laughed, somewhat nervously.

'So, now you can leave me.'

'What . . . what on earth are you on about this time?'

'Mathilde told me . . . what you'd told her in confidence.'

'This is ridiculous . . . Stay there, I'm coming.'
'I'm in a hurry.'
'I'll be right there.'

For the first time, in all the time he'd known her, he thought she was wearing too much make-up.

He had nothing to add.

He'd found a flat, he had to rush, had a flight to catch.

'Charles, just stop. It was nothing . . . women's talk. You know how it is . . .'

'Everything's fine,' he smiled, 'everything's fine. *I'm* the one who's leaving. *I'm* the bastard.'

'Right . . . if you say so.'

Right up to the end, he would have to admit she had class.

She said something else, but because of his helmet he could only nod his head without knowing what.

He tapped on the young man's thigh to urge him to slalom between the cars.

He *could not* miss this flight. He had a badger to unearth.

★

A few hours later, Laurence Vernes would go to the hairdresser's, smile at little Jessica while putting on her smock, sit down facing the mirror while another employee prepped her colour, pick up a magazine, leaf through the gossip columns, raise her head, look at herself, and burst into tears.

What will happen after this, we do not know.

She is no longer in the story.

6

Charles got started on a huge file entitled *P.B. Tran Tower/ Exposed Structures* and picked it apart until a flight attendant asked him to store his tray.

He reread his notes, checked the name of the hotel, looked out of the window at the grid patterns of towns, and mused that he was going to sleep well. That he'd finally recovered.

He thought about a lot of other things. About the work he'd just finished, which made him pleased, work that he could do anywhere in the world. From his office, from a stranger's two-room flat, from an aeroplane seat or from . . .

He closed his eyes and smiled.

Everything was going to be very complicated.

So much the better.

It was his job, to find solutions . . .

'Detail of a joint between the stone modules of columns showing the insertion of the steel counterbalancing system', said the caption on his latest sketch.

Gravity, earthquakes, cyclones, wind, snow . . . All the hassles that were part of what they called live loads and which, he had just remembered, he found very entertaining . . .

He sent a message to the Highlands and decided not to adjust his watch.

He wanted to live in the same time zone as she did.

★

He got up very early, checked with the concierge about the delivery of his hired tuxedo, drank a coffee from a paper cup on his way down Madison Avenue and, as always when he was in New York, walked around staring up at the sky. New York, for someone who as a child used to like playing with Meccano sets, meant one stiff neck after another.

For the first time in years, he went into boutiques and bought clothes. A jacket and four new shirts.

Four of them!

He turned round and looked behind him from time to time. Keeping a lookout, fearful of something. A hand on his shoulder, an eye in a triangle, a voice bellowing at him from a skyscraper, Hey . . . you. You have no right to feel so happy . . . What did you go and steal this time, what are you hiding there, against your heart?

No . . . but I . . . I think I have a cracked rib.

Raise your arms so I can check.

And Charles did as he was told, and was carried away on the flow of passers-by.

He shook his head, called himself an idiot, and looked at his watch to remind himself of where he was.

Almost four o'clock . . . Last day of school but one . . . The children must have emptied their cubbyholes into their worn-out schoolbags . . . She had told him that every evening she went with the dogs to wait for them at the end of the lane, at the spot where the school bus dropped them off, and they loaded all their stuff into the donkey's saddle-pack – 'when I manage to catch him!'

And she'd gone on to add that a hundred or more oak trees barely sufficed to give them time to tell her all the goss, and . . .

A hand had just closed on his shoulder. He turned round.

With his other hand a man in a dark suit was pointing at the traffic light: DON'T WALK. Charles thanked him and was told that he was *Welcome*.

He found the vitamin shop and made a clean sweep of the six remaining tins they had in stock. Enough to fill quite a few cracks. He left the paper bag on the counter and slipped them into his pockets.

He liked the idea.

To feel her weight, as it were.

He pushed open the door at Strand's. 'Eighteen miles of books' bragged the slogan. He couldn't go through them all, but spent a few hours. Ransacked the architecture section of course, but also treated himself to a selection of Oscar Wilde's correspondence, and a short novel by Thomas Hardy, *Fellow-Townsmen*, because of the blurb: 'Notables in the Wessex town of Port Bredy, Barnet and Downe are old friends. Yet fate has treated them differently. Barnet, a prosperous man, has been unlucky in love and now lives with the consequences of a judicious but loveless marriage. Downe, a poor solicitor, is radiantly happy, with a doting wife and adoring children. A chance meeting one night causes them to reflect on their disparate lots in life . . .' And a genial *More Than Words* by Liza Kirwin, which he read with delight while eating a sandwich on the steps, in the sun.

It was a selection of illustrated letters from the Smithsonian Archive of American Art.

Letters to spouses, lovers, friends, patrons, clients or close confidants, from painters, young artists, and total unknowns, but also Man Ray, the brilliant Gio Ponti, Calder, Warhol, and even Frida Kahlo.

Letters that were discreet or moving or purely informative, always illustrated with a drawing, a sketch, a caricature or a vignette showing a place, a landscape, a state of mind or even an emotion, when the alphabet did not suffice.

More than words . . . This book, which our laconic Charles had found on a cart as he was headed for the till, reconciled him with a part of himself. The part he had abandoned in a drawer with his cloth-covered notebooks and his tiny box of watercolours.

And who drew for the pleasure of it, back then . . . When he didn't just sketch to find a solution to a problem; when he couldn't give a damn about steel counterbalancing systems and other prestressed cables . . .

He developed a soft spot for Alfred Frueh, who would go on to become one of the *New Yorker*'s great caricaturists, and who sent hundreds of truly extraordinary missives to his fiancée. He told her about his trip to Europe shortly before the First World War, describing in detail the local customs of each destination and the world he discovered around him . . . He tucked a real dried edelweiss under his arm and, by means of a lead pencil, sent it to her all the way from Switzerland; he proved his delight in reading her letters, cutting them up into bits the size of postage stamps which he then used to tell her the story of his life so far: reading those same letters in his bath, or in front of his easel, at his table, in the street, under a lorry driving over him, in his bed, while his house was burning down or a crazy tiger was piercing his body with a sword. He also sent her his own art gallery, a thousand little three-dimensional cut-out figures, so that he could share with her the paintings that had most touched him in Paris – and all of it adorned with texts that were tender, full of humour, and oh so elegant.

He would have liked to be that man. Jolly, confident, loving. And talented.

And then there was Joseph Lindon Smith, with his perfect pencil stroke, telling his very worried parents about his ordeal as a painter on the Grand Tour in the Old World. Drawing himself beneath a shower of coins in a Venice street, or half-dead from eating too much melon.

Dear Mother and Father, Behold Jojo eating fruit!

Saint-Exupéry disguised as the Little Prince, asking Hedda Sterne if she were free for dinner and . . . Come on, you can have another look later on . . . then leafing through one last time before closing the book, spotted the self-portrait of a lost man, with his head in his hands, bent over a photo of his beloved . . . *Oh! I wish I were with you.*

Yes. Oh.

I wish.

He took a detour to see the immense Flatiron Building, which had made such an impression on him during his first visit. Constructed in 1902, it was one of the highest edifices at the time and, above all, one of the first steel structures. Charles raised his eyes.

1902.

1902, for Christ's sake!

Such genius.

And because he got lost, he ended up looking into a shop window full of bakery equipment. *N.Y. Cake Supplies.* He thought of her, thought of all of them, and spent a fortune on cookie cutters.

He had never seen so many in his life. Every possible, imaginable shape . . .

He made a pile, of dogs, cats, a hen, a duck, a horse, a chick, a goat, a llama (yes, there were llama-shaped cookie cutters . . .), a star, a moon, a cloud, a sparrow, a mouse, a tractor, a boot, a fish, a frog, a flower, a tree, a strawberry, a kennel, a dove, a guitar, a firefly, a basket, a bottle and, uh, a heart.

The salesgirl asked him if he had a lot of children.

Yes, he replied.

He went back to the hotel exhausted and loaded down with carrier bags like the good little bloody stupid tourist that he was, and he couldn't have been happier.

He took a shower, then donned his penguin suit, and spent a delightful evening. Howard gave him a big hug and called him, 'My son!', and introduced him to a load of fascinating people. He spoke at length with a Brazilian man about Ove Arup, and managed to find an engineer who had worked on the shells of the Sydney Opera House. The more he drank, the more fluent his English, and he even wandered out onto a terrace overlooking Central Park, chatting with a pretty young girl in the moonlight.

He eventually asked her if she was an architect.

'Nat meeee,' she drawled.

She was . . .

He didn't grasp what she said. He added that that was great, then listened to her spew a load of bullshit about Paris, which was *so romantic*, and the cheese was *so good*, and the French were *such great lovers*.

He looked at her perfect teeth, her manicured fingernails, her skinny arms, listened to her non-Queen's English, offered to get her another glass of champagne, and got lost on the way.

He bought some Sellotape and a pad of paper in a Pakistani corner store, hailed a taxi, yanked off his fake shirtfront, and stayed up late.

He wrapped each one separately: the dogs, the cats, the hen, the duck, the horse, the chick, the goat, the llama, the star, the moon, the cloud, the sparrow, the mouse, the tractor, the boot, the fish, the frog, the flower, the tree, the strawberry, the kennel, the dove, the guitar, the firefly, the basket, the bottle and the heart.

All of it nicely bundled and mixed up in a package, she'd be none the wiser.

He fell asleep thinking about her.

About her body, a little.

But mostly about her.

About her, with her body round her.

It was a huge bed, a sort of double-size obese King Size, so how was it possible?

That this woman, whom he hardly knew, was already taking up all the room?

Yet another question for Yacine.

He had his breakfast brought out to the patio, and on the hotel letterhead he drew the tribulations of a badger in New York.

His own tribulations, that is.

His pockets full of badger grease, his peregrinations around Strand's, his reading session surrounded by bums and rebellious teenagers (he went to a lot of trouble to make sure he reproduced the graphics on the T-shirt one of them was wearing: *Keep shopping everything is under control*), his smooth badger fur in his fine tuxedo, his tail wagging in the breeze as he chats on the terrace with a badgerette who keeps badgering him about France, his night spent tearing off bits of Sellotape, getting it all stuck in his claws and . . . no . . . he wouldn't tell her about how cramped the bed was . . .

He found the postal code for Les Marzeray on the Internet, went to the Post Office, and wrote *Kate and Co.* on the parcel.

He flew back over the ocean, immersed in the disparate lots of Downe and Barnet.

Terrible.

Then he read the letters Wilde wrote in prison.

Refreshing.

Upon arrival, he was annoyed at having lost five hours of his life. He put together his 'solvent tenant' file, went by Laurence's, put his clothes, a few CDs and a few books into a bigger suitcase, and left his key ring out where she was sure to see it, on the kitchen table.

No. She wouldn't see it there.

On the shelf in the bathroom.

A completely idiotic gesture. He still had loads of things to pick up, but oh well . . . Let's chalk it up to that dandy's bad influence. The same one who, after everyone had abandoned him and he was dying in a drab Paris hotel room, with wallpaper that he despised, still had the swagger to declare, 'Either that wallpaper goes, or I do.'

So Charles went.

7

Never had he worked as hard as during that month of July.

Two of their projects had got past the first round. One was not terribly interesting – an administrative building that would pay the bills; the other, more exciting but far more complicated, was one that Philippe cared greatly about. The design and realization of a new urban development zone in a new suburb. It was a huge project and Charles was not easy to convince.

The land was on a slope.

'So what?' retorted his associate.

'Well, let me give you just a random example . . . Here, last January 15, for instance: "When a slope is necessary in order to overcome a difference in level, it shall be less than 5%. If it is above 4%, a landing will be installed at the top and the bottom of each gradient and every 10 metres continuously. A support railing will be required at any point where the level is broken at a height of more than 0.40 metres. If this should prove technically impossible, due in particular to the topography or the disposition of existing edifices, a ramp of greater than 5% will be tolerated. This slope may attain 8% over a length less than or equal to two metres and up to . . ."'

'Stop.'

He sat down at his work table, shaking his head. Somewhere in the midst of all those arcane Ubuesque figures, regulations were notifying them that the average slope on any plot earmarked for construction must not exceed 4%.

Oh?

He thought of the huge danger represented by the Rue Mouffetard, the Rue Lepic, the Fourvière Hill in Lyon, the *stradine* struggling up the hills of Rome . . .

And the Alfama and Chiado districts in Lisbon, and San Francisco . . .

Come on. Get to work. Let's flatten and level and make it all uniform, since that's what they want, to transform the country into a gigantic suburban sprawl.

And obviously it must all be sustainable development, right?

Naturally. Of course.

He consoled himself with keeping the footbridges for the end. Charles loved to draw and cogitate suspended walkways and bridges. There, at least, you could see the trace of the hand of man.

Where the void was concerned, industry still had to make concessions to the designer . . .

If he could have chosen, he would have been born in the 19th century, at a time when great engineers were also great architects. The most successful projects, to his mind, were those where certain materials were used for the first time. Concrete by Maillart, steel by Brunel and Eiffel, cast iron by Telford . . .

Yes, those fellows must have had a good time . . . Engineers in those days were also entrepreneurs, and they corrected their errors when they came to light. As a result, their errors were perfect.

The work of someone like Heinrich Gerber, Ammann or Freyssinet, or Leonhardt's Kochertal viaduct, or Brunel's Clifton Suspension Bridge. And the Verrazano . . . Well, you're wandering off, now, yes you are. You've got an urban development zone on your plate so zone in on it and get out your urban land use code.

'. . . up to 12% on a length equal to or less than 0.50 metres.'

But perhaps something good would come of all his doubts. If you set yourself up to win, you're also setting yourself up to lose. If you wanted a deal at any price, you'd end up being timid and conservative in your dealings. Not to shock . . . Philippe and Charles did agree on that point, so he worked on the project like a madman. But relaxed.

Supple, sloping.

Life was elsewhere.

He had dinner nearly every evening with young Marc. Together they discovered, at the end of the most improbable cul-de-sacs, the back rooms of dingy little bistros still open after midnight, where they would eat in silence and sample beers from all over the world.

Drunk with exhaustion, they always ended up declaring that they would write a guidebook. *A Very Sloping Gullet*, or, *Urban*

Intoxication Zone, and then finally, *finally*, their genius would be recognized.

Then Charles would drop him off by taxi, and collapse on the mattress on the floor of his empty room.

A mattress, a duvet, soap, and a razor: that was all he had for the moment. He could hear Kate's voice, 'this Robinson Crusoe lifestyle saved us all', and he fell asleep naked, rose with the first light, and got the impression that it was here, at this point, that he was beginning to build the bridge of his life.

He spoke several times by telephone to Mathilde, told her that he had left Rue Lhomond and was camping on the other side, at the foot of the Montagne Sainte-Geneviève.

No, he hadn't picked his room yet.

He was waiting until she got back . . .

He had never had such long conversations with her before, and he realized how much she had matured over the last few months. She talked to him about her father, about Laurence, about her little half-sister; she asked him if he had seen Led Zeppelin in concert, and why Claire had never had children, and was it true, this business about bumping into a door?

For the first time, Charles talked about Anouk to someone who hadn't known her. During the night, long after he'd kissed Mathilde goodnight, he found it perfectly normal. To have shared Anouk with a heart that was the age he'd been when . . .

'But you loved her – like, you were *in love*?' she'd asked eventually.

And as he hadn't been able to reply right away, while he searched for another word, a word more accurate and fair and less compromising, he heard her give a jaded grunt, which twenty years on had the effect of a slap in the face, bringing him back to his senses:

'What a dork I am . . .' she added. 'Like, how else can you love someone?'

★

On the 17th, he squeezed the huge paw of his Russian chauffeur for the last time. He had just spent two days tearing out the few hairs he had left over a phantom construction site. Pavlovich had disappeared, most of the men had gone over to the Bouygues project, the few who'd stayed behind threatened to sabotage the works if they weren't paid *syu minutu*, two hundred and fifty kilometres of cables had shrunk to twelve, and they still needed that authorization in order to –

'*What* authorization?' he fumed, without even bothering to switch to English. 'What sort of blackmail is it this time? How much do you want altogether, for fuck's sake?'

And where was that bastard Pavlovich? Gone over to Bouygues as well?

The project had been a shambles from the start. It wasn't even their project to begin with, it was a friend of Philippe's, an Italian bloke who had come and begged them *di salvargli*, to save *l'onore* and his *reputazione* and *le finanze* and *lo studio* and *la famiglia e la Santa Vergine*. He came that close to kissing their fingers on signing . . . Philippe had accepted; Charles said nothing.

He suspected that beneath it all there was a sort of devious under-hand game being played, the sort to which his incorruptible associate held the secret. If they rescued the site, it meant they'd have Whosit in their pocket, and Whosit was Thingie's right-hand man, and Thingie had 10,000 square metres to rebuild somewhere else now, and . . . In short, Charles had read the plans, thought it would be an easy job, had grabbed his dog-eared Tolstoy and, like the little Emperor, had set off with six hundred thousand men to show them what great tacticians the French were . . .

And like Bonaparte, he went home devastated.

No, not even. He couldn't give a damn. He'd simply held Viktor's hand in his own for a little while, and felt his knuckles, and their smiles, crack a little. In another life, they would have been good comrades . . .

He handed him a wad of roubles that he had on him. Viktor grumbled.

'For the Russian lessons.'

'*Nyet, nyet*,' he insisted, still squeezing his knuckles.

'For the kids . . .'

There, okay. He set him free.

Charles turned around one last time, and saw not the desolate plains, or the remains of famished soldiers with their frozen feet wrapped in rags or sheepskin, but a last tattoo. A barbed wire the length of an arm raised very high, to wish him lots of *shchastye* in his life . . .

*

It was hard going home, however. To live like an eternal student when life was a non-stop hectic joyride was one thing, but to skid to a stop when you had no more home – that was another sort of thrashing . . .

He didn't have the courage to take a taxi, so he mulled over the debacle in the RER.

A wretched journey. Dreary, and filthy. To the left, tower blocks, Roma camps, and to the right . . . Why call them Roma camps, anyway? Why be so tactful, when slum would be the proper word? Let us pay tribute to globalization for allowing us to enjoy the same sights as in other countries . . . Everywhere you looked on the ballast, nothing but refuse and rubbish – and then he remembered that it was somewhere around here that Anouk had passed away.

Nana in his pissoir, and Anouk back where she had started . . .

In just such a mood, of terrible waste, he reached his own camp on the other side of the Gare du Nord.

He went straight into his partner's office and opened his kitbag.

'*Terror belli, decus pacis . . .*'

'I beg your pardon?' sighed Philippe, frowning.

'Terror during war, shield during peace, I return it to you . . .'

'What are you on about this time?'

'My Marshal's baton. I shall not go back there.'

The next part of their conversation was extremely technical, financial, rather, and when Charles closed the door on all the bitterness he had just caused, he decided to get out of there without returning to square one, those well-worn armrests.

He had over 2,500 kilometres of retreat on his emotional dial, two additional hours on his biological clock, he was tired again, and he had to go by the dry cleaner's if he wanted to get dressed the next day.

As he was on his way out of the door, Barbara gestured to him without breaking off her phone conversation.

Pointing to a parcel on the counter.

He'd deal with it tomorrow . . . Slammed the door, stopped abruptly, allowed a silly smile to spread over his face, retraced his steps and recognized the postmark.

Which was proof enough, if any were needed.

*

He didn't open it straight away and, as he had done a few weeks earlier, he crossed Paris with a surprise under his arm.

And no more anxiety.

He went down the Boulevard Sébastopol with a lightness to his step, and his floating rib, and felt as chuffed as any ingénu who has just obtained his first walk-on part. Smiling at the pay-and-display machines and contemplating the address over and over and over again while the little pedestrian signal was red.

(The Boulevard had earned its name, should one need reminding, in memory of a Franco-English victory in the Crimea. Ah . . .)

He contemplated his parcel yet again on the zebra crossing. He'd had a good idea her handwriting would be like that. Fine, looping . . . like the design on her dress . . . And he knew, too, that she wouldn't manage to make her letters fit in the obligatory little boxes. And that she would pick out pretty stamps . . .

Her name was Cherrington.

Kate Cherrington.

What a doofus he was . . .

And how proud he was.

To be a doofus, at his age.

He made the most of this burst of energy to fill his cupboards. He left a huge trolley by the till at the supermarket, and promised he'd be home two hours later in time for the delivery.

He left the store with a broom and a bucket filled with cleaning products, cleaned the flat for the first time since the inventory inspection, plugged in the fridge, unpacked the water bottles, neatly stored Mathilde's cereal boxes, her favourite jam, her low-fat milk and her gentle shampoo, unfolded the bathroom towels, screwed in the light bulbs and prepared his very first steak on the Impasse des Boeufs.

He pushed back his plate, wiped away the crumbs, and went to fetch his present.

Removing the lid of a tin box, he discovered: dogs, cats, hens, ducks, horses, chicks, goats, llamas, stars, moons, clouds, sparrows, mice, tractors, boots, fish, frogs, flowers, trees, strawberries, kennels, doves, guitars, fireflies, baskets, bottles and . . .

Right. He lined them up on the table. The way he liked, methodically, and according to category.

All the shapes had been used for different kinds of biscuits, but as for the heart, there was only one.

Was it a sign? It was a sign . . . It was a sign!

The term 'doofus' didn't really live up to his situation, now, did it?

Dear Charles,
I made the batter, Hattie and Nedra did the cookies, Alice added the eyes and the moustaches, Yacine found your address (it is you?) and Sam is taking the parcel to the post office.
Thanks.
I miss you.
We all miss you.
K.

He didn't take a single bite, but lined them all up again, standing them this time, on the mantelpiece in his bedroom, and fell asleep thinking about her.

About the shape he would become, if she came over him like a cookie cutter.

The next morning, he drew a picture of his fireplace in the middle of the empty space and added, *I miss you too.*

And, recalling what she had told him about the word 'cook' and 'cooker', he found the ambiguity of her language very useful.

Because his 'you' could mean, just *you*, Kate, or *all of you*.

He'd let her choose . . .

He could have, perhaps should have, let his guard down a bit more, but he didn't know how to do that.

His split with Laurence, however admissible it might be, had left him with a nasty aftertaste of spinelessness.

Once again, he anchored himself to his table, his future prospects and his AutoCAD. It was software for work, where everything was perfect because everything was virtual. He'd set his sights elsewhere, in order to avoid any work on himself and, firmly buttressed against the differences in level, he was sure he would not stumble.

He did his sums. Again and again.

He thought endlessly about Kate, but never really thought.

It was . . . he was quite incapable of explaining it . . . Like a light.

As if the certainty of knowing she existed, even far away, even without him, was enough to calm him. Of course he harboured thoughts that were more . . . *incarnate*, at times, but not even that much . . . He felt ridiculously overconfident when he dreamt of playing cookie cutters with her. But in actual fact he felt . . . how to put it . . . impressed, maybe. Yes, why not, let's go with *impressed*. She may have done everything in her power to have nothing to do with it – sweat, burp, tell him to get lost with a wave of her ring, sulk, bitch, swear, blow her nose in her sleeve, drink like a fish, fuck the educational system – and the social services too while she's at it – fume at her curves, her hands, her pride, run herself down on numerous occasions, and abandon him without the slightest farewell – the word seemed appropriate.

It was stupid, it was a pity, it was inhibiting, but that's the way things stood. When he thought about her, he was designing a world, rather than a woman with a star-shaped scar.

Moreover, if he really thought about it, she'd done the casting right from the start. He was the stranger, the visitor, the explorer, the Columbus who'd ended up there because he'd lost his way.

Because of a little girl with crooked teeth, and an even more crooked mother.

And, by letting him head off again without saying goodbye, Kate had very cleverly misaligned his compass . . .

So we're back to operating instructions, I see . . . So what's all this business about bridges, and this monastic lifestyle, this sublime Grand Impoverishment? Are you missing your goose-feather bed, is that it?

No, it's just that . . .

Just what?

My back aches, fuck. It *really really* aches.

So go and buy a bed!

No, that's not all . . .

What then?

Guilt . . .

Aaah! Well, I wish you luck. Because you'll see, there are no operating instructions where guilt is concerned.

No?

No. If you look hard enough, you will certainly find some, the merchants of the Temple are everywhere, but you'd do better to save your money and buy a decent mattress instead. Besides, she just wrote to you, she said she misses you.

Pfff . . . *Miss you* in English, that's just an expression. Like *Take care* or *All my love* . . .

She didn't write *Miss you*, she wrote *I* miss you.

Yes, but . . .

But?

She lives in Timbuktu, she has a pile of kids, animals who will take thirty years to die, a house that stinks of damp dog and . . .

Stop, Charles. Stop. You're the one who stinks.

And because this kind of dialogue between his Cogito self and his Ergo sum self was getting his Charles self absolutely nowhere, and because — mainly — he had a lot of work, he preferred to work.

What a wanker.

Fortunately, there was Claire.

8

She had said, I absolutely have to take you to this new place. Not only is the food delicious but the guy is incredible.

'What guy?'

'The waiter . . .'

'Still fantasizing about waiters? Thumb in waistcoat and hips nice and tight in a long white apron?'

'No, no, not at all. This guy, you'll see, he's . . . I can't explain . . . I adore him . . . A sort of really classy toff. As if he'd landed here from the moon. A sort of cross between Monsieur Hulot and the Duke of Windsor . . .'

Writing down their lunch date in his diary, Charles rolled his eyes skyward.

His sister and her infatuations . . .

They met up early in August, time enough to close their files and wish their respective assistants a pleasant holiday. Claire would be taking the train at the end of the afternoon to go to a soul music festival in the Périgord Noir.

'Can you drop me at the station?'

'We'll take a cab, you know I don't have a car any more . . .'

'Exactly, that's what I wanted to tell you. After you drop me off, could you keep my car for me? My parking permit has expired . . .'

Charles rolled his eyes heavenward once again. It was a hassle, having to struggle with Parisian parking meters. Right . . . he'd take it over to his parents' place. He hadn't seen them in such a long time . . .

'Okay.'

'Did you write down the address?'

'Yes.'

'Are you all right? You sound funny . . . Is Mathilde back?'

Yes, she was, but he hadn't seen her. Laurence had picked her up and they'd gone straight to Biarritz.

Charles had not had the chance, nor the courage, to relate his conjugal adventures to his sister.

'I have to go, I've got an appointment,' he replied.

★

The description was apposite: the awkwardness, the poetry, the lankiness of a Monsieur Hulot, with the sense of class and flower in the buttonhole worthy of His Majesty King Edward.

He opened his arms wide, welcomed them into his tiny bistro as if they were on the steps of St James's Palace, greeted Claire's new dress in iambic pentameters, and stuttering ever so slightly, led them to a table by the window.

Tati de Windsor brought them two glasses of wine as a matter of course and had turned round to explain the menu on the slate when a loud grumble came through the serving hatch:

'Telephone!'

He begged them to excuse him, and rushed to grab the mobile phone held out to him.

Charles and Claire watched him blush, go pale, lift his hand to his forehead, drop the telephone, bend down, lose his glasses, put them back on skew-whiff, hurry towards the door, grab his jacket from the coat rack, and slam the door just as said coat rack crashed to the floor, taking with it a tablecloth, a bottle, two place settings, a chair, and the umbrella stand.

Silence in the room. Everyone looking at one another absolutely flabbergasted.

A litany of swear words exploded from the kitchen. The chef appeared, a young guy with a frown, who rubbed his hands on his apron before picking up his mobile phone.

Still muttering into his beard, he placed the phone on the bar, leaned over, pulled out a magnum of champagne and began to jiggle the cork, taking his time.

Time enough for his frown to change into something that might actually pass for a smile . . .

'Right,' he said, addressing all the diners, 'it would seem that my associate has just provided an heir to the throne . . .'

The cork flew out. And he added, 'This one's on the uncle!'

He passed the bottle to Charles and asked him to serve the others. He had work to do.

He walked away with a glass of champagne in his hand, shaking his head as if this were something he simply couldn't believe – how was it possible to feel so much happy turmoil inside?

He turned round again, and with his chin pointed to the order pad that had been left on the counter:

'Please, if you don't mind, take your own orders, tear off the top sheet and put it on the serving hatch,' he said grouchily. 'And keep a copy. I'll let you add up the bill, as well.'

The kitchen door swung shut and they heard, 'And write in capital letters if at all possible! I'm illiterate!'

And then a laugh.

A gigantic, gastronomic laugh.

'Holy shit, Philou . . . Holy shit!'

Charles turned to his sister.

'You're right, this place is really, er, quaint . . .'

He poured their glasses and passed the bottle to the next table.

'I can't get over it,' she murmured, 'I'd have imagined that bloke to be completely asexual . . .'

'Hah! That's a typical woman's way of thinking. As soon as a fellow is kind, you castrate him.'

'Bullshit,' she shrugged. Then, taking a sip, 'Look. You . . . you're the kindest boy I know and . . .'

'And what?'

'No, nothing. You live with a woman who is, uh, totally fulfilling . . .'

Charles said nothing.

'Sorry,' she apologized. 'Forgive me. That was stupid.'

'I left, Claire.'

'Left where?'

'Left home.'

'Noooo,' she said, on the verge of a laugh.

'Yeeeees,' he countered glumly.

'Champagne!'

And when he did not react: 'Are you unhappy?'

'Not yet.'

'And Mathilde?'

'I don't know . . . She says she wants to move in with me . . .'

400

'Where are you living?'

'Near the Rue des Carmes . . .'

'I'm not surprised.'

'That I left?'

'No. That Mathilde wants to go with you.'

'Why?'

'Because teenagers love generous people. Later on, you get a thick hide, but at that age, you still need a certain amount of kindness . . . Hey, how are you going to manage with work?'

'I don't know . . . I'll organize things differently, I suppose.'

'You're going to have to change your life . . .'

'So much the better. I was tired of the other one. I thought it was jet lag but not at all, it was . . . what you just said . . . An issue with kindness . . .'

'I can't get over it. When did this happen?'

'A month ago.'

'Since you saw Alexis, then.'

Charles smiled. One smart customer.

'That's it . . .'

Claire waited until she was hidden behind the wine menu to let fly a little, 'Thank you, Anouk!'

He didn't answer. Was still smiling.

'Oh, look at you . . .' she said, giving him a sidelong glance, 'you've met someone . . .'

'No . . .'

'Liar. You're all pink.'

'It's the bubbles.'

'Oh, yeah? And how well stacked are the bubbles? Are they blonde?'

'Amber.'

'Well, well . . . Wait. We'd better order if we don't want to get ticked off by that Neanderthal, and after that (she looked at her watch) I've got about three hours to worm it out of you. What are you having? Artichoke hearts? Heart of romaine?'

'Where do you see that?'

'Sitting across from me.' She giggled.

'Claire?'

'Hm?'

'How do they manage, the guys who are up against you in the courtroom?'

'They cry out for their mothers . . . Right, I've decided. Well? Who is it?'

'I don't know.'

'Oh fuck, no. Don't give me that.'

'Look, I'll tell you the whole story and you will tell me, since you're so clever, if you can see what it's all about.'

'A mutant?'

He shook his head.

'What's so special about her?'

'A llama.'

Claire looked at him, startled and stunned.

'A llama, three thousand square metres of roof, a stream, five children, ten cats, six dogs, three horses, a donkey, hens, ducks, a goat, entire clouds full of swallows, loads of scars, an intaglio ring, martingales, a pocket cemetery, four ovens, a chainsaw, a gyratory crusher, a stable from the 18th century, roof beams to make you fall on your face, two languages, hundreds of roses, and one sublime view.'

'What on earth?!' said Claire, opening her eyes wider still.

'Ah! So you can't make head nor tail of it, either!'

'What's her name?'

'Kate.'

He took their order and left it by the entrance to the bear's den.

'And . . .' continued Claire, 'is she pretty?'

'I just told you.'

★

So Charles sat down to eat, and told all.

The grave by the waste depot, his spray job on the tombstone, Sylvie, the tourniquet, the dove, his accident on the Boulevard de Port-Royal, Alexis's empty gaze, his little substitution therapy life with neither dreams nor music, the figures dancing round the fire, Anouk's legacy, the Tin Can Alley, the colour of the sky, the police captain's voice, the winters at Les Vesperies, Kate's neck, her face, her hands, her laugh, her lips that she could not keep from badgering, their shadows, New York, the last sentence in the short novel by

Thomas Hardy, his hardwood floor bed full of splinters, and the biscuits he counted every evening all over again.

Claire hadn't touched her food.

'It's going to get cold,' he prompted.

'Yeah. If you stay in your flat like a halfwit playing with biscuits, you can be sure something's going to get cold.'

'What else do you want me to do?'

'You're the project manager.'

'You haven't seen the project.'

She emptied her glass, reminded him that this meal was on her, checked the prices on the slate, and left the money on the table.

'We've got to get going.'

'Already?'

'I don't have my ticket.'

'Why are you going this way?' he asked.

'To drop you off.'

'And the car?'

'I'll leave it with you when you've put a travel bag and your notebooks in the back . . .'

'Pardon?'

'You're too old, Charles. You've got to get a move on, now. You can't start behaving with her the way you were with Anouk . . . You're just . . . too old. Do you see what I mean?'

He didn't see anything.

'I can't promise you it will work, you know, but . . . You remember when you made me go to Greece with you?'

'Yes.'

'Well . . . we each get our turn.'

He carried her case and went with her as far as her compartment.

'And you, Claire?'

'Me?'

'You haven't told me a thing about your love life.'

She made a dreadful face so that she wouldn't have to answer him.

'It's too far away,' he went on.

'From where?'

'From everything.'

'That's true. You're right. Go back to Laurence, go on carrying a torch for Anouk, go crawling to Philippe, and tuck Mathilde in every night until she leaves home, that will be less of a hassle.'

She gave him a resounding kiss on the cheek before adding, 'And feed the pigeons some bread while you're at it . . .'

And she disappeared without turning round.

Charles stopped off at the Vieux Campeur shop, went by the agency, filled the boot with books and files, turned off his computer, his lamp, and left a long memo for Marc. He didn't know when he'd be back, it would be hard to reach him on his mobile, he would call in, and he wished him good luck.

Then he made a detour by the Rue d'Anjou. There was a little shop there that would surely have what he was looking for.

9

A whole scenario in his head. Five hundred kilometres of trailers and almost as many different versions of the opening scene.

It was just like something out of a Lelouch film . . . There he'd be, and she'd turn round. He'd smile, she'd be petrified. He'd open his arms, she'd rush into them. He'd be in her hair, she'd be in his neck. He'd say, I can't live without you, she'd be too full of emotion to reply. He'd lift her off the ground, she'd squeal with laughter. He'd carry her off towards . . . um . . .

Right. By now it was time for the second scene, and the set, no doubt, would be full of extras . . .

Five hundred kilometres, that made for a lot of celluloid. He'd imagined *everything* – and of course nothing happened as he'd foreseen.

It was nearly ten o'clock in the evening when he crossed the bridge. The house was empty. He could hear laughter and the sound of cultery and plates in the garden; he followed the light of the candles and, as on the previous occasion at the far end of the meadow, he saw many faces turning round before he saw hers.

Unfamiliar faces and figures, of adults he'd never seen. Shit . . . He was good for a long rewind.

Yacine rushed forward to greet him. As he leaned over to give him a hug, Charles saw Kate getting up in turn.

He had forgotten that she was as lovely as in his memories.

'What a nice surprise,' she said.

'I'm not disturbing you?'

(Oh! The dialogue! The emotion! The intensity!)

'No, of course not . . . I have some American friends visiting for a few days. Come on. I'll introduce you.'

Cut! thought Charles, get all those guys off the set! Those fuckers shouldn't be in this shot!

'With pleasure.'

'What's all this?' she asked, pointing to the stuff he had tucked under his arm.

'Sleeping bag.'

And, just something out of a film by Charles Balanda, she turned round, smiled to him in the darkness, and lowered her head, which enabled him see her neck, then she placed her hand in the small of his back to show him the way.

Instinctively, our young leading man walked more slowly.

From where they are placed, the viewers probably don't realize, but that palm, those five long fingers slightly spread, with their burden of an image of rural sacrifice and a young ephebe with a perfect slope of the hips, all pressing gently into the warm cotton of his shirt: that was something else . . .

Charles sat down at the end of the table, was offered a glass, a plate, knife and fork, some bread, a napkin, some *Hi! Nice to meet you!* greetings, kisses from the children, snuffles from the dogs, a smile from Nedra, a nice nod on the part of Sam of the Howdy gringo type, (you can go ahead and try to piss on my territory, but it's huge and you'll never aim far enough), the fragrance of flowers and mown grass, glow worms, a crescent moon, a conversation that went too quickly so he didn't understand a thing, a chair whose left rear leg was slowly sinking into a mole's living room, an enormous slice of pear tart, another bottle, a track made of crumbs in a dotted line from his plate to everyone else's, altercations, questions, and moments of violent protest about a topic he hadn't been following. The word 'bush' was often evoked but . . . um . . . were they referring to the man or the plant? And . . . In short, a sort of delicious floating sensation.

But there was also Kate, her arms rolled around her knees, her bare feet, her sudden mirth, her voice that wasn't quite the same when she was speaking her own language, and her sidelong glances that he'd grab hold of between swallows and which seemed, each time, to say, 'So . . . Is it true? You came back . . .'

He returned her smile and, as silent as ever, he got the feeling he'd never been this talkative with a woman.

And then they had coffee, and the kids put on some skits, and they had brandies, and the kids did some imitations, and bourbon, and more laughter, and more private jokes and even a little bit of architecture, as they were well-brought-up people . . .

Tom and Debbie were married, professors at Cornell, and the other man, Ken, a tall bloke with a lot of hair, was a researcher. It seemed to Charles that he was spending a lot of time around Kate. Well, it was hard to tell with these Americans, who were always hugging and patting for the least little thing. All sweetie and honey and hugs and gimme a kiss every which way . . .

Charles didn't care. For the very first time in his life, he'd decided to let himself live.

Let. Himself. Live.

He didn't even know if he'd be able to meet the challenge.

He was there on holiday. Happy and slightly drunk. Taking sugar cubes and building a temple to the mayflies that had died for the Light and that Nedra brought to him in beer capsule coffins. He answered Yes or Sure when necessary, or No when that was better, and concentrated on the tip of his knife to give a more Doric touch to his pillars.

There'd be time enough, later, for his urban development zones and land-use plan and other three-word headaches.

He glanced at his rival between two convoys of dead mayflies.

Anyway, long hair at that age was . . . pathetic.

And he had a huge chain bracelet just in case he couldn't remember his name. And as for his name, well, it was downright Barbie.

All that was missing was the camper van.

But above all – and this was something the hairy monster in his Hawaiian shirt seemed to be *totally* unaware of – the model Charles had brought with him was *Himalaya Light*.

It cost a fortune, okay, but was filled with duck feathers treated with Teflon.

Hear that, Samson?

Teflon, mate, Teflon.

Which just goes to prove I am more durable than I seem . . .

Himalaya, maybe, but *Light*.

That was his programme for the summer.

When Charles set off towards the courtyard with his candle in his hand, Kate had tried to resuscitate the perfect housewife who lay dormant inside her by offering him the soba-fed, uh, the sofa-bed.

But frr . . . they were all too wasted to play at good manners.

'Hey,' she called, 'don't – don't set the place on fire, okay?'

Charles raised his hand to gesture that he wasn't *that* stupid, after all.

'Already on fire, baby, already burning,' he chuckled, stumbling through the gravel.

Oh, yes. He was as tanked as a Panzer.

He found his niche in the stables, had the worst time imaginable locating the opening of his bloody bivouac, and fell asleep on a mattress of dead flies.

Bliss . . .

10

Naturally, it was Ken who went to fetch the croissants this time.

At a run . . .

With his handsome Nikes, his ponytail (!), and the sleeves of his T-shirt rolled up onto his (gleaming) shoulders. (Gleaming with sweat, that is.)

Right then.

Charles cleared his throat and put away his torrid scenarios.

If, at least, the guy had been an imbecile . . . But he wasn't. He was a good-looking egghead. A very likeable sort. Fascinated and fascinating, and funny. As were his compatriots.

The tone had been set. The house would be filled with an atmosphere – give me five – of comradeship, Baden Powell with a dash of ten in the bed roll over roll over. Never mind. So much the better. The children were happy to have all those adults about all of a sudden, and Kate was happy to see the children happy.

Never had she looked so lovely . . . Even this morning, with her hangover hidden behind her big dark glasses . . .

Lovely as only a woman who knows by heart the price of solitude can be, when she is finally laying down her weapons.

She was on leave for a few days and, little by little, she distanced herself from them. She didn't want to take any initiatives, she left them the house, the children, the animals, René's interminable weather forecasts, and the meal roster.

She read, sunbathed, slept in the sun and didn't even try to pretend to pitch in.

And that wasn't all. She didn't lay a hand on Charles. No more sidelong smiles or meaningful gazes. No more kidding me or teasing you. No more treasure troves in the hay or missionary dreams.

He suffered initially from this apparent coldness which manifested itself, painfully, as *conviviality*.

So that was the way things stood? However unexpected his presence, Charles was now relegated to playing his role as one of the gang. She never called him by his name, only addressed them all as 'you guys'.

Shit.

Could it be she was hooked on that big lump of a bloke? Not necessarily . . .

She was hooked on herself.

She played, fooled about, disappeared with the children and set herself up to get told off *with them*.

As if she were one of them.

She blessed all the adults, raised her glass in a toast a dozen times during meals that lasted longer and longer, and took advantage of their presence to slip away from the Board of Guardians.

And, as a result, she was perfectly happy.

Charles, who – and this was unconscious on his part – could have, or should have been . . . how to put it . . . intimidated? hobbled? by those budding little wings beneath the strap of her bra, only loved her all the more for it.

But. He was careful not to show it. He had had his fair share of slaps in the face recently, and that bone, just there, which was supported by his spine in order to protect his heart, was in the process of healing, as it happens. This was not the time to be opening his arms any old which way.

No. She wasn't a saint . . . She was a major idler who didn't lift a finger, who could really knock it back with the best of them, was growing marijuana (oh, so that was her 'comfort pharmacopoeia' . . .), and she didn't even hear the bell ring.

She had no sense of morality at all.

Phew.

This discovery was worth a bit of indifference.

Patience, little snail, patience.

What on earth was he doing that gave him the time to mull over all this besotted perpetual teenager nonsense?

He was sweeping up dead flies.

He wasn't alone. He dragged along behind him both Yacine and Harriet who, obliged to relinquish their rooms to the star-spangled banner, decided to go into exile with him.

410

They drew straws for their rooms and spent two whole days swallowing cobwebs and wandering through the various barns as if they were in some dusty flea market of abandoned treasures. Commenting, patching, stripping and painting tables, chairs, mirrors and other relics nibbled by termites and capricorn beetles. (Yacine, somewhat annoyed by such inaccuracy in matters of worm holes, gave them a lecture: Holes, that's capricorn beetles; and if it looks rotten and crumbly and brittle, that's termites.)

They organized a little housewarming party and Kate, upon seeing his room – bare, stripped, whitened with pure bleach, austere, monastic, with all those files piled at the end of the bed, and his laptop and his books on the clever little desk he'd installed beneath an alcove – stood silent for a moment.

'You came here to work?'

'No. This is just to impress you.'

'Oh?'

Everyone else was in Harriet's room.

'There's something I would like to say,' she added, leaning out of the window.

'Yes?'

'I . . . you . . . well . . . if I . . .'

Charles clung to the brass bedstead.

'No. Nothing,' she said, turning back, 'you've made it very cosy here, haven't you?'

In the three days that he'd been here, this was the first time he'd had her all to himself, so for two minutes he put aside his good cub scout badges: 'Kate . . . talk to me . . .'

'I . . . I'm like Yacine,' she said abruptly.

Charles looked at her.

'I don't know how to tell you this, but I . . . never again will I take the slightest risk of suffering, ever.'

Charles didn't know what to say.

'Do you understand?'

He was silent.

'It's something Nathalie told me . . . A lot of foster children, when they sense there's a change in the air, suddenly become unbearable and absolutely torment their host family. And do you know why they act like that? It's a survival instinct. To prepare themselves mentally and physically for a new separation. They make

411

themselves unbearable so that everyone will think their departure is a relief. To destroy the love . . . That . . . that hideous trap where they almost got caught, once again . . .'

Her finger traced the edge of the mirror.

'And so I'm like them, you see. I don't want to suffer any more.'

Charles was at a loss for words. One, two, three. More even, if he couldn't make do with less, but words, for pity's sake, some words . . .

'You never say a thing,' she sighed.

And, moving away towards the next room, 'I don't know a thing about you. I don't even know who you are or why you came back, but there is one thing you have to know. I've had a lot of people to stay in this house and, it's true, there is a Welcome sign on the doormat but . . .'

'But?'

'I will not give you the opportunity to abandon me.'

She peered back round the doorframe, made sure that the feather-weight was well and truly knocked for six, and stopped counting: 'To get back to more serious things, you know what's missing here, darling?'

And as he was really almost out for the count, she added, 'Une Mathilde.'

He spat out his gumshield and a few teeth along with it, and returned her smile before following her to the buffet.

And, while watching her laugh, raise her glass, and play darts with the others, he thought, well shit, she wasn't going to rape him, so . . .

And then he remembered a joke Mathilde had told him: 'D'you know why snails are so slow?'

'Uh . . .'

'Because drool is really sticky.'

So he stopped drooling.

11

What follows is what is known as happiness, and happiness is a very awkward thing.

It can't be told.

So they say.

So it is said.

Happiness is flat, soppy, boring, and always hard going.

Happiness bores readers.

Kills love.

If the author had even the slightest good sense, that author would immediately resort to an ellipsis.

Thought about it. Had a look in the dictionary:

ELLIPSIS. *Suppression of words that would be necessary for the plenitude of the construction, where the words that are expressed convey the meaning clearly enough to avoid any obscurity or uncertainty.*

What on earth?

Why do without words that would be necessary for the plenitude of the construction of a story that has been missing so many words already?

Why deprive oneself of the pleasure?

On the pretext that one is writing, simply write out, 'Those three weeks he spent at Les Vesperies were the happiest of his entire life,' and send him back to Paris?

It's true. Those six words: the, happiest, of, his, entire, life, would convey neither obscurity nor uncertainty.

'And he lived happily ever after.'

But the author is feeling a certain reluctance.

There have been taxi drivers, family dinners, loaded letters, jet lag, insomnia, chaos, lost tenders, muddy building sites, an injection of Valium/potassium/morphine, cemeteries, morgues, ashes, closed cabarets, a ruined abbey, renunciation, repudiation, break-ups, two overdoses, one abortion, bruises, too many lists, judicial decisions, and even hysterical Korean women.

Might have liked a bit of grass, too . . .

Sorry, a bit of greenery.

What is to be done?

Dig deeper into this lexicon of literary devices.

OTHER DEFINITIONS: *An elliptical story strictly observes the unity of action, avoiding any pointless episodes and uniting everything essential in a few scenes.*

Thus, we are entitled to a few scenes . . .

Thank you.

Too kind of you, dictionary.

But which scenes?

Since *everything* is a story . . .

The author refuses to take responsibility. To determine what is 'pointless' and what is not.

And, rather than judge, shall entrust what follows to our sensitive hero.

He has proven his worth.

Let's open his notebook.

In which an ellipsis could be a Roman amphitheatre, the colonnades on St Peter's Square, or Paul Andreu's Performing Arts Centre in Beijing – but under no circumstances an omission.

On the left-hand page, a sales receipt from the DIY where Ken, Samuel, and Charles had gone the previous day. You should always save sales receipts. Everyone knows that.

It's never the right thing. Never the right bolt, or the right length nail . . . You always forget something, and then they hadn't bought enough sandpaper. The girls complained because of the splinters.

Opposite, some sketches and some sums. Nothing insurmountable. Child's play.

A real game for children, as it happens. And for Kate.

Kate, who never went bathing with them in the stream . . .

'There's too much silt,' she said, making a face.

Charles was the head, Ken the right-hand man, and Tom in charge of the refreshment stand, cold beers at the ready at the end of a rope attached to the rowlock.

The three of them had designed and manufactured a magnificent landing stage.

And even a diving board on piles.

They'd gone to collect huge oil drums at the nearby waste depot and placed pine planks over them.

Charles had even thought of steps and a railing in the 'Russian Dacha' style, for drying towels and leaning against during the endless diving contests that would ensue . . .

He'd even thought about it some more during the night, and the next morning he climbed up a tree with Sam and stretched a steel wire from one bank to the other.

And here's what you can see on the third page.

A strange contraption made out of old bicycle handlebars: the children's zipwire.

He'd gone back to FixItFreddy for the third time and brought back two ladders that were sturdier. Then with the other 'grown-ups' they'd spent the rest of the day lolling about on their elegant wooden beach, encouraging any number of little scamps who would fly over their heads with a cry of Banzai! before dropping into the current.

'How many of them are there?' he asked, dumbfounded.

'The entire village,' smiled Kate.

Even Lucas and his big sister . . .

The ones who didn't know how to swim were desperate.

But not for long.

Kate could not stand desperate children. So she went to get a rope.

Thus, the ones who didn't know how to swim were only half-drowned. They were pulled back to shore, and they had to recover from their excitement and all the mouthfuls of stream they'd swallowed before they were allowed to go back in.

The dogs yapped, the llama chewed its cud and the water spiders moved elsewhere.

The kids who didn't have a swimming costume wore their knickers, and their wet knickers became transparent.

The more modest among them would sit astride their bikes. Most of them came back with a swimming costume and a sleeping bag on the bike-rack.

Debbie was in charge of tea and snacks. She loved the Aga's pastry oven.

The drawings on the following pages have only one subject: little Tarzan figures suspended between sky and water, hanging onto a pair of old handlebars. With both hands, with one hand, with two fingers, one finger, right side up, upside down, head first. All for one and one for all.

But Tom is there, too, in his rowing boat, to pick up the dazed ones; there are a dozen pairs of sandals and trainers lined up along the bank, spots of sun sparkling on the water through the branches of a poplar tree, Marion sitting on the bottom step handing a piece of cake to her brother, and a big ninny standing behind her about to shove her into the water with a laugh.

Her profile, for Anouk, and Kate's, for himself.

Quick sketch. He didn't dare sit drawing her for too long.

He was trying to forestall any social worker discussions.

Alexis came to fetch his brood.

'Charles? What on earth are you doing here?'

'Offshore engineering . . .'

'But you . . . How long are you here for?'

'Depends . . . If we find oil under the stream, for quite a while yet, I suppose . . .'

'You'll have to come over for dinner one evening!'

And Charles, our kind Charles, declined.

Said that he didn't feel like it.

And Alexis went off, and took it out on his kids, What are all those marks on your thighs? And what is Mummy going to say? And how'd you get that hole in your swimming costume and where are your socks and niggle niggle nag and naggle naggle nig. Charles turned round and realized Kate had heard him.

You still haven't told me your story, said her gaze.

'I have a bottle of Port Ellen in my briefcase,' he replied.

417

'*Really?*'

'*Yes.*'

She put on her dark glasses and smiled.

She hadn't been in the water once, let alone put on her swimming costume.

  She'd tricked them good and proper.

  She wore long white shirts in cotton canvas, split high up, usually missing a few buttons . . . Charles didn't draw her, but what was behind her, so that he could eye her calmly. A lot of the drawings in these pages are based on her skin. If you look at the foreground you can always see the top of a knee, a bit of shoulder, or her hand placed on the railing . . .

  And that handsome lad, there?

  No, it's not Ken. It's her ancient Greek boyfriend, the one she wears on her finger.

The next two pages have been torn out.

The same landing stage, and the same zipwire, but neatly drawn, with all the dimensions conscientiously indicated.

For Yacine. Who sent them to the editor of a junior science magazine, to the column entitled 'Innovation Competition'.

'Look,' he'd said one evening, climbing onto Charles's lap.

'Oh, no,' Samuel had moaned, 'you're not going to start with that, again . . . He's been driving us nuts for over two years . . .'

And since Charles, as usual, didn't know what was going on, Kate interrupted: 'Every month he rushes to that page to see which little genius, never as brilliant as he is, has won the thousand euros . . .'

'A thousand euros . . .' came the languishing echo, 'and their inventions are always useless . . . Look, Charles, what you have to send in –' he said, grabbing the magazine from his hands, '– is the "prototype of an original, useful, clever and even entertaining invention. Send your application with diagrams and a precise description . . ." Isn't that exactly what you've got? Right? Could you send it? Could you?'

So the two pages were sent, and from the very next day and every day thereafter, until the end of the holidays, Yacine and Hideous would rush out to meet the postman.

The rest of the time was spent wondering what they would do with all that money . . .

'You can pay for your pooch to have a facelift!' squawked the jealous bystanders.

A few lines . . .

My dear, my angel, my little pumpkin, my favourite down-
loader . . .
Where are you? What are you up to? Are you into surfing, or
surfers?
I often think about . . .

*The draft stopped there. The bell had rung and Charles, still groggy from
thinking about Mathilde, had gone to join the others, taking a detour via
the hill. The only spot where you could get a bit of satellite reception,
provided you stood on one leg, with your arms in the air, and wriggled
around to face west.*

He'd heard her voice, her laugh, vague echoes, and clinking cocktail glasses.

*She asked him when he was going to join them, but didn't listen to
her stepfather's mumbling reply to the end. They were waiting for her.*

She sent a kiss and added, 'D'you want to speak to Mum?'

Charles lowered his arms.

'Emergency calls only,' flashed the screen.

*Why was she pretending not to understand, this child of divorced parents?
Did she think he'd taken a bachelor flat for the summer?*

*He didn't drink much that evening, and went back to his garret room well
before curfew.*

He wrote her a long letter.

Mathilde,

Those songs you listen to all day long . . .

He hunted for a second envelope.

*No hope of winning. He hadn't invented anything original, and for the
first time in his life, he was quite incapable of providing a precise diagram.*

Pastern, withers, fetlock, hock, cannon, gaskin, and dock. Charles wasn't familiar with any of these terms, and yet these drawings are probably the most exquisite ones in the notebook.

Kate had taken the tourists on an outing and he had worked all morning.

He had lunch the way he'd been taught, with a few warm tomatoes nicked from the garden and a piece of cheese, and then he went for a stroll along the edge of the property with a book she had lent him, 'A fantastic treatise on architecture'.

The Life of the Bee, *by Maurice Maeterlinck.*

He went in search of a good vantage point to vent his spleen.

For he was cogitating later and later into the night, restarting his calculations ten times or more, and breaking his neck on those 4% gradients.

He was a family man without a family. He was forty-seven years old and he was having a hard time finding his position on the curve . . .

Could it be that he had already gone halfway?

No.

Yes?

Good Lord.

And now? Wasn't he wasting the little time he had remaining?

Should he leave?

To go where?

To an empty flat with a bricked-up fireplace?

How could this be? After he'd worked so hard — to find himself with so little at his age?

That other cow had been right, after all . . .

He had followed her to the stream, like a rat.

And now?

The rope!

It could well be that at night she was having it off with Monsieur Barbie, while he was manufacturing his bloody housing estates.

And something in his crotch was itching terribly.

(Harvest mites.)

He leaned into the shade of a tree.

First sentence: 'I have no intention of writing a treatise on apiculture or beekeeping.'

Contrary to expectation, he devoured the book. It was THE thriller of the summer. All the ingredients were present: life, death, the necessity of life, the necessity of death, allegiance, massacres, madness, sacrifice, the foundation of the citadel, young queens, nuptial flight, the massacre of the males, and the females' genius in construction. The extraordinary hexagonal cell which 'attains absolute perfection from every perspective, and it would be impossible, even were one to unite all the geniuses, to improve on it.'

He nodded. He looked around for René's three hives, and reread one of the last paragraphs:

'And just as it is written in the tongue, stomach, and mouth of the bee that it must make honey, so is it written in our eyes, our ears, our nerves, our marrow, in every lobe of our head, in all the nervous systems of our body, that we are created to transform what we absorb of the things of the earth into a particular energy that is of a unique quality on the planet. No other creature, that I know of, has been so equipped to produce, as we are, this strange fluid, that we name thought, intelligence, understanding, reason, soul, spirit, cerebral power, virtue, goodness, justice, knowledge; for it has a thousand names, although it is all of one essence. Everything in us has been sacrificed to it. Our muscles, our health, the agility of our limbs, the equilibrium of our animal functions, the tranquility of our life: all bear the growing burden of its preponderance. It is the most precious and most difficult of states in which to raise matter. Fire, heat, light, life itself, and then the instinct more subtle than life and the majority of all those elusive forces which crowned the world before our advent, all pale upon contact with this new fluid.

We do not know where it is taking us, nor what it will make of us, nor what we shall make of it.'

Well, well, mused Charles, that doesn't half leave us in a bloody fix . . .

He stretched out, chuckling to himself. As far as he was concerned, he was more than ready to produce the strange fluid that would necessitate

422

the sacrifice of his muscles, of the agility of his limbs, and of the equilibrium of his animal functions.

What an idiot.

He awoke in a very different state of mind. A horse — huge, fat, terrible — was grazing not three feet away. He thought he would pass out, and was overcome with a fit of anxiety the likes of which he'd rarely known.

He did not move an inch, only blinking when a drop of sweat tickled his eyelashes.

After a few minutes of wildly racing heartbeat, Charles reached gingerly for his notebook, wiped his palm on the dry grass, and drew a line.

'When there is something you do not understand,' he never failed to tell his young students, 'something that escapes you, is beyond you, draw it. Even poorly, even just a rough sketch. When you aim to draw something, it obliges you to sit still long enough to observe it, and if you observe it you'll see that you have already understood it.'

Pastern, withers, fetlock, hock, cannon, gaskin, and dock — he wasn't familiar with any of these terms, and the little round handwriting that inserted the caption beneath each watercolour sketch, still crinkly from his sweat, was Harriet's.

'Brilliant! You're really good! Can I have this one?'

So, another page torn out.

He made a detour by the stream to wash his hide and, while he was rubbing himself with his damp shirt, he decided that he'd take advantage of the others' departure to prepare his own.

He wasn't really getting much work done and, all in all, he would have preferred it if she had drowned him outright.

This life just below the surface was making him stupid.

He decided to prepare dinner while waiting for them, and went into the village to do some shopping.

He took advantage of the fact that he was back in civilization in order to listen to his phone messages.

Marc briefly enumerated a whole list of setbacks and asked that Charles return the call as soon as possible; his mother complained of his ingratitude and brought him up to date on all the mishaps of the summer; Philippe wanted to know how far he'd got and told him about his meeting at Sorensen's offices; and Claire, finally, while he stood in front of the monument to the dead, told him off in no uncertain terms.

Had he forgotten that he had her car?

When did he intend to give it back to her?

Had he forgotten that she was going next week to Paule and Jacques'?

And that she was too much of an old bag to get herself picked up if she hitch-hiked?

Why couldn't she reach him?

Was he too busy fucking to spare a thought for others?

Was he happy?

Are you happy?

Tell me.

He sat down at an outdoor café, ordered a glass of white wine and pressed the return call button four times.

Began with the most unpleasant one and then was very pleased to hear the voices of those he loved.

And came up with a really amazing thing.

He licked the wooden spoon, put all the lids back on, went round humming as he set the table, *Ne me quitte pas, ne me quitte pas and all that rubbish.* Fed the dogs and took the seed to the hens.

If Claire could see him now . . . Calling the hens, with all the majestic gestures of the sower . . .

On his way back he spotted Sam and Ramon training in the large meadow, generally referred to as the château meadow; they were slaloming in and out among the haystacks.

He went over to them. He leaned against the gate and greeted all the teenagers who'd been sleeping in the stables with him, and whom he'd been spending more and more time with, playing endless poker games.

He'd already lost 95 Euros, but he figured that wasn't a lot to pay if it kept him from brooding in the dark.

The donkey didn't seem very motivated, and when Sam went by, grumbling and cursing, Mickaël called out, 'Why don't you whip him?'

Charles was delighted with Sam's reply.

True horsemen require legs and hands; incompetent riders need a whip.

A revelation like that was well worth a blank page.

He closed his notebook, and welcomed the mistress of the house and her guests with glasses of champagne and a feast beneath the arbour.

'I didn't know you were such a good cook,' said Kate, with wonder.

Charles served her seconds.

'It's true I don't know a thing,' she added, stiffening.

'You've got it coming to you, then.'

'I hope not . . .'

Her smile drifted for a long time across the tablecloth and Charles reckoned that he had reached the last refuge before the mountain pass. Before the final assault on Mons Veneris . . . What a dreadful expression. Ha, ha! He was pissed again, and got himself roped into the conversations on all sides, without really following a single one. One of these days he would grab her by the hair and drag her the length of the courtyard before delivering her to his Teflon thing so that he could lick her scrapes.

'Penny for your thoughts,' she said.

'I put too much paprika in.'

He was in love with her smile. It would take him some time to get round to telling her, but then he'd tell her for a long time.

He was over two score in years, and he was sitting across from a woman who had lived twice as much as he had. The future had become a terrifying prospect, to both of them.

Because the amazing plan was indeed amazing, for a few days he abandoned his notebooks.

Only one drawing remains as testimony . . . Spoiled with a pastis watermark as well . . .

It was evening, and they were all in the village square. The evening before, his beloved Parisians had arrived, with great fanfare (crazy Claire, honking all the way along the oak avenue . . .); now Sam and his consorts were ravaging the pinball machine, while the little ones played around the fountain.

Charles had formed a boules team with Marc and Debbie, and they'd taken a terrible beating. Kate had warned them, all the same: 'You'll see, these old fellows will let you win the first round to make you feel good, and then, they'll kick your ass!!!'

With their well-kicked asses – what do you expect from bloody Parisians and Yanks – they sat nursing their anisettes to find some consolation while his sister, Ken, and Kate were laboriously trying to save the day.

Tom was keeping score.

The more they lost, the more they had to pay another round, and the rounder they got, the harder it was to locate that fucking little co-sho-nay.

Claire is the one who is rolling the boule on that solitary drawing of a very colourful weekend.

She isn't concentrating very hard. She's flirting with Barbie boy in English that is basic at best but very quaint: 'You teer my bioutifoule Chippendale or you teer pas? Bicose if you teer pas correctly, nous are in big shit, you oondairstonde? Show me please, what you are kah-pabble to do with your two boules . . .'

The super genius, researcher into the atom's atoms, could not oondairstonde a thing, other than that this woman was completely barmy, that she could roll a joint like no one else, and if she continued to cling to his arm like that while he was desperately trying to save the last round, he would 'push elle dans fontaine, okay?'

426

Later, and in somewhat more precise English, Charles set out to explain to Ken what his sister did and how she had become one of the most feared attorneys in all of France, if not all of Europe, in her particular field.

'But . . . what does she do?'

'She saves the world.'

'No?'

'Absolutely.'

Ken looked up at the woman who was busy fooling around with an old geezer, spitting her olive pits in the direction of Yacine's head, and he looked extremely puzzled.

'What the hell are you telling him now?' *shouted Claire to Charles.*

'About your profession . . .'

'Yes!' *she exclaimed, turning to Ken, who was transfixed,* 'I am very good in global warming! Globally I can warming anything, you know . . . Do you still live chez your parents?'

Kate was laughing. As was Marc, who had driven down with Claire to join them, and according to whom Claire was the most disastrous navigational system on the market.

But she had great music in the car . . . So much the better, they'd got lost no less than six times, after all . . .

Between two thrashings they all savoured ventrèche de porc *and very greasy* pommes frites, *and with their nonsense and their laughter they managed to lure the entire village under the linden trees.*

This was Kate's gift, mused Charles.

To create life wherever she went . . .

'What are you waiting for?' *Claire would ask, two evenings later, on the other side of the bridge, before starting to load kilos of fruit and veg into her little car.*

And as her brother would not interrupt his scrupulous wiping of her windscreen, she would aim a big kick directly at his arse.

'You're bloody stupid, Balanda.'

'Ouch.'

'You know why you'll never be a great architect?'

'No.'

'Well, because you're too bloody stupid.'

Laughter.

★

427

Tom had just shown up again, his hands full of ice cream for the kids, and Marc was picking up the stray boules when Kate announced, 'Right! La consolante, and after that, we'll head home.'

With a nod the old geezers pulled the rags from their pockets to wipe the boules.

'What is it? Some sort of rotgut?' asked Charles worriedly.

She blew on her lock of hair: 'What, la consolante? You've never heard the expression?'

'No.'

'Well . . . there's the first game, the second, the decider, the revenge, and then finally the consolation match. It's a game for no reason at all . . . nothing at stake, no competition, no losers . . . Just for the pleasure, really.'

Charles played a perfect game, thus enabling his team to win – no, not win – to honour the magnificent notion.

Consolation.

As he was getting ready to head off to bed, he said good night to everyone, and was leaving his sister to her private lessons (he suspected she spoke English much better than she was letting on, in order to create new challenges with her tongue), when she came up to him and said, 'You're right, go and get some sleep. You have to be at the station in Limoges tomorrow at eleven.'

'Limoges? What the fuck d'you want me to go to Limoges for?'

'It was the most practical route I could find for her.'

'Who, her?'

'Hmm, what's her name, already?' she said, pretending to frown, 'Mathilde, I think . . . yes, that's it, Mathilde.'

The-happiest-of-his-entire-life.

Here's why.

On arriving back from Limoges with Mathilde he found them all still, once again, and as always, sitting round the table.

They moved over to make room and gave a distinguished welcome to the new recruit.

They spent the rest of the afternoon by the stream.

For the first time since he had come here, Charles did not take his notebook with him. All the people he loved on earth were here around *him, and there was nothing else he could dream, imagine, conceive, or draw.*

Absolutely nothing.

★

The next morning they ran into Alexis and Madame his wife at the market.

Claire hesitated for a few seconds before deciding to give him a kiss.

But she did give him a kiss.

Cheerfully. Tenderly. Cruelly.

They were already gone when Corinne turned around and asked who the girl was.

'Charles's sister.'

'Oh?'

She turned to the cheesemaker: 'Hey, you haven't forgotten the grated Gruyère like the other time?'

Then, to her ghost of a husband: 'What are you waiting for? Pay the man.'

Not a thing. He wasn't waiting for a thing. That is exactly what he was doing.

He would go to Les Vesperies the next day under the pretext that he wanted to borrow some tool or other, and one of the children would inform him that she had already left.

Charles, who was working with Marc in the living room, didn't bother to get up.

Tom, Debbie, and Ken, who had already postponed their departure for Spain any number of times, finally left, too.

And Kate's mother, who had arrived the day before, took Hattie's room in their wake.

Hattie was already managing really well at poker and very kindly gave up her second room to Mathilde . . .

For two nights only.

After that, Mathilde took her mattress down to the saddle room.

Charles, who had worried about whether the 'city mouse country mouse' transplant would take, was quickly reassured. Mathilde had got back in the saddle after the second day, plugged in her headphones, and fleeced them all.

He already knew what a good bluffer she was. He could have warned them . . .

He went to bed, disgusted, as he heard her laugh and bid higher than all the others . . .

One morning when they were alone, she asked him, 'Just what is this house?'

'Well . . . it is what is called a house, actually.'

'And Kate?'

'What, Kate?'

'You in love?'

'You think so?'

'You're a case,' she confirmed, rolling her eyes skyward.

'Shit. Is it a problem?'

'I don't know. And what about the flat I haven't even seen, yet?'

'That doesn't change anything. But incidentally . . . There's something I've been meaning to ask you . . .'

He asked his question, and got the answer he had hoped to hear. Then he remembered Claire and her story about kindness.

Always the right pleadings, his learned friend . . .

He recognized his sister's writing and the shape of a CD.

If the goat hasn't eaten your laptop, put track 18 on repeat. The words aren't very difficult, and with your stentorian voice, you should do a good job with it.

Good luck.

He turned over the box: it was the soundtrack of a Cole Porter musical. The title?

Kiss me, Kate.

'What's that?' asked Mathilde.

'Oh, just some silly nonsense your aunt sent me,' he said with a daft smile.

'Pfff . . . you guys are such babies.'

Later, reading through the libretto, he would learn that this was an adaptation of Shakespeare's Taming of the Shrew.

Of the Shrew, no doubt about it; Taming, *however, was a lot more hypothetical . . .*

The next four pages are a catalogue of little wooden houses.

One morning, Charles suggested to Nedra, who spent long hours playing alone in the depths of a huge box shrub behind the henhouse, that he build her a real little house.

The only answer she gave was a slow batting of her eyelashes.

'Rule number one: before you build a single thing you have to find a good location. So come with me, to tell me where you'd like it.'

She'd hesitated for a few seconds, looking around for Alice, then got up, smoothing her skirt.

'From the windows, would you rather see the rising sun or the setting sun?'

He felt bad to be putting her through such an ordeal, but he couldn't manage it any other way, it was his profession . . .

'Rising sun?'

She nodded.

'Right you are. South, south-east would make the most sense.'

They went silently round the house in a big loop . . .

'This would be a good spot because you've got a few trees for shade and then the stream isn't too far away . . . Very important to have water nearby!'

When she saw him in this light-hearted mood, she gradually brightened, and at one point, because they had to make their way through some brambles, she forgot herself and gave him her hand.

The foundations were laid.

After lunch, she brought him his coffee, as she had done ever since his first visit, and leaned against his shoulder while he drew the entire range of chalets offered by Balanda and Co.

He understood her. Like her he believed that a picture was worth a thousand words and he drew innumerable variations for her. The size of *the windows, the height of the door, the number of window boxes, the length of the terrace, the colour of the roof – and what should they carve in the middle of the shutters: lozenges or little hearts?*

He could have guessed which model she would point to . . .

Charles really had intended to leave, but now Mathilde was there, and Kate, between her nutcase of a mother and Mathilde, had given him a summit to aim for. All the more reason to stay and embark on this new childish undertaking.

He'd covered a lot of ground with Marc, and he'd let him head off to his parents' place with most of their files in the boot. Now, in order to find a new foothold, he had to keep his hands busy.

And then . . . building miniature houses was something he'd always done particularly well, so far. If he scrounged around enough he would surely find a slab of marble in the barns somewhere . . . He thought he'd seen a broken mantelpiece somewhere the other day . . .

At first Kate was annoyed when she found out that he was paying Sam and his mates, but Charles would not listen. Young apprentices deserved a salary.

But the mates were more idle than venal and very soon let them down, so this gave Charles and Sam a chance to become better acquainted. And to appreciate each other. As is often the case when two blokes are sweating it out together digging ditches, tossing back beers, bellowing bloody hells, and comparing their blisters.

On the third evening, as they were getting undressed on the pier, Charles asked Sam the same question he'd asked Mathilde.

Charles understood his hesitation better than anyone. He found himself in exactly the same situation.

There's a photo slipped between the next two pages. He printed it out long after his return, and left it lying around on his desk for weeks before deciding to put it in the notebook.

Inventory statement for end of project.
 Inventory statement full stop.

It was Granny who took the photo, and it had been an epic event, trying to explain to her how to press the shutter without worrying about anything else. Poor Granny was not well versed in digital hybrids . . .
 They are all there. Standing just outside Nedra's house. Kate, Charles, the children, the dogs, Captain Haddock and the entire barnyard.
 They're all smiling, they're all beautiful, they're all hanging expectantly on the trembling of an old lady who is about to go into her classic clueless diva routine, but they all have faith.
 They'd known her for so long . . . Let their indulgence set her free.

Alice was in charge of the décor (the day before she'd gone to fetch her books and had introduced him to the work of Jephan de Villiers . . . And that is what Charles appreciated most about these children, the way they always managed to lead him into unexplored territory . . . Whether it was Samuel's principles of dressage, or Alice's talent, or Harriet's dark humour, or Yacine's fifty anecdotes a minute . . . In all other respects they were totally typical: wearying, always wanting something, disrespectful, full of bad faith, noisy, unruly, bone idle, artful, and constantly squabbling with one another, but there was something about them that you didn't find in other kids . . .
 A freedom of spirit, a tenderness, a quickness of mind (even courage, because one had only to see them take on all the chores that their huge house required, without ever making a sour face or complaining), a zest

for life and a sense of ease with the world which Charles found endlessly fascinating.

He remembered something Alexis's wife had said about them: 'Those little Mormons . . .' but he did not agree with her at all. First of all, he'd seen them tear each other to pieces over the joysticks on the video games, spend entire afternoons in chat rooms or polishing up their blogs or selecting the best from YouTube (they'd forced Charles to sit through every single episode of 'Have you ever seen'?) (which in fact he didn't regret, he'd rarely laughed so heartily), but above all, he did not for one minute get the impression that they were entrenching themselves on the other side of their bridge.

It was just the opposite . . . Everything that still throbbed with life came to them. To rub up against their joyfulness, their valour, their . . . nobility . . . Their farmyard, their dinners, their meadows, their mattresses – all were a stage for endless procession, and each day brought with it a crop of new faces.

The latest receipt for their food supplies measured over one metre long (Charles was the one who'd been in charge that time . . . hence the aberration . . . he shopped, it would seem, like a Parisian on holiday), and at peak hours the beach nearly sank.

What did they have that made them different from other children?
Kate.

She was so unsure of herself – she had confided as much, said that every winter she succumbed to a depression that could last for days, where she was physically incapable of getting up in the morning; so the fact that she had been able to give so much confidence to these children – orphaned of both mother and father, as the official forms required one to specify – seemed to Charles nothing short of . . . miraculous.

'Come back in mid-December,' she scoffed, to calm the zealous worshipper, 'when it's five degrees in the living room, and you have to break the ice on the hens' water ever morning, and we eat porridge at every meal because I've got no strength left to cook anything else . . . And then Christmas comes . . . a wonderful family holiday with me all alone to stand in as the entire family tree, and then we'll talk about miracles . . .'

(But another time, after a particularly depressing dinner during which our four professionals of the planet had drawn up an alarming balance sheet, with all the figures, irrefutable with . . . well . . . we know what . . . she had poured out her feelings: 'This life . . . this very singular life – perhaps discriminating in some way – that I've imposed on the children . . .

It's the only thing that might absolve me. In this day and age the world is in the hands of grocers, but tomorrow? I often tell myself that it's only people who know how to tell a berry from a mushroom or how to plant a seed who will be saved . . .'

And then, elegant as ever, she had laughed and spouted a lot of nonsense in order to be forgiven for her lucidity . . .)

So Alice had taken charge of the décor, and Nedra had invited everyone to come and visit her palace.

No, that's not quite it. They were allowed to look, but not to go in. She had even stretched a rope in front of the door. The others were indignant, but she held her ground. This was her home. Her home on this earth that hadn't wanted her and, with the exception of Nelson and his mistress, no one had right of asylum.

You just have to have your documents in order.

Charles and Sam had done things properly. The wolf could blow and blow, the bunker would hold. The stud partitions were supported by a cement screed, and the cladding nails were longer than Nedra's palm.

Besides, it's visible on the photo − you can see she's stressed out.

When Granny finally allowed them to disperse, Kate turned to Nedra: 'Tell me, Nedra, did you say thank you to Charles?'

The little girl nodded.

'I can't hear what you said,' insisted Kate, leaning lower.

Nedra looked down at her feet.

'It's all right,' said Charles, embarrassed, 'I heard her.'

For the first time he saw Kate get angry: 'Oh for goodness' sake, Nedra − two little syllables in exchange for all this work, that wouldn't rip out your tongue now, would it?'

Nedra was biting her lips.

The legal authority, who had become as white as her shirt, added before walking away: 'You want my opinion? I don't bloody care if I go into this selfish child's house or not. I am disappointed. Terribly disappointed.'

She was wrong.

The little word she had so hoped to hear was on the following page, and it would take a form that would leave them all speechless.

The drawing isn't one of Charles's, it takes up two pages, and it isn't really a drawing.

It was Sam who copied out a rough draft of the required course, in order to memorize it.

Squares, crosses, dotted lines and arrows in every direction . . .

So here we are. The famous competition that had unseated him.

Third weekend in the month of August. Charles had not yet had the courage to mention it to Mathilde, but their days were numbered. His voicemail was saturated with threats, and Barbara, crafty woman, had managed to find Kate's number. Everyone was expecting him, there were already a dozen or more appointments set up, and already Charles could sense that Paris meant a workload worthy of an ass — to get back to the time we were talking about . . .

A few hours earlier, Sam had won the final qualifying races hands down, and they were all camped out on the far side of the paddocks.

What an expedition . . .

Ramon and his driver had left the night before, at their own pace and to have time to warm up, so they had slept on site.

'If you make it through the first round,' said Kate, putting her basket under her seat, 'we'll come with our sleeping bags and camp out under the stars with all of you to lend you our support in your ordeal . . .'

'Only lend, Auntie Kate? Why not give?'

'Thank you sweetheart but I know what I'm saying . . . Because I've been giving my support to you and your ass for ten years already . . . Does that suit you, Charles?'

Oh, Charles . . . Everything suited him . . . His thoughts were already being invaded by clauses about late penalties . . . And this would give him the chance to sleep less than a hundred metres away from her, for once . . .

He was saying that just for the hell of it, no? He'd abandoned any

*dreams of getting his leg over a long time ago . . . This woman needed a
friend more than she needed a man. That was it. Thank you. He'd got
the picture. Bah . . . Friends, as Jacques Brel would say, are less perish-
able . . . On the quiet in his little room he would pour himself little drams
of Port Ellen, and drink to the health of the wonderful holiday companion
that he'd become.*

Cheers.

*Naturally, the children had jumped for joy and rushed off to their rooms
to stock up on heavy jumpers and packets of biscuits. Alice painted a
magnificent banner,* Come on, Ramon!, *but Sam made her promise not
to unfurl it unless he was victorious.*

'It might make Ramon lose his concentration, you understand?'

*They all rolled their eyes. They knew that that stubborn beast would
balk at a fly farting or a blade of grass pointing in the wrong direction.*

They weren't up on the podium just yet . . .

*So, there they all sat, cross-legged round a campfire, some roasting sausages,
others roasting marshmallows, some Camembert, others bits of bread, and their
laughter and stories melted into the, um, pleasantly contrasting aromas. Every
last one of their friends had come along. Bob Dylan was practising his scales,
the little women were reading the palms of the little girls, Yacine was explaining
to Charles that this particular spider's web had been woven close to the ground
in order to catch jumping insects, like grasshoppers, for example, whereas that
one, see, up there, well, that's for flying insects . . . Logical, isn't it? Logical.
And Charles is very friendly with his best mate. After fixing her a club sandwich, he went to steal a bale of bay to place behind the small of her back . . .*

Sigh . . .

Kate had been particularly agitated since her mother arrived.

*'Is it to get away from her that we're all having a wild time over here
tonight?' he asked.*

*'Could be . . . It's stupid, isn't it? At my age, to still be so sensitive to
my old mum's moods . . . It's because she reminds me of other times. A
time when I was the youngest and the most carefree . . . I feel down,
Charles . . . I miss Ellen. Why can't she be here tonight? I imagine that
the reason people have children is to experience moments like this, no?'*

'She is here, since we're talking about her,' he murmured.

'And why haven't you ever had any?'

Charles said nothing.

'Children, that is.'

437

'Because I have never run into their mother, I suppose . . .'

'When are you leaving?'

He wasn't expecting this question. 'A word', 'a word', 'a word', growled his brain, in a panic.

'When Sam has won.'

Well done, my hero. You had to go a long way to find that smile . . .

★

It was nearly eleven o'clock, they were wrapped up in their blankets, keeping watch over the embers, 'like cowboys', and trying to come up with the appropriate lullabies. What was that cry? That hissing sound? That rustling? What sort of bird? Or beast? And what was that distant braying?

'Courage, comrades! In a few hours we won't have to entertain these stupid bipeds any more!'

And then a voice, Leo's perhaps, came quavering: 'You know what . . . it's time to tell ghost stories . . .'

A few raptor-like shrieks encouraged him. He embarked on a very gory tale full of viscera and haemoglobin, with cruel Martians and transgenic bumble bees. Nice try, but . . . it was hardly the sort of thing that would keep them from sleeping.

Kate raised the stakes even higher: 'Heliogabalus? Does that ring a bell?'

Nothing but the crackling of the flames.

'There were a lot of nutters among the Roman emperors, but I think this one took the biscuit . . . Right, he came to power when he was fourteen, entering Rome on a chariot pulled by naked women . . . Off to an excellent start . . . He was mad. Mad as a hatter. The story goes that he would sprinkle crushed gems on all his food, and put pearls in his rice, and he liked to eat bizarre, cruel dishes, and he craved stews made from tongue of nightingale and parrot, and coxcomb torn from the live animal, and he fed his circus animals with foie gras, and one day he massacred six hundred ostriches to eat their brains while they were still warm, and he adored the vulvae of I don't remember which sort of female, and he . . . Well, I'll stop there. This was just for starters.'

Even the flames did not burn as bright.

'The anecdote which I'm sure Leo wants to hear goes like this: Heliogabalus was renowned for the orgiastic banquets he hosted . . . Every time had to be better than the previous one. Worse, in other words. He had to have ever more massacres, more terror, more rapes, more orgies, more food, more alcohol . . . In short, more of everything. The problem was that he got bored very quickly.

438

So one day, he asked a sculptor to make him a metal bull that would be hollow inside with just a little door on one side and a hole where the mouth was so that he could hear the sound emerging. At the beginning of his lovely parties, they'd open the door and then lock a slave inside. When Heliogabalus began to get a little bored, he'd ask another slave to light a fire underneath the bull, and at that point all his guests would draw closer with smiles on their faces. Oh yes. It was really funny because the bull, you see, would start bellowing.'

Gulp.

Dead silence.

'Is that a true story?' asked Yacine.

'Absolutely.'

While the children wiggled and shivered, she turned to Charles and murmured, 'I won't tell them this, obviously, but – for me it's a metaphor for all humanity . . .'

My God. She really did have a bad case of the b̒es. Something had to be done.

'Yes, but . . .' *he continued, fairly loudly in order to drown out the sounds of their disgust,* 'that guy died a few years later, I think he was only eighteen, in the toilet, by suffocating on the sponge he used to wipe his own arse.'

'Is that true?' asked Kate, astonished.

'Absolutely.'

'How do you know?'

'Montaigne told me.'

She pulled on her blanket, winking: 'You are brilliant.'

'Absolutely.'

But not for long. The story he told, about how they always found bones whenever they started digging a construction site, and how they mustn't let anyone find out, otherwise the investigation would spoil the concrete that was ready to be poured, and make them lose a lot of money, well, all that failed to leave anyone remotely shaken.

That one fell flat.

As for Samuel, he recalled the only French lit. class during which he had not fallen asleep:

'It was the story of this young bloke, a peasant, who refused to enlist as just another piece of meat in Napoleon's army . . . Something they called the blood tribute . . . It lasted five years, and you were sure to die

439

like a dog, but if you had money, you could pay someone else to go in your place . . .

'He didn't have a brass farthing, so he deserted.

'The prefect summoned the bloke's father, gave him hell and humiliated him, but the poor old guy really didn't know where his son had gone. A bit later he found him starved to death in the forest, with the grass he'd been trying to eat stuck between his teeth. So the old man put his son over his shoulder and carried him without saying a word to anyone for three leagues until he got to the prefecture.

'That bastard of a prefect was at a ball. When he came home at two in the morning he found the poor peasant on his doorstep, and the old man says, "Well, you wanted me to find my son, Monsieur le Préfet, and here he is." Then he put the corpse up against the wall and cleared off.'

Now that was spicier . . . Sam wasn't dead sure, but he thought it was by that Balzac bloke.

The girls didn't have any stories, and Clapton wanted to keep the mood just the way it was . . . Gling, gling. He plucked some really macabre staccatos in the meanwhile.

Yacine volunteered.

'Right, I warn you, it'll be short.'

'Is it the one about the slug massacre?' someone asked worriedly.

'No, it's about the lords from the Franche-Comté and Haute-Alsace. The counts from Montjoie and the lords of Méchez, if you prefer . . .'

Some grumbling from the cowherd quarter. If this was going to be some intellectual stuff, thanks a lot.

The poor storyteller, tripped up just as he was hitting his stride, didn't know whether he should continue.

'Go on,' hissed Hattie, 'give us the one about the dubbing and the salt tax. We love it.'

'No, it's not about the salt tax, that's just it, it's about something called the "the right to lounge".'

'Oh, reeeally? You mean, like sling hammocks between the battlements?'

'Not at all,' said Yacine, clearly annoyed, 'you're really dumb. During the harsh winter nights, the lords had, so to speak, and I quote, "the right to disembowel two of their serfs in order to warm their feet in their smoking bowels", close quotes, by virtue, as I just told you, of this "right to lounge". There. That's all.'

It wasn't a flop at all, actually. There were a few calls of 'yuck' and 'gross' and 'are you sure?' and 'that sucks', all of which warmed his heart just as effectively.

'Right then,' announced Kate, 'we're not about to improve on that one this evening . . . Time for bed.'

There were already a few shouts of irritation against sleeping-bag zippers when a faint little voice rose in protest: 'But I have a story, too . . .'

No. They were not stupefied. They were petrified.

Sam, with his usual class, said jokingly to defuse the moment, 'Are you sure your story's horrible, Nedra?'

She nodded.

'Because if it's not,' he added, 'you'd do better to keep your mouth shut for once.'

The laughter that followed made him want to go on.

Charles looked at Kate.

What was the word she'd used the other night? Numb.

She was numb.

Numb and with deeply etched dimples on the lookout.

'It's the story about a urtwur . . .'

'Huh?'

'What?'

'Speak louder, Nedra!'

The fire, the dogs, the raptors, even the wind, were hanging on her every word.

She cleared her throat: 'A, um, earthworm.'

Kate was on her knees.

'Well, um, one morning he comes out and sees another earthworm. And he says, "Fine day, isn't it?" But the other one doesn't say a thing. So he says it again, "Fine day, isn't it?" Still he doesn't answer . . .'

It was tricky because she was speaking more and more softly, and no one dared interrupt her.

'"Do you live round here?" he went on, wiggling 'cos he was all embarrassed, but the other one still didn't say a thing, so the earthworm that was all annoyed turned round in his hole and said, "Oh drat, there I went talktootelgen."'

'What?' protested the audience in frustration. 'Speak more clearly, Nedra! We didn't understand a thing! What did he say?'

She looked up, her little face a pout of confusion, and removed the lock of hair that she'd been chewing on at the same time as her words, then *valiantly uttered once again, '"Oh drat, there I went talking to my tail again!"'*

It was a sweet moment, because the others didn't know whether they ought to smile or pretend to be horrified.

To break the silence, Charles applauded very gently. Everyone followed suit, only soon they were clapping fit to break their knuckles. This startled the dogs who woke up and started barking, so Ramon started braying, so all the donkeys in the campsite asked him to kindly shut up. Swearing, clamours, more yapping, whips snapping, banging and clanking rose in the night from all around, as if the entire sky were celebrating the courtesy of an earthworm.

For Kate the emotion was too much; she could not join in the Mexican wave.

Much later, Charles would open one eye to make sure there were no coyotes at the door; he sought out her face on the far side of the embers, and tried to make out her eyelids, and saw them open and thank him in turn.

Perhaps it was something he had dreamt . . . It did not matter, he snuggled deeper into his Himalayan feathers, smiling with happiness.

At some point he must have believed that he would build great things and earn the recognition of his peers, but now he was resigned to the fact that the only buildings that would ever really count in his life were dolls' houses.

★

For a reason that will remain a mystery to this day, Ramon refused to cross the last open water just before the finish line. The very same stream where he'd splashed about dozens of times . . .

What happened? No one knows. Perhaps some duckweed had drifted down, or a facetious frog had cocked a snook at him . . . The fact remains that he stopped short a few metres from his title, and waited for all the others to ford the water before condescending to follow them.

Yet God knows he'd been pampered . . . the girls had brushed him, combed him, made him shine, coddled him all morning until Samuel came along and grumbled, 'That's enough, now, he's not My Little Pony y'know.'

They hadn't unfurled the banner, they hadn't taken any photos or put on any dark glasses, to avoid any annoying reflections that might cause Ramon to shy, they'd encouraged him carefully and squeezed their buttocks painfully, but all in vain . . . He had preferred to teach his master a lesson.

442

What was important was working hard at school, not acting the idiot between two haystacks . . .

His master, who for the occasion had put on his great grandfather's tail-coat, was the sole competitor to drive without a whip.

The most powerful, therefore . . .

All he had to say when everyone was pressing round him, each one more sorry than the next, was: 'I suspected as much. He's very highly strung. Huh, treasure? Come on, let's get out of here . . .'

'And your reward?' said Yacine worriedly.

'Bah. You go and get it . . . Kate?'

'Yes?'

'Thanks for the great support. I appreciate it.' They continued in English.

'You are welcome, darling.'

'And it was a fantastic evening, right?'

'Yes, really fantastic. Today I feel like we're all champions, you know . . .'

'We sure are.'

'What are they saying?' asked Yacine.

'That we're all champions,' translated Alice.

'Champions of what?'

'Well, donkey champions!'

Charles offered to go with him. Sam thanked him, but Charles was too heavy. And besides, he needed to spend some time alone . . .

Charles adored that kid. If he'd had a boy, he would have chosen exactly the same model . . .

The next drawing is the only one that is not finished.

And there are tiny strands of hair all along the fold by the spine . . .

When Charles was about to put the notebook away in his briefcase, once he had packed everything, his initial reflex was to blow on the hairs to get rid of them but then, no, he closed the page on them, for ever.

Like a bookmark.

For the page he had turned.

He had spent the morning, and the entire previous day, with Yacine, obsessed with building a Spud Gun. He'd had to go back to FixitFreddy's for the second time (no comment) because the PVC tubing wasn't good enough. Now he wanted a metal one.

For a chemical Spud Gun . . . one that could send a piece of potato as far as Saturn, on condition that the reaction between the Coke and the Mentos Mints was properly calibrated (the one between bicarbonate of soda and vinegar only went as far as the moon, and that wasn't nearly as much fun . . .)

God knows it had kept them busy, that thing . . . They had had to nick a few potatoes on the sly from René, and when they had returned Kate's special vinegar from Modena they had got yelled at, even though the vinegar was completely useless; they had had to rush back to the bakery because those idiot girls had eaten all the Mentos, they had had to keep Sam from drinking the Coke, beg Freaky to spit out the valve he was chewing on, do a whole bunch of test runs, go back to the grocery to buy a can of Coke because the big bottles weren't gassy enough, they had had to get everyone out of the way, run to the stream to rinse their hands because their fingers were too sticky to screw the top on, run a fourth time to the grocery – the woman who ran it was beginning to wonder (although . . . she'd had no illusions about the mental health of that household for a long time now) – because Diet Coke was supposed to work better than normal Coke and . . .

444

'You know what, my dear little Yacine? I think it's easier to build a shopping mall in Russia with Sergei Pavlovich,' sighed Charles in the end.

Sheepishly, they came back to the house. They could have made ten kilos of chips with all the spuds they'd just wasted, and they needed to check one more thing on the Internet.

Kate was cutting Sam's hair in the courtyard.

'Yacine, you're next.'

'But . . . we haven't finished the Spud Gun . . .'

'Precisely,' she said, standing up straight, 'with all that hair gone, you'll be able to think more clearly . . . And leave Charles alone for a change.'

He had smiled. He didn't dare say so, but he was beginning to be pota-totally fed up. He went to fetch his sketchbook and another chair, and sat down next to them to sketch them.

Yacine was scalped, the girls had a trim, or a cut, or layers, depending on their mood and the latest trend at Les Vesperies, and locks of hair of every size and colour fell into the dust.

'You know how to do everything,' said Charles, full of wonder.

'Almost everything . . .'

When Nedra got up, the hairdresser shook out her big tea-towel cape and turned to the man with his pencil: 'And you?'

'What about me?' he answered, without looking up.

'Wouldn't you like me to cut your hair, too?'

A sensitive topic. His pencil lead snapped.

'You know, Charles,' she continued, 'I don't have many principles or theories here on earth . . . Yes, you know as much . . . you've seen the way we live . . . And where men are concerned, even less, alas . . . But there is one thing about which I am absolutely certain.'

He was clicking on his propelling pencil like a lunatic.

'The less hair a man has, the less hair he should have . . .'

'What . . . what?' he choked.

'Shave it all!' she laughed. 'Get rid of the problem once and for all!'

'You think so?'

'I know so.'

'And, uh . . . You know, that thing about virility . . . When Delilah shaves Samson, he loses all his strength, and I feel like I'm being scalped and . . .'

'Come on, Charlie! You'll be a thousand times sexier!'

445

'All right . . . If you say so.'

Oh, woe. Twenty years he'd been nurturing his meagre little down like some mother hen, and now this upstart of a girl was going to ruin it all in the space of two minutes . . .

He was headed for the block when he heard the words uttered very surgically:

'Sam, the clipper.'

Oh, woe.

'Kate, let me turn my chair towards the statue of the faun . . . I'll draw his pretty curls to console myself . . .'

Her associate came back with the little torture kit, and the children had a field day pulling out all the different size combs:

'How short are you going to do him? A five?'

'Nooo, that's way too long. Do two . . .'

'Don't be daft, he'll look like a skinhead! Take the number three comb, Kate . . .'

The condemned man kept mum, but had no trouble reproducing in his sketchbook the gentle sneer of the satyr facing him so proudly.

Then he drew the line of his neck, and went as far as the lichens on his . . . Closed his eyes.

He could feel her belly against his shoulder blades, leaned into her as discreetly as possible, lowered his chin while her fingers brushed his skin, then felt him, touched him, stroked him, dusted him off, smoothed him, pressed him. He was so troubled that he pulled his sketchbook higher up on his thighs and kept his eyes firmly shut without caring any more about the noise of the machine.

He wished his skull were endless, and was prepared to lose all the virility in the world, if only this delicious cramp could last forever.

She put the trimmer down and took her scissors to finish him off with a flourish. And while she was standing like this before him, concentrating on the length of his sideboards, and leaning over, giving him whiffs of her warmth, her smell, her perfume, he lifted his hand towards her hip . . .

'Did I hurt you?' *she asked, concerned, stepping back.*

He opened his eyes, realized that her audience was still there, or at least the little ones, waiting to see his reaction when he'd next look at his reflection, and he decided the time had come to ensure his snow anchor was firmly fixed before he tossed his last rope: 'Kate?'

'I've nearly finished, don't worry.'

'No. Don't ever finish. Sorry, that's not what I meant to say. I've been thinking about something, you see . . .'

She was behind him again, scraping the back of his neck with an open razor.

'I'm listening.'

'Uh . . . could you maybe stop, there, for a few minutes?'

'Are you afraid I'll cut your throat?'

'Yes.'

'Oh God. What is it you have to say?'

'Well, I'll be living on my own with Mathilde once school starts up, and I was thinking that . . .'

'That what?'

'That if Sam is really too unhappy at boarding school, I could take him in.'

The blade fell silent.

'You know,' he continued, 'I'm lucky to live in a neighbourhood where there are any number of excellent lycées and —'

'Why once school starts up?'

'Because it's . . . It's the end of the story that is in the bottle of Port Ellen . . .'

The blade beginning, gently, to warm up again.

'But do . . . do yoū have room for him?'

'A very nice room with parquet floors, mouldings, and even a fire-place . . .'

'Oh?'

'Yes.'

'Have you mentioned it to him?'

'Of course.'

'And what does he think about it?'

'He likes the idea but he's afraid to leave you on your own. Which I can understand, actually. But you would see him —'

'During the holidays?'

'No . . . I was thinking of bringing him back here every weekend . . .'

The blade stopped again.

'Sorry?'

'I could pick him up at the end of the school day on Friday, take the train with him, and buy a little car that I could leave at the station in —'

'But,' she interrupted, 'what about your own life?'

'My life, my life,' he said, pretending to be annoyed, 'never mind *about my life! You haven't got a monopoly on self-sacrifice, you know. And then, this business about adopting Nedra, I don't want to hurt you but you know it would be a lot easier for you to do it if you could show proof of some sort of . . . male presence here, even if it were feigned . . . I'm afraid that people working in administration are still rather . . . old-fashioned, so to speak . . . or even downright misogynistic . . .'*

'You think so?' she said, pretending to be upset.

'Alas.'

'And you would do that, for her sake?'

'For her. For Sam. For me . . .'

'What, for you?'

'Well . . . for the good of my soul, I suppose. To be sure of going to paradise with you.'

Kate went back to work in silence while Charles lowered his head still further, waiting for the verdict.

'You . . .' she eventually murmured, 'you don't say a lot, but when you do, it's . . .'

'Regrettable?'

'No, I wouldn't say that . . .'

'What would you say?'

With the tip of her cloth she wiped his neck, blew gently and for a long time into the gap beneath his collar, giving him shivers all down his spine, and hairs all over his notebook, then she stood up straight and declared, 'Go and get it, that bloody bottle. I'll meet you over by the kennels.'

Charles walked away, disconcerted, while she went up into Alice's room.

Mathilde and Sam were there, too.

'Listen . . . I'm taking Charles to do a bit of botany. You look after the house, all right?'

'How long will you be gone?'

'Until we find what we're looking for.'

'Find what?'

She was already tripping down the stairs four at a time to put together a survival basket.

And while she was busying herself with this chore, failing to remember where the kitchen was, opening, shutting, banging doors and drawers, Charles was blown away.

★

This was him, surely, but he didn't recognize himself.

He looked older, younger, more virile, more feminine, gentler, perhaps, and yet beneath his palm he found a very rough self . . . He shook his head without having to worry which way his locks might fall, then lifted his hand in front of his face to give himself back a familiar point of scale, touched his temples, his eyelids, his lips, and tried to smile to help himself adjust.

He slipped the bottle into one jacket pocket (like Bogart in *Sabrina*) (but without the hair), and his notebook into the other.

He took the basket from her hands, placed an eighteen-year-old bottle into it, and looked where her index finger was pointing.

'Do you see that tiny little grey spot down there?' she asked.

'I think so . . .'

'It's a lodge. A little house where the people who were slaving in the fields could go to rest . . . Well, that's where I'm taking you.'

He was careful not to ask her what they would do there.

But she could not help elaborating. 'It's the ideal place to put together an adoption file, if you want my opinion . . .'

The last drawing.

The back of her neck.

The place where Anouk had touched her, so furtively, and where he, Charles, had just caressed her, for hours.

It was very early, she was still sleeping, stretched out on her stomach and, through the tiny arrow slit, a ray of light revealed all that he had rued not being able to see in the dark.

She was even more beautiful than anything his hand had led him to believe . . .

He pulled the blanket up over her shoulders and reached for his notebook. Gingerly, he parted her hair, and refrained from kissing her beauty spot yet again, for fear of waking her. And drew the highest point on earth.

The basket was tipped on its side, and the bottle was empty. He had told her, between embraces, how he had come to her. From the marbles games to Mistinguett, held tight to his chest between the pavement and the little bit of himself still faintly beating that morning . . .

As he was telling her about Anouk, his family, Laurence, his profession, Alexis, and Nana, he confessed he had loved her from the very first moment, round that big campfire, and he hadn't taken his trousers to the cleaner's because he wanted to keep, deep in his pockets, the wood dust she'd left in his hand that first time she'd held it.

And it wasn't only about her, either. It was her children, too . . . And they were 'her' children, not just 'the' children, for no matter how she might protest to the contrary, however different they might be, they were all in her image. Absolutely, marvellously sparky.

At first he had thought he would be too overwhelmed, or too troubled, to make love to her the way he had fucked her in his dreams, but then

450

there were her caresses, her confessions, her own words . . . The beneficial effects of the bottle and the notes of honey and citrus . . .

His life, his story, had all come out, and he loved her accordingly. Honestly, chronologically. First as an awkward teenager, then a conscientious student, an ambitious young architect, a creative engineer, and finally – and this was the best bit – a man who was all of forty-seven: rested, shorn, happy, who has attained a distant goal he'd never thought possible, let alone dared hope for; and with no flag to plant other than these thousands of kisses which, if strung together, would go to make the most precise of cookie cutters.

Her body. To be savoured crumb by crumb, nibbled, gobbled. That is how she would like it.

He felt her hand searching for his, so he closed his notebook and checked that he had not got the perspective wrong.

'Kate?'
    He had just opened the door.
    'Yes?'
    'They're all here.'
    'Who, all?'
    'Your dogs.'
    'Bloody hell . . .'
    'And the llama.'
    'Ooooh,' moaned the blankets.

'Charles?' she said, coming up behind him.
    He was sitting in the grass, savouring a peach the colour of the sky.
    'Yes?'
    'It will always be like this, you know.'
    'No. It will be better.'
    'We'll never have any peace and –'
    She couldn't finish her sentence, savouring lips that tasted of peach.

12

'Well? Did you find a four-leafed clover?'

'Why do you ask?'

'No particular reason,' laughed Mathilde.

She was perched on the windowsill.

'So it seems we're leaving tomorrow?'

'I have to go back, but you can stay a few more days if you want to. Kate will take you to the station.'

'No. I'll come with you.'

'And you . . . You haven't changed your mind?'

'About what?'

'The arrangements for your room and board . . .'

'No. We'll see. I'll get used to it. I think it's my dad who's going to be given the push, but, oh well, I'm not even sure he realizes . . . As for Mum, it will be good for us.'

Charles put his papers aside for a few minutes and turned to face her.

'I never know when you're serious and when you're just putting on an act . . . I get the feeling you're going through a lot at the moment so I find all this cheerfulness a little bit suspicious.'

'What am I supposed to do?'

'I don't know . . . be angry with us?'

'But I am *totally* angry with you, I assure you! I think you're useless and selfish and a big let-down. Typical adults, in other words. On top of that I'm jealous as hell . . . Now you've got a whole bunch of other kids besides me and you're going to be off in the country all the time . . . Except there's things that can't be downloaded in life, y'know.'

'And the fact that Sam's coming with us . . . does that bother you?'

'Nah. He's cool. And I'm really curious to see what a bloke like him is going to be like at the lycée Jean-Paul Sartre . . .'

452

'And if things don't go well?'

'Well then, you're the one who'll be pulling out your hair . . .'

Ha ha ha.

The entire household accompanied them as far as the ticket barrier and Kate didn't have to run away to say goodbye: he would be coming back the following week to fetch his young boarder.

He got rid of the kids for a moment by giving them some change for the sweet machine, then grabbed his lover by the neck and –

A chorus of 'houuuuuuuhh' came from all around, so Charles closed his mouth to turn and tell them off, but Kate opened it again, gesturing with her middle finger just in case anyone had forgotten who was in charge.

'They're useless,' muttered Yacine. 'In the *Guinness Book of Records* there's an American couple who snogged for thirty hours and fifty-nine minutes without stopping.'

'Just you wait, Mr Potato Head. We're going to practise.'

13

Charles was a huge hit with his shorn head. He was tanned, he'd put on weight and filled out; he got up early, worked effortlessly, made an offer to Marc to join the firm, took care of Samuel's enrolment, bought beds and desks, gave the bedrooms to the kids and settled into the living room.

He was sleeping in a single bed and was mortified to have so much room.

He had a long conversation with Mathilde's mother, who wished him luck and patience, and asked him when he would come and collect all his books.

'So? I hear you've gone into intensive breeding?'

He didn't know what to say. So he hung up.

He flew to Copenhagen and flew back via Lisbon. He was preparing the ground for a new career as advisor and consultant, instead of tenders and procedures and responsibilities. He sent illustrated letters to Kate every day, and taught her how to answer the telephone.

That evening, it was Hattie who answered.

'Charles here, everything all right?'

'No.'

It was the first time he'd ever heard this scatty little miss complain.

'What's going on?'

'Big Dog is dying.'

'Is Kate there?'

'No.'

'Where is she?'

'I don't know.'

He cancelled his appointments, borrowed Marc's car and found her, in the middle of the night, curled up in front of her ovens.

The dog was one long death rattle.

He came behind her, put his arms around her. She touched his hands without turning round: 'Sam is about to leave, you'll never be here and now he's abandoning me too . . .'

'I am here. It's me, just here behind you.'

'I know, I'm sorry.'

She paused, then said, 'We'll have to take him to the vet's tomorrow.'

'I'll go.'

He squeezed her so tightly that night that he hurt her.

It was deliberate. She had said she didn't want to cry over a dog.

Charles, thinking of Anouk, watched as the syringe drained, and he felt the dog's dry muzzle breathe its last in the palm of his hand. Then he let Samuel carry him out to the car.

Samuel was crying like a baby, telling him the story about the day Big Dog had saved Alice from drowning . . . And the day he ate all the *confits de canard* . . . And the day he ate all the ducks . . . And all those nights he'd watched over them and slept outside the door when they were camping in the living room, to protect them from the draughts . . .

'It's going to be hard for Kate,' Sam murmured.

'We'll look after her.'

Silence.

Like Mathilde, this young man did not have too many illusions about the adult world . . .

If he had not been so sad, Charles would have told him: he was both a natural person and a legal entity, subject to the yoke of decennial liability. He would have said this with a laugh of course, and would have added that he was prepared to restore their bridge every ten years to prevent them from drifting away without him.

But Sam kept turning round to check whether the great totem of his childhood was comfortably settled in the rear before blowing his nose in the shirt that had once belonged to the father he had hardly known.

Out of a sense of decency, therefore, Charles held his peace.

★

They dug the hole together while the girls wrote poems.

Kate had chosen the spot.

'Let's have him lie on the hill, that way he can go on protec . . . sorry,' she wept, 'sorry.'

All the kids from the summertime had gathered. All of them. Even René, wearing a jacket for the occasion.

Alice read a very moving little piece which said, more or less, you gave us a run for our money but we will never forget you, you know . . . And next to speak would be . . .

They turned round. Alexis and his children were climbing up the hill to join them.

Alexis. His children. And his trumpet.

. . . next to speak was Harriet. Who didn't manage to get to the end of her tribute. She folded it up and between two sobs she spat, 'I hate death.'

The children tossed lumps of sugar into the hole until Samuel and Charles filled it up and, while the two of them were bent over their spades, Alexis Le Men played his trumpet.

Charles, who up until that point had respected and understood their emotion without sharing it, paused in his grave-digging work.

Lifted his hand to his face.

Drops of . . . of sweat blurred his vision.

He had forgotten that Alexis could cry like this.

What a concert.

Just for them.

On a late summer's evening.

With the last swallows in flight . . .

On top of a hill overlooking luscious countryside on one side and, on the other, a farm that had survived the Terror.

The musician kept his eyes closed and rocked gently back and forth, as if his notes were restoring his own breath to him before fading into the clouds.

The *bras d'honneur*, the final fuck-you. The ballad. The solo piece of a man who had not played, not since the era of little spoons heated in a flame; and now he was using an old dog in order to mourn all the deaths in his life.

Yes.

What a concert.

*

456

'What was it?' asked Charles as they were heading back down the hill, one after the other.

'I don't know . . . *Requiem for a stupid mutt who ruined two trouser legs . . .*'

'You mean you –'

'Oh, this time, yes! I was way too jittery not to improvise!'

Charles, thoughtful, followed him for a few more steps and then clapped him on the shoulder.

'Yes?'

'Welcome, Alex, welcome . . .'

Alexis thumped him in his fragile rib.

Just in order to teach him: don't break out the violins when you're so utterly tone deaf.

'You'll stay for dinner, the three of you, won't you?' asked Kate.

'Thanks, but no. I've got to –'

His gaze met his former neighbour's, and he made a little face and continued in a jollier tone, 'I'll have to ring, first!'

Charles recognized that smile, it was the one he used to make when he was about to throw all his ammunition into the ring, to get Philippe Lerouge's prize marble . . .

He played again that evening, for the red-rimmed eyes. All the daft nonsense of their childhood, and the thousand and one ways they had found to pester Nana.

'And *La Strada*?' asked Charles.

'Some other time.'

They stood by the cars.

'When are you leaving?' asked Alexis anxiously.

'Tomorrow at dawn.'

'Already?'

'Yes, this time I just came for . . .'

He was going to say an emergency.

'. . . the revelation of a young talent.'

'And when will you be back?'

'Friday evening.'

'Could you swing by the house? I'd like to show you something.'

'Okay.'
'Right, ducks, shoo!'
'You said it.'

Kate did not understand the last words he murmured in the hollow of her ear.

You are very? Something merry? You're a fairy?

No, it must have been something else. Fairies don't have such ugly hands.

14

There he was, once again standing by the entry phone at 8 Clos des Ormes . . .

God, it pissed him off to spend even a second of his precious time away from Les Vesperies, in this bloody place . . .

'Coming!' shouted Alexis.

Good. At least he wouldn't have to wear felt slippers and put up with the careful figure skater.

Lucas jumped up to hug him.

'Where are we going?' asked Charles.

'Follow me.'

'Here.'

'Here what?'

The three of them were in the middle of the cemetery.

And since Alexis did not reply, Charles gestured to him that he had understood: 'Look, it's perfect. Here, she'll be exactly midway between your house and Kate's. When she needs peace and quiet, she'll come to your place, and when she's in the mood for something more exotic, she'll go to Kate's.'

'Oh, I know where she'll go . . .'

Charles found his smile a bit sad, and returned it.

'No problem,' continued Alexis, looking up, 'as for me, I've had my share of exotic . . .'

They went to find Lucas, who was playing hide-and-seek with the dead.

'You know I . . . I meant what I said when you called me the first time. And I still think that –'

Charles gestured to him that it was all right, that he didn't need to justify himself, that . . .

'And then when I saw everything they were doing for their dog, I . . .'

'Balanda?

  'I'd like you to make the journey with me.'

  His friend agreed.

★

Later, walking along the road: 'Tell me, is it serious with Kate?'

  'No, no. Not at all. I'm just going to marry her and adopt all the kids. And the livestock, while I'm at it . . . I've asked the llama to be maid of honour.'

  Charles recognized that laugh.

  After they had walked for a moment in silence: 'Don't you think she resembles Mum?'

  'No,' said Charles, to protect himself.

  'Yes. I think she does. Just like her. But more solid.'

15

Charles met him at the station and they went straight to the waste depot.

Both were wearing a white shirt and a light-coloured jacket.

When they got there, two heavy-set men were already pulling her up.

Their hands behind their backs, without exchanging a single word, they watched as the coffin came up to the surface. Alexis was weeping, but not Charles. He remembered what he had looked up in the dictionary the night before:

Exhume, verb [trans.] Recall from oblivion, bring back.

The suits from the funeral director's took over the next stage of the operation. They carried her to the van and closed the doors on all three of them.

They were sitting facing one another, separated by a strange coffee table in pine . . .

'If I'd known, I'd have brought a deck of cards,' joked Alexis.

'Have mercy, no . . . She'd be perfectly capable of cheating as usual!'

Over the bumps and in the curves they instinctively placed their hands on her, despite the fact that she'd been cinched round and round to prevent any sliding. And once their hands were where they were, they left them there for a long time, feeling the gnarls in the wood, as if they were gently caressing her.

They did not talk a lot, and only about topics of no interest. Their jobs, their back problems, their teeth, the difference in cost between a city dentist and a country dentist, the car that Charles ought to buy, the best used-car lots, the cost of a car park season ticket at the station, and the crack in the stairwell . . . What the assessor had said, and the form letter Charles would give Alexis for the insurance company.

Neither one of them, that much was clear, felt like exhuming anything other than the body of the woman who had loved them so much.

At one point, however – and of course it had to be about him, because he was always the one who set the mood and lowered the lighting – they evoked memories of Nana.

No. Not memories. His presence, rather. His vitality, the energy of a little fellow all covered in jewels, and who had always had their chocolate croissant waiting for them when they got out of school.

'Nana . . . we're sick of your chocolate croissants . . . Can't you get us something else, next time?'

'And the myth, duckies, and the myth?' he replied, dusting off their collars. 'If I get something else, you'll end up forgetting me, whereas like this, you'll see, I'm leaving crumbs behind for your entire life!'

And now they saw.

'Some day, we ought to go and see him, with the children,' said Alexis, a more cheerful note in his voice.

'Pfff . . .' sighed Charles, exaggerating the 'pfff' somewhat (he was a very poor actor), 'do you know where he is?'

'No . . . But we could find out . . .'

'Find out how?' retorted Charles, fatalistic. 'Ask the Association of Friends of Old Queens?'

'What was his name anyway . . .'

'Gigi Rubirosa?'

'Shit, that was it. And you remembered that?'

'No. In fact I've been hunting for it since your letter, and it came to me just now.'

'And his other name . . . his real name?'

'I never knew.'

'Gigi . . .' murmured Alexis thoughtfully, 'Gigi Rubirosa . . .'

'Yes. Gigi Rubirosa. The great friend of Orlanda Marshall and Jacquie the Jam Tart . . .'

'How can you remember all that?'

'I don't forget a thing. Alas.'

Silence.

'Well that is, when it's things that deserve to be remembered.'

Silence.

'Charles . . .' murmured the erstwhile junkie.

'Shut up.'

'It'll have to come out someday . . .'

'Okay but not today, all right? We'll each have our turn. Hey, what is it with you,' he said, pretending to get annoyed, 'you piss me off in the end you Le Mens with all your psychodramas! It's been going on for forty years now! What about some respite for the living, no?'

He lifted up his briefcase. After a split second of hesitation he placed it before him, pulled out his files, and proved to Anouk, leaning on her, that no, you see I haven't changed, I'm still that diligent little old schoolboy who . . .

Nana would have loved that song . . .

And instruction leaflets, just like autumn leaves, can be shovelled into piles. Memories and regrets too. When autumn leaves . . . na na na . . .

Yves Montand, that was something else. Nana had known him well.

'What are you humming, there?'

'Rubbish.'

★

It was nearly one o'clock when they arrived in the village. Alexis invited the undertakers to lunch at the grocery-store-bistro.

They hesitated. They were in a hurry, and didn't like leaving the merchandise out in the sun.

'Go on . . . just something quick,' he insisted.

'Just a boxed lunch,' joked Charles.

'With a good stiff hot dog,' added Alexis.

And they had a good laugh, still the two young jerks they had always been.

Once they'd swallowed the last of their beer, they went back to their ropes.

★

When she was once again in the cool earth, Alexis approached the edge of the grave, stood still, lowered his head and . . .

'Excuse me, Sir, would you mind getting out of the way?'

'Pardon?'

'Well, we're really in a rush now. So we'll put the other one in right away, that way you'll have all the time you need afterwards to meditate –'

'The other what?' he said, startled.

'Well, the other . . .'

Alexis turned round and saw a second coffin waiting on a trestle near the Vanneton-Marchanboeuf family, raised his eyebrows, then saw his friend's smile.

'What . . . what's all this about?'

'Come on . . . Make an effort . . . Can't you see it – the boas and the pink ruffles around his wrists?'

Alexis broke down and it took Charles forever to console him after the added shock.

'How . . . how did you manage it?' he stammered, while the experts were packing up their gear.

'I bought him.'

'Huh?'

'To start with, I actually did remember his name. I have to admit I've had time to think about it over these last months . . . Then I went to see his nephew, and I bought him.'

'I don't understand.'

'There's nothing to understand. We were sitting round having a drink, having a chat, and this Norman bloke wasn't going along with it, it was shocking, he said, and it made me laugh to see that these people, who'd had nothing but bad things to say about him when he was alive, had suddenly got so mindful of his maggots . . . so I brought myself into line with their vulgar behaviour and pulled out my cheque book.

'It was grand, Alex . . . Grandiose, even. It was like . . . something out of a short story by Maupassant. There was this stupid fool trying to pass off his crass stupidity as some kind of dignity, but after a while his wife came over and said, "Oh, all the same, Pierrot . . . The boiler wants replacing . . . and what's it to you whether Maurice has his final rest here or elsewhere, huh? He's had his last rites . . . Huh?"

Last rites . . . Sublime, isn't it? So I asked how much it cost for a new boiler. They told me some amount and I copied it out without batting an eyelid. For that price, I reckon you could heat the entire Calvados region!'

Alexis was lapping it up.

'And the best is yet to come: I'd filled everything out – the stub, the date, the place, but just when I was about to sign the cheque, up went my pen: "You know . . . given what this is costing me, I need at least . . ." Long silence. "Pardon?" "I want six photos of Na— of Maurice," I said, "it's that or nothing."

'You should have seen the way they went into action. They could only find three! They had to call Aunt Whatsit! But she only had one! But maybe Bernadette, well she ought to have a few! So the son goes rushing over to Bernadette's place, and in the meantime we went through all the albums, going berserk with all that fiddly transparent paper. Oh, it was a fine moment . . . For once, I was putting on the show for Nana . . . Well, anyway . . .'

He pulled an envelope out of his pocket.

'Here they are. Look how sweet he was . . . Of course, the one where you recognize him best is the baby photo, naked on an animal skin . . . Yes, there you can tell he really is in his element.'

Alexis leafed through the photos and smiled, 'Don't you want one?'

'No . . . you keep them.'

'Why?'

'It's your only family.'

Alexis was silent.

'And Anouk's too, actually . . . That's why I went to get him.'

'I –' he began, rubbing his nose, 'I don't know what to say, Charles . . .'

'Don't say anything. I did it for myself.'

Then he bent forward all of a sudden and pretended to be tying one of his shoelaces.

Alexis had just taken him by the shoulders, 'brothers in arms', and the embrace upset him.

He'd done it for himself, the purchase. As for the rest – their complicity – that was no longer part of this world.

Alexis was astonished to see Charles heading off towards the van, and he called out, 'Where are you going?'

465

'I'm leaving with them.'

'But . . . and . . .'

Charles didn't have the courage to listen to the end of his sentence. He had a site meeting the next morning at seven, and the night would not be long enough to prepare it properly.

He squeezed in next to the two vultures, and just as the *Les Marzeray* road sign with its red diagonal stripe disappeared behind them on the right, he felt – he suffered – his only sorrow of the day.

He had been so close to her, and to go away again without having kissed her – it was . . . mortifying.

Fortunately, his travelling companions turned out to be regular bricks.

They began by wiping off their graveyard expressions, loosened their ties, took off their jackets and finally let their hair down completely. They told their passenger a whole slew of stories, each one more macabre and salacious than the next.

Dead bodies farting, mobile phones ringing in the satin, secret mistresses showing up with the holy water sprinkler, the last will and testament of certain late merrymakers which, as the undertakers put it, were 'literally killing them', survivors so off their rocker that you ended up with enough bloody anecdotes to carry you through retirement, and any other thing you could think of that was mortally hilarious.

When the source of the stories had run dry, the *Grosses Têtes* quiz show on the radio took over.

Bollocks. Just in time.

Charles, who'd accepted their offer of a cigarette, took the opportunity as he tossed the butt out the window to offload his black armband at the same time.

He laughed, asked Jean-Claude to turn up the volume, left behind his mourning, and concentrated on the next question from Madame Titi.

From Brest.

16

Mid-September. Last weekend Charles picked two kilos of black-berries, put paper dust jackets on twenty-four schoolbooks (twenty-four!), and helped Kate to trim the goat's hooves. Claire had come with him and took Dad's place by the copper cauldrons, where she chatted for hours with Yacine.

The day before, she'd gone completely crackers over the black-smith, and decided she would change professions and go into the Lady Chatterley line.

'Did you see that torso under his leather apron?' she pined, all day long and well into the evening. 'Kate? Have you seen him?'

'Forget it. He has a hammer in his head.'

'How do you know? Have you tried him out?'

She waited until Claire's brother had gone into the other room, then winced, yes, she had played the, er, anvil a while back . . .

'Yeah but still,' sighed Claire, drooling, 'that torso . . .'

A few hours later, on happy pillows, Kate would ask Charles if he thought he would last the winter.

'I don't understand the meaning of your question . . .'

'Okay, forget it,' she murmured, turning over and giving him back his arm so she could lie on her stomach.

'Kate?'

'Yes?'

'What did you mean?'

She didn't know what to say.

'What are you afraid of, my love? Me? The cold? Or time?'

'Everything.'

The only answer he would give was to caress her, for a long time.

Her hair, her back, her bottom.

He wouldn't struggle with words any more.

There was nothing to say.

Make her moan, once more.

And lull her to sleep.

Now he was in his office and trying to understand the graphs for the analysis of the arches subjected to unequal weights provok—

'What is this bloody shit?' Philippe burst into his office like a jack-in-a box, shaking a wad of papers at him.

'I don't know,' answered Charles without looking up from his screen, 'but you're going to tell me.'

'Confirmation of an application for a design contest for a shitty village hall in Back-of-Beyond-on-Bullshit! That's what it is!'

'It won't be shitty at all, my village hall,' he answered calmly, leaning over his table of graphs.

'Charles . . . what *is* this insanity? I just found out you were in Denmark last week, and that you might start working for old Siza again, and now this –'

Caught in the line of fire, Charles switched off his screen, rolled back and reached for his jacket: 'Have you got time for a coffee?'

'No.'

'Well, make time.'

And as Philippe started heading towards the kitchenette, he added, 'No, not here. Let's go out. I've got two or three things to tell you . . .'

'So what do you want to talk to me about this time?' sighed his associate in the stairway.

'About our marriage contract.'

★

Five empty cups sat between them now.

Naturally, Charles hadn't filled him in on the details about how dicey it could be, holding the horns of a terrified goat having a pedicure, but he'd said enough for his team-mate to realize that he'd embarked on one hell of a strange ark.

Silence.

'But . . . but how on earth did you ever get involved in such a set-up?'

'I needed a place to shelter from the flood,' smiled Charles.

Silence.

'You know what they say about the country?'

'Go ahead . . .'

'"During the day, you're bored, and at night you're scared."'

Charles was still smiling. He found it very hard to imagine how you could be bored for an instant in that house – and what could you possibly be scared of, when you were lucky enough to sleep in the arms of a superheroine.

With beautiful breasts . . .

'So you have nothing to say,' continued Philippe, despondent, 'you just sit there, smiling like a daft bugger . . .'

Silence.

'You're going to be bored out of your mind.'

'No.'

'Of course you are. Just now you're on your little cloud because you're in love, but . . . well, shit! You know what life's like, don't you?'

(Philippe was in the process of consummating his third divorce.)

'Well, no . . . I think I didn't know what life's like, actually.'

Silence.

'Hey!' said Charles, slapping him on the shoulder, 'I'm not giving you notice or anything, I'm just making you aware that I'll be working differently . . .'

Silence.

'And all this turning everything upside down for some woman you hardly know, who lives five hundred kilometres away, who already has five kids, each more knocked about than the other, and who wears socks hand knitted from nanny-goat yarn, is that it?'

'I can't think of a better description of the situation.'

Longer silence than ever.

'You want my opinion, Balanda?'

(Ah . . . That paternalistic little tone of voice . . . sucking up to him . . . Odious.)

His associate had turned round to get the waiter's attention, and now he came back to his question mark and said, 'It's a fine project.'

And while he was holding the door for him: 'Hey . . . Do I detect a faint odour of cow manure about your person, by any chance?'

17

For the first time, his father had not come to greet them at the gate.

Charles found him in the cellar, at a loss because he could not remember why he had gone down there.

He gave him a kiss and helped him back upstairs.

He was even more dismayed when he saw him in the bright light. His features, his skin had changed.

His skin seemed thicker. Yellowish.

And the . . . the elderly gentleman had cut himself so badly with his razor, in their honour . . .

'Next time I come, I'll bring you an electric razor, Papa . . .'

'Oh, my boy . . . Keep your money, now.'

He walked him over to his armchair, sat down across from him and gazed at that face full of gashes until he thought he found something else there, something more encouraging.

Henri Balanda, a prince among men, could sense this, and made a huge effort to distract his only son.

But as he was entertaining him with news about the garden and the latest great events in the kitchen, Charles could not help but drift away still further.

His father too would die soon . . .

So it would never end?

Not tomorrow. With a bit of luck, not the day after, either, but in any case . . .

Anouk's words continued to echo in his brain.

He'd given Mistinguett to Alexis; and the only keepsake he had of her, her legacy to him, was simply this: life.

A privilege.

His mother's whinging roused him from his third-rate philosophizing:

470

'What about me? Aren't you coming to give me a kiss? Is it only the old men in this house who get any attention?'

Then, shaking her chignon, 'Oh dear Lord. Your hair. I shall never get used to it . . . You had such lovely hair . . . And why are you laughing like an idiot now?'

'Because that's the sort of remark that's worth all the DNA tests on the planet! Such lovely hair . . . You really cannot be anyone but my mother to come out with such utter rubbish.'

'If I really were your mother,' she winced, 'you would surely realize that you should not be so vulgar at your age.'

And he let her embrace him round his neck, now so clean and smooth behind his ears . . .

No sooner had they finished the meal than the kids went upstairs to watch the end of their film, while Charles helped his mother to clear away, and his father to organize his papers.

He promised that he'd come back one evening the following week to help him fill out his tax return.

Having said that, he promised himself that he'd come back to see him every week of the current fiscal year . . .

'Don't you want a little brandy?'

'Thanks, Papa, but you know I'm driving . . . Where are the keys to your car, anyway?'

'On the console.'

'Charles, it's not a good idea to head off at this time of night.' His mother sighed.

'Don't worry. I've got two chatterboxes in the glove compartment.'

The keys . . . the console . . .

'Well!' he exclaimed. 'What have you done with the mirror?'

'We gave it to your older sister,' answered his mother from the depths of her dishwasher. 'She wanted it so badly . . . It's her advance share of the inheritance . . .'

Charles looked at the mark which the removal of the mirror had left on the wall.

It was here, he mused, I mused, that I lost sight of myself, almost a year ago.

It was there, on that tray, that the letter from Alexis was waiting for me.

It's no longer the absent stare of a bloke who's been devastated by four syllables that meets my gaze, but a big white rectangle set almost incongruously against a greyish, dirty background.

Never has my reflection resembled me more.

'Sam! Mathilde!' I shout, 'do what you want, but I'm out of here!'

I kiss my parents and hurry down the front steps with the same feverishness as when I was sixteen, when I'd go over the wall to meet Alexis Le Men.

To get into bebop, and nicotine, and anything that remained in the bottom of those bottles belonging to the woman who, that night, was on duty, and the girls who never stayed for very long because jazz was 'dullsville', then I'd listen to him belt out Charlie Parker at me until I couldn't take it any more, to console ourselves for the fact that our giggling prey had left . . .

I blow the horn.

The neighbours . . .

My mother must be cursing me . . .

I'll wait two more minutes, but after that, too bad for them.

No, really! They're going too far, those two! I've taken on a double load of maths, a triple one of physics, photos of Ramon in my kitchen, knife blades smeared with Nutella, and even a literary essay on *The Sufferings of the Young Werther* at quarter past midnight last Thursday!

I bring them a fresh baguette every evening, and I try to give them a balanced diet of vegetables, protein, and starch, I empty out their pockets and rescue a pile of rubbish every time I wash their jeans, I put up with them when doors slam and they don't talk to each other for days on end, I put up with them when they close the doors and giggle half the night, I tolerate their shit music then get told off because I can't bloody see the subtle differences between techno and tecktonik, I . . . None of all that really weighs too heavily on me, but they had better not try and make me lose a single *second* more when it's time to go and be with Kate.

Not one.

They've got their whole life ahead of them, those two.

And because I've been bloody soft enough to drive very slowly,